THE
Granddaughter

for
Katherine, Robert and Denise
with love

Gratefully . . .

I thank the many people who gave me their advice, friendship and help during the writing of this book. I am particularly indebted to Edward J. Acton, Liza Antelo, Herbert Bialosky, Patricia Ferlin, Lee Guber, Pamela Hartford, Lee Kohrman, Phyllis Levy, Jerome Lurie, Robert Rivel, Lewis Steel, Richard Voehl, Rose Wohlgemuth Weisman and Katherine Wyse.

Most of all, I hope that Hope Dellon knows how deeply I appreciate her insight, talent, confidence and patience.

LOIS WYSE
New York
Spring 1981

Walking away is much harder than carrying on. I've done both.
John Lennon
Interview, *Playboy* Magazine
January 1981

THE
Granddaughter

August 1957

I have a little shadow
That goes in and out with me . . .
Robert Louis Stevenson
A Child's Garden of Verses

I

SHE WAS A PECULIAR CHILD, not cuddly and full of feminine wiles like her little sister, but direct and strong like him.

Her body held no promise of duplicating the ethereal, willowy mold of her mother's. Instead, she was square and compact like him.

She never looked at the world in the bored, contemptuous manner of her father; instead, her blue eyes were as penetrating as his.

That made Alexandra Cassman at ten years of age as hard to deal with as the old man.

"For the last time, Alexandra, get dressed or I'll tell your mama, and she will be very angry."

Cassie looked up from the floor, where she was sitting in white underpants. Cross-legged and grim-faced, she was clutching her Raggedy Ann doll. She looked at her nanny with contempt.

No one, not even—no, especially not—Miss Evans could get Alexandra Cassman up from that floor.

Not to put on a baby dress.

Not a dumb little baby dress.

Not even for Grandpa's birthday party.

"All right, then, I'm going to tell your mother," Miss Evans said as she planted her hands firmly on her hips.

"Tell her," Cassie hissed. "Go ahead, tattletale. See if I care."

Miss Evans threw her shoulders back and strode down the hall.

Peculiar child, she muttered.

Very peculiar child.

She'll grow up to be a terror.

Just like that grandfather, Samuel Cassman.

Diane Winters felt lighter than air.

"Excuse me, Mrs. Cassman." It was the clipped tone of Miss Evans, the English nanny. "Mrs. Cassman, do you hear me?"

Diane did not turn. "What is it?"

"It's Miss Cassie. She says she won't wear the dress you want for the party tonight. She just sits on the floor."

"And you'll let a ten-year-old child tell you what to do?"

Miss Evans emitted a long, loud "harumph." As if that child didn't tell *her,* too. And her the mother. The one who should get the respect.

"Just leave," Diane said, irritation edging her voice. When she was certain that Miss Evans had left, Diane went to her closet and rearranged two pairs of black shoes under the proper handbags.

There. The patent looked better under the suede.

Or did it?

She took three steps back.

No. No. It looked better the other way. The patent under the patent.

Ahhh! Lovely. It was all so lovely.

Her closet was prettier than the Gucci shop on Fifth Avenue. Diane hugged herself, the better to hold on to her delicious secret.

She had lined up 279 pairs of Gucci shoes under 279 matching Gucci handbags.

And to do it she'd run up a bill for sixteen thousand seven hundred forty dollars at Gucci's this month.

And guess who'd have to pay for it?

Good old Grandpa.

S.C.

Samuel Cassman.

She laughed out loud.

Then Diane walked down the hall, her high heels clicking on the bare floors. She loved bare floors. In a wall-to-wall carpeted world, she loved the sound of her own heels rat-a-tatting out her rhythm. She loved this house, too. A duplex on Fifth Avenue. So right for the rich young Cassmans. So perfect for Bill and Diane and their rotogravure family.

Diane stood at the door of her elder daughter's room. Before she could say a word, Cassie looked up from the floor and said evenly, "I'm not going to the party."

"What?" Diane snapped.

Cassie shook her head. Mommy must really be a dumbbell to make her say it again. Grandpa would get it all the first time.

"Cassie, listen to me," Diane commanded. "Get ready at once, and put on your dress. I designed it, and Madame de Lys sewed it by hand." Diane paused; her daughter's expression had not changed. She'd have to try to lure Cassie. "There's a big party at '21.' It's going to be so much fun." Still no movement. Now the ultimate: guilt. "What will everyone think if you're not there?"

"It doesn't matter what they think." For a minute Cassie felt sorry for her mother; she really cared what *they* thought. Poor Mommy.

"What will I tell Grandpa?" Diane asked. "You know he's coming to pick us up."

"Tell him the truth. I won't wear a baby dress."

"He'll be furious. You know how much he loves you. Your sister wouldn't behave like this. Stephanie," she called, turning nervously toward the next room as she suddenly remembered the obedient daughter.

"I'm just getting on my gloves," Stephanie called, her postnasal drip snuffling her voice.

Cassie shivered.

She was comparing them again. Always comparing. Didn't Diane know there was nothing to compare? Stephanie was hollow, a shell, her mother's guided missile.

And Cassie was full—full of life, of resolution.

No, she wasn't going to sit still for comparisons.

She jumped to her feet.

Diane smiled. "There's a good girl." She tried to remember what she'd said that had brought Cassie to her feet. She'd have to try to say it again sometime. Diane went over and patted Cassie's head. "Now get dressed, and don't disappoint Grandpa. This is going to be a party you'll remember all your life." Suddenly she thought of something important. "Listen to me, Cassie. I'm your mother, and I know. Don't ever miss a party."

Cassie stood, arms folded, lower lip jutting out—just the way she pictured Grandpa in the same situation. Then Cassie turned her back to her mother. She didn't hear Diane leave.

But minutes later she did hear Grandpa Sam coming up the stairs. And then he was hugging her fiercely and saying in that big booming voice, "What's this I hear? You're not going to the party? You have to come. It's my birthday, and you're always my best present. From the day you were born, Cassie, you looked like me. You still do, and I love that little face."

"Oh, Grandpa." She put her arms around his neck and cried until she couldn't find any more tears. "I love you, Grandpa, but I can't go."

He pulled away and shrugged his shoulders, palms upraised. "I never heard such foolishness. Your mother says you won't go because you don't want to wear a beautiful dress. Is that true?"

She nodded.

Grandpa looked around the room. "I suppose it's that dress rolled in a ball on the floor. Why won't you wear it? You like Stephanie's better?"

Cassie gulped. "No. Hers is just like it."

"The same dress?"

She nodded, and the tears started once again.

Suddenly Sam Cassman saw it all. "And you don't want to be compared with Stephanie?"

She looked up and gasped. How did he know? How could he read the mind of a little girl when her mother didn't even begin to understand?

She nodded.

Grandpa sat heavily in the white rocking chair in the corner of the room. He reached in his pocket and pulled out a big cigar. "Got a match?"

Cassie shook her head.

Grandpa laughed. "After this, if you're going to entertain a gentleman in your bedroom you'd better have ashtrays and matches."

Cassie sniffled.

"Give me that saucer," Grandpa said.

She went to her dresser and took the tiny saucer that held her add-a-pearl.

"Make do," Grandpa said. "That's the first rule." He lighted his cigar, sat back and puffed. "Grandma never let me smoke in the bedroom," he confided.

Cassie nodded sympathetically. See. Grandpa had problems, too.

"All right. Now let's talk about this party," Grandpa said. "You're not mad at me, are you?"

She shook her head.

"That's what I thought. But you're mad at your mommy because she likes you and your sister to look like Singer's Midgets—"

"What?"

"That's an old vaudeville expression. I mean she wants you two to look like trained seals."

Cassie smiled. Grandpa got it all right.

"You want to be yourself. Is that it, Cassie?"

"Yes, Grandpa." She wouldn't have been able to say it, but Grandpa had found the words for her.

Sam smiled. He'd known from the minute she was born that this was an independent one. She had guts, Sam Cassman kind of guts. He'd train this one, not let her get away the way her father had. He felt waves of love wash over him. He'd never loved any of them like this. Not his own parents. Not Bertha, his wife. Not his only son, William. What a disappointment that one was. Looked like his mother, was like his mother. He'd waited for the grandchildren. This one had it. All she needed was a little confidence, some reassurance. Okay. He'd give it to her. He cleared his throat. "I don't blame you for what you're doing. Listen, Cassie, I'm a pretty old fellow, and I'm still fighting to make people see me for myself. You have to start early. Assert yourself."

Noting the puzzled look on her face, he tried another tack. "So let me say it simple. You have to be pushy. You have to let people know who you are and what it means to make the deal. See, here's how I figure it. This is a deal. Your mother wants you to wear a dress like your sister's, but where's the prize for you? Your mother and your sister win everything. Your mother looks like a doll with two dolls. And your sister is a prettier doll. See? You thought I didn't know. But pretty, shmitty—what counts is the brains. Brains is what you have, Cassie. Remember this, baby. The face goes. The brains stay. All right. Now back to the deal . . ."

Cassie was fascinated. She couldn't take her eyes off Grandpa. He was gesturing, acting. He was better than Sir Laurence Olivier. "Now remember, in every deal there's got to be something for you. Any time someone asks you for something, ask what you're getting in return. Now sometimes all you get is the satisfaction of making someone else feel good. To tell the truth, that's usually not a good enough reason. Do it sometimes—but not often. Your mother thinks that making her happy is the reason for every deal. That's what's wrong with your mother."

Cassie giggled. That Grandpa really knew his stuff.

"You want a different dress; she won't give it to you. You know what you do?"

"No."

"Sure you do. It's what you're doing."

"You mean I don't go?"

"Exactly. You're born smart, Cassie. You're my granddaughter, for god's sake. Listen, I'm about to tell you the Samuel Cassman rule of success. I never told it to anybody before. Listen."

She knelt in front of the chair, and he took her face in his hands. She held her breath so she wouldn't have to smell the cigar, and Grandpa, his face almost touching hers, said, "Make your best offer, and if you can't get what you want—walk away."

"Walk away?" She was puzzled. She even breathed a little and almost fell over from the cigar fumes.

"Sure. Walk away. But first, fight for what you want just the way you did. Then, when you see you can't get what you want—walk away. That only makes everybody want to give it to you more. You're right not to go to this party, Cassie. Next year Diane will let you go, and she'll let you wear the dress you want. You won't wear the same dress as Stephanie, after all. Diane will say you're grown up now so you don't have to. But the real reason is she'll remember that you could walk away. And I'll tell you something else. There *will* be another party next year. And next year it won't be just a room at '21.' It'll be the whole third floor."

"You don't care if I don't go tonight?"

"I care, but I understand. Always do what you think is right. The trouble with your father is he can't even think, let alone know wrong from right."

That Grandpa sure was smart. Cassie reached up to kiss him. Then she rubbed her nose, tied her robe tighter and went downstairs to watch television. On her way she stopped at her mother's bedroom. "Mommy," she called, "I told Grandpa I'm not going to the party. He said it was okay."

Diane heard her and dropped the hairbrush she was holding. How did Cassie always know how to get to the old man? It certainly wasn't her good looks.

"What was that about?" Bill Cassman called from his dressing room.

"Cassie won't go to your father's party," she said dully.

"How do you like this tie?" Bill asked as he came into the bedroom.

"I said Cassie won't go to your father's sixtieth birthday party."

"Oh shit. There's a spot on it."

"Bill, Cassie won't go to the party in the dress I designed and had made for her, and your father says that's all right."

"Hey, Diane, do you have spot remover or do I have to wear another tie?"

"You didn't hear me, did you?" She sat on the edge of the bed and watched her husband look for a tie. No, he hadn't heard her. He was always so busy. Changing ties, arranging golf games, finding tennis partners. He was to the country club what his father was to the office. They'd each disconnected themselves from the world, the father with mergers and acquisitions, the son with tournaments and trophies. And she? What had she used? Charge accounts and luncheon dates. That was her escape from them all.

Bill Cassman walked out of his dressing room once more. He was five feet ten inches tall, good-looking in a pretty-boy, magazine-model way. He was wearing his black hair long, and his lean body was geared to show off the French and Italian clothes that lined his closets. One look, and you knew he was Stephanie's father. Both of them had what Diane knew to be the Cassman look of indifference. But it came from Bill's mother. It was a soft and sullen look. Slightly sensuous. Poor Cassie didn't have it. She had the same look as her grandfather. Tough. Hard. That wouldn't get a girl very far in this world. Softness was what men really wanted in women; they wanted to control their wives and daughters. Hadn't she seen that all her life?

"Diane, why aren't you dressed? You know this is a big night. Dad's not going to stand for anyone being late."

"Good, then since I can't be prompt I won't go," she said softly.

"Won't go? Since when don't you go to a family party?"

"Your father will have everything he wants at that party. He'll have you. He'll have my father. They can sit in the corner together and discuss tomorrow's *Wall Street Journal* and buy and sell everything in the world they don't already own."

"Diane, just shut up and get dressed."

"I don't have anything to wear."

"Diane, you're crazy. There's a closet filled with every designer's clothes and over sixteen thousand dollars worth of Gucci shoes and bags in case you've forgotten."

"Oh, are we discussing that again?" Diane asked, her voice rising.

"Discussing it? For god's sakes, it's all my father talks about. I don't have the money to pay for it. I don't know what gets into you. How can you spend sixteen thousand dollars at Gucci in one month?"

"Easily," she said laughing uncontrollably at her joke.

"What's wrong with you? You're really disgusting. Always proving how rich you are."

Her laughter slowed. "No. I'm proving how rich you are, how much you and Sam Cassman love me. You'll even pay my bills."

"Well, my father wants me to pay your bills. He won't, and I can't."

She stood, and now the laughter stopped. "But Sam won't give those bills to my father, will he? He won't because Sam Cassman doesn't want Charles Winters questioning his daughter. Your father doesn't want my father to know what really goes on in this house. You see, my dear Bill, Sam's afraid that Charles might pull back on a few deals, renege on a couple of pieces of land, isn't he? But if little Diane looks happy and has all those pretty things from Gucci, then the Cassmans must really be wonderful to our daughter. But my father's no better than your father. Each of them would sell us for a block of midtown real estate. My price this month is a Gucci bill."

[10]

"You're rotten, Diane. I can't stand you," Bill said.

"Join the crowd," Diane smiled.

"Listen to me, Diane. I don't have the money to pay that bill. I'm not a rich man. I'm a rich man's son."

"Good. Then you can go to the party and grovel in front of your father. And take Stephanie. She ought to be worth a few dollars from a grandfather. You can tell everyone that Sam's beloved Cassie isn't feeling well, and her mommy's taking care of her. That should go over well with all the relatives."

Diane walked back to her closet and looked at the rows of shoes. She was still standing there when she heard the front door slam and Bill leave with Stephanie.

Finally Diane walked into her bathroom, filled the tub and took two vials of sleeping tablets.

Cassie never knew just why she looked in her mother's room on the way upstairs. She didn't even realize Diane had stayed at home. But there was some strange, intuitive feeling that made her gravitate toward the bedroom. When she saw her mother's ashen face and heard the labored breathing, she knew something was wrong. Cassie screamed, and Miss Evans came at once. Minutes later an ambulance rushed Diane Cassman to Lenox Hill Hospital. Bill got the emergency call at "21," left quietly and hurried to the hospital, where he sat in the waiting room until four A.M. when the doctors assured him that his daughter's quick thinking had saved her mother's life.

The next morning Bill went into Diane's bathroom.

Floating in the bathtub were sixteen thousand seven hundred forty dollars worth of ruined Gucci handbags and matching shoes.

June 1968

Time cannot break the bird's wing from the bird.
Bird and wing together
Go down, one feather.

> Edna St. Vincent Millay
> "To a Young Poet"

II

CASSIE LOOKED AROUND her old room.

The Raggedy Ann doll still sat in the corner, her shoe-button eyes unchanged by the years. Cassie flung open her closet doors, searched for something—what? what?—to wear to Grandpa's party at noon today, a party to celebrate her graduation from Wellesley. As she opened the closet, memories of another Grandpa party came back to play a ghostly game. She shut the doors quickly and leaned against them. It would be awful today—all the family gathered at Grandpa's. But she had to do it for him, didn't she? It would be boring. So boring. Unless—of course!—unless she did something to liven up the party. She flung the doors open.

Stephanie stood in front of her closet and chewed her lip. What would Cassie wear today? She didn't want to upstage her sister. "Cass," she called down the hall.

"Coming in a minute," Cassie answered.

Stephanie stood in front of the three-way mirror and inhaled. If she could just keep her breath in, her stomach wouldn't go out. And nowadays, now that everybody was eating grains and all that terrible-tasting stuff, most women had thick waistlines. She squinted. There. Still an acceptable twenty-two inches. She let her breath go—whew!—and the hook and eye popped from the waistband of her fly-front skirt. Damn! Sal liked her thin, loved that little waist.

Sal! Just the thought of him made her smile. Wait 'til she told Cassie about him. Maybe she'd tell her now.

Stephanie hadn't really talked to Cassie about Sal yet. Well, she hadn't really talked to Cassie about very many things in the past four years. Not since Cassie went away. Before that they'd been close in the way that sisters finally grow close: somewhere in midchildhood, when they reach the age when both understand that parents, not siblings, are the enemy. Did any sisters unite out of love?

But make no mistake. Cassie had turned into a loving sister. Cassie was good, really good. Five years ago when Stephanie had had a crush on a classmate's father, hadn't Cassie said those telephone calls to California were hers? And later when "they" ("they" being their code word for their parents) had learned the truth, "they" had been annoyed. But by then that crush had ended, and Stephanie had been wildly in love with the lead singer in an Upper East Side rock group.

Love was so much fun. Falling in love was the best feeling in the world. Stephanie knew; she did it all the time. Funny that Cassie wasn't like that at all. Cassie was always doing boring stuff like reading. Still, she loved Cassie, and even though they weren't as close as they had been that year before Cassie went away to school, that year had bonded them for life. Once every two or three months Stephanie would call Cassie—all breathy and teary-voiced—with news of her latest romantic calamity. Each time Cassie listened and advised. But she never criticized. That's what made Cassie so good. She cared, but she didn't keep telling you what was wrong with you the way Mother did.

Mother. Muh-ther. Oh, how she wanted everything to be proper and social and perfect. Life just wasn't that way. Oh well, pretty soon she and Sal—

"Now what is it?" Cassie walked with a small bounce into her sister's room.

No one walked quite the way Cassie did: small, springy steps that made her seem even smaller than her five feet two inches. It was not a particularly feminine or graceful walk. Instead it was a funny kind of walk, full of promise, the bounce barely hinting at the explosive action that might erupt if ever the walker were to release more of the energy that made possible those buoyant steps.

The sharp, strong face that had marked Cassie as "an unusual-looking child" at best and "homely as sin" at worst had mellowed into a contemporary sort of look. Cassie's cinnamon-colored hair was cut very short and curled around her face. But the pugnacious look in her blue eyes had not been replaced by a more feminine one. Her look was still as much a defense as it was a statement. Cassie knew she'd never be a traditional glamour girl, but she didn't care. No, she didn't care at all. Not a bit. Not a particle.

Oh, who was she kidding? Of course she cared. Who wouldn't prefer being tall and willowy like Stephanie? Who wouldn't rather have the perfect features of Diane? Why would any girl want to be short and square when the world gave the best jobs and the best men to women who were hard-working but slender, intelligent but pretty, equal but better?

Like Stephanie.

Yes, Stephanie. Still perfect. Still the pretty sister. Smart, no. But oh, so pretty, with that black, straight, silky hair worn almost to her waist. So lovely with that perfect white skin where no blemish dared appear. Ah, so lovely. The one boys liked. "Pretty as a model," people said and added, "so different from—" From her. That's what they meant. So different from Cassie. Someone was always sure to ask, "Are you two really sisters?" From the time she was four years old until she was eleven, Cassie hated the people who asked, and her heart ached with envy. By twelve she—no, not she; it was Grandpa who did it really—Grandpa had come up with an answer for her to use. "No, we're not really sisters"—pause pause—"we're brothers." When she began to get laughs with that line, Cassie decided it was best to have a sense of humor about yourself, and as her wit developed she began to feel better. Humor didn't attract boys, but it helped with girls, teachers, and parents. And your sister. It helped make your gorgeous sister feel less guilty about her gorgeousness. At least humor had helped bring them closer.

Stephanie was picking the hook from her skirt off the floor. She looked up. "What are you wearing today, Cassie?"

"Who wants to know?"

"Don't get hyper. Not Mother. Just me."

"Oh well, Mother'll get hyper soon enough."

Stephanie stopped her movement. "Now what?"

"I'm going to wear jeans."

"You're kidding. You're always kidding."

"No, I'm not. I'm going to Grandpa's fawncy fawncy party in blue jeans."

Stephanie laughed. "They'll die," she said. Then, catching herself stating the family fear, she added hastily, "I mean, they'll have a fit."

"Jeans at a family party," Cassie mused, "that's what would excite our family. Isn't that awful, Stephanie? I graduated with highest honors, a Durant scholar, and the only thing that would matter to Mother is what I wear to a family party."

"Oh, that's not the only kind of thing that'd excite Mother," Stephanie said darkly.

"What's that supposed to mean?"

"If she doesn't like the man you fall in love with . . . if he doesn't turn out to be a Warburg or something like that . . ."

"Well, she certainly doesn't have to worry about the men in my life," Cassie interrupted angrily; then she stopped. What was the point of explaining her life to Stephanie? How would Stephanie ever understand what it felt like to be Cassie? How would Stephanie know about the stomachache you get when you sit around a dorm listening to girls talk about the men who love them? How would Stephanie know the humiliation that comes when you go to the mixer, and nobody mixes with you? Well, Cassie knew about those feelings. She knew only too well. She knew about telephones that didn't ring and girls who paid no attention to you. And boys. Oh sure, the new, feeling men. They still saved their feelings for the girls with the pretty faces. Who cared if you had all A's? Or wrote well? Or edited the college literary magazine? Only your grandfather. That's who. Your mother was too busy checking the family tree of the boys your sister saw, and your father—where was he anyway?

The magazines said that men were different these days. Oh sure. Really different. She made a face.

"Cassie, come off it," Stephanie said sharply. "You haven't heard a word I said."

"Sure I did. What did you say?"

Stephanie sighed. "I never know if you're being smart or funny."

"Or neither," Cassie mumbled.

"There you go again," Stephanie said, now really annoyed.

Cassie put an arm around her. "Sorry," she said. "You said something about men, and I just started thinking—"

"Is there someone?" Stephanie asked, a note of hope in her voice.

[18]

Cassie dropped her arm. "No. Nothing's changed. You still have the men, and I still have the grades. It's getting boring, isn't it?"

Stephanie looked at her sister and smiled, a beatific smile. A familiar smile. Oh, such a familiar smile.

And from that smile Cassie could predict her sister's next statement. But she didn't want to spoil Stephanie's dramatic timing. She waited.

Stephanie drew her breath, held it an instant, and then whispered, "I'm in love."

Cassie moaned, "Not again."

"Never like this," Stephanie said softly.

Cassie shook her head. Never like this? Dare she remind her that at least seven other times she'd stood in this very room hearing Stephanie's same teary voice and seeing Stephanie's same dreamy look as she proclaimed yet another undying love?

"No, never like this," Stephanie repeated. Now her eyes were closed.

"Wake up and tell me who he is," Cassie said in a flat tone.

"Sal Romano. You know, the singer."

"Sal Romano! I don't believe it. He's—he's—" Cassie stopped short. She wanted to say he's a third-rate singer who's old enough to be our father. Instead she asked, "How did you meet?"

"At Cousin Michael's bar mitzvah last year."

"What was he doing there?"

"Don't tell me you don't remember? He sang with the band."

"Have you seen him since?"

"Of course. I see him all the time. We're in love."

"Love?"

"Love. Madly, wildly, passionately. He's so good to me, so sweet. He can't get enough of me, Cassie. He sings those songs to me. He says for the first time in his life he knows what the words mean. He's had three wives, and he's never been in love before. This is it for me."

Cassie cringed. No, she wasn't jealous of Stephanie. Not this time. No man in your life was better than a Sal Romano. "How do you see him, Stephanie?"

"Well, we can't go out. His divorce isn't final yet. His wife is suing for child support and custody and all that kind of stuff, so we don't want to do anything to delay the divorce, and well—well, Cassie, we have an apartment near Lincoln Center."

Cassie shuddered. "I'll bet they don't know this at Finch College."

"Finch College!" Stephanie said the word as if it were an epithet. "What snobs. They're so—so chemically reproduced there that those girls wouldn't even recognize a real man anymore."

"This is pretty heavy stuff, Stephanie. I mean the idea of you and Sal Romano! He must be forty-five years old if he's a day."

"Fifty-one. He's three years older than Daddy. But age doesn't mean a thing. I love him; I absolutely adore him. He takes care of me, Cassie. No one ever has."

As she spoke, Cassie remembered Sal from the bar mitzvah, a tall slick man with dyed black patent-leather hair—the whole world looked different from him—a black suit that was too sharply tailored, a flashing diamond ring. Cassie had been repelled by him. Why wasn't Stephanie? Everything about him was something Cassie had seen before—only it had been done better. Even his singing style was stolen—an attempt at Sinatra's shading mixed with a touch of ersatz Tony Bennett.

"I'm going to marry him," Stephanie said with pride.

"Married?" Cassie shrieked. "Who gets married nowadays?"

"Men like Sal. Old-fashioned men."

"Don't marry him," Cassie said quickly. "You've got to stop looking—" She stopped suddenly and lowered her head. How could she tell her beautiful, popular sister to stop looking for a daddy outside the family and do what she, the homely one with no dates, did—use one of the grandfathers.

Instead Cassie asked, "Do Mother and Daddy know about him—and, and you?"

"Are you crazy? You're the first person I've told."

"What about Grandpa?"

"Grandpa doesn't know. Papa Charles doesn't know. Only you know, Cass." She said the last with a slight lift in her voice, a small note of hope. Cassie would help, wouldn't she?

Cassie stood rooted to the spot, silently facing her sister. Of all the secrets in the world she didn't want to hear, this was Number One. Stephanie, the adored daughter, the heiress apparent to the family's title of Most Likely to Continue the Social Line of the Winters Family—that first-rate beauty, Stephanie, was about to follow a secondhand siren song.

Cassie took a deep breath and gathered strength to go back to her room. Another mess. Another hard decision for Stephanie. What to do? She'd tell Grandpa. She'd find a way to talk to him today. He'd know what to do. Sal Romano. Oh God. She shuddered. They had to keep this from Diane. She reached in her closet and took out a black skirt and white sweater. She'd forgotten all about the jeans.

Cassie always felt a little thrill going across town to Grandpa's, and despite her preoccupation with Stephanie this last hour, it was still Cassie's day, even more of a graduation than the one earlier in the week at Wellesley. This was Grandpa's acceptance of the fact that his granddaughter was now a college graduate.

The four Cassmans settled in a cab; Grandpa had never permitted Bill to have a limousine and driver. As they drove through the park, Diane said what Cassie remembered her saying every time the family made the trip to Grandpa's. "You'd think that with your father's money he'd move to the East Side."

"For God's sake, Diane, he's not living in Altoona," Bill answered. "So my father likes the West Side. So what? So he's not chic like your father. Tough."

"Forget my father. Your father's the only one of his friends still there. You don't see any of the other people he knows living on the West Side. They moved to the East Side years ago."

"He'd never get that view he has from the San Remo on the East Side," Cassie said.

"Oh, of course. You'd defend him," Diane said. "Whatever Grandpa does must be perfect."

Cassie slumped in her corner of the cab. Right. Grandpa was perfect.

"Come on, Diane," Bill said as a small stab at diplomacy. "It's Cassie's party, so let's all relax."

"Who's going to be there?" Stephanie asked, eager to keep a peaceful conversation going between her parents.

"Sixteen. Just family," Diane answered.

All four were silent. Nothing could be worse than "just family."

Home.

That's where she really was. She was home the minute she got off the elevator on the sixteenth floor to find Grandpa waiting to put his arms around her and kiss her soundly on the lips. He took her face in his hands and his own blue eyes filled with tears. "My girl," he said again and again.

Of course he was right. She was Grandpa's girl, just as surely as he was her grandfather-daddy-beloved.

"Come on in and meet Elyse," Grandpa said, one arm around Cassie. Together they made a fetching picture—the adoring grandfather and his counterpart, separated by sex and years, yet bound inextricably by both looks and feelings.

"Elyse? Is she the reason you missed graduation?" Cassie asked.

"You didn't need me to graduate," Grandpa said quickly. "I don't like all those ceremonies; they're for women. I was here making money. Elyse had nothing to do with it."

"Then who is she?" Cassie asked again.

"The new one your father hates," he laughed. Cassie nodded knowingly. When Grandma had died thirteen years ago Grandpa had become what Bill called the Playboy of Central Park West. "He thinks he's Cary Grant," Bill said belligerently to all the family.

Grandpa himself laughed and told the family he couldn't help it; he was simply God's gift to widows. Those widows, Grandpa would say—his head shaking in mock compassion—they all came running with their chicken soup and roasts as soon as Grandma died. Then Grandpa would sigh. "You know what their problem is? They scare me. They're all too quick on the brisket." Then Grandpa's whole body would shake with laughter. Cassie laughed in return, but Bill didn't. Diane sneered. The old fool. In Charles Winters' heyday the women had been chic and elegant, the ad-

[22]

vance runners of today's jet set. Of course Papa Charles no longer saw any of those women—but that was another story.

Now Sam Cassman was proudly leading Cassie through the apartment. When they reached the huge living room with the leaded glass windows overlooking the park, the sun was streaming in. This was Cassie's favorite room in all the world. The high wainscoting was of dark-stained oak, and the plaster walls above were cream-colored. The dark wood floors were covered by Aubusson rugs; each piece of furniture had been selected by Grandpa and Grandma on their travels throughout the world. On the wall were two Braques, a Chagall, a Picasso, and a van Gogh. "I buy only what I like," Grandpa always said. "Who cares if it matches?" Diane, who never moved an ashtray without approval from her decorator, tried to get similar professional help for the Cassmans. Grandma had been willing to listen to the elegant daughter-in-law, but Grandpa said, "Nobody's going to tell me how to live."

Now in this room stamped with the toughness and the sweetness of Grandpa, Cassie was meeting the newest of his ladies.

"So you're Cassie," Elyse Fenton said.

"Yes," Cassie answered smartly. Well, what was there to say to these carefully coifed and girdled Mah-Jongg players Grandpa found? Small wonder Bill was nervous, but Cassie sensed that her grandfather would never marry any of them.

"Your grandpa certainly loves you," Mrs. Fenton was saying. Now Cassie smiled. This Elyse was no dummy. Cassie liked her—pink dress, Florida suntan and all.

"Where's the rest of the family?" Cassie asked, looking around the room.

"Oh, they're in the back watching the television," Grandpa answered. *The* television. Grandpa never watched television or telly or TV; it was always "the television."

As soon as Cassie heard "the television," she nodded knowingly. That meant the Cassmans had arrived. Family dinners were divided into two groups: the Cassmans and the Winters. The Winters drank and talked about Gstaad and Nice; the Cassmans ate and watched TV.

[23]

Grandpa always evinced a certain sentimentality before each family affair. "We're such a little family," he would sigh. Cassie agreed; they were a small family, but in a crowd they stood out like a set of unmatched china.

In her sophomore year Cassie had invited Marcia, her roommate, for Thanksgiving dinner, and when Marcia had quickly accepted, Cassie had cautioned her, "Outside of Grandpa they're not so terrific."

"Don't worry," Marcia answered, "on holidays any family is better than your own."

Cassie remembered Marcia's words as she walked to what Grandpa called "the back." It was formerly a maid's room, now converted to a small television room. She knew she'd walk in to find Uncle Izzy, Grandpa's brother. "Sam got the brains; I got the looks," Uncle Izzy was fond of saying. To Cassie only half the statement was true—the part about the brains.

Uncle Izzy's wife, Aunt Sarah, a heavy-set blonde with a quick tongue, was ever aware of the Cassman pecking order, an order that made Sam the head of everything and Izzy the brother who worked for the boss. "Listen, girls," Aunt Sarah would ask her friends in Miami, "where do you think Sam would be without Izzy?" Out of courtesy no one ever answered the question. Herbert, Izzy and Sarah's son, was married to a girl named Shirley. Herbert and Shirley, alike as Tweedledum and Tweedledee, had, appropriately enough, produced a set of twins named Donnie and Donna, now six years old.

"Bang, bang, I killed you," Cassie heard a twin yell as she entered the room. Was it Donna or Donnie?

"You're dead, you dumbbell," screamed the other child.

"Herbie, make them stop." No mistaking that voice. It was Aunt Sarah.

Donna turned toward her grandmother and hissed, "Bitch."

Aunt Sarah stiffened and stuttered, "H-H-Herbie, did you hear that?"

"Leave Herbert out of this," Shirley snapped at her mother-in-law from her position on the floor. "I am not going to let you turn Donna into a repressed child."

Now Donna lay down flat on the floor, stiffened her body and let out a bloodcurdling scream.

"What did I do?" Sarah moaned, moving toward her granddaughter.

"Leave her alone," Shirley commanded. "You didn't do anything. Just let her get rid of her frustration and anger."

"She's mad because her grandma loves her?" Izzy asked.

"Donna has negative feelings, and she has to resolve them in the way that's best for her. Now the natural reaction is to redirect the negative feeling outside one's own self—" Shirley explained.

At that moment another long and loud scream came from Donna.

"Herbie, turn off that set," his father shouted.

Herbie-Herbert obediently clicked the set off, but Donna's screams continued. A moment later she was joined by Donnie.

"What kind of craziness is this screaming?" Izzy asked.

"Look, Pa," Herbie explained, "Shirley and I think that it's very unhealthy to bury anger. You have to express it; otherwise a lot of little hurts can add up and do terrible damage to you later in life. If children let the anger out, they feel clean and good again."

"You don't tell them to stop?" Sam asked.

Herbie shook his head. "Never, Uncle Sam. Never."

"Then watch me," Sam commanded. He cleared his throat and thundered, "Stop that, Donna."

The little girl looked up and stopped screaming as suddenly as she had started.

"Now you stop, too," he ordered Donnie.

The little boy, caught in midscream, simply let out air like a deflated balloon.

"And you stop, too," Grandpa said pointing a finger at Shirley and Herbie. "Stop telling your children they can do whatever they want. Maybe this foolishness goes in your house but not in mine. This is Cassie's party and nobody's going to spoil it."

"Come on, Herbert, I think we'd better leave," Shirley said, standing and smoothing her skirt.

"Sit," Grandpa commanded. "You go when I tell you to go. Now remember, you're a guest in my house, and so are your children. You're here because my Cassie graduated from college, and I want to celebrate with the family. Listen, Shirley, we're all the family Herbert's got," he emphasized *Her-bert,* "so quit telling your children to scream, and act like a lady."

Shirley stood frozen.

Cassie smiled. She squeezed Grandpa's hand. Grandpa could do anything. He could make the sun shine, part the sea, and turn boiled spinach into caviar. Yes, he was the one to save Stephanie.

"Now come on, Cassie," Grandpa said. "I bet the others are here."

As they walked back through the long hall Grandpa confided to Cassie, "Families all in one room can drive you crazy."

"Then why did you have this party?" she asked.

"To show you off," Sam beamed as he hugged her.

Cassie shook her head. It was wonderful to be loved like this, but what if she ever disappointed him the way Stephanie was going to? Thinking of Stephanie reminded her to whisper, "I need to talk to you before I go."

Grandpa frowned. "What's wrong?"

"Nothing," she assured him. "It's not about me."

"Good, Cassie. From you I don't need surprises."

She locked her arm through her grandfather's and braced them both for the onslaught of Winterses.

The New York Winters family had more elegance and about as much money as Sam Cassman. German Jewish bankers, the Winters had come to the United States long before the Civil War and had established beachheads in such exotic places as San Francisco, Cincinnati, and Dallas. The San Francisco branch was in mining, the Cincinnati branch in retailing and the Texas branch in oil. Only the New York branch had stayed in banking. The same names had been used down through the generations, so there was a Selig Winters in New York and one in San Francisco. Similarly there were two Benjamins, three Alexes and four Leopolds. They were distinguished from each other by their city of origin and their place in family history, so there was "the first Alex in San Francisco," or "the second Leopold from Dallas." There was only one Charles. Now, generations later, he represented the New York branch with roots still deeply entwined in Wall Street. Charles advised the far-flung branches, the cousins throughout the United States, cousins who were now distant enough to intermarry and keep money from being tainted by other blood. Diane had just such a Winters match in mind for Stephanie; there was a Cousin Alex in Texas, twenty-six, a bachelor and supposedly a little wild. But a beautiful woman could always tame a wild man. Hadn't she done just that with Bill? Life, after all, hadn't been so easy for beautiful Diane Winters. Her mother had died when she was born, leaving Charles with a three-year-old son and the newborn daughter. He had immediately hired a staff for the Long Island home—nurses, maids, housemen, gardeners—and then Charles Winters had taken off to roam the world. Diane and her brother Dick would see their father on the high holy days when he came to New York to go to Temple Emanu-El and recite the prayer for the dead, Kaddish, for the wife he still mourned. He was home for Christmas, often on birthdays, always on March 15 to file his income tax. In 1960 he had been hit by a taxicab at three A.M. as he was leaving a lady's apartment. He had spent six months flat on his back in the hospital and come out a helpless cripple, paralyzed from the waist down and confined to a wheelchair. Now the nurses, maids, housemen and gardeners were summoned for him. Now Diane and Dick were parents to the man who had been a shadowy father to them. Each day a chauffeur took Charles Winters in a specially equipped limousine to his office on Wall Street, where it was generally agreed that Charles Winters's accident had only made him tougher, sharper, and more mentally agile.

Today he entered the living room, his wheelchair tended by Dick. Cassie went to kiss Papa Charles, the grandchildren's name for Charles Winters. "Hello, Uncle Dick," Cassie added as an afterthought. That's really what Uncle Dick was in the family—an afterthought. Dick Winters smiled absentmindedly. If he could only hold out for an hour, then he'd be able to slip away and no one would notice his departure. Behind Dick were his two children: Elizabeth, a seventeen-year-old with a rock-and-roll mentality, and Michael, a solemn fourteen-year-old with a passion for

[27]

business. At four he had announced his career goal: he would be president of United Air Lines. In ten years nothing had happened to cause Michael to change his mind. Nothing—not his father's lack of interest nor his mother's desertion. Dick's wife, Marilyn, had left him four years earlier and was now married to his best friend. But they saw each other and got on well. "Too well," Papa Charles often said. "If they'd hated each other more, they'd probably still be married. I guess the Winters blood is so thin we lost our passion over the generations."

Cassie looked around the room at each face. She saw boredom, hatred, anger. Then she laughed to herself. What did she expect? The Waltons?

"Cassie," Grandpa called, "come with me and pick out the wine for your party."

She looked at him in surprise. Since when was she the wine expert?

Grandpa winked broadly, and Cassie threw her head back and laughed. Foxy Grandpa once again. She'd said she wanted to talk to him, and Grandpa—ever eager to know what was happening— couldn't wait to get her into a corner. She followed him to the pantry.

"Now what do you have to tell me?" he whispered.

"I can't tell you here."

"What's wrong with this place?"

"All the help is here."

Sam Cassman walked into the kitchen. "Don't anybody go near that pantry for ten minutes." He walked back, turned to Cassie and said, "Now talk."

She looked down at the floor.

"Look up and talk," Grandpa commanded. "I got everybody out of here; don't waste time. You only have ten minutes. What is it? Your mother again?"

Cassie tried to rehearse the story, but she couldn't find the words. Finally she blurted, "It's Stephanie. She wants to marry Sal Romano, that old singer."

"So?" Grandpa asked. "That's all you wanted to tell me?" He reached in his pocket for a cigar. "I thought it was important."

"But it is important. He's older than Daddy. He's in his fifties. Grandpa, we have to stop her. It'll kill mother."

Grandpa shrugged. "It'll take more than that to kill her. Look, Cassie, in a family filled with bad marriages, what's another?"

Didn't he understand? She'd try again. "Grandpa, we just can't let her marry him."

"We?"

"You and I. We have to stop her."

Grandpa put his arm around Cassie. "Let me tell you something, sweetheart. You're a young girl, and there are some things you don't know yet. You can never keep people from doing what they really want to do. So your sister thinks she loves a broken-down comedian—"

"Singer," Cassie corrected him.

"Comedian, singer, what's the difference? Your sister's going to marry wrong, no matter what. If your mother had her way, Stephanie would leave to marry one of her rich cousins in some other city. Would that be good? Who knows? Look at Stephanie's life so far. What's been right for her? She's a sweet little puppet of her mother's; she has to break away. And who are we, Cassie, to know what way she should go? Your other grandfather and I were sure we planned the greatest match in the world when your parents got married. Outside of producing you, their marriage has been a disaster. I thought when they got married . . . good. So now she'll make him go to work. No more being a bum. I was wrong. He ran instead to play more golf, more tennis. Anything to get away from her. I pushed for that marriage. So did Charles Winters. We were wrong. The smart fathers. We were very wrong. But oh, how we thought we were doing good. What I'm saying, doll, is, don't get mixed up in anybody else's love affairs. Just tell your sister you love her, give her a kiss, and let her do what she wants."

"I don't think she knows what she wants," Cassie said sadly.

"Well, it's not up to you to decide for her. It's her life, Cassie. It's a big temptation to play God with your younger sister. But you'll be damned if you don't let them get married and damned if you do."

[29]

"But she confided in me, Grandpa. I think she told me because she wanted me to end it for her."

"Don't give me that psychological stuff, Cassie. I get enough of it with your mother and her Park Avenue analyst. Forget all that Freud stuff. Let's look at it coldly. I deal in figures. Now what are the chances of this being a good marriage? Zero. But at least when this marriage goes down the drain, Stephanie won't be able to say, 'My sister made me do it.' "

"Grandpa, I want to help her."

"Then walk away."

Sam Cassman threw his head back, inhaled, blew one perfect smoke ring, smiled and said, "Let's go back to the party, Cassie. Enough of Stephanie already."

III

LUNCHEON WAS SIMPLE, hearty, and catered down to the last roll by "21." It was what Cassie called "Grandpa food." Shrimp cocktail, fillets, baked potatoes, salad. "For this you need '21'?" Aunt Sarah sniffed in an aside to Shirley.

As the graduation cake was wheeled in, Grandpa stood and tapped his wine glass carefully. The small conversation died. Cassie sat back and smiled; it was all for her, all done out of love. "You all know why we're here today," Grandpa began. "When Cassie was born, I said to Diane and Bill that when Cassie was twenty-one, I'd have a birthday party for her at '21.' But Cassie's birthday was in April when she was away at school, so I decided to wait until June and celebrate two things: her new adult status and her graduation from Wellesley. Maybe it's hard for some of you who look around this house to understand what it means to a boy who began with nothing, a boy who grew up in a cold-water flat with an outhouse in the backyard, to come to this point in life. I have everything a man could want: a beautiful home, a fine career, plenty of money. But I have more. I have a granddaughter who is a graduate of Wellesley. That's something money can't buy."

Charles Winters cringed. These people were so—so maudlin.

"Here, hear," came a male voice. Everyone turned as Uncle Izzy rose and raised his glass. "May I propose a toast to Samuel Cassman, all of us, the family, and especially Cassie. I thank you."

Sam threw his napkin down on the table. "For God's sake, Izzy, not yet. I didn't want that yet."

Cassie and Stephanie shot knowing looks at one another and contained their laughter. Poor Grandpa. He'd orchestrated everything, but Izzy, with his usual faulty timing, had stood up too soon.

Sheepishly, Izzy sat down.

"Okay, forget it, Izzy," Grandpa said.

Charles Winters laughed out loud.

Sam shot a black look at Charles Winters. Then Sam turned to his granddaughter. "Come here; stand by me, Cassie. Now I'll talk in front of everybody. So tell the family. What are you going to do now that you're a graduate?"

Cassie looked at her grandfather. What was he expecting her to say? She'd tell the truth; that's all she could do. "I have a job at Doubleday, the publishing company. I got it through the Wellesley placement office," she added apologetically. How could she explain that a job in publishing was only the most sought-after job of a seven sisters English major?

"And what will you be?" Grandpa asked.

"Be?"

"Yes. Be-come. What will you be-come?"

She dug her toe in the carpet. What was Grandpa leading up to? She looked up, "I think I will become an editor, and since I'm ambitious and smart, a Winters as well as a Cassman"—there was an audible sigh of relief as she named both sides of the family, credited everyone for her brains; they scarcely heard the rest of her statement—"I'll probably be the best editor in New York within ten years."

Grandpa laughed and pinched her cheek playfully. "So, Cassie, is that all there is? Is that all you want out of life? To be an editor?"

[31]

She looked at her grandfather soberly, and she thought . . . no, no, that's not all I want out of life. I want a man who will love me a lot and be good to me . . . and I don't ever want to see my mother try to kill herself . . . and I hope I never hear my father complain about bills again . . . and I hope everybody will survive if Stephanie marries that creep . . . and I hope you never walk away from me, Grandpa . . . and I especially hope I never have to ask any person in this room for money.

But of course she said none of that aloud.

Instead she squared her shoulders, stared straight at Grandpa and said in a low voice, "There are three things I want in life. I want to be rich, famous, and live to the year two thousand."

Grandpa smiled. "I can only help with the rich and famous."

"How?" called Papa Charles.

Sam Cassman's back stiffened. Who was Charles Winters to question his intentions?

"I'll do plenty," Sam said.

"Now's the time to tell," Charles said.

"All right, Cassie," Sam said, his face beet-red. "Forget Doubleday. Come to my office."

"No. Come to my office," Papa Charles called out.

Cassie looked from Papa Charles to Grandpa Sam. Had this been planned? No, it was a fight—not a fight really, but a contest—between the two men. And she was first prize. Maybe Stephanie was smart to run away and get married.

There was not a sound in the room.

Then Cassie looked straight into her grandfather's blue eyes. "No," she said. "No, I won't work for you."

Then she turned toward her other grandfather. "And Papa Charles, I won't work for you."

Again there was silence.

Bill was distraught. Who was Cassie to say no to two such grandfathers?

Diane fingered the hem of her napkin. Was Cassie crazy? The fortunes she and Bill couldn't touch were being thrown at Cassie's feet, and she was turning away.

Bill stood up. "Why don't you go to Europe for the summer,

dear? That's part of the graduation present Mother and I want to give you." He blew the perspiration from his upper lip. God, get the kid out of town before she screwed everything up.

Cassie shook her head. "I don't want any more in-between things. I've been to Europe other summers. I can't wait for my life to begin. I'm starting to work at Doubleday on Monday."

"That's ridiculous," Bill said, his vexation toward his older child now showing plainly. "Take the trip and think things over."

"We know better than you," Diane added.

"No, you don't," Cassie said, her voice barely audible.

Diane closed her eyes, and for a moment she could see the ten-year-old Cassie in the perfect little sister dress.

"Just a minute," Grandpa said slowly. "You won't go to work for Charles Winters or me. You know something? I think maybe you're right. But I'm not sure Doubleday is the best place for you. I have a couple of other ideas. Will you listen? Saturday, nine o'clock sharp in my office?"

She nodded.

Sure, Grandpa.

Sure, I'll be there.

Nothing will keep me away.

Because this is the beginning of Alexandra Cassman.

Until now you've been the one with the brains.

Until now Stephanie's been the one with the men.

But look out, world.

My name is Alexandra Cassman, and my time has come.

I'm never going to sit out another dance.

Or wait for a job to find me.

I'm on the loose. I'm free. I'm out to get the best.

The best job.

The best man. School and those wimpy boys are all behind me.

Hello, world.

Here comes Cassie.

And nobody had better get in my way.

Sam Cassman smiled.

He'd finessed Cassie right out of Charles Winters's hands.

They'd learn someday.
They'd all learn.
Sam Cassman always got his way.

IV

SATURDAY MORNING AT eight forty-five Karl, Grandpa's driver, came to pick up Cassie to take her to the Empire State Building. "You're still Grandpa's little girl," Karl said. "Plenty of Saturdays I came to your house, always eight forty-five sharp, to get you and take you away with him."

"My favorite part was lunch," she laughed.

"He used to take you to '21'. "

"Only at the beginning. Later he took me to other places."

Karl said nothing, but Cassie thought of the other places, the ethnic restaurants of New York in Little Italy, Chinatown, Harlem, and the Lower East Side. Grandpa wasn't just a grandfather; he was an experience. She felt waves of love as she counted the blocks, and when she arrived at the office and saw her grandfather behind the big partners' desk where he'd wheeled and dealed for fifty years, she ran over to kiss him, just as she had when she truly was Grandpa's little girl.

"Sit. Over there," he commanded. "No, not the couch. The other side of this desk. Why do you think I have a partners' desk?"

She grinned.

"I bought this desk because I knew someday I'd have a son, and he would sit across from me. I have a son, but he's not good enough to even try out that chair. You I'll let try it out."

She slid into the chair. It was too big for her. Too big in every way. What was Grandpa up to?

"Look, let's not fool around. You can go to Doubleday and be happy and have a very good life. I wouldn't stop you."

"You really wouldn't try to stop me, Grandpa?"

"No, that's not true. I guess I'll try. Cassie, what do you want with a company where you can't be the president? President. That's what a job has to lead to."

[34]

She paused. Grandpa was right. The chances for becoming president of Doubleday were not exactly as rosy as the chances of becoming president of any company in which Samuel Cassman had as much as an eyelash of interest.

"So what do you think I should do, Grandpa?"

"Remember my attorney, Jerry Farber?"

"No, I don't think so."

"He's the nice fellow who's a theatrical lawyer, handles some authors, a little real estate, some union work. I know him because I've bought and sold theaters over the years. Anyway, I talked to Jerry, and he said he could use a smart young girl graduated with highest honors . . ."

"What could I do for him?"

"Look, listen, and then move on to a real job."

"How do I know what's real?"

"You ask your grandpa. He'll have all the answers."

She said nothing. She wasn't sure she wanted all the answers.

"Now let's go to lunch. Is "21" all right?"

"Come on, Grandpa. Let's go to the good place."

He smiled and nodded approvingly. He buzzed his secretary. "Tell Karl we won't need him today." The good place, of course, was the Lower East Side, where they'd walk and talk just like in the old days, before Wellesley.

"It's good you're back; we'll have our Saturdays together again."

As he said the words she could see the continuing pattern, the ever present Grandpa pressure in her life. Suddenly she felt as if she were suffocating. She had to try to get her breath and do it now. Now. She gripped the edge of the desk and found her voice. "No, Grandpa. We won't have our Saturdays. I need them for myself."

"I'm not yourself?"

"I'll see you a lot, not just Saturdays."

He started to speak, then stopped. The little girl was growing up. He wasn't sure he liked it.

Cassie started on June 15 as Jerry Farber's girl Friday at Farber, Flynn and Fogel. The office was in the Corning Building

[35]

right on Fifth Avenue; the salary was seventy-five hundred dollars a year.

On August 1, Cassie moved into an apartment on East Fifty-seventh Street, a one-bedroom penthouse apartment with a small living room and a narrow terrace with a sweeping view of absolutely nothing. Every view was blocked by yet a taller building. Diane's decorator, Harold Quince, offered to do a few little things "just to make it livable, darling," and Diane offered to pick up the bill. So Cassie ended up with a tiny apartment that reeked of money and chic—and Diane. Each night Cassie came home, put her key in the door, and entered a place where she felt like a visitor. Even her dorm room at Wellesley had seemed more her own. This place was Diane Junior.

Cassie bought a few things to wear to work, and at least she did that without Diane. Her wardrobe consisted mainly of two longish skirts (one black, one brown) and tailored shirts. She thought she looked terrible, but she noticed that for the first time men's eyes rested on her. Instead of dismissing her with a glance or—even worse—bypassing her, men now seemed to smile when they saw Cassie. At least the men at Farber, Flynn and Fogel did. Those smiles made her feel at least an inch taller. And she knew the smiles she gave those fortyish men made them feel at least a year younger.

There was one man, however, who didn't stop at Cassie's desk to exchange pleasantries about the weather, the work load, or the news of the day. His name was Jimmy Brown, and he was so beautiful that Cassie's heart practically stopped every time she saw him. Jimmy Brown had long blond hair and blue eyes and a perpetual suntan. She knew it was a perpetual suntan. Sure, this was June, and you could expect the beginnings of a suntan now. But Jimmy's tan was a part of Jimmy—just like those deep, intense blue eyes.

Cassie's job was interesting in its way. It didn't sound as impressive as Marcia's: working for the public television station in Boston. And it certainly wasn't as important as the careers of some other classmates of hers, at least six of whom had gone to Washington to work in senators' offices, the space program, and various government agencies. Cassie had no illusions about this job; she was really a secretary's secretary. And she had no dream of becoming the secretary. Indeed, she liked her job better because she did the research on Jerry's clients, who were an interesting bunch: Broadway producers, film stars, writers. But the one person she really wanted to research was Jimmy Brown. She began her research with Jerry's secretary.

"Jimmy's a nice kid, about twenty-three or twenty-four. He was just graduated from law school—don't ask me which one—and he's waiting around here while he takes the bar. You know, sort of a paralegal." Cassie thought he seemed more like an office boy.

In the meantime, she began dating. More dating than she'd ever done in all her life. Diane sent a procession of young men—she seemed tuned in to everyone who had a son looking for a new lady—and they all seemed like carbon copies of Cassie's parents. These young men took her to the fashionable restaurants, the private clubs, the places where you saw your parents or their reasonable facsimiles. But these were one- or two-date fellows; they were always stopping en route to somewhere or something. And she wasn't very interested in any of them anyway. They all seemed so, oh, so sort of *vapid*. The only young man within sight who didn't look vapid was Jimmy Brown.

"Jimmy Brown?" Jerry said when Cassie asked. "Oh sure. I know who you mean. Nice-looking boy, isn't he?"

Cassie could scarcely breathe as she nodded yes.

Jerry shrugged. "H-m-m, I wouldn't guess he's your type."

Cassie's heart sank. What was that supposed to mean? He's so good-looking he wouldn't want you? She felt her juices bubbling. In anger and frustration, Cassie waited until her lunch hour, then stormed out of the office. "Don't hit a truck," the receptionist called after her.

"Ha, ha," Cassie snapped as she stood at the elevator and punched the button. Once on Fifth Avenue she strode down to Saks and went to the makeup counter. "Give me a good face," she said to the surprised cosmetician. And thirty minutes and one-hundred twelve dollars later she was armed with cosmetics and a new—if not better—face. Then she went over to Madison Avenue and bought a short black dress with white collar and cuffs. It wasn't like anything she'd ever worn. She didn't even look like the same Cassie who'd left the office an hour before. But she was cooling down now. Getting calm. Relaxing. She could breathe easier. She'd show Jerry. And everybody else.

When she went back to the office she felt less confident. What if no one noticed? Of worse, what if they didn't recognize her because she looked so good? She came into the reception room with her head down.

"Whom are you seeing?" the receptionist asked.

Cassie lifted her head.

"Oh, my God, it's you," the receptionist blurted.

Cassie quickly moved toward her office. She didn't know whether the surprise was good surprise or bad surprise.

About ten minutes later she looked up to see—oh, was it really true?—could it be?—Jimmy Brown sitting on the edge of her desk. Nobody ever sat better. She grinned foolishly. She didn't know quite what to say.

"Hi, Cassie."

So! He knew her name. He must have done some asking, too. She sat straighter. She wasn't such a bad number after all. No indeed. Not if Jimmy Brown knew her name. "Hi."

"I'm Jimmy Brown."

She fought the temptation to say "I know." Instead she smiled. "My name is Alexandra Cassman, but everyone calls me Cassie."

"I know," he said.

She smiled, a big wonderful happy-to-be-me smile.

Jimmy Brown knew.

The first date with Jimmy was perfect.

Not like the ones with Mother's friends' sons.

None of those middle-aged restaurants.

Not for Jimmy Brown.

He took her to Chicken Little, the hottest disco in New York, and they danced until four in the morning. The music was so loud you couldn't talk. But who had to talk when there were bodies and movement and feeling? Oh such feeling! It was beyond words.

The first date was followed by another, and another, and another. Cassie had never seen so much of any man unless he'd needed help with schoolwork. Here was a man who didn't want help but gave it.

By the fourth date she felt she knew Jimmy well enough to ask, "Did you think I looked different the day you stopped to talk to me?"

"You mean because you were made up?"

She nodded.

"To tell the truth, Cassie, I'd been waiting to talk to you for about three days, and I'd decided that that was the day, and when I went over to introduce myself, Jerry's secretary said you were out to lunch. So I decided that whenever you came back from lunch, I'd be there."

Cassie laughed. "So my new face didn't mean a thing."

He squinted and framed his hands around her face. "Honest opinion?"

"Honest opinion."

"All right then. Do more with those cheekbones."

"Cheekbones?"

"Yes, cheekbones. You have marvelous facial structure."

"I do?"

"Of course you do. I took an art class, and I know lines and planes—"

"Where did you take the art class?"

"University of Pennsylvania."

"Is that where you went to school?"

He nodded.

"And to law school?"

"Penn."

"And now?"

"I'm working at Jerry's until I pass the bar, and then I'll have to make some big decisions. I don't know if I want to be a lawyer."

"What do you want to be?"

"A mover. A shaker. Law's so damned slow. I'm a young man in a hurry, Cassie."

She smiled. He was a man after her own heart.

"Look. Just look at that face when it smiles. Oh, you are a beauty, Miss Cassman."

"Oh, I am not."

[39]

"Stop the modesty. You are an absolutely beautiful woman. None of those cotton-candy looks. I hate those. I like your looks, Alexandra."

"Nobody calls me Alexandra except Papa Charles. He's my grandfather.

"I hope that's all I have in common with him."

"Well, I have nothing in common with him. He's my mother's father, and I've never spent any time with him at all. But my other grandfather . . . oh, my other grandfather's fabulous. You'd be wild about him. I know you would."

"In that case I hope I get to meet him."

"You will. I'll see that you do." She paused as the idea came to her. "What do you do on Saturdays?"

"Saturdays I just kind of hang out."

"Great. Want to go with Grandpa and me one Saturday?"

"What do you do?"

"You'll see," she promised.

Sam was pleased when the call came from Cassie. "So I'm back on the Saturday list?"

"Will you let me bring a friend?"

"If that's the price, I'll pay it."

Cassie thought about the conversation as Karl picked her up on East Fifty-seventh at eight forty-five. Jimmy was waiting on the corner of Fifth Avenue and Fifty-fifth, and the car slowed down for him.

"A Mercedes? Nice generous grandpa you have, Cassie."

"Oh, it's his car, not mine," she reminded him. "I'm still standing in the wings."

Jimmy leaned over and kissed her. "I like those wings."

Cassie wondered how Sam would react to a boyfriend of hers. She'd never really brought anyone home. Would he be jealous? Sweet? Understanding? After all, he had plenty of girlfriends.

"So this is the young man," Sam Cassman said. "Sit down. Sit down. Want a cigar?"

"No thanks, sir. I'm glad to meet you. I've heard so many fine things about you—"

"What did she tell you?" Sam asked pointing to Cassie.

[40]

"Only that she loves you and you're smart—"

"Which proves you should never ask a relative an opinion. What do the other people say, Mr. Brown?"

"Call me sir, Jimmy. I mean call me Jimmy, sir."

Sam threw his head back and laughed. "Sir Jimmy. That's a hot one."

Cassie flushed. Grandpa hadn't been rude. In fact, nothing had gone wrong, but everything had. It was time to step in. "Where are we going to lunch today, Grandpa?"

"Oh, kitten, I made a lunch date," Grandpa said.

"But I thought—" she finished lamely.

"I guess you thought wrong, doll. I had another date. Now I suppose you and Sir Jimmy will be able to figure out a few things to do. Two healthy young people don't need advice from an old man on how to spend a few hours."

Wordlessly they rode the elevator to the lobby.

Finally Jimmy said, "Can you cook, Cassie?"

She shook her head. "Well, I can," he said. "Let's go and buy some pasta and fresh vegetables, and we'll make one small Italian luncheon for you and me. I've got a couple of bottles of red wine at my place—"

"Let's go," she said, the relief flooding her. It could have been so awkward, but Jimmy, deft, adorable Jimmy, covered over the inexcusable rudeness of Samuel Cassman.

The publishers' spring lists included a book by one of Jerry Farber's clients, and it was decided to send Cassie as a sort of super-schedule arranger to Dallas, Houston, and Atlanta with John O'Rourke, an old-time movie actor who had written a book about how he gave up liquor and latched onto religion. What he didn't mention in his autobiography was that he had also latched onto young boys, and Cassie had her hands full keeping the tit-. illating news from the media.

The day she came back to New York Jerry came into her office. "How did it go, kid?"

She smiled. Jerry was a little like an uncle. In his midfifties, gray-haired and soft-spoken, he looked like the firm and gentle man he was. Cassie realized that Grandpa had arranged the job because it was the closest thing he could find to the publishing business, but both Cassie and Jerry knew it wasn't exactly the same as editing star authors.

"You didn't tell me everything about that fellow, did you, Jerry?"

"Cassie, you've been here almost a year now. I figure you know the score."

"Come on, Jerry, you never told me how he kept score."

His eyes opened wide. "I didn't?"

"You'd make a great attorney. Too bad you're an actor instead. Jerry, don't tell me you didn't know that our author had a little problem with—u-m-m, little boys."

Now he looked truly concerned. "I thought that was a long time ago. Did you have any trouble?"

"Nothing serious. But once I got the drift, I just went into his room and said, 'Hey, what you're doing is probably terrific. But don't do it in Dallas, Houston, or Atlanta, or you'll not only have a few show bookings but some police bookings, too."

"And?"

"Once he knew that I knew, it took the fun out of it. He was good from then on."

"You're tough, Cassie." Then, seeing the look on her face, he added, "I mean that in a good way. I've been watching you around the office, and I get great reports on your work. There isn't much you can't do."

"There's a lot I don't know."

"Sure, but you can learn. Now are you ready for the next step?"

"What is it?" She felt a little thrill; it was like that anticipatory feeling she was just starting to know when you're with a man who's interested in you and you're waiting for his next move.

Jerry chewed his pipe and finally said, "I think you've got to get a look at the business you know instinctively. Let's get you into real estate. I've got a project for you."

"You are so subtle, Mr. Farber."

"Come on, Cassie. This is far from the Cassman interests, so relax. You've worked with Betsy Blakely on contracts. Betsy trusts you. Now she wants to buy a co-op, and she's asked if you'll

[42]

go with her. You know, sort of look things over and help her make the deal."

"Why me? Why doesn't she get a broker?"

"Because Betsy's like all those actresses. Tight with her own bucks. Before she parts with a quarter, she flies the eagle. She thinks that's getting her money's worth."

"I still don't understand why she won't get a real estate agent. It's the seller who pays the agent, not the buyer."

"Betsy thinks an agent will push her into a deal just to make the commission. She says she can trust you. Will you do it?"

Cassie smiled. Maybe it *was* in the blood; the thought of real estate made her feel suddenly alive. "I'll do it," she said quickly. She didn't want Jerry to change his mind.

When she told Jimmy about the assignment, he took her out for a drink. "You're moving up, Cassie."

She put her hand on his. He was so generous, so good, so giving. Suddenly she felt pangs of guilt. "What about you, Jimmy? What's happening to you? When do you take the bar?"

He drew her to him and kissed the top of her head. "This is your day, Cassie. Thanks for caring, but we'll talk about my options another day."

"Your options?"

"Sure. The things I want to do."

"But you want to be an attorney."

"Now are you saying that or am I?"

"But you ought to at least take the bar."

He smiled. "Would that make you happy?"

She nodded.

"Then I'll do it."

She ran her fingers through her curls—

"That's so adorable. Do it again," he said.

She did.

"Now what were you going to say, Cassie?"

She shook her head. She couldn't remember.

Betsy Blakely didn't want to spend the time needed to look for a place to live, but on the other hand she wanted to see every apartment personally. Cassie scoured the pages of the *Times* every morning and called each likely lead.

"How's it going?" Jerry asked one morning as he poked his head in the door of the tiny, windowless cubicle Cassie called an office.

She looked up from the paper, stopped her pencil in midair, and said, "Betsy Blakely is one tough cookie."

Jerry sat on the edge of her desk. "No tougher than Sam Cassman."

"Meaning?"

"Meaning that nobody's easy when it comes to money. Especially Sam."

Cassie's eyes narrowed. What was Jerry really trying to say? She stood up. "Look, Grandpa—no, I mean Sam—no, I mean Grandpa is generous. Look what my grandfather has given to this city—a vest-pocket park, donations to every charity regardless of—"

"Whoa, horsie. Who said he wasn't charitable? There's a difference between selling it and giving it away. And don't you forget it."

She nodded and sat down quietly. But he didn't have to worry. She wouldn't forget that Jerry Farber thought Grandpa was as tough as that bitch Betsy Blakely.

"Now back to Miss Blakely," Jerry said with a smile. "What's happening?"

Cassie regained her composure instantly and answered, "I can't find anything she doesn't pick apart before she's past the foyer. 'Too high up.' 'Too low.' 'Terrible lobby.' 'Dark rooms.' 'Too much sunshine.' 'Wrong exposure.' And that's *before* she sees the plumbing."

Jerry laughed. "I've got an idea. Fold up your newspaper, kid, and find yourself a good agent."

"But I thought you said—"

"*I* didn't say; *she* said. And why does she have to know how you're working?"

Cassie smiled. "No wonder Grandpa wanted me here. You're one smart fellow."

He patted her head. "Now listen carefully, Cassie," he said

reverting to his usual crisp style. "The best agent in town is Hilda Taylor. Call her, take her to lunch—no one ever does—and tell her your problem."

Hilda Taylor had twenty business years and two husbands behind her. At forty-three she was a woman whose professional and social lives were so intertwined you couldn't tell where one began and the other ended.

Cassie invited Miss Taylor to meet her in the Regency Hotel dining room. It seemed businesslike yet a good woman's place, and Cassie was surprised to find Hilda Taylor already at the table when she arrived five minutes ahead of schedule.

"I always come early," Miss Taylor explained. "Then the client is on the defensive from the start."

Cassie nodded knowingly, as if she shared that business trick.

"Call me Hilda," her guest said quickly. "We'll get down to business in due time. But first let's get rid of the vital statistics. As you probably know, I've been married twice. My first husband was a lot older; my second husband was the same age. Now I live with a man twelve years younger than I am, and I'm still waiting to get the score on that one."

Cassie, wide-eyed, could hardly order her omelet. Wasn't this supposed to be a business lunch? All this didn't have much to do with Betsy Blakely and an apartment, but why not play the game Hilda's style? "Are you going to marry the man you live with?" Cassie asked.

Hilda laughed loudly. Cassie smiled in embarrassment. What was so dumb about asking? Wasn't that what Hilda wanted?

"Honey, I wouldn't get married again if I were pregnant with the South American sextuplets."

"You don't believe in marriage?"

"Hardly. What did marriage ever do for a woman?"

"My mother seems to like it."

"Did you ever ask her? Really ask her?"

"I guess not."

"Marriage was invented by men to keep women in place. Don't you think it's kind of wonderful the way they do it? We dress ourselves up so the men will grab first. They do, and then

[45]

we say we're interested. And they act as if we want to rob them of their precious freedom. Finally they agree under great duress, pain, and pressure that yes, they'll marry us. And the next thing you know we're the ones who've been robbed of our freedom."

"Oh, it's not that way any more," Cassie said.

"How do you know? Have you ever been married?"

Cassie shook her head.

"Well, no matter what all those women's lib leaders say, I'll tell you from experience that nothing's changed between men and women. You see, all those men had mothers, and those mothers and sons are out to get the next generation. Meaning us," Hilda said pointing to herself and Cassie. "Don't look so shocked, my dear. I know we're not the same age, but in the business world all of us women have to be the same age, the same color and the same size. You see, we're all wearing the same jersey."

"You really think it's us against them?"

"I know it is. Now let's see how we can outsmart them. Come on, what do you want me to do for you? What's the purpose of our lunch really?"

Cassie leaned forward and told Hilda about Betsy Blakely. Hilda took notes as Cassie spoke, and when Cassie finished, she flipped her black notebook to the back pages. "I've got some listings," she said looking up, "but I can't give them to you now."

"When will you?"

"Meet me here at the Regency for breakfast at eight o'clock Monday morning."

Good. Cassie smiled. Someone else could think about Bitchy Betsy for a while.

Hilda asked Cassie some questions about herself and Cassie found that suddenly she was talking openly about things she'd never discussed with anyone. Meeting Hilda Taylor was a little like meeting a stranger on a plane; you knew your paths would never cross again, and so you felt free to tell the things that everyone else would judge you for doing. Probably it had been Hilda's refreshing openness at the beginning of the luncheon that set the tone, but in this atmosphere of intimacy Cassie felt surprisingly grown-up. Maybe that was because Hilda was the first

[46]

person she'd met in business who didn't treat her like Sam's granddaughter. Openly and with no hesitancy she told Hilda about her romance with Jimmy and her love of business. But there was one thing she didn't tell. She never told Hilda Taylor that she was Samuel Cassman's granddaughter. Somehow she didn't want Hilda to know that a man had put her into her job.

When luncheon ended Hilda stood and shook hands with Cassie. Hilda was six feet tall with curly black hair, black eyes, and big bones. Cassie was surprised to see just how tall she was; she felt like a circus midget next to her.

"Don't let my size scare you," Hilda winked at Cassie. Obviously, Hilda was used to people being awed by her imposing height; Cassie wondered fleetingly if that was the real reason she always arrived early—in order to be seated before she was judged. Yes, Hilda was certainly what Grandpa would call a lot of woman. But her strong personality seemed right for that strong body. Which had come first?

As they left the dining room, Hilda said to the maitre d', "I'll see you Monday. Miss Cassman is joining me."

"You didn't tell him what time we'd be here Monday," Cassie said as the two women retrieved their coats from the check room.

"I didn't have to," Hilda said. "No one eats anything but breakfast in this room."

Cassie flushed. "I guess I'm no one."

"You'll learn," Hilda Taylor said crisply. "The Regency dining room is where New York makes its business deals over breakfast. At noon the wives of businessmen from Minnesota who've been brought along on the trip come down for brunch. And dinner is for hotel guests who don't have anyone else to eat with. But breakfast at the Regency. Ah, that's where New York deals."

By the time they met Monday, Hilda had four good leads for Cassie, and by Wednesday Betsy agreed to close on an apartment on Fifth Avenue.

"It's really too good to sell to her," Hilda confided to Cassie.

Cassie laughed. "I think so, too. That apartment won't look nearly as good with Betsy living in it."

"I like you," Hilda said and shook her hand firmly.

[47]

Cassie felt good about herself; Hilda was her first real business friend, her first round without Grandpa watching over her.

Two days later Cassie and Jimmy were standing in line at a West Side movie house waiting to see *Psycho*. It was their seventh date.

Seventh date! Imagine! Cassie, the one nobody thought was cute or adorable or beautiful or even mildly attractive, was seeing the best-looking man she'd ever laid eyes on, and for the seventh time. There was a sparkle to her, a liveliness in her face to match the alertness of her mind. As a result Cassie was looking quite pretty. To a casual observer, the nice-looking young man and woman were well suited, but Cassie didn't know that.

"It's hard to believe you never saw this movie," Jimmy said. "I thought everyone had seen it."

She shook her head. "I'm the one who missed it."

"But you like films, don't you?"

She nodded. He was an old-movie buff. For him movies were an art form and one of life's joys. And the proof was that he called them films, not movies or flicks.

"I like the oldies better," Jimmy said.

She was silent. It was so hard to think of things to say to him. Work. Books. They were her safe topics. She decided to try work. "I hope you meet Hilda Taylor; she's so smart."

"You're lucky," Jimmy said.

She looked puzzled.

"Lucky because you get to meet people and have an interesting life. I feel like a goddamned office boy. I never meet anyone with more than a third-grade education."

"That's a slight exaggeration, isn't it?"

"Not in an office like that. When you're waiting around to take the bar, they don't give you anything interesting to do. I feel as if I'm stuck, just waiting—"

"And you are. You'll take the bar, and everything will be great."

He looked at her. "You really think so?"

"Sure."

[48]

"I don't. I'm thinking of forgetting about the bar and just going to work."

"But how can you?" Her face showed a slight tension.

"I can go to Wall Street."

The tension was replaced by concern. "Would that make you happy?" His face lit up. He was obviously touched by her question. "You're a very nice person, Cassie. You didn't ask if it's a lot of money or the first step on a career path or any of those corny things people say. And you didn't make a speech about law school. You asked about me. You're different. What I mean is that most women aren't like you at all."

She grinned foolishly.

The ticket line began to move. "And another thing," Jimmy said, "You're really good to stand in a line like this."

"Oh, I don't mind. It's really a nice night."

"But don't think I don't notice that you're willing to stand. You get points for this."

She felt herself growing under his praise. This must be what love felt like. This kind of blooming and expanding.

"Anyway, Cassie, I think you ought to be the first to know. I'm looking for a job."

"And you're looking on Wall Street?"

"I've had three interviews. One at a small banking house called Blore and Miller. And I saw the people at Merrill Lynch, and I went to Winters and—"

"Winters?" she interrupted. "Who saw you at—at Winters?"

"Not old man Winters, of course. Say, did you know he's a cripple?"

"Jimmy, you're not putting me on, are you?"

"What? Why?"

"Mr. Winters—Charles Winters—is my grandfather."

"I thought Sam Cassman was your grandfather."

"They come two to a customer."

He lowered his eyes. "Dumb of me. No, I didn't know that. I didn't know at all, Cassie. But I'm not going to work there."

"That's good. I'm glad."

"Under the circumstances, I am too," he assured her. "But that's really weird. I had no idea—"

Were his wheels turning or was she paranoid? Was he using her? "I'm not rich," she said quietly. Then she added. "At least not yet."

"Oh, come on, Cassie." He laughed. "Don't worry. I'd like you even if you were rich."

The facial tension was there again, and he noticed it.

"Don't be upset, Cassie. What I'm saying is that I care for you. I really do. I don't care what you *have*. I like what you *are*. You're not one of those crazy, sexy bitches that the East Side calls its own. Fashion and beauty. That's what the East Side is all about. You're different. You're smart. You're a worker. I know you want a career. But I hope you'll want a man, too."

She nodded. "I do want a man," she said in a strong voice. "I definitely want a man."

Jimmy put his arm around her, and they walked into the theater. He led her to two seats in the back, and when the horror movie was about to begin, he took her trembling hand in his. She felt her eyes mist. It was all too good to be true. This was a wonderful life.

A week later Cassie was in her office when Hilda stopped by. "How would you like to come to work with me?" Hilda asked.

"But you don't know anything about me," Cassie said in surprise.

"Sure I do. Remember our first lunch? You told me all I needed to know."

"I did?"

"Of course. You told me about school and men. But I fell in love with you, Cassie, because you have confidence in your own brains and talent. You never once mentioned your grandfather's name. I thought that was really nifty."

So Hilda had known all the time. "I didn't want you to think—"

"I know what you thought. Now listen to what I think. You and I can be a terrific team. I admit we look a little strange standing side by side, but the world's changing, and we're going to be judged by more than the way we look together. There are openings for smart women in real estate, and I can teach you the business the right way. I'll teach you things your grandpa doesn't even know."

Cassie nodded; that was probably the truth. Sam got to his place in life in another time. Nothing would ever be the same again; you needed to learn the new style of business from the new style of businessman—businessperson. Now back to practicality. "How can I leave Jerry?"

"Tell him the starting salary is twelve thousand five hundred."

Cassie blinked. She was making eighty-five hundred now, and she knew her job at the law firm could be filled by somebody else's daughter or granddaughter. She sensed that since Jerry had a hand in getting her to Hilda in the first place, he wouldn't be too surprised at her leaving. "I'll talk to Jerry and give him two weeks' notice—"

"Then the answer is yes?" Hilda asked, her big face wreathed in smiles.

"Yes," Cassie said, a small hesitation in her voice. Then, in response to Hilda's warmth she said loudly and firmly, "Yes. Yes, I am going to work for you as soon as possible."

"Good," said Hilda, "but since I'm on my way to Jerry's office on another matter, let me tell him first so he'll know I didn't kidnap you, and you didn't defect to the lady with the big pocketbook."

Hilda turned on her heel and went around the corner into Jerry's office. She threw her bag on the chair across from his desk. "Well, you can call Sam and tell him it worked," she said triumphantly.

"No kidding," said Jerry.

"She's going to be great. What's more, she could have done it on her own. But Grandpa doesn't want to keep his hands out of his granddaughter's life. Give Sam a ring and tell him that Cassie's leaving to come to Hilda Taylor and Associates. But tell him one thing for me. I'm not starting her at ten thousand. That's what he wanted, but the old guy's still a tightwad when it comes to paying for anything."

"Don't tell Cassie," Jerry warned. "She sees red when you say it."

Cassie wasn't sure just how she wanted to break the news to Jimmy. They were having dinner at a little neighborhood bistro, and all through dinner Jimmy watched her closely.

"Cassie, something's bothering you," he said as the espresso was being served.

She looked straight at him. "Yes, you're right."

"That's what I love about you, Cass. No shit. No fumbling and fussing. You answer everything directly. You are so adorable."

"Come on, I'm honest, but I'm not adorable."

"*I'm* honest. You are adorable. You're a beauty because you don't use your looks the way those professional good-looking women do."

It was such heady stuff to hear, but Cassie had more on her mind. "Let me tell you what I want to discuss with you. I'm leaving Jerry. Hilda Taylor wants to hire me."

He smiled. "Fabulous."

"But—I mean—I thought you might feel I was trying to move ahead of you. Is it too soon? Too fast?"

"Nobody moves too fast in this world, Cassie. And that settles it for me, too. I'll definitely get out of there. I'll go back to Blore and Miller. They made an offer, but it wasn't very big."

"But what about the bar? Aren't you scheduled to take the exams next week?"

"Sure. But first I can take this job. The market's moving. There's money to be made. Cassie, you go to Hilda Taylor, and I'll go to Wall Street, and then you can sell me my co-op."

"Is your building going co-op?" she asked.

"No. My co-op is my next place, the one I'll live in when I—when we—oh well, you'll see soon enough."

She smiled at the unspoken words.

V

HILDA TAYLOR was old enough to show Cassie the ropes and young enough to swing from them. Born in California during the Depression, Hilda had come of age during World War II and gone to college in the postwar boom years. But college and Hilda weren't compatible, so after a semester at UCLA she quit school, married a veteran returning from duty in the Pacific—he stopped briefly in L.A. en route to the East—and with her new husband moved to New York. From the moment Hilda arrived in New York, she knew she'd found her home.

Hilda's husband had his separation pay from the Army, and the newlyweds bought a town house on the Upper East Side. Hilda didn't know anyone in New York, but she knew she soon would. The first step would be to preside over her own salon in a home where Sunday night suppers would attract the crème de la crème. From the beginning she was a success. Hilda was so famous for her suppers that an invitation to Hilda's (even now, no one could remember that husband's name) was the most sought-after invitation in a city of never-ending invitations. She ran a salon where the rich mingled with the soon-to-be-rich, and society rubbed shoulders with show business people who were married to businessmen who, in turn, knew politicians. It was a society all locked together in a kind of Chinese puzzle, and Hilda not only played the game, she wrote the rules.

She became an expert in French cooking, served the finest wines, hired the best caterers. Shows were auditioned in her music room; business deals were given their trial run on the stairway leading to her second floor, and then—then one day her husband's money ran out. Shortly thereafter her husband ran out.

It was a shock, and the memory still sent shivers up Hilda's back. But now she was to find her real role. She was a survivor. And the role of a survivor is to survive.

So the music became a little louder, the parties a little bigger, and the invitations a little more desirable.

That was about the time the bill collectors became more insistent. Hilda went to her friends for advice.

The bankers shook their good gray heads. Don't come into our business, they said. Banking's not for women. The Wall Street people also gave their best advice: stay off The Street. Not one of them mentioned that he didn't want Hilda Taylor lassoing the customers he'd met at her house. The only person who was truly helpful was the one she'd least expected to help.

Sam Cassman, a blonde on his right arm and a scotch in his left hand, had stood in the corner of the drawing room at one of Hilda's parties on a snowy Sunday night. Sam's eyes had traveled the room, but he'd heard every word Hilda was saying, and he read between the lines and knew what she wasn't saying. Hilda was broke, and she was asking her friends to find her a dignified way to be rich. Sam poked her shoulder with his finger and said, "Kid, I just got a great idea. You ought to go into my business. Real estate. And I'll show you how."

Sam, true to his word, had shown her. But he hadn't shown her his business. "Don't sell commercial like me," he'd advised. "Go into the business like a woman. You got everything going for you, Hilda. You're as smart as any man, and you're as pretty as any woman."

So Hilda Taylor had begun selling residential real estate and had gone to work for the sales company where Sam placed her. Two years later, with Sam's blessing (and a good word from him to the banks), she'd gone out on her own. By 1965 she was earning over two hundred thousand dollars a year.

Hilda was a success on all counts, but like all successful people she had her detractors. Some were jealous; some truly didn't like her. Hilda could understand the jealousy, but she never could figure why everyone didn't love her.

After all, wasn't she the smartest, most entertaining, rich woman in New York?

When Cassie called Grandpa to tell him she was changing jobs, he didn't seem greatly surprised. "What did I always say, Cassie? Didn't your grandpa predict you'd be in his business someday?" He quickly caught himself. "I mean *the* business. And see? You knew all by yourself when it was a real job. You didn't have to ask anybody."

A small suspicion was kindled as Cassie put the phone back. Was Grandpa telling her something? And what if he were? What if she hadn't really been given the job on her own? Well, so what? Lots of people got jobs through connections. Besides, how could Grandpa possibly know Hilda Taylor? But then again that was faulty reasoning because Grandpa knew everybody. Everybody except the most important person in her life.

He didn't know Jimmy. Not really. She wanted to talk to

[54]

Jimmy. What did he think? Was Grandpa using her? Making her his tool? Manipulating her life? She dialed Jimmy's number.

Before she could ask, he shouted, "Oh god, this is ESP. I was just about to call you. Cass, listen. Véronique, you know, Véronique, the one with the nightclub in Paris, is opening a place in New York on Park Avenue. There's a whole series of celebrity openings, and I'm invited to the one Monday night. Rollo Vanderhoof, the man who got me to Blore and Miller, invited me. Imagine, Cassie, I haven't even started there, and . . ."

Fantastic. Sensational. Marvelous. She said all the right words. She was delighted; she really was. But she still needed to talk to someone. She'd call Marcia. Hadn't she listened to enough of Marcia's triumphs and disasters all through school? Now Marcia could take a few minutes away from her job at the TV station and listen to her.

"Good news, Marcia. I just—"

"Don't tell me your news yet. Just wait until you hear this. I'm joining your ugly world of business. I just found out I've been accepted for the executive training program at Macy's. Get it? I'm coming to New York."

Before Cassie could say a word, Marcia added, "And since I don't have an apartment yet, I figured I could crash at your place."

Sure, Marcia, sure. Why not?

Again Marcia didn't wait for an answer. "I knew you'd be fantastic about it, Cass. It won't be a long time. A week or two. I'm not coming down for at least three weeks—"

"How did you get out of television?" Cassie asked.

"I was surgically removed," Marcia admitted, "and I figured I'd better go someplace where they really want women. There's always room for another female in retailing, so here I come."

"I'm in real estate now," Cassie added.

"Nice," Marcia commented. "Yes, that's really nice. Very good for a woman." Now Marcia went back to her own life, forgetting all about Cassie's news. "I can't tell you how excited I am to be moving to New York. It will be so wonderful. We'll go to plays and the ballet and concerts and meet a lot of terrific

[55]

men—just like college. Oh god, Cass," she said, the longing filling her voice, "do I ever miss you."

Cassie hung up. Nothing had changed. She still couldn't get a word in edgewise with Marcia.

Well, when all else failed, couldn't you turn to your very own sister? That's who'd she call. Call her at the dorm at Finch. Stephanie was probably in class, but Cassie would leave a message anyway. After waiting on the line seven minutes, Cassie heard a bewildered-sounding student ask, "Stephanie's sister? You said this is Stephanie's sister? I thought she was staying with you this week." Cassie could scarcely breathe as she put the phone back on the hook. There was only one reason Stephanie would lie like that. The reason was spelled Sal Romano.

Or was Stephanie at home?

Was something wrong with Diane?

Maybe that young woman answering the phone got the relationship confused.

She'd call home.

The phone rang eight times, and Cassie's throat felt parched as she heard each ring. Stephanie, are you there? Mother, where are you?

Nine rings.

Ten.

Hang up?

On the eleventh ring came Diane's little girl voice saying, "Hello."

Oh, blessed relief. "Mother, it's me, Cassie. How are you?"

"Cassie? What a surprise."

"Ha ha. It's not so unusual for a daughter to call her mother."

It is for you, Diane wanted to say. She bit her tongue. But Dr. Phillips wouldn't approve of holding back. He wanted her to get everything out; get it on the table. Well, it took time to learn to say things after a lifetime of not talking. But she'd try. She was going to be very good at saying things. Very good. Even if it killed her.

"Sorry . . . sorry. What did you say, Cassie? Lunch today? Oh, how nice. Yes, I'd love it. Stephanie? She's at school, of course, so she couldn't possibly join us. Twelve-thirty? Oh, that's a bit early for me. I have a doctor's appointment. No, no. There's nothing wrong with me. It's just Dr. Phillips. Oh, didn't I tell you? He's my new shrink."

Diane giggled nervously.

There.

That was getting it out on the table.

Cassie walked briskly into La Grenouille and saw her mother at her usual corner banquette. Diane had picked the restaurant, and Cassie didn't have to ask why. Convenience was the least likely reason. Cassie assumed her mother would have flown back from the moon in order to lunch at La Grenouille at one P.M., for this was the season of the "Frog Pond "(Women's Wear Daily's name for the chic restaurant), and Diane Cassman was so important that she never sat in the Catsup Room—the not-so-nice name for the perfectly nice area in the back of the restaurant, the tables where Nobody was seated. Diane was Somebody. Her name was in the "eye" column of WWD in bold type every time she lunched there, and she was frequently photographed in her latest Valentino outfit or Missoni knit as she walked out after lunch. Cassie wondered if her own name would be in the papers along with Diane's. She could see it now, "Ms. Cassman of Hilda Taylor."

She reached the table, gave her mother the obligatory peck on the cheek, ordered wine along with her mother. Why not? She had exciting news to tell.

"How have you been?" Diane asked. "It seems like such a long time since we've seen each other. I wish I saw you more." Diane fingered the silverware. There. She'd said something important. Dr. Phillips would be proud of her.

"Something really terrific happened to me, Mother. I met Hilda Taylor."

Diane swallowed. Cassie hadn't even answered. What was she talking about now? She asked in a puzzled tone, "Hilda who?"

"Hilda Taylor. You know, the real estate woman who sells everybody—"

"Oh, I know. You mean the one they call the Barracuda."

"She's really smart," Cassie said. "Honestly she is. I've seen her firsthand."

"You saw her? How can you know she's smart just because you saw her?"

"I didn't just see her. I've worked with her. Betsy Blakely—you know, the actress—was looking for an apartment, and Jerry had me use Hilda and so I got to work with her and she saw me and she thought I was good so she offered me a job," Cassie finished triumphantly.

Diane blinked. What exactly did this mean? She wasn't sure, but she knew she had to be supportive. "Congratulations. That's wonderful, dear."

"It means I'm going to be in real estate, Mother."

Now Diane laughed. She thought of something really funny. "Wait until Samuel Cassman hears he's not the only real estate genius in the family—"

"Mother, he knows. I've already told him."

Diane's stomach slid. The black pit was opening again. "Oh well, I guess he'd always be first with you."

So she had disappointed Diane once again, and she fished for another subject. "How do you like the clothes this year, Mother?"

"Nice. Nice."

Cassie didn't really know enough about fashion to ask more. There was a long, awkward pause.

Finally Diane said, "Oh yes. Hilda Taylor offered you a job. Are you going to take it?"

"I am, and I'm going to real estate school, and I'm getting a broker's license, and I'm really pleased, Mother. Really pleased."

"I hope so, darling."

Cassie nodded. She was running out of things to say to her mother. How awful.

Diane, too, searched for the next topic. She looked sideways at Cassie, sitting next to her on the red banquette. The child looked better than usual, but she was certainly no Amanda Burden. She wondered what Cassie's social life was like. "Do you have any fun at all, dear?" she asked sympathetically.

"A little," Cassie answered. Then she remembered Jimmy's call. Oh, Diane would like that kind of party. "I'm going to the opening party at Véronique's," Cassie announced.

"How wonderful." Diane smiled. "We're going, too. Who's taking you?"

"Jimmy Brown invited me."

"Jimmy Brown? Who's he?"

"The man I'm seeing."

"But who is he? Who's his family?"

"I don't really know. I think he comes from Long Island—or maybe Philadelphia. I—I guess I don't know. I met him at work."

"Oh well, if it's just a business thing, you know you'll probably be going Monday night."

"We are," Cassie said.

"Oh then that explains why you wouldn't know his family. Monday's not Véronique's party for the real people. That's just for the business crowd."

Cassie had a hard time swallowing the rest of her lunch. She couldn't wait to go back to the office.

Work was more than exciting, wonderful, and a woman's identity. It was also a place to escape from your mother.

VI

VÉRONIQUE HAD BEEN the toast of Paris when Cassie was still on zwieback. Now in her early fifties—and admitting to forty-one—Véronique had magically subtracted years and added cafés, restaurants and nightclubs to a constantly growing chain of international watering holes for the jet set, that group formerly known as café society. Véronique was not the arbiter of café society but a fulcrum around whose enormous presence movie stars, businessmen and assorted hangers-on glittered brightly in the media.

Diane and Bill were part of the Véronique crowd that attended every benefit, junket, and opening, for they had the money, the clothes, the home, and the ability to carry off publicity with panache. Bill was handsome, Diane beautiful—certainly not a prerequisite, but definitely a plus in that milieu.

Young people were admitted regularly to the set, and for the young, proper parents were an absolute necessity. But parentage wasn't the only reason for entry. Style was important, too. Some had it, some didn't, and those who were "in" and those who were "out" changed with the season. In 1969 Stephanie, the Finch College undergraduate whose mother made sure she went to the right parties with the right escorts, was in; Cassie, whose best friend-beau-suitor, Jimmy Brown, was a boy from the office, was out. No one—least of all Diane Cassman—dreamed that Stephanie had a thrice-wed, still married lover who had fathered children before she was born.

At first Cassie had been ecstatic about being invited to Véronique's New York opening. Did it mean she was finally to be accepted? No, her mother made it quite clear when she put the invitation in its proper perspective. Cassie, however, was determined not to let Diane's rating system spoil her good time. Especially since Cassie was now able to afford her own good time.

When she'd graduated from college, Grandpa had put a building in her name, and starting in January the income from the property started. "No trust funds," Grandpa said. "That's no fun. You have to have a good time making money, Cassie. What kind of good time when the bank sends a check? But when the property pays you money—ah, that's a good time."

Now, Cassie thought, was the time to take some of that money and buy herself a really good time. "I think I'll buy a new dress for the Véronique party," she said to Jimmy over a quick lunch.

He stopped unwinding his spaghetti and threw his napkin in the air. "I'll go with you." Then he got up from his chair, pulled her by the hand and headed for the door of the restaurant.

"Hey, hey," the waiter called. "You forgot something, bud."

"The check," Cassie whispered. "You forgot to pay the check."

"I've got something better to do," he laughed. Then Jimmy reached in his pocket and threw a twenty-dollar bill on the table. Cassie blinked. Their check couldn't have been more than seven or eight dollars. Jimmy was a dashing man all right.

"This way," Jimmy shouted as they reached the street.

Dutifully she followed him. Dutifully, cheerfully, excitedly. Life with Jimmy was one grand adventure, unpredictable and exhilarating.

"Up Madison Avenue," he sang to a passing cab, and crowded together in the back seat he put his arms around her and kised her nose.

"Jimmy," she said, slightly abashed.

"You are going to be the most beautifully gowned woman at that party."

"But Jimmy—"

"But nothing. To St. Laurent, my good man."

Jimmy was wonderful. Right out of F. Scott Fitzgerald. Right out of the movies. Right out of her dreams.

Jimmy watched carefully as she tried the clothes. Big skirts that overpowered her small frame. Tops that made her look as if she were under a tent. "Let me pick something," Jimmy said to the salesgirl. He went to the window and pointed out a black silk coat and tapered skirt. "This with a white shirt," he said.

She tried on the outfit and turned slowly in front of the mirror, then clapped her hands in delight. She'd never looked so good. The light in her eyes and the glow on her cheeks softened her look. What had magically changed her? Was it the clothes—or was it the young man sitting there with a careful, caring look saying, "Yes, it's good. I think it's very good."

"Indeed it is," the saleswoman said. "It's a charming little day outfit."

"But I want to wear it for the Véronique opening," Cassie said quickly. She didn't see any point in confessing that it was the déclassé Monday night opening, not the glittering one next Saturday.

But Jimmy wouldn't let the event go unexplained. "This is an important dress," he said, "because it's not for the glitzy Saturday night affair. This is the serious opening, the Monday night party."

Cassie shot him an appreciative look. Wait until Diane heard this one talk!

The saleswoman pursed her lips thoughtfully. "Then you cannot wear this outfit. It's simply not important enough." She slipped out of the dressing room and returned a minute later with a chiffon dress in graduated shades of pink and red. "This is a dress to remember."

Cassie tried it. She'd never felt so beautiful. "She'll take it," Jimmy said.

"But how—how much is it?" Cassie asked.

"Fourteen hundred dollars," came the reply.

Cassie hesitated—but only for an instant. Fourteen hundred wasn't too much to pay for a dress that caused a man to look at you the way Jimmy Brown was looking at her.

Cassie gasped when she walked through the velvet ropes and entered Véronique's, for beyond the gleaming steel doors was a chrome and mirrored room that glistened. It was spectacular, but at the same time there was no way it could overwhelm the people who would drink, eat, and play there. In this room the people were the art. "It's so beautiful," Cassie whispered to Jimmy. She didn't add, "And so are you," But no man could have been more handsome. At the office, good-looking Jimmy was special; in black tie he was a show stopper. She smiled broadly; Jimmy's appearance gave her great confidence.

Véronique had decorated her new cabaret with mirrors and grapes: the mirrors to reflect the beautiful people who would be able to come there regularly, and the grapes to remind them of Véronique's trademark.

"Let's go find Rollo," Jimmy said, looking around anxiously.

"You seem nervous." Was casual, easy-going Jimmy scared because he was out with his prospective boss?

"I'm not exactly nervous," he assured her. "It's just that Rollo's always judging me."

"Fairly or unfairly?"

"We'll see. All I can tell you is that Rollo is not what he seems. Don't worry, though. Just put on a happy face."

"I put on a happy dress. Remember? Do you like it?"

"Hey, I'm sorry. You know how much I love it. It's really pretty. You look beautiful. I'm a heel. Why didn't I say something without being prompted?"

"Relax, Jimmy."

"Okay . . . hey Rollo. Here. Rollo."

Rollo Vanderhoof waved from the other side of the bar. He was sixty years old and impeccably tailored, the fringe around his bald head groomed to perfection. On his arm was a blond powder puff in a sequin dress.

"I don't believe it," Jimmy said, teeth clenched.

"This must be Cassie," Rollo said flashing a toothy, almost lecherous grin.

"Cassie, may I present Rollo Vanderhoof. Alexandra Cassman. And this is Anne Compton."

Cassie forced a smile. How did Jimmy know Anne Compton? And who *was* Anne Compton?

"Come on, Cassie, let's dance," Rollo said. Cassie looked helplessly at Jimmy, but Jimmy had already handed her over to Rollo who was an expert dancer, a superb conversationalist, and clearly a real ladies' man. "That's a spectacular dress, Cassie. Obviously St. Laurent. I knew that S.C. had two granddaughters, a beautiful one and a plain one, but I never did get the names. Delighted to meet you and find I lucked out and got the beautiful Cassman girl."

Cassie's heart fluttered. What a joy. She was so taken with the idea of mistaken identity that she forgot to ask Rollo just who Anne Compton was. But when she returned to Jimmy, she asked him.

"Who is she?" Jimmy repeated the question as Cassie stood at the bar with him.

"Yes," Cassie repeated, curious now about Jimmy's hedging. "Who is she?" she repeated.

"Just a girl in the office."

Anne sidled up to the bar and locked her arm through Jimmy's. "Jimmy has told me so much about you, Cassie."

Cassie said nothing for a few seconds, then asked quietly, "What do you do with Jimmy?"

"What don't I do is more like it," she answered, a catlike smile spreading across her face.

"Anne's a secretary," Jimmy said quickly.

"And a little bit more," Anne added, now squeezing Jimmy's arm.

Cassie's hand shook as she drank the scotch.

"Oh, you might as well know who Anne Compton is," Jimmy said. "I don't like playing these silly games. Her father is the senior partner in our office. And Anne works as a secretary at CBS."

Cassie felt her mouth go dry. It was worse than she expected. Anne, like Cassie herself, was no ordinary career woman. She was a well-connected New Yorker. Anne obviously liked Jimmy a lot. A whole lot. It was there in her eyes, in the way her hand rested lightly on his when he handed her a drink. Cassie looked at Jimmy again. Handsome, sweet, attentive. In that instant she knew she, too, wanted Jimmy. She wanted his waking up and sleeping with her, his teasing and his sweetness. In between she wanted her work, the sense of success. She wanted to be in business alone, but she knew now she wanted someone to share the success. She needed a career. She must have this man. She wanted everything. And a woman today could expect everything. Everything was possible. Everything. You just had to go out and get it. As she sat at the bar watching the man she wanted with another woman, Cassie knew she'd fight Anne Compton down to the last whiskey glass at Véronique's if she had to.

"They're serving dinner," Jimmy said.

The four made their way to the big round table set near one of the mirrored pillars in the barroom. At each table were place cards set in a bunch of frosted green grapes. Ten people sat at each table, and as soon as the last drinkers and dancers were seated, Véronique herself appeared. She looked like a Titian beauty, with long red hair (there were whispers that it wasn't really hers) and a milky complexion. She wore a pale green Grecian toga that hid her ample curves and made her look tender and girlish. Véronique moved from table to table, flitting here and landing there. And as she moved, she seemed to orchestrate the entire dinner.

"Some woman she is," Rollo said with admiration.

"And she did it on her own," Jimmy added.

Cassie looked at Anne. Was he saying Cassie hadn't? Or Anne? Well, let the ball bounce in Anne's court. Cassie smiled sweetly and said, "You either have talent in business or you don't, and everyone eventually makes it on her own."

"Her own?" Anne asked.

Cassie looked at her in surprise. Was she dumb or antifemale? "Or *his* own," she added.

Anne nodded, pleased that God was in His heaven.

Cassie knew from the silence—the ten-second silence—that followed that there was more to be said on the subject. "Regardless," she continued, "nobody can give you the fire or drive for success."

"No," said Rollo, "they just hand you the keys and let you open the door all by yourself."

Cassie flushed. "I suppose you think you're talking about me, and I imagine you're referring to my career."

"My dear," said Rollo, "I'm simply stating the truth. Look, your grandfather had the chutzpah, the temerity, the temper for success. Fine. Dandy. And all I'm saying is . . . isn't it nice that he's handing it all to you?"

So. Rollo had known exactly which Cassman sister she was. "He's not handing it to me," Cassie said, the sparks igniting her words. "Look, business is something that's always been a part of my life. When I was a little girl, Grandpa used to take me to his office, the one at the Empire State Building, and I watched him at work. I saw him in action; I saw him make people buy what they didn't want and sell what they swore they'd never part with. I saw things they don't teach at the Harvard Business School and that's going to make me the best damned businesswoman in this town."

Rollo clapped politely. "That and Grandpa's influence will get you someplace. I agree. Not to mention the Winters wealth."

"I don't need my grandfathers," Cassie said. "I can do it on my own. In fact, Mr. Vanderhoof, just for your information I have already done it on my own. I just happen to have been hired by Hilda Taylor. And that was because she met me, not because one of my grandfathers arranged it."

"Wrong, Cassie." Now Jimmy was speaking. "Everybody who knows S.C. says he has been looking for something for you. Hilda Taylor was his choice."

"His choice?" Cassie was stunned.

Rollo smiled. "Cassie, you've got spunk. You're a great successor to S.C. He knew what he was doing when he picked you.

You know, the meek may inherit the earth, but the spitfires own all the land."

Jimmy laughed appreciatively.

"Do you laugh at all his business humor?" Cassie asked sharply. God, how she hated Rollo. He'd insulted her, and now Jimmy was playing up to him. Disgusting. She'd show them what she thought. Cassie stood and threw her napkin on the table, "I don't think you're very funny, Mr. Vanderhoof."

Jimmy ran his fingers around his collar and wet his lips. "Cassie, sit down," he said softly. "Look," he said in an effort to blunt her wrath, "they're serving the first course. Oh, Cassie, you'll love it. It's that fantastic egg with caviar you read about in the *Times*. Come, be my good girl. Sit down and eat."

She drew her breath and exploded. "Good girl? *Girl?* What do you think I am? Your child? Well, listen to me. I'm not your good little girl, Jimmy. I'm not even your girl. I'm not your old lady. I'm not your anything. I'm me. I'm Cassie, and I'm also Sam Cassman's granddaughter." Now she looked directly at Rollo and shook her fist, "But that isn't what anyone's going to remember me for. They'll know me because I'm going to have the hottest career New York has ever seen. Now go ahead and eat your eggs, boys. And while you're at it, you can eat mine, too."

In one quick movement Cassie picked up the eggshell filled with soft scrambled eggs and black caviar and threw it at Jimmy. He ducked, and the egg landed on the sequined bodice of Anne Compton. She shrieked.

"Sorry," said Cassie, "but that's what happens to women who keep quiet these days."

Two women at the next table and one waiter applauded. Then Cassie bowed to them, picked up her handbag and left. She smiled. Samuel Cassman's granddaughter was walking away.

And breathing free. Yes, that's what walking away really did. It freed you. It made you feel like a real person. She hadn't felt this alive since the day she was ten years old and walked away from Grandpa's party. Maybe that was her role in life—to walk away from parties.

The consequences of that old walking away had made her stronger in her family's eyes. What would the results be now?

Would Rollo tell Wall Street that Cassie was a mean bitch? Probably. But then even if she hadn't thrown the egg, he would, wouldn't he? For that was the ultimate weapon of men. That single word. *Bitch.*

And Jimmy? What of Jimmy? Well, she'd wait and see.

Meanwhile she'd have to get home from Park and Fifty-sixth Street. Cassie walked to the door of the club.

"Your car is waiting?" the doorman asked.

She shook her head. He was an old doorman from another place and another year. He recognized Sam Cassman's granddaughter. But tonight she didn't have a car. Tonight she was just plain Alexandra Cassman, and although she could have called for Grandpa's car, she didn't want his protection. No, not tonight. "I'll take a taxi," she said.

The doorman smiled. "It's teeming. Just started, and in this rain, ma'am, you won't find a taxi for hours. Better go back to the party, dance a little, and wait."

Cassie shook her head. No way would she go back into that lion's den. No. Instead she clutched her fur jacket closer to her body, stepped over the curb and into water that covered her ankles, and she started walking. Walking away. And she didn't mind at all that the rain was turning her fourteen-hundred-dollar St. Laurent dress into rags as she waded the five blocks east to her apartment.

She was soaked to the skin and shivering by the time she reached Sutton Place. The new doorman opened the door, saw her and in shocked surprise asked, "Miss Cassman, what happened?"

"I got sunburned," she said wryly. Then, seeing the confused look on his face, she reassured him. "Don't worry. I'm all right. Just get the elevator, and take me upstairs."

"Yes. Certainly," he said as he scurried to the elevator. "Oh," he added just as the doors were about to close, "there's a young lady been waiting for you since seven in your apartment."

"A young lady?"

"Yes, she said it would be all right."

Cassie leaned against the elevator wall. Oh no. Marcia had

promised not to come for another two weeks. Cassie couldn't face her. Not tonight anyway. She wanted a hot bath, hot tea, and a warm bed—not a fast-talking roommate.

Cassie slipped the keys into both locks, opened the door to her apartment reluctantly, and called, "Marcia. Marcia, I'm here."

A small voice came from the depths of the sofa. "It's not Marcia. It's me. Stephanie."

Cassie snapped on the lights. "Stephanie, what are you doing here?"

Wordlessly Stephanie pulled herself out of the sofa and stood in the light of the lamp.

Cassie gasped.

For even in this soft light Cassie could see that her sister had two black eyes.

VII

OH, GOD," Cassie cried out, "who did this? What happened? Let's call a doctor."

"I can't. No, I can't. Oh Cassie," Stephanie cried as she fell forward to embrace her sister.

"What do you mean, you can't?" Cassie demanded. "Why?"

"It's nothing, just a little accident. I walked into a door—"

"A door? You didn't—you wouldn't—oh! That bastard. That rotten—"

"Don't," Stephanie begged. "Don't say anything. I deserved it." She clutched Cassie.

Cassie shivered. She was cold and wet, but the words "I deserved it" made her shiver. She needed time. Time to think. "Stephanie, let me get out of these wet clothes." She unlocked Stephanie's grasp and took a step toward the bedroom.

"Let me go with you," Stephanie pleaded.

Cassie nodded, and Stephanie followed her across the dark-stained parquet floor to a bedroom decorated in cinnamon and white, a room that matched Cassie's spice-colored look.

Cassie looked at the bed longingly. How she wished she could crawl under the eiderdown and shut out the world. "Why don't you change too? I'll give you a robe," Cassie said.

Stephanie slipped out of her dark slacks and sweater while Cassie watched. Were there marks on her body? No. She breathed a sigh of relief and handed her a wool robe. Then Cassie wrapped herself in her white terry robe and put a white terry towel around her wet head.

Stephanie looked around. The walls were covered in a subtle cinnamon pattern that was repeated in the draperies, and the wall-to-wall carpeting took the tone from the paper. The linens were white, fresh, crisp, and inviting. "I feel so safe now," Stephanie said.

"I guess my world is safe."

"Mine's not."

Cassie could see that, but she held her hand up. She was still too full of her own bewildering evening. She needed a little time before she could absorb more shocks. "Before we talk I'll make some tea," Cassie said. "Wait here."

Minutes later Cassie came back to the bedroom with two steaming mugs. The sisters sat on the edge of the bed and sipped silently.

After a few minutes Stephanie asked, "Can we talk now?"

"Now," Cassie answered.

"This is so tough for me, Cassie. I don't have any place to turn. There's nobody but you. Please help me. Oh God, please."

"Promise to tell me the truth?"

"Promise."

"When did he hit you?"

"Tonight. About an hour before I came here."

"Did he ever do it before?"

"No. I swear this is the first time."

"Why now?"

"You're sort of part of it."

"Oh, no," Cassie moaned. Was she part of every fight in New York tonight? "Before you tell me more, I'm going to put some cool tea bags on your eyes. Now lie back, Steph."

Cassie adjusted the kitchen remedy and looked at her sister. She was so beautiful. She could be with anyone. And here she was, lying on her sister's bed with two black eyes. And god only knew what other bruises to her soul.

Stephanie sighed deeply.

"Don't go to sleep—not yet," Cassie warned. "Tell me what happened."

"You had lunch with Mother the other day and told her you were going to the Véronique opening, so of course I had to go, and she had to arrange it. She had to upstage everybody. So she called Cousin Alex Winters in Dallas and invited him—" Stephanie's voice was rising; she sat up and tossed the teabags from her eyes. "Ouch!"

"Lie down."

"Later. Listen, Cass, she called this creepo cousin I've never seen and said we'd love him to come to New York"—now she mocked Diane's little girl voice—"and come to the party of the year. Divine. Absolutely divine. I couldn't get out of it; I just couldn't. So when I went to see Sal at six o'clock tonight he blew his top. You see, Cass, that would have meant I'd miss our last night together. Well, damn, how'd I know next Saturday would be our last night?"

Now Cassie saw some light. "Why is it your last night?" She dug her nails in her palm. Please say the affair is ending, she prayed.

"It's the last night because he's going on the road to play one-nighters, and his agent wants the apartment back. You know, as I said that to you, I just realized something. That's why that no-good agent got him out-of-town work. Sure, he wants his apartment back. Money grubber. Takes all that money for making phone calls and won't even give us his apartment."

Cassie shook her head. Didn't Stephanie know how ridiculous this sounded? Did all our stories sound ridiculous to the rest of the world? Any temptation ever to tell anyone her side of tonight's Véronique affair vanished as she heard Stephanie's version of the apartment story.

"Don't you think that's rotten of the agent?"

"Oh, Stephanie," Cassie said softly, "get out. Leave Sal. Next time he could kill you."

"No, don't be silly. He loves me. That's why he got so mad when we couldn't be together. We need each other desperately. The only time I'm really alive is when I'm with him."

Cassie wanted to add, *It's also the only time you're almost dead.*

"Cassie," Stephanie said, her voice almost a whisper, "would you let us use your apartment?"

Cassie debated silently. Finally she said, "You'll stay here tonight."

"Oh, I knew you'd say yes. You're the best sister in the world."

Cassie picked up her pillow and walked to the living room. If it was more blessed to give than receive, why did the givers always end up on the couch?

Early the next morning Cassie phoned Jerry Farber; she still had a week to go at his office. "Jerry, I have a small family crisis. My sister's not feeling well, and she's at my house. I'll be in by noon."

He paused. She said nothing; I know what he's thinking. He thinks I am about to have the office girl ailment, an abortion. Finally Jerry said, "Aw, stay home all day, kid. You're a lame duck anyway."

"You're a love. Thanks."

Cassie made coffee and took it to the bedroom. Stephanie was standing at the dressing table looking at herself in bright daylight. "I'm a mess, Cass. What am I going to do?"

Now, in addition to the black eyes, Stephanie had red welts on her cheekbones.

"What are you going to do? Leave him, I hope."

"I love him."

"Is he divorced yet?"

"Almost."

"That's what you said a year ago."

"Well, stop pushing me."

"I'm not pushing you toward him; I'm pushing you away."

"No one can do that. Not ever. Look, Cass, he only gave me what I deserved."

"What?" Cassie's voice went up.

[71]

"I was baiting him. He knew it."

"Did you ever hear of fighting back with words?"

"He's a real man; he uses his fists."

"I didn't know that was the sign of manhood," Cassie snapped.

"Why don't you come off your high horse and meet him?"

"I never said I wouldn't."

"You're right, I guess. I just figured you wouldn't. You know you're pretty scary, Cassie. He doesn't have a lot of education. You have to remember that he may not have had all the advantages—"

"Please, don't lay the whole guilt trip on me. I can't help it if you and I weren't born poor. Look, I'm willing to meet him, but I won't until you're all right. There's no way he and I can be in the same room with your eyes like that. When he comes back from Vegas, invite him here for dinner."

"Thanks, Cass. One more thing. Will you let me stay here this week? I can't go to school or see Mother."

"Yes, of course," Cassie said.

"I'll give you back your bed."

But not my privacy, Cassie thought. A whole week without Jimmy. Then she remembered. Jimmy wouldn't be around anyway. Not after last night.

Three days went by. Stephanie was still there, and Jimmy still hadn't called. And he wasn't at the office.

Twice Cassie dialed his number, then put the phone down before she could find out if he was home.

Thursday the switchboard operator said, "Well, I hear the boyfriend is leaving, too."

"What?" Cassie asked, trying to appear cool and aloof.

"The boyfriend. Your fella. He got a new job."

"Oh, I know," Cassie said airily, "and he's studying for the bar."

"Yes, sure. And I know which bar," the operator said, her voice dripping with insinuation.

"What's that supposed to mean?"

"Whatever you want it to," she said and turned her back to Cassie.

Cassie felt confused and very much alone.

By midweek Cassie had decided she needed someone to talk to about Stephanie. Not her parents, of course. She couldn't call Jimmy. No, she'd have to wait and see. There was only one other person in whom she could even think of confiding. Grandpa.

"Just a sandwich in your office, Grandpa," she said lightly.

"You don't want to go out like a real career lady?"

"I want to eat in like a real career lady," she answered.

Walking over to his office, Cassie knew what she'd have to do. She'd have to beg for help. Make him reconsider.

Slowly, minute by minute, she told Grandpa of her concern about Stephanie. Her sister wasn't just walking into disaster; she was running toward it. When she came to the part about the black eyes, Cassie expected Grandpa to rise out of his chair, give vent to a biblical wrath and ask an eye for an eye.

Instead, he shrugged. "She never had your brains, so what do you expect? Your mother thinks she was meant to marry one of her Winters German Jewish banking heirs, or Prince Charles— but this?" Grandpa threw his hands up in the air. "It's not anything. You know, if he were a poor Jewish boy, we'd all say—so too bad she didn't get money when she's so pretty. But a woman beater? For God's sakes, what do we need that for? But you know something? Maybe that's all she should have."

"Grandpa! Stop!"

"Listen, Cassie. All through life we take our dreams and tailor them for our children and then wonder why they don't fit. Our children don't fit in our clothes, so why should they fit in our ambitions? You know something? Most people don't understand that, and so they keep pinning their dreams on everybody else. That's the real reason children disappoint their parents so much. Who gets what he wants? Where is it written you get what you deserve? I worked hard all my life, and look, just look at your father. I get a son who'll never be a man. He's nothing but a playboy, a bum, At least when he got married, I figured he'd settle down. Not him. Not Mr. Tennis Player. So when they were going to have a baby, I said to myself . . . Sam, don't expect already. Because from this nothing good can come. Best maybe is another beautiful one. So can you imagine how excited I was when you were born and you weren't pretty? I said, 'Finally there's hope. A girl who's not too pretty will have to be smart.' I went home that night and I said to Grandma, 'It's not so bad. The genes skipped a generation but we're all right now.' "

Cassie smiled at Grandpa's version of her birth. "So the day I was born you decided all that. What if I hadn't been smart?"

Grandpa raised his hands. "It would have been another disappointment. I've had plenty; I'll have more. That's life. Look, Cassie, you weren't pretty, so for your parents that was a disappointment. They couldn't wait until they had another baby so they'd get a pretty one. And when I saw the second one was pretty, I knew for sure you'd need to have it here." Grandpa tapped his forehead. "You'd never get in the kind of mess your sister's in."

Cassie was getting impatient; Grandpa was avoiding the subject. "Come on, Grandpa, let's talk about Stephanie. She doesn't know how to get out. What can we do for her?"

"You have two choices, Cassie. Walk away or see your other grandfather. I don't like talking about Stephanie. She's a boring little girl with a servant's problem. Tell me about you. What about the job you're getting?" Now there was a big smile playing on his broad features.

Cassie sat back. So Stephanie was boring, and Cassie ought to walk away. That wasn't the kind of help she'd expected for her sister. But maybe the reason Grandpa had survived was that he manipulated only those things he thought he could control—like Cassie and her jobs. Wasn't that what she'd heard at Véronique's? Wasn't that why Jimmy wasn't around these days? She took a deep breath. Okay, Grandpa. You asked for it. "So you want me to tell you about the job. Come on, Grandpa, stop playing your cute little games with me. I hear you're the one who got it for me. And let me tell you something. I don't like it. More than that, it makes me damned mad. I don't like people in this town saying

[74]

S.C.'s paving the road for Cassie. Grandpa, I've got to make it on my own."

"Why? Who else did?"

"You, for one."

"No, Cassie. I didn't make it on my own. Look, Cassie, don't believe the newspapers. I'll tell you myself how I made it. Made it? Who knows what 'made it' is anyway? But let me tell you about my first business success. Back in 1922 there was a theatrical producer named Louis Rothschild, and he needed a stable."

"A stable?"

"Right. A stable, because in those days the theaters were moving north of the garment center. So I sold Rothschild one stable, and from that I got into all kinds of theater investments. But if Mr. Rothschild hadn't decided I was a nice, honest boy, you know what? I'd still be selling stables, and today—outside of Bethlehem in December—there's no market for stables."

Cassie laughed. "You're impossible."

"I don't see you walking away," Grandpa said.

Sam Cassman chewed on the end of his cigar until he was certain that Cassie was well out of the office. He shook his head sadly. Why did Stephanie have to complicate everybody's life? He tapped his fingers along the desk top as he inched closer to the telephone. Should he do it? Well, what choice did he have? He picked up the phone, dialed, heaved a long sad sigh, cleared his throat and waited.

He smiled. You always had to sound happy on these calls.

A low, guttural voice said, "Hello."

Sam's response was loud and cheerful. "Vince, it's me, Sam. How are things out in Vegas? I see you're doing good business at the Gypsy. Somebody told me you got two big conventions this month. Wrong? You got six. Ha. You're some comedian, Vince. Say, Vince, I want to thank you for the oranges. I didn't think you'd remember. It's already a year since I told you Florida oranges are better than California oranges. Some memory you got, kid."

But Sam knew what it really was that Vince never forgot. The land deals. The money Sam laundered for the boys. That, not orange juice, bound them. But the charade was important to them both. So Sam smiled, nodded, and exchanged pleasantries.

"And how's that grandson? He made his first communion? That's what it's all about, Vince. The grandchildren." Sam knew that Vince's son, like Sam's son, was the disappointment of his life, but good form still dictated that he ask. "How's your son doing? Uh-huh. Well, maybe he'll like the dry cleaning business. I know. I know. I've got one, too. What is it we do, Vince? How come we don't get sons like us?"

Those were the magic words. Now Vince poured his heart out. Sam listened, clucked at the key words: never smart . . . no good . . . sweet . . .

Vince would have gone on talking all day. Sam had to jump in now. This was the opening. "Nobody knows better than I do, Vince. I understand. Oh, do I understand. Guess what happened to my Stephanie. Remember last year when you got me that Sal Romano to sing at the bar mitzvah in our family? Sure you remember. It was that big party. Diane's brother's boy. Well, you wouldn't believe what happened from that night. My granddaughter Stephanie took one look at that bum, and they're having what they call a relationship. Sick? Of course I'm sick. You and I got a problem, Vince. Let me ask you something first. How much does Sal know? You sure nothing? No, I don't agree. You're just saying that, anyway. Who knows what he knows? I'm never sure how much those dummies learn without realizing what they know. In my opinion we should get him out of town. I was thinking . . . maybe he should suddenly get a date to play Vegas, and maybe . . . just maybe it would look better if he got married."

Sam let Vince react, then he said softly, "It breaks my heart to think she would marry somebody like that. But what can we do? She loves him. He sang her a couple of songs, and she's hooked."

Again Vince spoke, but Sam knew the words were perfunctory. Now Sam's voice was soft again as he said, "Look, who knows better than you, Vince, what it is to have kids who can't take care of themselves? You have to help them. So we put them out there, and in the long run we have to figure it's better for everybody. I'm thinking now about my crazy daughter-in-law.

Sure, you know it's not enough Bill is no good in the business, but he married that society girl who's crazy altogether. She has a sickness called buying things. I think if we get the kid out of here, everybody's better off."

Now Sam repeated the only argument he knew Vince heard—and agreed with. "I don't want Sal opening his mouth to anybody in New York. Out there you can take care of him, watch what happens. Look, nobody's suspicious this way. You put him in the show and they move out there. Out of New York . . . right . . . right . . . . that's the ticket. You'll do it? Fine. Fine."

Sam pulled out a white handkerchief and mopped his forehead. Vince was still talking.

Sam chuckled. "All right. All right, I owe you one. But a small one. This schlemiel isn't worth a big one."

VIII

WITH INTENSITY, new love quickly becomes an old, accepted love. In Cassie's mind there had been no time before Jimmy; she couldn't contemplate life without him. Now he had vanished, and Cassie was finding that love does not appear on the doorstep every morning with *The New York Times*. Jimmy's short absence had left a hole in her life that the prospect of a new job and concern for her sister didn't fill.

"Marcia," she moaned long distance to her old roommate, "you're experienced. You've had a million affairs—"

"Two by actual count, Cassie. But thirty-seven if you figure—"

"Don't quibble. Just tell me what to do."

"Nothing."

"Really?"

"Absolutely nothing. Don't call. Above all, don't call."

Cassie thought piously of the times she'd dialed and hung up.

"Cassie, they never come back if they're asked."

"They?"

"Men, dummy."

[77]

Cassie stared at the phone. Dummy. That was the right word for her. Oh, how stupied she had been to leave. She missed him so.

Stephanie had planned to stay a week, but Friday night when Cassie came home, she found a note propped on the kitchen counter:

> Cassie,
> I know you won't understand,
> but Sal came for me. I'll call
> you next week. Thanks for every-
> thing.
> Kisses,
> S

Had Stephanie really wanted to go with him?
Had he beaten her once more?
And how could Cassie ever find them? Confused by her own life, Cassie needed advice to cope with her sister's. It was time to see Papa Charles.

The Wall Street offices of Winters & Co. were austere. Charles Winters occupied a corner office from which there was a commanding view of the Statue of Liberty on one side and up-town New York on the other. Cassie had rarely visited this office; she had, in fact, been there only four times in her life, and that had been when she was a young girl accompanying her mother, who was signing some papers.

Viewing Charles Winters behind his desk, a visitor never realized he was operating his empire from a wheelchair. There were neat piles of papers (Grandpa Sam's desk was a jumble of match-book covers, contracts, and scribbled deal sheets), a small bank of telephones (Grandpa Sam didn't even have a hold button on his black telephone), a ticker tape (Grandpa Sam called his broker), and a secretary in constant attendance (Grandpa Sam just yelled "Get me a girl" whenever he had something to dictate). Papa Charles's secretary was a male named Burlington. He'd been with

Papa Charles ever since Cassie could remember, but she knew so little about him that she wasn't even aware whether Burlington was his first or last name. All she knew was that he was always present as the go-between in the shadowy world of Winters finance.

Cassie went around the desk, gave Papa Charles the Winters kiss—a small peck in the air aimed at the cheek—then sat down opposite him.

"To what do I owe this visit?" Papa Charles asked. No hello, how-are-you, how-are-your-parents sociability. No offer of coffee, tea, or soda. (Grandpa Sam poured the coffee himself from the pot in the corner in his office).

"May I see you alone?" Cassie asked. Burlington's heavy black eyebrows made her nervous. He always seemed to be looking through her, but he in turn was protected by those bushy brows.

"Burlington is my right arm. Since I already lost two legs, don't make me give that up, too," Papa Charles said brusquely.

Cassie flushed. He was a tough old bird, all right. "But I'd like to talk to you about a family matter," she insisted.

"Burlington is family," Charles Winters said, enunciating each word carefully.

Cassie nodded. All right. She'd lay the story on him and see how he liked the embarrassment of hearing an ugly story about his granddaughter and the way it could affect an even uglier story about his daughter.

Again, as she had for Grandpa Sam, Cassie recounted the events leading up to Stephanie's seeking refuge with her.

When she finished, Charles Winters touched the fingertips of both hands in an inverted V. He bowed his head.

Good, thought Cassie. He knows now that we should have been alone. And he's shocked. He can't even look me in the eye. He'll help. What's more, he'll know what to do. Private detectives. Lawyers. Just you wait, Grandpa Sam. Just you wait and see how Papa Charles will take care of things.

Papa Charles raised his head slowly. "Don't you think the news of this would kill your mother?"

Cassie nodded. "That's exactly what I think."

Papa Charles cleared his throat. "Now let me get all the facts in order once again, Alexandra." Papa Charles never called her Cassie; that was a Cassman family name. He preferred Alexandra, the feminine of Alex—a Winters family name.

"Do you want me to tell the story again?"

"No. Just let me review it in my fashion. Fact number one: Diane is sick. Fact number two: Bill is incompetent. Fact number three: Stephanie is stupid. Now do you think that I, a man who is not sick nor incompetent nor stupid, should waste time on those people? No, Alexandra, the only person in the whole family who is strong, smart, and well is you. And you, my dear, have never come to me with your strengths. No, those go to Samuel Cassman. I must assume, therefore, that since you first take your triumphs to him, you first took your troubles to him. I have to assume further that he turned you down when you requested help. You must therefore assume that I will turn you down as well. I also am willing to leave Diane and Bill and Stephanie to muddle through life. But when you, Alexandra, are ready to come to me with your strengths, I will match your strengths with mine."

Only the sound of Burlington's heavy breathing could be heard.

"And that's all you have to say?" Cassie asked.

"No, I want to say one thing more. Don't come to me in my office for family help, Alexandra. Not now or ever. My office is for business. If you ever again want to see me on a family matter, kindly remember that I have a residence on Fifth Avenue: I assumed when you came to my office that you were here to discuss your future. I thought you wanted a place in this company. I would have made a place for you. But like all women, you're occupied and preoccupied with affairs of the heart. Now that I have seen that, I'm glad you didn't ask to come to Winters & Co., Alexandra. There's no room for emotional women here. They belong in the kitchen."

Cassie stood up and walked out without saying goodbye.

Papa Charles hadn't stood up once, but he had walked away.

Monday morning when Cassie went to work with Hilda Taylor, she was determined to put her family concerns behind her, bottle her emotions where Jimmy was involved, and be the best damned real estate saleswoman in New York.

Hilda's office was in a converted brownstone on East Sixty-sixth Street. "Is there a reason you don't have your office in one of the big buildings?" Cassie had asked her earlier.

Hilda had smiled when she'd answered, "Sure there's a reason. You'll learn, honey. You see, this way I can put my home and business at one address. That makes my living deductible. Not only that, but we use this address for listings in the *Times*, and it says quality to people right away. A good address is a comforting thing in New York. It makes it look as if we know what it's all about. And we do."

"We" was now to include Cassie. She felt a new sense of sisterhood; she would be part of a new family, one that would be responsive and loving.

When Cassie entered the office at nine o'clock, Hilda was already on the telephone. So were four other staff members, all female. No one spoke to Cassie. She didn't know what to do. Hang her jacket on the hanger behind the door? Sit? Stand?

Hilda finally motioned Cassie to take a chair, and poured coffee for her as she talked. Cassie couldn't fathom the conversation because Hilda wasn't selling; she was just saying things like "yes . . . no . . . sounds good . . . you never know . . . we'll see."

When she hung up, she learned back, raised her arms in the air, and shouted, "Whoopee. You've brought us luck already, Cassie."

Cassie looked around. What had she done?

"That was the listing for the Bucker duplex on Park. Douglas Elliman would give their eyeteeth for it, and we have an exclusive."

The other women, all on the phone, didn't miss a word. They smiled, nodded, and acknowledged the deed of the day.

"You didn't sound very enthusiastic when you talked," Cassie said.

"Of course not, silly," Hilda replied. "Enthusiasm is for selling. When you list, you have to make them believe they're lucky to get you."

"I see I have a lot to learn," Cassie said.

"You sure do," Hilda told her as she poured another cup of coffee. "The first thing you're going to do is get your real estate license."

"I have to take a course for that, don't I?"

"You'll do it at night while you work during the day," Hilda said tersely. Then, seeing the disappointment on Cassie's face, she added, "But that doesn't mean you won't start selling right away. Don't worry, kid. I'm not going to waste you."

During the next few minutes Hilda introduced Cassie to the women in the office. Ginny, Linda, Fran, and Terry. Cassie wasn't sure which was which. As Hilda showed her the desk where she would work, Cassie asked, "Why don't you have any men here?"

Hilda patted Cassie on the hand. "Because women and real estate go together. If you're divorced, female, over thirty, and out of the job market for twelve minutes in your adult life, just see what's available. There are four women here; one is damned tired of lying about her age on job applications; another hates making cookies for the school bake sale; two are bored, one with volunteer work and one with marriage. Now you figure out which one is which. Doesn't make any difference, though. They're all here because in the real estate business you can come right in, sell a house, and understand exactly what you're doing—for god's sake, these women don't have to take a computer course to know why a kitchen is good—and they have the satisfaction of making something happen."

Cassie started coming to work at eight, began staying until eight at night. Each day she learned something new.

"Hey, English lit. major, we're going to let you write some ads," Hilda said.

Within two days Cassie learned the shorthand of real estate ads. She found that a *lux drmn bldg* was as good as a *fpl*; she began to spell bright *brite* (every letter counted, Hilda reminded her), and she learned the value of a hot headline: 7 *LARGE RMS*.

There was a rhythm to this business, and Cassie was learning the steps.

Toward the end of the third week, Cassie and Hilda were

working late, trying to get the best possible language for the ads for two buildings that were going up on the East Side, buildings for which Hilda Taylor was the exclusive rental agent. When the telephone rang at eight, Hilda said, "I knew I should have turned the damned thing off an hour ago."

"I'll take it," Cassie said.

It had been so long since she'd heard his voice—three weeks by actual count—that she almost didn't recognize it.

"Jimmy?" Her heart was pumping wildly.

"Yes, it's me. Good ole Jimmy. Hey, Cass, may I see you tonight?"

"About what?" Oh, what a stupid question.

"Just tell me. Will you see me?"

"Yes. Oh yes. But I promised to work late," she said lamely.

"I don't care how late."

"Okay, then, make it eleven o'clock. My place."

"Great. Hey, one more thing, Cass. I miss you. I miss you a lot."

She put the phone down. Tears came to her eyes. She was relieved, happy. It was exquisite joy—just the prospect of seeing Jimmy warmed her whole body.

She arrived home at ten-thirty. The telephone was ringing as she opened the door. She ran to answer the phone, but she was too late.

She went into the kitchen, opened the fridge, poked around and found some old cheese, orange juice, four eggs, two tomatoes, and a bottle of white wine. Not exactly Lucullan. She took the wine into the living room, found some nuts, and turned the radio to WQXR; it was a Beethoven night. She stepped into the shower and scrubbed away the past two weeks. Forget Stephanie. Forget that Jimmy had done a disappearing act. Forget that Anne Compton might be the reason. What was the difference? The water was warm, and the prospects were good. She buffed her body with the big terry towel until she shone from head to toe. Her coppery hair was curly and wet from the shower. She looked in the mirror over the sink. Not bad for a Cassie. She put on white pants and a sweater.

At eleven the doorbell rang and so did the telephone. She knew there was good news at the door . . . but what mysterious caller was still trying to reach her by phone? She hesitated for a minute and made the decision.

She let the telephone ring.

She could hear her heart beating as she opened the door.

"Hi, Jimmy," She lifted her face for a kiss, and as she did she felt suddenly shy.

"Hi," he said. Not, how've you been? What's new? I've missed you.

The kiss was sweet, not passionate. He grinned. "You look good enough to eat. Just like pralines from New Orleans. That's a compliment," he added quickly.

Cassie clasped and unclasped her hands. What do you say? Thank you? I tried? So do you?

"What do you have to eat?" he asked.

"Wine and nuts. Very nutritious," she said. Was that answer witty enough? Would he like it? He does. He's smiling. Shhhh. Now he's talking.

"In that case I'll take some." He followed her into the living room.

"Where've you been?" she asked. "Anne Compton get you in her clutches?" Oops. Dopey question. Too direct.

He grinned. He saw through it. "Anne Compton? You thought I was involved with Anne Compton? No, Cassie. Anne Compton isn't even interesting."

Isn't even interesting. That meant she was. She, Cassie, was interesting, and so he'd come back to her. And with him had come a new appreciation; he didn't say it, but she knew it. This time she was ready for him. Ready to declare her love for him. She'd never before felt this sense of rightness about herself. Suddenly everything was different. Beautifully different. Happily different. Lovingly different. This wasn't like a boy-girl or a parental love; it wasn't even blind adoration like Grandpa's love. This was love. Real love.

Cassie felt very good, very much a woman. She felt something new: she was a different Cassie. She raised her eyebrows in surprise when he asked, "Any other men for you lately?"

[84]

She shook her head. No. She didn't smile.

He poured his wine, lifted his glass to her. There was another question he had to ask. "Cassie, how experienced are you?"

"Experienced?"

"Yes, experienced. You know what I mean."

"Not very," she said, her eyes lowered. "Not very much at all." Now she looked at him directly.

"Honest?"

"Honest."

He nodded his head and said nothing. She felt the weight of the unspoken words between them. She longed to question the silence, but she said nothing.

Finally he cleared his throat. "Cassie, did any man ever mean more to you than I do?"

She shook her head. Her heart was too full to speak the words.

Jimmy took her hand and put it to his lips. "Do you trust me, Cassie?"

"I would trust you," she whispered. "I would trust you with anything in my life."

"Will you trust me with you?" He reached over and touched her shoulder.

Under the white sweater she felt a quiver of delight.

Jimmy sensed the first ripple of pleasure and put his arms around her. Slowly, expertly he unfastened the bits of silk and lycra that kept her a prisoner of herself.

The anticipation of joy was almost more than she could bear. She did not want it to end. She did not want it to begin. But it was not her decision. All at once Jimmy was free to explore; dimly she saw her clothes strewn about the room. Then his.

He was holding her so tight. So safe.

And then—at last—there was no question. She knew. For the first time she was certain. She cried out once to tell him, but she could not speak. Instead, the fullness spilled from her eyes. She did not will it, but she was crying, sobbing . . . and there was no sadness. Nothing before had ever been like this. Not any joy or any other sadness. There'd never been such intense emotion in her life. She couldn't stop the sobs.

"All right?" he asked anxiously. "All right?"

[85]

She wanted to say yes. Very all right. But she couldn't speak.

He held her and kissed her wet hair, her wet eyes. "I love you," he said with such sweetness she thought her heart would break.

Still she could not speak.

She sobbed aloud.

But she knew he knew.

She loved him with all her heart.

Cassie didn't answer the phone when it rang again at midnight; at twelve-thirty Jimmy took the phone off the hook.

So it wasn't until she was at work the next morning that Cassie got the telegram. The operator read it to her, and then Cassie had her read it again. In a shaking hand she wrote the words, *Sal and I married last night in Vegas. Please tell the family. Will call soonest. Love, Stephanie.*

March 1970

It's normal for a man to work hard
for a woman—it's the custom of the
country.
  Edith Wharton
  The Custom of the Country

IX

THE ELOPEMENT OF their daughter frustrated every dream of Diane and Bill Cassman. Until now, Diane had assumed that Bill simply rode in the backseat as his daughters bumped along the road of life. Now Bill suddenly wanted to move into the driver's seat. "I'm going to Las Vegas and have that marriage annulled. That filthy old man is after the money, the name. Everybody knows that." Diane took to her bed; Dr. Phillips prescribed some mood elevators, and the first full sentence Diane managed later that week was, "What will I tell Cousin Alex? He wanted to marry her." Cassie flushed; the two cousins didn't even know one another.

For the first time, Cassie understood what Grandpa meant when he said you couldn't interfere in the lives of others. Did Diane and Bill wonder why Stephanie had done such a thing? Did they question her needs? Did they ask why she chose not to be the pretty girl whose career goal was to marry well? Did they care that under the pink cheeks and white brow, under the demure manner and robotlike acquiescence to parental pressure was a young woman with a heart, a body, a need? Did they, in any of their long and tearful telephone conversations with Stephanie, ask if she was happy?

No. Cassie knew that both Diane and Bill were trying to interpret Stephanie's action in order to justify their lives, not to understand hers. It was unsettling. Would her parents try now to introduce Cassie to the Winters' relatives? Would they try to do what Grandpa said all parents do, alter the child to fit the dream?

As she walked to work each day—past the whistling construction workers, past the rock music lovers with the radios plugged into their bodies, past the panhandlers, blind beggars and sleepers in doorways—Cassie reflected on her own life and needs.

It was one thing to say blithely that you wanted to be rich, famous and live to the year two thousand. It was another to think about how. And with whom.

So even though Bill finally calmed down long enough to say he'd wait for Stephanie's return—presumably he thought she'd get tired of Sal before the Cassmans had to meet him—and even though Diane rose from her bed long enough to go to Saks Fifth Avenue, Cassie knew that they were casting long, anxious looks at her. She was the independent one, the free thinker. If marrying such a person was what the good one did, what would the other one do?

From the night Jimmy came back to Cassie, they were a couple. Not a couple who lived together but rather a man and woman—independent in action, thought and career—who had chosen each other as a preferred companion and spent three or four nights a week together. They never questioned each other about the nights they spent apart.

Lovemaking with Jimmy—after all, she had no real comparisons—was all she had dreamed it would be. There was passion, but a sweet tenderness, too. Jimmy courted her, lured her, made her feel a fragile woman. She knew from all the confidences she'd heard throughout her college years that Jimmy really was different. Jimmy gave her romance, then passion. From what she'd heard, some men—no, most men—skipped the romance.

During the day Jimmy went to work on Wall Street—"Rollo still let me come to work for him despite the crazy lady I took to Véronique," Jimmy said—and Cassie went from deal to deal at Hilda Taylor's. She'd never dreamed that she'd love the real estate business so much. It involved most of her waking hours, and Jimmy and Cassie found that their social life was an offshoot of their business life, for within the parameters of their careers they met the people with whom they partied and played.

A woman in Cassie's office had a sister who was an artist, and one Friday the sister-artist had an opening at a Soho art gallery. "Will you go?" Cassie asked Jimmy.

"Sure," he said.

So that was the reason he was standing now in the foyer of the Yoho Soho Gallery watching his breath paint small pictures on the glass door. He frowned.

Terrific. A party going full blast upstairs, and here he was—

downstairs waiting for Cassie and blowing frosty pictures of duckies and horsies.

Where was Cassie anyway?

Stuck in downtown traffic?

On the subway? Was somebody looking at her? Kind of a crazy look? Had she gotten off three stops too early to escape him?

Had she been reading and gotten off too late?

Maybe she was standing in a doorway waiting for the rain to let up. Sure, that was it. Cassie was practical, sensible.

But what if she ran across the street and didn't see the taxi? No, please God, no. He shut his eyes, terrified by the thought. When he opened them, Cassie—complete with polka-dot umbrella—had materialized.

He felt a tremor of joy and relief, "Hey, Mary Poppins, where did you come from?"

She laughed and shook her poodle-y hair. Droplets of water fell on her face. He put his arms around her.

"You'll get wet," she warned.

"Yes, but I'll also get kissed."

"Want to bet?" she teased. He pulled her close and kissed her hard.

She shrugged. "So I lost." Then she grinned. "But it sure felt like winning."

"What kept you?"

"Something wonderful—a new client."

"Then why go upstairs? Let's go and celebrate by ourselves."

She hesitated. Hadn't she promised—

"I have something to talk about," he said solemnly.

She felt the panic in her stomach; he'd had enough. He wanted out. He wanted to tell her now. She was instantly clammy and scared. She knew she couldn't go upstairs.

"There's a great little Chinese restaurant down here in Soho," Jimmy said.

"Let's go," she said, summoning up a note of gaiety. Funny, the way contemporary women still knew when they had to do old-fashioned things. Smile at the birdie. Agree with the man. "Whatever you say, Jimmy."

He put his arm around her. What did that mean?

The dinner seemed endless to Cassie. What was this about? Hadn't she skipped the gallery in order to hear something important? Why wasn't he saying anything? It was all small talk: the office, the headlines. She poured a cup of tea and realized her hands were shaking.

"What's the matter, Cassie?"

"You said you wanted to talk to me."

"I do."

"Then talk."

"Cassie, do you like us the way we are?"

"What does that mean?"

He sighed deeply. "There's a lot you don't know about me."

"I know everything I have to know," she said quickly.

"Do you really think so?"

"Oh yes."

He moved the chopsticks around his plate. For a moment neither of them spoke.

"Why don't you ever ask me about the bar and being a lawyer?"

"Well, I know you didn't pass the exam, and I think that was probably kind of painful to accept. But you did get a job on Wall Street, so I guess you're doing something that satisfies you, and if you ever want to take the bar again, I'm sure you will. Meanwhile—" she finished lamely. She knew that under the blusher she was turning pale. Didn't he understand she tried to put her heart in his body, his thoughts in her head? Then, as if she were framing his thoughts for him, she asked softly, "Are you worrying about money?"

He smiled a sweet, warm, understanding smile. "Doesn't everybody?"

"I don't."

"I—my family isn't rich, Cassie."

"Oh, I don't feel secure because of my family's money. I feel good because I can see that I can make money and don't have to ask for any of theirs."

"I don't want any of theirs either," Jimmy said. "I'll tell you

[92]

one thing about me. I'm no fortune hunter looking for an heiress."

She smiled. "I would've guessed that, but it will make my grandfather like you a lot more." Then she stopped. Her grandfather. Of course. That was what was troubling Jimmy. Sir Jimmy. How could she forget?

"I don't think your grandfather considers me a very likely prospect for his granddaughter."

"My grandfather won't really care. All he'll want is for me to keep working."

"That's strange."

"You don't know my grandfather."

"I guess I don't."

"Cassie, I like things the way they are now."

Then he wasn't going to leave. Relief warmed her body better than Chinese tea. But what was he going to do? What was this about? She wanted to ask, but she said nothing.

Finally Jimmy spoke. She had to lean across the table to catch his words. "I've never loved a woman the way I love you. I never thought I'd feel like this."

"But you're so handsome," she said in surprise. How could somebody so beautiful not be confident?

He shook his head as if to dismiss her words. "What I'm trying to say, Cassie, is that I'd really like to marry you, but I don't want to change things."

"I won't get mean and start fights," she said. "And I won't spend a lot of money," she added, thinking of Diane.

"What I mean is that I don't want to get bogged down in all the garbage of marriage."

"The garbage?"

"Oh, you know. Going here, going there. Like tonight. I mean I still need time to myself."

"So do I," she said quickly. "I have to work some nights."

"Then you'd understand?"

She nodded, but she wasn't quite sure what she was agreeing to.

"Nowadays," he said, his voice gaining strength, "women talk

[93]

so much about their needs, and I thought I'd better say up front that I have needs. And they're important to me. I don't want to be at your beck and call, Cassie. I still want to be able to go out when I want to go out and have my own business dates and keep up with some of the guys I see."

She felt relieved. Well, he wasn't asking for carte blanche in order to have assignations with other women.

"Cassie, maybe we should leave and go uptown and hire a carriage and take a ride around Central Park, and then this would be more loving and romantic."

"This is fine. Right here is just fine. Go ahead and talk, Jimmy dear." She squeezed her eyes shut. Oh please, let her hear the words she always dreamed of hearing.

"Cassie, if you can put up with me and stand my kind of life—" He paused.

She opened her eyes. "Your kind of life?"

"Oh, my kind of craziness. Well, Cassie, if you can . . . oh hell, Cassie, even if you can't, listen to me. I love and adore you and want you with all my heart. Please, please, please, Cassie. Will you marry me?"

And there, in the middle of a rundown Chinese restaurant in the heart of Soho, with tears falling into her *dim sum,* Alexandra Cassman sobbed, "Yes, yes, yes I will."

X

FOR THE FIRST TIME, Diane Cassman felt she had a role in her daughter's life.

She was the mother of the bride, the center of the caterer's attention, the keeper of the wedding gifts.

How different it all was from—from Stephanie. Diane couldn't bear even to think about the difference.

Instead she busied herself with designers and consultants, florists, Tiffany, Cartier, and James Robinson.

Diane rented the Grand Ballroom of the Plaza Hotel for a wedding ceremony, reception and dinner at seven o'clock on the second Saturday in June. She'd picked that room because, as she told Cassie, "If I'd had my way, that's where my wedding would've been."

"Why wasn't it?" Cassie asked.

"Someday I'll get around to telling you. Not just now," she said.

And Cassie didn't pursue the reasons.

So much went over her head these days.

She tried to keep her mind clear and free for work, and she tried to get more involved than ever with Jimmy, his life and his career. But she soon learned that her questions were better than his answers.

Whenever Cassie found herself with fifteen extra minutes, she ran off to lunch with Marcia.

"Let me ask you something," Marcia said one day as they sat at the Schrafft's counter. "Do you really feel you know everything about Jimmy?"

"Of course not." It was a disturbing question, but loyalty to Jimmy wouldn't let her reveal that. "I don't think women should know too much."

"Cassie, you're too smart to say something like that."

"Well, maybe if I'd slept around as much as you—oh, Marcia, I'm sorry." She truly was chagrined. After that Marcia never asked anything about Jimmy, and Cassie tried harder than ever to be nice to Marcia, but those words that shouldn't have been spoken seemed to come between them. They were still friends, both of them agreed silently that they were, but the quality of their friendship was different. Besides, Cassie now had another kind of confidante in her life. She had Hilda.

Mornings were her times with Hilda. Mornings over coffee in the office. Mornings when you waited for the phones to start ringing.

Cassie filled Hilda in on the wedding details on a daily basis. There would be a string quartet playing on the balcony of the Grand Ballroom. . . .

"Thank God you didn't want to get married in a field with only God and Kahlil Gibran," Hilda mused.

". . . Jimmy and his father—you know, his father's his best

[95]

man—well, they'll come in from the side and be at the altar. Then after the recessional, we'll have a receiving line and serve champagne."

"What vintage?" Hilda asked wickedly.

"Dom Perignon '66," Cassie answered in her matter-of-fact way. These days she was so preoccupied that she heard questions, but innuendo escaped her. Alexandra Cassman was taking herself very seriously. "And after the receiving line, we'll go into the Crystal Room for a formal sitdown dinner."

"Just like the movies," Hilda cracked.

"Mother calls it the perfect little summer menu. She had it planned by Les Frères Troisgros."

"Of course, Cass. Terribly simple. Doesn't everyone go to France to plan a wedding dinner?"

"Well, I can't help it," Cassie said defensively. "She is my mother, and I do owe her—"

"Cassie dear," Hilda said putting her coffee mug down and touching Cassie's arm. "Don't pay any attention to me. I think it's really sweet of you to let your mother have this last hurrah."

Cassie, somewhat appeased, apologized. "I guess it sounds like I believe it all, but the way she's carrying on you'd think it was a Mafia wedding."

"Better not say that in front of your grandfather," Hilda said, suddenly grim.

"What's that supposed to mean?"

Hilda dropped her arm, picked up her coffee cup and then said, "I told you, Cassie. Don't pay any attention to me."

Stephanie arrived in New York the week before the wedding. She came without Sal, and Diane and Bill never asked where he was. But Cassie did. Stephanie explained, "He can't get away; he's really going to be a big star, and you can't walk out on a Vegas show just for your sister-in-law's wedding. Oh, Cassie, you know I don't mean *just* for a wedding."

"Relax," Cassie said. "I understand. But you? Are you all right? Is he good to you? You know what I mean."

Stephanie's eyes were blank when she said, "Sure. Oh sure. Sal's very good to me."

If Cassie hadn't been so involved in her own plans, she would have tensed at that first alert. But happiness put a hazy mist between the real world and Cassie.

Cassie stopped working the day after Stephanie arrived and spent her time with her sister and mother. At first there was a kind of uneasy truce forged between the daughters and their mother as Diane led the way in what she did best: planning and shopping. But gradually the truce turned to genuine affection among the three.

Stephanie offered to give a dinner for Cassie's friends the night before the wedding, but Cassie declined. She couldn't offend the Browns, who wanted to give the rehearsal dinner that night. The Browns had really been very nice about accepting all Diane's plans. Sheldon Brown owned a printing plant in Garden City, and his wife, Joan, looked like a younger version of Grandpa's widows. Yet they had made no demands on Cassie or Jimmy. This one dinner would be their chance to be the hosts at an event.

Stephanie understood Cassie's refusal for that night.

But what about two nights before the wedding? And just Cassie's good friends?

Cassie started to say no, and then she realized that a party mattered more to Stephanie than it did to her.

"Stephanie, what I'd really like is to have a party with just Hilda and Marcia, you and Mother and me. And let's do it in my new apartment. It'll be the first party there. You can take care of whatever kind of serving you think should be done. Cheese. Wine. You know, our kind of food. Nothing fancy, and let's not compete with Mother."

Stephanie kissed Cassie. "Thanks."

And so tonight, forty-eight hours before the wedding, they—Cassie, Stephanie, Diane, Hilda and Marcia—sat in the middle of the floor in the no-furniture apartment on East Sixty-fifth Street. The apartment was on the twenty-third floor, the top floor, the penthouse floor—but it wasn't a penthouse. There was no terrace.

The apartment was a rental; Jimmy had insisted on that. "I can't afford to buy a co-op now; I won't live in your old apartment, and I refuse to let your Grandpa buy us one." Cassie respected that independence—besides who said Grandpa would

buy? Cassie and Jimmy's new apartment was luxurious by contemporary apartment standards, but ordinary when compared to
the fine old buildings of New York. It was no San Remo; it didn't
even have the charm of the Fifty-seventh Street apartment Cassie
had lived in.

The walls of the new apartment were painted white. Cassie had
the asphalt floors carpeted in her favorite color, cinnamon, and
was waiting for the furniture—new upholstered pieces ordered
from Sloane's and Bloomingdale's (Diane shuddered—no chic)
and their old things: the nineteenth-century French armoire from
Cassie's and the captain's desk from Jimmy's.

"It's a nice apartment, isn't it?" Marcia asked, expecting no
answer.

"It's all right for a rental," Hilda said, expertly sniffing the
space.

"You're an apartment snob," Cassie laughed.

Tonight even Diane was eating cheese on paper plates and
drinking chablis from the Baccarat wedding gift glasses. My first
party, Cassie had said wryly. She looked around the room, the
boundary of her new life, and she looked at the women, the
boundaries of her old ties.

"Show me around and let me see your closet space," Diane
asked.

"Mother, you are a closet maven. There isn't anything you
don't know about closets."

Diane patted her daughter's head. "It's important to have good
closets."

Cassie shot a look at Stephanie, and both smiled. She was their
mother, and they'd never change her.

"Come on; we'll take a tour." The others stayed in the living
room while Cassie quickly showed Diane where the china was
kept, the silver stored, and her clothes hung.

"What about Jimmy's things?" her mother asked as they stood
in the bedroom.

"That's his closet," Cassie said pointing to a closed door.

"Let me see the size of it," Diane said walking to the door and
turning the knob.

"Stop," Cassie shouted.

[98]

"What?" her mother asked in surprise. "I'm only looking, not taking, Alexandra."

"Mother, it's just that I promised Jimmy I'd let him have his privacy. I'd never snoop in his closets and drawers, and he'd never snoop in mine."

"Snoop? You call it snooping for a mother to see the size of the closets in her daughter's apartment?"

"No, I don't, but he does. So don't do it."

Diane took her hand from the doorknob and walked into the living room. The stubborn child was now a stubborn woman. Diane wondered whether Cassie had shown the closet to Marcia.

Marcia had turned into a New York woman thirty seconds after her arrival in the city. Always quick to latch on to the latest trend, Marcia had gone immediately from her low-key, nonprofit public television look to a Gucci–Vuitton–Fendi look. And she'd gone from crashing at Cassie's for that first month to a neat little apartment at Kips Bay. She'd also crashed into a neat little affair with a married man, a divisional head at Macy's who spent Monday and Thursday nights with her. "Yes," she'd told Cassie, "I'm just like the store—open two nights a week."

Diane and Cassie went back to the living room. To her daughters Diane seemed like a different person these past weeks, a real mother instead of a walking credit card and clothes critic. Cassie had suffered from years of Diane's appraisal, that slow intense looking: looking for a crooked hem, an outworn boot, too little makeup. The age-old scrutiny of the mother who seeks to find her faults turned to virtues in her daughter and instead finds new faults.

Hilda was talking. Was it marriage and men? Men and marriage? Diane tried to tune in. "Marcia, take it from me," Hilda was saying. "There's not a lot of difference between men and business, our two loves. Business will sweet-talk you just like a man, and just when you think you've got it all in place, you're dropped for someone younger and cuter and more in tune with the times."

"Did that ever happen to you—in business, I mean?" Stephanie asked.

"And how. And not just in business. It's happened to everybody. Come on, Diane, haven't you been dropped on your ass from time to time?"

Diane winced, and then she smiled. She understood that the language was the welcome, the audible signal of her acceptance by these modern women. Diane looked at her daughters and the other two women, and she felt a kind of sisterliness she'd never known before. Maybe she was becoming a New Woman, just like the others. Whatever was happening, it was making her feel as though the darkness, the pit, the empty blackness had never been.

"You're smiling, Diane," Hilda said. "What're you thinking about?"

Diane started; she'd have to give a good answer. "Oh, oh, I'm sorry. I guess I didn't hear the question. I was just thinking about my own wedding."

"Tell us about it," Marcia urged.

Tell? Yes. She'd tell. "I got married in nineteen forty-three to the best-looking second lieutenant in the United States Air Force."

"You mean Daddy?" Stephanie wondered aloud.

The others laughed.

"Of course. I was as head over heels about him as you were about . . . about . . ." She wanted to say "about Sal," but she couldn't bring herself to say the name of the son-in-law whose name was never spoken. Instead, she stammered awkwardly and then blurted, "In my day maybe it was easier to say no to a man." She blushed after she spoke. She hadn't meant to embarrass Stephanie. She was so sorry. What had loosened her tongue that way? The wine or just the warmth of the women? "Oh, I didn't mean to say all that," she added.

"Why do you think it was easier to say no?" Marcia asked.

"No one reason, I'm sure. The pill. The mores. It's all different now. And maybe we don't try to make men over the way we used to. In my time we'd meet a boy and then decide how to mold him so he'd be right. We never realized he was already everything we wanted. We were busy figuring out how to change him."

Is she talking to me, Cassie wondered. Am I expecting more

[100]

from Jimmy than he can give? Am I trying to make him me?

". . . and so," Diane was saying, "we went on and did the same things with our children, always trying to remake them."

Cassie felt a surge of tenderness towards her mother. It hadn't been easy raising girls at this time. She realized suddenly that she did love her mother. She loved her very much. Was she free to do so at this moment because Grandpa wasn't there stealing Cassie's heart? Maybe so. Obviously she couldn't feel love for Diane without Grandpa's image clamoring for equal time. The realization shocked Cassie.

"What are you thinking about, bride-to-be?" Hilda asked.

Cassie rubbed her hands nervously along the legs of her jeans. She lied. "I'm scared about Saturday."

"Oh, Cassie dear, don't be nervous," Diane said. "Maybe I shouldn't have insisted on this big wedding, but I wanted something wonderful for you. I don't want you to be nervous about it."

"Make *me* nervous instead," Hilda said. "Who's coming to the wedding? Who are the hot names?"

"She means important business people," Cassie translated for her mother.

Diane looked at Hilda. All right. So the real estate woman was crass and aggressive. Maybe some of the guests would even find her obnoxious. But at least Hilda was honest. No wonder Cassie liked her. Diane had lived with so much duplicity all her life that she found this whole evening as stimulating as one of those stinging showers at Elizabeth Arden.

"Did I offend you?" Hilda asked.

Diane shook her head. "After all I've said tonight? Hardly. I was thinking how nice it must be to say what you mean all the time."

Cassie looked at her mother. Diane was full of surprises tonight.

"Don't you usually say what you mean?" Hilda asked Diane.

Diane shook her head. "I've always been the perfect child."

"Like Stephanie," Cassie murmured to herself.

Hilda left first. Then Marcia.

And then they were three. The mother and her daughters. A

rare moment in the rarest week of their lives. A week of unity and love. It seemed to Cassie that this was the first time her mother had ever had an unobstructed view of herself. Cassie wanted it to go farther. She scooped up the remaining cheese, poured out the last of the wine, and as her mother followed her to the kitchen she asked, "Were you really the perfect child? It's funny, but I thought Stephanie was the perfect child in our family. I didn't realize you had been, too."

Diane leaned against the kitchen wall. She had the look of silk and softness. "I was even better than Stephanie when she was little. I always did what my governess wanted. I tried so hard to be perfect. I wanted my father to notice me. I wanted him to leave The Actress or The Duchess or whoever he was with that season and come home and play with me. So I'd pretend my governess, Miss Lindsay—don't ask me if that was her first or last name—anyway, I'd pretend Miss Lindsay was my mother. Sometimes I even called her Mummy. But I never had much chance to call my father anything. Miss Lindsay said he spent his whole life in mourning. My brother and I didn't see it that way. We thought he spent his whole life running away from us, so all those beautiful ladies wouldn't be turned off by two little children. So you see, Cassie dear, my life was very different from yours. I was set up to fall in love with the wrong boy. And I did. It was before your father. I was eighteen and the young man was twenty. He was wrong because he was sweet and young and Protestant. In those days religion mattered a lot. It still does to my father. You see, my dears, he thinks he's a Rothschild."

Stephanie shook her head sadly. "I never heard this story."

Diane reached out and touched her daughter's black hair. "Of course not. Because I never told it. I thought I was the heroine of every book I read and every movie I saw. I was Cathy in *Wuthering Heights,* and I was Elizabeth Barrett Browning, and this boy was the hero I so desperately wanted. I suppose I gave him qualities he never really did possess. But I'm not sure, and I'll never know. We wanted to be married in the Grand Ballroom of the Plaza Hotel. He was in the Navy, stationed at Columbia. That's where they trained officers in those days. Columbia and some other schools had a V-twelve program, and you learned to be an ensign by going to college. Well, he became an ensign, and then I followed him to Norfolk. All of a sudden, Daddy saw what I was doing. He said it was a bad thing. All the good things I'd ever done to get my father's attention went unnoticed. But the bad thing brought him home. Daddy dispatched two of his lieutenants, and they brought me—meek and subdued—back to New York."

"What happened to the Navy boy?" Cassie asked.

"He was killed at Guadalcanal. When it happened, my father said, 'See, it's a good thing you didn't marry him. Look how unhappy you'd be.' That's why, when you got married, Stephanie, I wanted it to be a real love match. I'd hoped it would be an Alex Winters you'd love, but it wasn't meant to be. But if this is what you want, I'm glad for you. When all this happened, I know all of you thought I'd crack. But I didn't. Because I pretended you were me, Stephanie, and I thought—oh god, at last I'm free of it all."

Stephanie took a step backward and looked at her mother for a full minute. "But I'm not you. I wish my father had done what your father did instead."

Diane looked at her, and her eyes filled. The pit. She was looking into the pit again. She put her head down.

Guilty. Always guilty. No matter what we do, we parents are guilty. My father turned his back on me. Grandpa Sam never took his eyes off Bill, so Bill never grew on his own. Instead he rebelled. "I suppose all parents are wrong, Stephanie. And so are all children. In S.C.'s eyes Bill can do no right. He's still not old enough to own a building. Darling Grandpa Sam emasculated his own son with attention; my father killed me with neglect."

"What are you talking about?" Cassie asked. "Daddy doesn't own buildings? He doesn't have his own income?"

"Oh, he has his own income because his father hands it to him every month, and he remembers to say thank-you. And I have money in Swiss bank accounts—so my father tells me. You see, Samuel Cassman and Charles Winters each plan to outdo the other. So they each do nothing."

"I don't understand," Stephanie said.

"Just think for a minute," Diane explained. "If Grandpa Sam gave us a building, then Papa Charles would have to give two. If

Papa Charles gave us a million-dollar trust, then Samuel Cassman would have to make it six million. By each doing nothing, they save their fortunes and keep playing their own war games."

Stephanie lowered her head. Her parents would never be able to give her what she needed now. There was a reason she'd come home for the wedding. A reason that had nothing to do with Cassie. But once again she'd have to turn to Cassie. Tonight was too soon. She'd have to wait.

But Cassie could not wait for further explanations. "Daddy doesn't own anything?"

"Cassie," her mother continued, "the first time anyone ever got income from a building without Sam Cassman handling it directly was the time you were given the income from a building as a graduation present."

"You must own the house you live in?" Cass questioned.

"No, we don't," Diane said. "He owns it. He lets us live there."

Cassie turned her head. So Bill Cassman said nothing and got nothing. And what the children—Diane and Bill—needed in terms of love and money went unheeded. The power was in the hands of the grandfathers. And as far as anyone could see, they'd never give it up.

They had no love to give.

And they had too much money to part with any of it.

Some revelation the night before you were to start a life and family of your own.

The wedding lived up to advance billing.

The bride wore an apricot silk satin gown with long pointed sleeves fastened with tiny wax calla lilies. She carried calla lilies fastened to her mother's white confirmation bible. Her veil was pale illusion, and she was attended by a maid of honor—her college roommate—and a matron of honor, her married sister.

Samuel Cassman came with his latest girlfriend, a widow named Dolores. The latest in a series of "a widow named ——"

Grandpa danced every dance with all the pretty women, but he saved a waltz for the bride, and he saved his wedding present for the waltz. "Know what I'm giving you for your wedding?" Grandpa asked.

"No," she said. What would he give her? Would he actually part with a building? Stock?

"I'm going to give you my house in Southampton."

"Grandpa, I love that house. Oh, how wonderful!" She hugged him. Everyone stood back. How sweet to see them like that. The old man and the young girl. So touching.

"One thing," he added, "I'll own it; you can use it. It's almost the same as having it yourself. Ask your parents."

They honeymooned in Bermuda at the Coral Sands, and like generations of honeymooners before them, they put sand in their shoes and promised one another to come back each year on their anniversary.

Cassie didn't know the color of heaven, but somehow she thought it must be filled with pink sand.

The last night as they sat on the beach and watched the ocean, Cassie said, "I wish this could go on forever."

"Could you be alone with me like this—nobody else—for the rest of your life?" Jimmy asked.

"Yes," she said emphatically.

"I couldn't," he said. "I love you, but you can't be my only stimulation, my only interest."

She felt as if the last cold wave had rolled over her.

They were quiet a few minutes. "Grandpa gave me our wedding present at the wedding."

"Oh?"

"Want to know what it is?" She tried to make her voice light. "Sure."

"His house in Southampton."

"Wow. That's some gift."

"We can use it; we don't get it outright."

"Still, that'll be wonderful."

"I forgot to tell you about it, but when you said something about more people, I thought you'd like it for summer. Business guests. Weekends. Things like that."

"I'd like to go out there all by myself sometime."

"You would?"

"Uh-huh. I'm—um—I'm writing a book, Cassie."

"Jimmy, I didn't even know you wrote."

"I don't like to talk about it."

"Will you let me read some of your things?"

"Not until they're ready for publication."

"Why?"

"Oh, you're emotionally involved with me, and I don't think that would be good for our marriage."

She nodded. As long as he put things that were good for their marriage ahead of worldly things, she knew she would be happy.

XI

"HILDA TAYLOR AND ASSOCIATES." Cassie Brown answered the telephone with the enthusiasm of the born salesperson. Although she had been with Hilda for six months, her honeyed tone had been there from the first day. You never knew who would be at the other end of each call; that was the fun of the business. Hilda Taylor was the city's reigning queen of the co-ops; the best listings started with a telephone call to her office. You could pick up the phone at Hilda Taylor any morning and hear the clipped syllables of a British secretary as she told you, ". . . The president of the network is calling . . . The man on the cover of this week's *Business Week* is calling . . . Paris is calling . . . Cairo . . . Rio." The whole world wanted to live in that one little piece of the world that Hilda specialized in selling: the Upper East Side of New York.

Listings, of course, were only half of what the co-op business was about. Selling was the other half. "Get the listing in this office, and we make twice as much money when we sell it," Hilda said tersely. Cassie soon learned that that meant the six-percent commission for the sale was kept by Hilda Taylor and Associates when they also listed the property. When the co-op was listed by another broker, then the selling broker had to split the six percent equally.

"I'll make a deal with you," Hilda said one August afternoon. "You've got a lot of enthusiasm, Cassie. Now let's see how hard you can really work. You and I have different friends, do different things; you ought to be able to bring in different leads. I'll give you one percent of every listing you get for our office, and you get the one percent no matter who makes the sale." Cassie licked her lips; she loved the taste of a challenge. It was like trying for dean's list all over again. It was like racing past your opponent in field hockey or making a slam or doing the Sunday *Times* crossword puzzle. It was the thrill of the chase and the reward, the things Cassie loved most.

"Any ideas on how to get listings?" Cassie asked.

Hilda hooted. "If I did, would I pay you?"

After that Cassie never asked. She kept her eyes open and watched her mentor. Hilda wasn't simply a business woman; she was a political and social presence in New York. Cassie began to understand what Diane meant when she called Hilda a barracuda. Hilda was an expert swimmer in the shark-infested waters of the Upper East Side.

Cassie watched Hilda's comings and goings, and soon she saw the correlation between where Hilda went and what came into the office.

Hilda went to a fund raiser for a congressman, Republican or Democratic, in the silk stocking district, and the next week three listings came to the office. Hilda served on the committee for a museum ball, and within weeks some of the biggest home real estate in New York changed hands without a listing ever appearing in the classified section of *The New York Times*. Hilda sent notes, gifts, congratulatory messages. Suddenly new listings appeared. No question. Hilda had legs in the silk stocking district. And Cassie had eyes and ears for the way Hilda made things happen.

At the end of August Cassie brought in her first listing, a forty-thousand-dollar one-bedroom apartment on the East Side with two significant selling points: low maintenance, the monthly sum that was paid as a kind of rent, and a kitchen with a window. The listing came from Marcia's married boyfriend. "How did he know about it?" Cassie asked.

Marcia shrugged. "Oh, it's so complicated. It's the apartment of his old girlfriend who's getting married."

"But I thought he was already married," Cassie countered.

"Listen," Marcia said, "Take it or leave it. I told you it was complicated. What do you want? His biography or his apartment?"

Cassie took the apartment and kept quiet. She even turned around and sold it to one of her customers. As a new broker Cassie was getting the customary fifty-fifty split with Hilda on commissions. On this deal Cassie was entitled to twelve hundred of the twenty-four-hundred-dollar commission, but because she'd brought in the listing, too, she got her extra point. "Just like the point after touchdown," she told Hilda.

Hilda shrugged. "Fair is fair," and paid her the extra four hundred. That was the first time Cassie made more than Hilda on a deal.

That night Cassie stopped at Sherry-Lehman for a bottle of red wine, put candles on the table, and made her best veal with pasta and a pesto. "What's this all about?" Jimmy asked, his hand tucked around her waist.

"I made two thousand dollars today," she said, pride and wine making her feel a little giddy.

"Good girl," he said.

"How's your business, Jimmy?"

"Very good. Very good."

She waited for more information; none was forthcoming.

Jimmy, as they'd agreed before their marriage, went out two or three nights a week. "Meetings," he said.

She never asked where to or with whom. She certainly wasn't going to be a comic-strip housewife who never let her man think or act or talk for himself. Besides, she had a fascinating business life of her own.

Cassie set a personal goal for the next six months: score better than the scorer. That meant she would try to make more on each of her deals than Hilda made. To do that she needed a systematic plan for developing leads. She needed an arena, an ambience, a milieu. Hilda had politics and East Side charities. What were Cassie's assets? She had to carve her own niche. But how?

Strangely, it was Diane who gave Cassie the key when she told her that Bill was spending the weekend in Westchester to play in a golf tournament at the Century Club. That was how Bill—not

Jimmy, who wasn't a golfer—became Cassie's accomplice. The Century was a perfect background for Cassie. She called her father and said she wanted him to get some games together. "To be quite honest, Daddy, get us some hot foursomes."

By fall Cassie had more than twenty listings plus leads, and by the spring golfing season her income was averaging four thousand two hundred dollars a month.

"No woman ever moved through this office this way," Hilda said in grudging admiration one evening as they were making up ads for Sunday's *Times*.

"Who else ever had this kind of inspiration?" Cassie asked in the flip manner she used with Hilda.

"Cut that," Hilda said sharply. "Stop conning me, Cassie. What the hell are you after? Me or my business?"

Cassie put her pencil down. "I don't get it."

"Then let me make it plainer. Whose arm are you biting? Are you out to get me or S.C.?"

"I'm not out to get anybody, Hilda. I'm out to win for me."

"I'm not so sure, Cassie. There's something vicious about the way you attack a deal."

"I think you're wrong," Cassie said. But she vowed silently to watch herself the next time around. She didn't have long to wait.

It was very warm for April, and when Cassie came from the golf course into the locker room at the Century she was hot and thirsty.

She stood at the sink, splashed water on her face, looked up and saw—"Chichi Fink. How've you been?"

"Great, Cass. What're you doing here?"

"Playing with my father and some friends."

"Since you're playing again, why don't we go out one day?"

"I'd love that, but I think you're too good for me. Aren't you still club champ?"

"Yes, but I think we'd have fun playing together. Shall I call you?"

"I work now. I don't have much time."

"What do you do?"

"I sell real estate. Co-ops in the city."

Chichi smiled. "Would you believe I want something in the city? Something Park Avenue, sixty-ish in location, sixty-ish in price."

Cassie smiled. She could fit Chichi's numbers on location but never on price. But Cassie wasn't worried. The way Chichi wiggled that little bottom of hers meant she knew just how to wiggle the money out of Herbie, her psychiatrist husband, her daddy, or some very rich in-laws.

From that day Cassie courted Chichi with all the ardor of a potential swain. She had learned the value of small courtesies from Hilda. To prove to Chichi that it wasn't money that was important—but just the joy of finding the right place—Cassie courted her with the de rigueur gifts of the New York hunter: wine, books, and a silver Tiffany keyring. The wine was a single bottle of René Lalou champagne (the card said simply "Open when settled . . . in new home"). The book was a Picasso art book (this time the card instructed the receiver: "Place in conspicuous place in new apartment."). And the note with the keyring said, "Give me a ring now. Have I got a key for you!"

The first apartment Cassie showed Chichi was on Fifth Avenue, park view, contemporary, ninety-five thousand. "I hate the turquoise carpeting," Chichi said.

"Hey," Cassie assured her, "you don't have to take the turquoise carpeting. They'll take it with them." (Of course, she didn't bother to say that the owners had just put the turquoise carpet in—wall to wall—in hopes that it would make their apartment worth ninety-five thousand instead of the seventy Hilda Taylor herself had advised them to ask. But one thing Cassie had learned from Hilda was: sell first, change later. Nonetheless Chichi was firm; she didn't want the place on Fifth. Besides it was too far uptown.

"Would you consider Sutton Place?" Cassie asked.

"Let me look," Chichi said magnanimously.

The Sutton Place apartment was built in the 1930s and had a living room twenty-two by twenty-eight feet, a full-size dining room, a kitchen with a window, and appliances that postdated the Civil War (a rarity in New York), two bedrooms, two baths, a powder room and a foyer. There was even a terrace. "Perfect, isn't it?" Cassie asked.

Chichi sighed. "Cassie, do you think for one minute I would live on Sutton Place in a house with a terrace that faced *away* from the river?"

"No, but I was just testing you."

And so she was. Cassie was testing her quarry, testing the times, testing herself. She'd know the big one. She'd know when to make her move. By showing those other apartments to Chichi she'd learned far more than Chichi had said. Cassie now knew that what Herbie thought didn't matter because Chichi never once referred to him or his parents. That meant Chichi had her own money and was on her own with this apartment. She also knew that Chichi would rather have an underdecorated apartment that needed "doing" because she had very definite tastes. And she also knew that location, in all its subtleties, mattered. Chichi was not about to live on the wrong side of anything just for a good address. Very important to know. Information like that was worth money.

The Park Avenue apartment that became available when a Dutch widow decided to return to the Netherlands to spend her last years was a gem. Cassie was so breathless she could scarcely describe it. The listing came in from Hilda, and when Cassie saw the apartment, she begged Hilda to give it to her exclusively for one day.

"It won't sell that fast," Hilda assured her.

"Doesn't matter," Cassie said. "I'm going to give this a kind of urgency you've never seen."

"Baby, the co-op market ain't that hot at the moment," Hilda said.

"It's heating up today," Cassie said, the fire mounting in her.

By midafternoon she had shown the apartment to Chichi. And even the usually calm Chichi had a mild attack of Great Excitement.

The building was one of the distinguished apartment houses on Park Avenue in the sixties. The long marble foyer was tended by two doormen; the elevators looked like something out of Radio City Music Hall. The apartment was on a single level but was so interesting in layout and decor that it gave the appearance of a multilevel home. "The only thing wrong with the whole place is this room," Chichi pouted as she looked around the heavy-looking, paneled dressing room. "It's so masculine. Why isn't it for me?"

"But the bedroom is feminine," Cassie countered. "Maybe you can take the maid's room behind the kitchen and fix that as a small retreat for yourself."

"That's where I want to put Herb," she said in her matter-of-fact voice.

Cassie decided to ask no questions. Chichi, however, had many questions. Down payment? Possession? Title? Escrow?

"Hold it," Cassie said. "Don't you think we ought to talk to Herb? You know Dr. Herbert S. Fink, husband?"

Chichi smiled. "He'll do whatever I say. This is my marriage, Cassie. He married me for my connections; I married him for his. You know, in this day and age everybody thinks we are all like dandelions, just blowin' in the wind. Let me tell you I'm pre-planned. And the reason I decided to work with you is that I think you are, too. You always think on the backswing."

Cassie smiled in appreciation. It was as close to a compliment as Chichi could come.

"All right," Chichi continued, "we'll call Herbie now and ask him to come down the street, but I'm making the decision. Remember that. No matter what he says. Herbie tends to sound a little pompous, but after all, he's a doctor, so he's allowed."

Herbie, like Orca the whale, lived up to his advance. He was intense, slightly pompous, and very concerned about getting a good deal.

Cassie explained that the usual rule of thumb about what one could afford to pay for a home probably didn't apply in the case of the Finks. "The rule is that a monthly payment, including taxes, principal, interest, and insurance should not be more than one fourth the family's monthly income. But since you have no children and have your greatest earning years ahead of and not behind you, I think you can waive the rule."

"The price again?" Herbie asked. Cassie had noticed doctors always asked financial questions. Even men on Wall Street asked less about money than doctors, who always assumed someone was going to make too much on them.

"Price?" Cassie repeated. "I always let a wife tell her husband."

Chichi didn't miss a beat. "Seventy thousand," she answered.

The apartment cost one hundred and seventy thousand. But the moment Cassie heard Chichi give the price, she knew it was a sale. A woman who would lie for a hundred thousand dollars wanted something. Badly.

"I thought we were going as high as sixty," Herb said to his wife.

"Real estate is a super investment," Chichi said, "and I've got a couple of thousand left from our wedding money I can add to this."

"No," Herb Fink said righteously, "I'm doing this on my own."

Cassie blinked.

"Well, let's do it," he said.

Chichi smiled. "Thanks, Cassie."

Only Cassie knew just what she meant by that thank-you.

"What's the next step?" Herb asked.

"We'll work with your bank," Cassie explained. "We usually ask the bank to order title insurance policy, prepare the loan documents, and prorate the taxes and maintenance. The bank will also arrange title insurance and prepare a final statement."

"It sounds like the house is going into analysis," Herb moaned.

Cassie smiled. "In a way it is. It takes about four weeks to do all this. Then we have the signing, and several days later the closing."

"The closing meaning when we take over?" Chichi asked.

Cassie nodded. There was one question she was itching to ask. But she said nothing.

Herbie excused himself; he could already picture the next patient fantasizing the reasons for his tardiness.

When the door closed behind him, Chichi extended her hand. "You're a pro, Cassie. Thanks."

Cassie shook hands solemnly, although she wanted to jump up and down. It was the biggest sale of her life. She tried to still the excitement inside her and asked the question she wanted so much to know, "Whose name is this in?"

There was a pause. Chichi wet her lips. "Put the apartment in my name. I'll pay with a cashier's check. I know you realize it's not my money, but I'm not ready to have you know whose it is."

Cassie put her hands over her eyes. "I see nothing, Chichi."

How was Cassie to know that sale would come back to haunt her?

"Can you believe this?" Cassie squealed when she got the check in her hand. "We made ten thousand two hundred dollars this afternoon."

"Fantastic," Hilda said. "You've got the technique kid. What did you do? Tell the husband that the apartment was a hedge against inflation, old age, and fear of darkness?"

"He didn't have much to say," Cassie admitted. "He's not too interested in what houses look like. He only cares what they cost."

"From what I hear, he doesn't have a wife fetish either."

"What's that supposed to mean, Hilda?"

"It means, my dear, that theirs is a New York marriage made in heaven. He has a girlfriend; she has a lover; and you, dear Cassie, even without understanding their curious ménage, have managed to find the perfect apartment for them."

"Hilda, how do you know all this?"

"Because," she said, pinching Cassie's cheek, "in my world the best psychiatrists sell real estate."

Cassie sighed. "Until I learn all that stuff about people, I'm not really going to make it to the top in this business, am I?"

Hilda put an arm around Cassie. "I want to tell you something. I once said you were vicious and going about your deals in a kind of tough way. I was wrong. You see, Cassie, it's been such a long time since I've seen a classic case of ambition that I had a hard time recognizing it. The last person I saw who wanted to be good for the sake and the sheer joy of being good at her work was me. Then when you came along, I said . . . no, no, relax, Hilda, there can't be two of you. But I was wrong. You're not vicious, Cassie. You're hungry. And there's a difference. You've got one hell of a future kid."

August 1972

Business? It's quite simple. It's other people's money.
    Alexandre Dumas the Younger
    La Question d'Argent

XII

CASSIE HAD NO INTENTION of voting for George McGovern, but it didn't seem politic to say so. Marcia was so passionate, so committed, that any disagreement now would only add to the tension of an already tense weekend. It had all started so happily, a weekend at Southampton—a little sun, some surf, and—the snap of Marcia's voice brought Cassie back.

"Sure." Marcia pointed her finger at Jimmy, "you think McGovern is some kind of nut, and Nixon is perfect—"

"I didn't say Nixon was perfect," Jimmy interrupted. "I just said McGovern wasn't."

"Typical Wall Street opinion," Cassie said with a wave of her hand.

"Now, now," Grandpa smiled. "You know what the trouble is with all of you?"

The circle of five was quiet. Samuel Cassman was about to speak.

Grandpa, with the timing known to all good actors, paused, stared at his hands, then lifted his eyes and said, "We all try to be different. Nobody wants to be like anybody else. You young people all talk about doing your own thing. What you're really doing is struggling to find new mistakes to make."

The group stared not knowing what to answer. What had he said? Was it really smart? Or did it just sound smart?

Cassie laughed to herself. Leave it to Grandpa to focus the attention back onto himself.

The second summer of her marriage, Cassie had invited small groups to the Southampton house, and this time Grandpa was the stellar attraction. "Use Twelvetrees to make deals," Grandpa had said. "If you only knew how much of New York I bought and sold there—and that was just in the cabana."

The house itself had a large, square entrance hall with a two-story ceiling and two brass chandeliers. The wood-banistered stairway led to seven bedroom suites on the second floor; servants' quarters were over the garage. But the second floor saw little use; the main floor was the center of the action. The living room was cheerily furnished in eighteenth-century antiques and rich damasks. Each item in the room had been selected by Grandpa on trips to London, and when pressed, S.C. could still tell exactly where, when and how he'd bargained for each of the antiques. The room had two focal points: a huge bay window overlooking the twelve trees that lined the entrance drive and, on the opposite wall, a walk-in stone fireplace.

The first summer of their marriage Jimmy used the house during the week for client meetings. Each time Cassie asked, "Who's going with you?" Jimmy was too handsome and interesting not to be noticed by the increasing number of women money managers on The Street. "Some of the fellows whose portfolios I plan," was his standard answer, and then seeing the small furrows appear on her forehead, he would smile. "There'll never be another woman in the world for me, Cassie." That was all the reassurance she needed.

Typically, Jimmy went to Southampton on Wednesday afternoons and returned Friday mornings. If the Browns were to use the house together for the weekend, she would join him Thursday afternoon. Most weekends, however, Jimmy returned to the city because her work required her presence in New York on Sundays.

Jimmy never complained about the time apart, but by summer's end Cassie found herself increasingly uncomfortable with the arrangement, and this time she told Hilda in May that she wouldn't be in the city any weekends. "Then you might as well forget the residential real estate business," Hilda said. Cassie knew that Hilda wasn't kidding. Torn between her husband and her career, Cassie was now experimenting with a Solomon-like choice: half her weekends were spent working in the city, half in Southampton. And she was discovering that she liked the Southampton weekends more than the city weekends. You not only left the city; you left the city behind. At Twelvetrees Jimmy was jovial and clever; he had a gift for the wickedly delicious one liner, and everyone—every single one of Cassie's friends—adored him.

In the sophisticated setting of Twelvetrees, Cassie loved him more than ever. Jimmy was more than her husband; he was a host and the man in residence. At least he had been all summer. This weekend was different, and Cassie knew the difference. This time Grandpa was there.

The first sign of Jimmy's temper showed when Karl came to pick them up at their apartment. "Why is Grandpa coming?" Jimmy wanted to know as he threw his weekend clothes into a small bag. "You know I like to drive out to the country myself. I don't like sitting in the back seat like a trained monkey while Karl takes the curves."

It was an old story; she was tired of the reasons. She ignored the last part of the statement and answered the question. "Grandpa's coming up because I've invited Holt Hayward, and he'll be impressed to meet Sam Cassman."

"Holt Hayward. That's a new one."

"Holt's an attorney who's into real estate. Hilda knows him from—oh, from wherever Hilda always meets these people. When we sold the town house on Sixty-ninth Street to that gallery owner, Holt handled the deal as a courtesy because he does the gallery's legal work. Then when Hilda was away—"

Jimmy held up his hand. "Enough explanation. Is he the Holt Hayward who managed the Simpson family trust? The one the papers call 'The Young Baron'?"

She nodded.

"I figured there couldn't be two Holt Haywards," Jimmy said. "He's important, all right. You've caught a big fish, Cassie."

Cassie smiled. Jimmy didn't often talk about her business. "Have you ever met him?"

"Rollo mentions his name; he'll probably know who I am because I'm married to you."

"He didn't seem to when I told him about us and invited him here."

"Maybe I'm not as important as I think I am," Jimmy said. Cassie thought she detected a note of relief in his voice, as Karl pulled up in front of the San Remo to pick up Grandpa and Grandpa's lady of the weekend, one Queenie Kest. She was in the usual mold, blonde and widowed.

[119]

Jimmy, his good humor momentarily restored at the thought of going to Twelvetrees, bowed low to Queenie, then whispered to Cassie, "Where does he find them all? In the checkout line at Zabar's?"

That was Jimmy's last joke.

From the moment Grandpa entered the car, Jimmy's smiles ended. Instead of Jimmy organizing the activities of the weekend as he usually did, Grandpa took over. Cassie realized how much of the summer had been Jimmy's doing when she saw Grandpa take on the role that would be Jimmy's undoing. Other weekends Jimmy organized the tennis games and talked Wall Street. This weekend Grandpa presided over financial seminars. Not that his audience wasn't attuned, appreciative, and informed—it was just that Grandpa didn't play tennis, and he did play all markets. So the six of them sat on the rolling slope next to the tennis court. Occasionally Holt and Jimmy hit a few balls. Cassie had invited Marcia for Holt. "Who needs another married man?" Marcia had asked.

"He's not married," Cassie insisted.

"Well, Holt Hayward is the most married name I ever heard," Marcia said.

"Holt and Marcia are not going to win the couple-of-the-year award," Jimmy said the first night as they were undressing for bed.

"I think they're very cute together," Cassie answered.

"Cute!" Jimmy hooted. "He looks like the world's curling-polo-soccer-skeet champion, and she looks like an assistant buyer at Macy's."

"That's what they both are," Cassie said.

"They go together like ham and lox," Jimmy said.

"Oh, Jimmy, the world's different now."

"Not that different," he insisted.

The next evening, as they sat in the cabana on the chintz-covered chairs, Jimmy knew for certain there were differences these people would never resolve. Marcia was fighting desperately for McGovern; Holt was for Nixon; and Grandpa was talking about mistakes. Time for levity.

Jimmy cleared his throat. "You know who Cassie's going to vote for?"

She felt her face flush. Somehow she sensed the joke would be directed at her. Just don't let him embarrass me too much, she prayed silently.

"She," said Jimmy kissing her lightly on the forehead, "will vote for anyone who lets her turn the White House into a co-op."

Cassie squirmed. It wasn't the wet bathing suit that made her uncomfortable; it was the soggy humor.

Grandpa nodded. "Why not, Jimmy? Cassie's always looking for a deal. She doesn't ever quit. I'll bet if she'd failed the bar the first time she'd still be trying to pass."

That was the last straw. "I'm tired. I'm going upstairs," Jimmy said. He stood stiffly and walked across the flagstones, past the pool and up to the house. Everyone noticed that Jimmy hadn't said good night to his wife. There was an uncomfortable pause while each of them tried to think of something that would bring a bantering tone back to the conversation.

Just when Jimmy was out of earshot, Grandpa leaned forward and said, "Cassie, why isn't he a lawyer like Holt?"

There was no generosity in Grandpa's question. Cassie was embarrassed for them all, the questioner, the subject, the respondent, and the audience. "It's not easy to study when you've been out of school a long time," she said quietly. She looked at Grandpa as she spoke; there was a disbelieving, sardonic smile on his face. Cassie was all right until she saw that look. Jimmy wasn't here to protect himself. She had to say something. She had to stop Grandpa's silent comparison between Jimmy and her. "Well, we don't all do what we begin doing. This isn't my first job. It's my second."

Grandpa laughed. "Who knows better than I?"

She flushed. Now she knew for certain that Grandpa had masterminded her jobs.

"Jimmy's on Wall Street, isn't he?" Marcia rushed to inquire, in order to cover everyone's embarrassment at Grandpa's rudeness.

Cassie nodded and shot her friend a thank-you with her eyes. "He loves it," Cassie reported as dutifully as if she were telling of a child's progress at school.

"He loves it so much? Why? What does he do?" Grandpa asked.

"He's—he buys and sells," Cassie stammered.

"Who doesn't?" Grandpa snorted.

"Stop it, Sam," Holt said. "It's none of your business."

Cassie felt her eyes grow bigger. She'd never heard anyone under the age of sixty ever call Grandpa "Sam." They said "S.C." or "Mr. Cassman" or "Sir." But they never said Sam.

Grandpa turned to Holt, opened his mouth to speak and instead slapped his knee. "You have guts, young man," he said. He pointed to Cassie. "Teach her how to have guts, too, will you?"

"I think she already has quite a teacher. You." Holt Hayward smiled innocently and leaned back against the stone column.

Cassie turned and looked at Holt more closely. Until this moment she'd seen only his credentials, not his face. Now she blinked and looked closer. He was almost six feet tall, curly-haired, and slender. His body looked at home in the jeans and sweat shirt he wore. It would have looked equally at home in a blazer, tuxedo, or J. Press suit. Cassie liked what she saw.

"I don't think Cassie should be your only pupil," Holt said. "I came out here this weekend, Sam, because Cassie promised me I could meet you. I could have sailed with some friends at the Cape, stayed in the city, or gone to Easthampton. Instead I came here, and with all due apologies to my charming hostess, I must confess that you—not she—attracted me."

Grandpa smiled. Flattery had no age limits. "What do you want to talk about? Interest rates? Real estate prices?"

"I want advice," Holt said. "I'm forty years old, born in the Depression to a man who went broke. That's when you made your money—or so I'm told. How did you do it, Sam? The rest of the world was jumping out of windows, and you supposedly were making a mint."

Grandpa lit a cigar. "Some young man you found," he said slyly to Marcia.

"Come on, what's the story?" Queenie asked.

"Oh, it's probably too dull for all of you. Besides, Cassie's heard it a thousand times," Grandpa protested.

"I've never heard it, and you know it," Cassie said. She shook her head. The old fox.

"In that case," said Grandpa rubbing his hands together, "let's pour another drink, and I'll tell you how it was to make money in the thirties and forties."

"Begin at the beginning," Holt said.

Cassie looked around the group. Too bad Jimmy'd gone off in a huff. Grandpa in top form was going to be some show; she could sense it. She motioned to Williams, the butler, and quickly the glasses were filled.

Grandpa settled in the big chair, sipped his scotch, lit his cigar and began. "You have to go back to the turn of the century to understand New York real estate. Now this will probably sound modern to you, but more than fifty years ago the city of New York passed a major pollution control measure. It meant that steam engines were banned from the city, and electric engines had to be used instead. Well, when that happened the New York Central had to cover up the railroad tracks from Forty-fifth Street to Ninety-sixth Street. Just close your eyes and think of it. They had to take forty blocks of city real estate, cover it up and put those engines underground. And the street they covered was—"

"Park Avenue," Holt said.

Grandpa nodded. "Exactly. It's all there in the history books. You can read it. Park Avenue was developed because the New York Central had to obey pollution laws. The Central fought the whole thing at first, but once the area was resurfaced, they found they were the owners of an incredible real estate empire. It was more than they could possibly handle. By the early nineteen-twenties, the Central was turning to outside dealers to negotiate some of its leases. New companies were formed. Why, just think of the kinds of ground leases they had. The Barclay Hotel. The Park Lane. The Yale Club. I started meeting some of those gentlemen dealers, partly by chance, partly by choice."

"How?" That was Cassie's question.

"Oh, I always liked good living." He winked at Queenie. "In those days I had my regular table at the Ritz Carlton Hotel."

"Where was that?" Marcia asked.

"There's a Uris building there now," Grandpa said. "A lot of deals just walked in the door of the Ritz Carlton in those days. You see, I always had this philosophy. The minute you get a little money, put it to work."

"Did your money always make money?" Holt asked.

Grandpa smiled. "Of course not. Joe DiMaggio never batted a thousand, but wasn't he a champion? Champions, young fellow, are the people who can stand losing, not the people who win."

"Come on," Cassie said, "what happened next?"

"I did some investing around town in the twenties and thirties, and I always managed to stay enough ahead of the game so I wouldn't go belly up. I was becoming well known around town as a manager of buildings. I was involved with theaters, banks, restaurants. I knew everybody. But it wasn't until nineteen-forty that I really started to roll."

"What happened?" Marcia asked.

"You'll like this story," Grandpa smiled, "because it's the reason you're all here. In 1940 one of the old-line real estate brokers came to my office and asked if I'd be interested in buying one of the fine, fashionable buildings on East Sixty-second Street. I explained that that wasn't really my style. I was basically a broker and manager, not a dealer. Then I went out to see why a first-rate building like this was for sale. It turned out that the rich man who owned the building had married a woman even richer than he and moved to London. The price was one hundred seventy-six thousand dollars, the cost of converting the house to an apartment building. I thought I could swing the deal with fifteen thousand down, but I knew first I had to meet the owner."

"And was the owner just another rich man?" Holt asked.

Grandpa freshened his drink with the bottle on the table next to him. "William Worthly was more than that. He was the right man at the right time. Worthly came to my office and got right down to business. Said he was in the investment business and didn't like mortgages; he liked cash. So I asked him to lend me the money to buy his building—and, incidentally, during our conversations I got the price down to one fifty."

Cassie groaned. "I get that for single co-op units on East Sixty-second Street now."

"Wait," Grandpa said holding up one hand. "William Worthly didn't like the deal. It still involved a mortgage. Finally, after one more afternoon of negotiations, Worthly turned to me and said, 'Give me cash, and it's yours.'

"I knew what I had right down to the last penny, but you don't think I'd tell him. I said I had to talk to my treasurer. My treasurer! Some laugh. I was the treasurer. I walked into the next office, poured myself a nice glass of cold water and decided what I'd offer. I came back in the room and told Worthly I'd give him sixty thousand in cash. At that time I had three thousand in cash to my name. Worthly took three days to think about it, then accepted. And then my problems really began. I had to raise fifty-seven thousand. I had three thousand. I knew I'd never get the money from a New York bank, so I took a little trip on the New York Central and went upstate to visit a bank in Albany. I showed the bankers the hundred-seventy-six-thousand-dollar balance sheet, and they shook their heads and said they were very sorry, but the most they could lend me was one hundred thousand with four percent interest. I smiled and took it. I had title to the property and forty thousand in cash with one deal."

Holt whistled.

"Oh, that wasn't the end of it," Grandpa said with a sly smile. "I went through the tenant list and found that the penthouse was occupied by a relative of the man who'd owned the place. A very nice widow she was. I have always had a soft spot for widows," Grandpa said and patted Queenie's head. "Well, I visited that widow and suggested she buy the house. It was a fine deal for her. She talked to her lawyers and agreed—but only if I'd take her house in Southampton for fifteen thousand as part of the deal. The house, of course, was Twelvetrees. So here's how that deal ended. I sold her the house for one hundred seventy-six thousand, a very fair price. I paid off the hundred-thousand-dollar mortgage and wound up with another seventy-six thousand. So for a three-thousand-dollar investment, I found myself one month later with one hundred sixteen thousand in cash and Twelvetrees. Incidentally, I took a mortgage on this house."

"Okay, Sam, you living legend, what did you do next?" Holt asked.

"I had another talk with my treasurer," Grandpa said. "I said to the treasurer—that's me, remember?—I said, if you can make this much money selling property, why manage it? But you know the best thing I learned from that whole deal? Don't be afraid of debt.

[125]

That was the greatest lesson of all. Debt gives you leverage. I had finally become aware that there was a Depression sellers' market, a market of people like Worthly who would take any price—so long as it was cash. And in those days many financial institutions had plenty of cash to lend. What I'd done was give three different people three different reasons for acting on a property. I gave a seller the cash he wanted; I gave a lender the high-quality property he needed in order to justify the loan; and I gave an investor a self-liquidating income property."

"That's an extraordinary story," Holt said.

"I've got a million more," Grandpa laughed, "but I'm not going to tell you. Well, not tonight anyway."

Marcia was the first to move. "If you're not telling stories any longer, I really must be going."

"But I thought—" Cassie began.

Marcia shook her head. "I'm not going to stay tonight, Cass. I'm going to a party at the Shepards', and then I'll pick up a ride back to the city."

"Sure?" Cassie asked.

"Yes," Marcia said aloud and then whispered in Cassie's ear, "Your friend Holt isn't for me, and the Shepards promised me a fresh male."

Cassie nodded. At least Marcia wasn't going to the same old married man. "I'll walk you to the door, Marcia," Grandpa said. "I'm going upstairs."

"I will, too," Queenie said.

As the three started on the path to the house, Holt remained at the pool house with Cassie. "I always wanted to meet S.C. He is incredible," Holt said.

"That's what I've always thought. He seems to scare most people, though."

"You mean they can't compete with him?"

"I guess that's it."

"How do you feel about him, Cassie?"

"Very mixed feelings, Holt, very mixed. I think he's emasculated all his family—yes, even me, a woman—and I also think he's been very brave and tough and gutsy. I admire him in a lot of ways, but he's got a black side."

[126]

"He obviously loves you a lot."

"Well, 'love' is a word we don't use much in our family."

"Why?" His eyes were focused on hers.

"I—I don't know. Please, I, um, uh, let's go. I'm sure Jimmy's wondered what happened to me."

"I'm not so sure," Holt said. "But I won't press you, Cassie. Relax. I loved listening to your grandfather, and then I enjoyed watching his story reflected in your reactions. A couple of times there, Ms. Brown, you actually licked your lips. Did you learn some new financial maneuvers?"

She laughed. "I hope so. I really want to be good."

"I know you do, Cassie," he said evenly. "So do I." He paused and looked once more in those electric blue eyes. "Do you think we'd be good together?" There was no mistaking the double meaning.

She felt desire and apprehension in one mighty chord. "I don't know."

There was a half smile on his face. "You invited me. What did you have in mind?"

"Just to meet Marcia—"

"Bull. Why am I here?"

"I don't know. I figured we'd—"

"No, Cassie. You figured I'd be knocked out by S.C. and want to work with you. Well, you were half right. The one who really knocks me out, though, is you. I love the alive way you respond, the way your eyes light up when deals are discussed. I like your no-politics approach to politics and your all-business approach to business. Listen to me, Cassie. I've got some land out on Long Island, and I'd like to build a shopping center and apartments, a real community. I think I'm the one to do it because I'm not just an investor; I'm a lawyer. What's more, I even have three thousand dollars," he teased. "I figure you do, too. Want to buy a piece of my dream, Cassie?"

She smiled.

"It's not for now. Other deals will come along now, and they'll help finance the big dream."

"I don't know that I'm ready for those other deals you're talking about. Maybe you ought to talk to Hilda."

[127]

"I have over the years. But Hilda eats, drinks, and sleeps residential real estate. On the other hand you've got lots of reasons to get your feet wet with a few deals of your own. Come on. Tell the truth. Aren't you ready to try your wings and see just how good you really are?"

"I'm not sure I'm another Grandpa."

"That's all right, too. I'm not sure the world could handle two Sam Cassmans, but it may be ready for one Cassie Brown."

For a few minutes they said nothing, and only the sound of the ocean could be heard. Finally Cassie asked the question she really wanted answered. "Do you think I could do it?"

"Yes," he said quietly, "but only if you use your ambition as if it were your biggest talent."

.

XIII

"USE YOUR AMBITION as if it were your biggest talent."

The words burned in Cassie's mind, even now, months after Holt had first spoken them.

"Penny for your thoughts," Holt said, as he leaned against the banquette opposite Cassie. They were in the bar at the Sherry Netherland Hotel, one of her favorite uptown meeting places.

She paused and smiled at him. "I'm sitting here facing Fifth Avenue, watching that parade of women out there. It's fantastic. They all look so purposeful and kind of wonderful. Too bad your back is to the window."

"Wrong, Cassie Brown. I'm facing just one woman, and she's fantastic."

Cassie shook her head in disbelief. If there was one thing she'd learned from selling co-ops and dealing with men, it was to laugh away all business flirtations. She reached for a line. "Are you Irish or does the blarney go with the territory?"

"Both."

"Good. Then it's safe to have another glass of wine before I meet my next client."

This was the first time she'd seen Holt since the weekend in the country, but they'd telephoned one another several times because as a wheeler dealer in commercial real estate, he had recommended Hilda Taylor & Associates—and Cassie Brown in particular—to potential co-op owners. The drink this evening had been his idea.

Holt motioned the captain for another round. "How's business?" he asked in his deceptively offhand manner.

"Slowing down."

"I sense it in the residential market. I think we're coming to the end of the apartment boom."

"Meaning?"

"It's time for you to take your next step or else be prepared to sit out the next few years."

"What are you talking about?"

"An historic, recurring phenomenon. It's called boom and bust. Don't look so surprised. I didn't invent it. At regular intervals our country in its business cycle has a period of tight money. When that happens, the interest rates go up, mortgages get tough to get, and the Hildas and Cassies of the world don't make too many deals."

"What are you trying to tell me, Holt?"

"Simply that the apartment craze is going to top out soon, and you'd better have some viable alternatives. Remember the night we talked out at the pool house at your place in Southampton?"

"Of course."

"I told you then that—both as an attorney and an investor—I wanted to get into some deals with you. That was two months ago. I'm ready now. I've got our first deal."

She looked puzzled. "What kind of deal?"

"A fair one, Cassie. If it doesn't work for us both, then it isn't any good."

She blushed. "I didn't think you were going to cheat me."

"Don't be too sure, Cassie. Just because I went to Princeton, had my own consulting company at thirty-two and am now forty, single, and acceptable in most saloons doesn't mean you ought to trust me. In fact, my credentials are so good you should be suspicious."

"I'm ambitious, not suspicious."

[129]

"In that case here's the story. There's a company called Alpha. Bottle manufacturer. In 1960 Alpha decided to leave Louisville and relocate in the Sunbelt. Put their building and land up for sale. A Louisville distiller offered to lease the building for twenty-two years. So, with the backing of the lease, Alpha said—hey, wait a minute—let's buy the building ourselves for a million dollars. They arranged a million-dollar loan from a local bank, payable in twenty-two years at five percent, pledged the lease as security, applied all rents to the loan."

"Perfect," Cassie concluded. "Alpha moved—no penalty. Liquor company gets use of facility. Mortgage company has no big risk. Alpha owns building, no money down."

"Smart kid," Holt acknowledged. "Now do a quick cut to New York, office of one Holt Hayward. Enter Holt's old college pal from Wall Street who, incidentally, is Mr. Alpha's broker."

Cassie nodded. "What's the problem? The liquor company wants out?"

"No. Nothing that fierce. The problem is more commonplace. Income tax. Mr. Alpha is paying income tax on earnings he won't realize until he sells the building—and it will be ten years before he owns it free and clear."

"So accelerated depreciation has caught up with him," Cassie said.

A knowing smile played in Holt's eyes. "Feed you the straight lines and you come up with the biggie."

She shrugged modestly.

"You're adorable, Cassie. Hey, don't look at me like that. It's not a put-down. Smile. It's all right to be the smartest kid on the block."

As long as I'm not smarter than you, she thought.

"So obviously they want to sell the building," he said. Then he added, "To you."

"I don't have that kind of money to invest," Cassie said quickly.

"I don't want you to buy it alone. I'd like us to buy it."

"Us doesn't have that money unless us is you. I don't have a million-dollar allowance," she answered.

Holt reached over and pinched her cheek. "Did you ever hear a

[130]

fellow named Cassman talk about something called leverage? Here's what we do. Borrow two hundred seventy-five thousand from a bank, and assign our interest in the distiller's lease."

"Have you been to the bank yet?"

"No, Cassie. That's where you come in."

"What do I have to do?"

"Go to Louisville, see the lending officer at the bank, and tell him why it's to his advantage to have to be in court for two weeks."

The idea was exhilarating. Go to a bank. Arrange a deal. Do it in a new city. Buy a commercial property. Suddenly a thought struck. "Will you coach me, tell me what to say?"

"Sure. Now will you do it?"

She paused. "I think there's just one other person I should talk to."

"I'm sorry," he said. "I should've realized you'd have to talk it over with Jimmy—"

"Jimmy?" Her eyes widened. She'd forgotten all about Jimmy. No, it wasn't Jimmy she had to phone.

There was only one person who could advise her now.

XIV

CASSIE DIALED FROM one of those sidewalk telephone booths. "Hilda . . . what do you think? Is Holt . . . is he . . . no, no. I'm not suspicious, just curious. Would you? . . . Yes, be honest . . . Tell me . . . please . . . would you . . . You wouldn't? . . . Just because it's not your kind of deal? And . . . because . . . he'd be trading on Samuel Cassman's name . . . you're right. I can't really do it without his permission, can I? Damn! Grandpa closes more doors than he opens. I'm going to talk to him tomorrow."

"Cassie!"

The sight of his granddaughter entering his office lifted years from Samuel Cassman. He stood up to greet her, the blue eyes open wide, the arms extended.

As they embraced, Cassie saw that they were not alone. Standing to one side with his eyes lowered was a man in a tan raincoat, a sheaf of papers stuck in his pocket. Cassie drew away from Grandpa at the sight of the stranger, and as she did Sam Cassman said, "Mr. Hawkins, this is the girl I was telling you about. This is my Cassie."

She flinched. My Cassie. No, she was her Cassie. Somehow she'd have to get that across to Grandpa today. He'd have to stop playing chess with her life, moving her here, checking opponents there.

"I'll come back later," Mr. Hawkins said, waving his hand and taking little backward steps toward the door.

Like homage to the king, Cassie thought. *They leave him as if he were royalty, never turning their backs.*

"Stay," Grandpa said, beckoning the visitor with his finger. "We can finish our business in front of Cassie; she's family."

Hawkins was a putty-colored lump of a man who acted as if his presence were an apology. Now forty-seven, he had probably looked the same at twenty-seven and would be but a bit more stooped at sixty-seven. But Wayne Hawkins had something Samuel Cassman wanted. Ten years earlier, in a sudden attack of foresight, Hawkins's father had bought a piece of corner property in North Miami. And Samuel Cassman wanted that corner; he wanted it because he was going to build a vast shopping center and office building complex. Mr. Hawkins, of course, didn't know why Sam Cassman wanted the property—but he could guess it wasn't for sunbathing. Under the putty-colored body of Mr. Hawkins was a putty-colored mind, where bits of colored glass sometimes formed a glimpse of things to be.

"I want to buy a small, insignificant piece of land from Mr. Hawkins," Grandpa said, obviously relishing his role as buyer, the powerful one in this transaction.

"If it's so insignificant, why don't we just forget it?" Mr. Hawkins said peevishly.

"Because," Sam Cassman said, "I hate to put things off."

"Then just pay me my price, and let me go," Hawkins snapped.

"Your price is too high, Hawkins."

Mr. Hawkins sighed, and his coat moved slightly to record the exhaled breath. "Mr. Cassman, you're a rich man. I'm just a small fellow. Give me my price. We'll shake hands. We'll be friends. I'll go."

"Mr. Hawkins, whether I'm a rich man or not has nothing to do with the price of your property."

"Listen, Cassman, if you weren't a rich man, you wouldn't be able to buy this land and build a shopping center or a big apartment that gives you fancy rents. If I had your kind of money I wouldn't sell the corner. I'd build there myself. But I can't. Now take it or leave it. My price is one hundred thirty thousand. That's it, and that's final. One hundred and thirty thousand dollars."

"And I'm telling you, Hawkins, I'll pay you one hundred thousand."

"That isn't fair. I tell you I'm a small man. I have no money. You have the money, the talent—"

"Not true, Mr. Hawkins. You have all the talent that's needed in real estate. You selected property that can increase in price."

"But you won't pay me my price."

"Ah, Hawkins, maybe I have more talent than you do. A hundred thousand and that's final."

"Cassman, listen, my father paid a hundred seven thousand for it."

"And where is it written that you have to get more than you paid?" A small smile curled around Samuel Cassman's lips. He walked Hawkins toward the door and bowed slightly.

"Written? Where is it written?" Hawkins asked, his voice rising in vexation and anger. "I'll tell you where it's written. It's written in the contract you'll sign to buy that land."

Samuel Cassman shook his head. "Wrong. You made the mistake of your life, Hawkins. You see, I don't really need you or your land. Keep it. Keep it all. You can have the corner. And let's see what you'll do with it. Because you see, I own the air rights."

"Air rights?"

"Everything above the second story is mine. You put a store on that corner, and I'll build a parking lot above you and let the fumes go into your store. You think an apartment house can go there? Did you ever see a one-story apartment house? While you were counting your money, Hawkins, I went to the city and bought the air rights. But I was going to be a good guy. I wasn't going to tell you this. When you came in, I thought . . . poor fellow. I'll be generous. A hundred thousand dollars I'll give him. But you're annoying me, Hawkins. And now you're whining. I hate whiners. I want this ended. This is your last chance. I'll give you a hundred thousand now. Today. Take it or leave it. Ninety-five thousand tomorrow. And five thousand dollars off that every day you wait." Sam Cassman took two steps toward Hawkins, who was now wetting his lips nervously, trying to move back into the office. "Take it or leave it," Sam Cassman repeated.

"Wait, wait," Hawkins begged.

"Take it or leave it," Sam said once more.

"You got me, Cassman. You goddamned miserable bastard. Give me the one hundred thousand dollars now."

"A very good decision," Sam said soberly. Then Sam Cassman closed the door on his visitor.

Cassie let out a shriek as the door closed. "Grandpa, how can you do that to that poor man?"

"That poor man, Cassie, owns eight parcels of oceanfront property in Miami."

"That little man?"

"That little man had a smart, rich father, and when the father died he took the brains and left the money."

Of course. Grandpa was really talking about her father.

S.C. smiled. "See what I mean?"

"After you hit me over the head with it, yes."

"Oh, Cassie, this business isn't easy. You know everybody says it's so simple. But you know what? The only people who think it's easy are those who never tried."

"Then why do you stay in real estate?"

"Because real estate is the only game where one player rules. I can write a deal on the back of an envelope sitting on a park bench." Grandpa put his arm around her and walked her back into his office wordlessly.

"And this office is your park bench?" she asked.

"Sit down, Cassie. Let me tell you something. It's beyond the park bench now. This business is even bigger than I dreamed it

[134]

would be. Let me explain. Since 1920 I've been putting deals together, and always with just one goal: to build something that will be more valuable when it's finished than the actual cost of land and construction. Today I've got properties in forty states. Shopping centers. Office buildings. Apartment houses. Now, for Florida, I want to build a planned community."

"Who's doing it with you?"

"Nobody," he said proudly. "I'm doing everything. Buying, selling, developing, managing."

"But how do you begin these things? How do you think about locations? Where do you find deals?"

"Ah, that's the real thing. Where do you find deals? Let me tell you. Once you're a deal maker, deals find you. I don't have to look too hard."

She nodded. Of course that was true. Hadn't Holt come to her? Grandpa's money cut a wide swath.

"When it comes to locations," Grandpa said, leaning back in his swivel chair, "I go places and sniff things out. With all due modesty, I must admit I have a nose for that kind of stuff. I can tell when it's good."

"Instinct and money? Is that what you use?"

He leaned forward. "My fortune is based on sweat plus leverage. When I was a young man, I didn't have any money at all, so what was the difference what a building cost? A million dollars or a thousand dollars. I didn't have either. All I had was the understanding that you should buy everything in life with no money down."

"Did you ever buy some bad stuff?"

"Every time I listened to somebody else, I went broke," Grandpa explained. "That's the only reason I had failures. Taking other people's advice."

Cassie wasn't sure she believed his glib answers, but his wealth was evidence of good decisions. "Where're most of our—I mean, your—assets now, Grandpa?"

"Shopping centers. Small ones. I like those babies because you can predict construction costs a lot better when it takes only six months to build. But I've still got plenty in Manhattan real estate. It'll be the hottest thing in the world to own in the eighties."

[135]

Cassie smiled. Past, present, fortune. Grandpa knew them all.

Suddenly Sam clapped his hands. "All right. Enough about me. Cassie: you've been married one, almost two years. When are you having a baby?"

"Grandpa, that's none of your business."

"Wrong. Everything's my business. How smart is your husband?"

"Smart enough to get me."

Grandpa smiled. She was fast with the answers, all right. Just what you needed in the real estate business. But he already knew how smart she was. He even knew the answers to the questions he was asking, but he wasn't sure Cassie did. Besides, she had to say the words aloud before she'd believe them. Saying the words always turned guessing into knowing. But Cassie wasn't talking.

"Can't fool your old grandpa. I see more than you think." He leaned back in the high leather chair.

Cassie sighed. How many times had she come to this office, first as a little girl with her father, now as a woman, but always as a visitor? She'd never felt a part of anything here; she had no kinship with the autographed photograph of Franklin Delano Roosevelt that hung behind Grandpa's English desk, nor did she relate to the pictures of buildings—had they been sold or bought by Grandpa?—that hung on the walls. Even the obligatory family photograph that Bachrach had taken when she and Stephanie were four and two was something from which she was now removed. Had she ever been the little girl in the picture?

Grandpa put his arm around her. "You've got a nice marriage. It's good for weddings and bar mitzvahs. The real life is at the office."

"I hope you're wrong, Grandpa. Jimmy's a nice man."

"So who ever said you needed a nice man?"

"Stop," she said sharply. Maybe there hadn't been very many ecstatic nights of love lately. But her love was as strong as ever; it just wasn't underscored with an active sex life these busy days— and nights.

She heard Grandpa's voice trailing off ". . . and I hope you and Jimmy stay married, if that's what you want."

Cassie pursed her lips. "What's this conversation leading to, Grandpa? What do you want? Come on. Stop fooling around."

Sam Cassman walked to the window. "Take a look, kid."

The view from the forty-fifth floor was thrilling. To the south lay the lower tip of Manhattan, the heart of the financial district. To the north was the expanse of the park, and both east and west offered a glimpse of water.

"Not a place like it," Grandpa said.

"How much of it have you owned, Grandpa?"

"You asked the question right, didn't you? Well, I've been up and down in this business. But you see that building over there?"

"Over where?"

"Look. Near Forty-seventh Street on Eighth Avenue. In the theater district. Remember when I told you how I got started?"

She nodded. "You sold a stable when the theater district moved uptown."

"Right, and from that I built a business. The little building right there was the start."

"Do you still own it?"

"Bought and sold it four times. Well, to be exact I bought it four times and lost it three."

"Did it cost more each time?"

"You'll never learn, Cassie. It didn't cost anything each time. I built it without putting a penny into it, and each time I bought it I didn't spend a cent. But you girls went to college on that building."

"That little building?"

"It wasn't little to me when I bought it. It was more money than I expected to earn in a lifetime."

"It took courage to buy it."

"Not if you think big, Cassie. Remember one thing, doll. Big deals are easier to make than little deals. So you might as well make big deals."

"I'm trying, Grandpa. I really am."

"Sure you are. And when you're ready, I'm going to have you here running things."

Cassie shook her head. "You wouldn't let me run anything, Grandpa. It's not just me. You wouldn't let anybody run anything. You've got your own style. It's unorthodox, I know, but it works for you. You run by the seat of your pants and the sparks of your mind. I'm more organized. I want to use my education."

"Use your education? For what? You get an education so you can enjoy museums and theater and books. But in business? Education kills deals. The smart guys, the lawyers and the bankers, they kill all the deals with their education. It's the men with the feeling for the business, the sense of what works who make it big in our business. It's instinct, Cassie. And you don't get that at Harvard."

"I'm taking some real estate courses now. I don't want to have to depend on the lawyers and the bankers for my advice. I want to know things myself."

"I'll teach you what you have to know."

"Grandpa, I want to go into my own deals."

"What are you talking about?" Sam Cassman asked angrily. He reached in his desk drawer, pulled out a cigar, bit off the end and spat it out.

Cassie waited, then said softly, "Holt Hayward, the man you met at—"

"Don't tell me where I met him. I know. In my own house. In my own house he was stealing my granddaughter."

"He's not stealing me. Listen. Grandpa, he's helping me. He sends me customers for co-ops, and now Holt wants to let me in one of his deals—"

"Sure, he sets you up with customers, and then he goes after you with a promise. Does he want money from you?"

"Well, yes. I have to go to Louisville and see the bankers and borrow the money—"

"Aha. So that's it. And on whose name do you think you'll borrow the money?"

She lowered her head.

"Sure. You don't answer those questions, do you, Miss Wellesley Education? That's because you need me. But you're not running to Louisville to borrow money on my name. You're staying right here."

Cassie had never felt so confused, angry, or frustrated. She cried, "Don't order me around."

"Order you around? Who do you think you're talking to? I'm not some fancy Wall Street fellow or a lazy do-nothing like your husband. I'm Sam Cassman and nobody talks to me that way. Not even you, Cassie. Now listen to me. I didn't know it would be so

[138]

soon, but you're coming into the business. You're not waiting. You're coming in now. Today. This minute."

"What about my deal? What about my life? I don't want to be in your business."

"You don't have a choice."

"It's a free country, Grandpa. Lincoln freed the slaves."

"Sure, but I didn't free you. Or your father. Or your mother. Or your sister."

Cassie looked squarely at Grandpa. It was as if she were seeing him for the first time. Had there been a gun or a knife handy, she would have used it.

"I don't understand you," she hissed. "What are you trying to do? Own me? You can't. I won't let you."

Samuel Cassman smiled. "I can't?"

"No. I'm your grandchild through and through. I can walk away."

Sam sat down heavily in the big chair. "No, no you can't Cassie. I thought I could sweet-talk you into the business, but I see I can't. So if I have to use force, then that's it." He threw his hands up in the air.

"There isn't one thing in the world you could offer me or say to me that would make me come into your business, Grandpa."

"Yes, there is, Cassie."

"Then say it."

"I'd rather not."

"Just as I thought," she said triumphantly. "You don't have one earthly way to push me into that business."

"I do, but I won't say it."

"Stop that," she screamed. "Stop taunting me and say it."

He sighed. "All right, I'll say it. Cassie, I don't plan to leave a big estate."

She smiled. That was his big threat? All it meant was that he'd start parceling out his real estate now.

"That is," he continued, "I won't leave *them* a big estate."

Still okay.

"I mean your father and sister—I'm not leaving them anything."

What was Grandpa leading up to?

"And you, Cassie, I'm not leaving it to you."

[139]

Now one eyebrow went up. The flush began in her neck and crawled upward.

"No, there's not going to be anything for you."

Okay, Grandpa, you old shrewdie. I'll play along. Aloud she said, "Are you planning to go broke, or are you going to take it with you?"

That was a Sam Cassman kind of question. He smiled. "Neither. I'm leaving it all to Mount Sinai Hospital to build a wing for genetic studies."

"What?" Her mouth fell open in surprise.

"Yes. I want to help future generations know why men like me can't reproduce themselves. For instance, why isn't my son like me?"

Now Cassie tried to hide a smile. But what if he were serious? He could be. "How will that help you?"

"Well, it would be too late for *me* personally to be helped, but look how good it would be for future generations. What if you, Cassie, have a child who's—God forbid—like your father instead of you?"

"Grandpa!"

"Or worse . . . like your mother."

"Stop."

"See? Even you can't stand thinking about it."

"And this decision is final?"

"No, not necessarily." He lighted his cigar. "I'd reconsider if you came here to work."

She waited while he relit the end of the cigar. She wanted his attention, damn it. "But I want to do something on my own—have my own chance—"

Sam regarded the burning end of the cigar. "Is God going to wait for me?"

"But just let me get started with my own—"

"Why? Just work here. That's what you should do. This business is in your blood. You don't know it. But thank God, my genetics studies will help so in the future no granddaughter will give her grandfather such a headache."

"Grandpa, give me a break."

"A break? Don't you know that's what I've always given you? Why do you think I brought you down here to the office from the time you could count? Why do you think I showed you my business the way I never showed it to anybody else? Now you want a break? For what? To meet fancy fellows like Holt What's-his-name so he can steal you from me?"

"Grandpa, he doesn't want to steal me."

"Sure he does. That's why you'd better work for me now. Your father has been in this business all his life, and he still doesn't understand it. Besides, he's too busy with his girlfriends to care."

She felt her nostrils flare. What kind of locker-room talk was this? If he couldn't get her with one story, he'd try another. No excuse was too outrageous for Samuel Cassman.

Sam saw the look of disbelief on her face. How was it that she didn't know? What did she think was going on with her father? Didn't she realize he was never at home? He shrugged. "Cassie, I thought you knew."

Tears filled her eyes. "I don't believe you."

"Then don't believe me, but it's the truth. Your father had girlfriends from the time he was old enough to tie his shoes. He was in one scrape after another. I bought his way out of trash you wouldn't believe. When he finally married, I was so relieved. Thank God. A girl from a good family. Pretty, even. That should straighten him out. But did it? Not your father. In business he's no good. But one thing about his girlfriends. They're good at business. They all come to see me, and they leave with a check. The latest is Mrs. Fink."

"Chichi Fink?"

"Sure, the one he bought the co-op for."

"What do you mean?"

"You know what I mean. You sold it to her."

Cassie fell back in her chair. Her father, Bill Cassman, represented the mystery money in Chichi Fink's apartment deal? "Are you sure?" she asked, but even as the words formed she knew the answer. There was just too much coincidence in Chichi's dealings with the Cassmans. The golf games with Daddy. Choosing Cassie as the real estate agent in the first place. Of course. Perfect sense. Chichi knew she was safe with Cassie. How could Cassie ever tell anyone even if she were to find out? How could she betray her father and hurt her mother? Cassie felt sick. She clutched at the last straw. "But Daddy's always broke."

"That's what he lets Diane think. There's not enough money in the world for your mother. So we let her think there's no money in your father's name. Your mother is a shopping nut. I remember one time she went to Gucci—"

"Stop!" Cassie cried.

"So you see. Your father is independently wealthy, but no one knows. I think family money will be part of the genetics study, too," Grandpa mused.

"The genetics study?" She'd see if he was serious or not.

As if he were reading her mind, he answered, "I'm not kidding. The genetics study that I'm sponsoring at Mount Sinai Hospital so people can learn why grandchildren like you don't go into the family business."

He had her. Coming. Going. Frontwards. Backwards. She stood up. "Forget your genetics study, Grandpa."

"What? I wouldn't—" he blustered.

She shook her finger under his nose. "Stop this play acting. You're not going to walk away from me and go to Mount Sinai Hospital."

He smiled. "I'm not?"

She felt her blood boiling, her temperature rising. "You're some conniving son of a bitch, Grandpa, but you're mine, and I'm yours. You can do your genetics study right here and watch me. I'm coming into the business."

His eyes filled; his face lit up. "That's my good girl. Now, Cassie, take some time. Relax. Go away, and then you'll come to work. And I'll find something just for you."

She nodded and tried to catch her breath. "I'd like that. I'll take a little time off. When do I start?"

"Monday."

Three whole days. Grandpa really was something.

XV

Cassie reflected on Grandpa's bombshells as she walked home. You had to be strong to accept these things. Very strong. Nothing scared Cassie more than the possibility of mental depression.

Ordinarily she tried to avoid fatigue, eat a balanced diet, get some exercise, and keep herself fit. But how did your body and mind handle the pressure of all your lives?

Now as she entered her building, Cassie thought how relatively simple life was for Jimmy. None of these conflicts for him. No, for men the sexual and occupational roles fused into a single aggressive personality. No wonder men could spend so much time on business; they didn't have to spend time developing two other subservient personalities—one for a spouse and one for a grandfather.

The telephone was ringing as Cassie came in; she dove for it. It was Jimmy's familiar voice. "You're home? I'll bet you just got there; I've been trying to reach you, dear. Rollo and I have a big deal on the fire, and we're going to run now to catch the seven o'clock shuttle to Boston. I know it's Friday, and I hate to leave on a weekend night, but it's business, so what can I do?"

She started to say, *Don't go. Please don't go. I need you. My father's not what he seems, and my grandfather offered me a job, and I'm scared. Please come here and hold me.* That's what she wanted to say. But she knew she couldn't. If the shoe were on the other foot, if she—not Jimmy—had a big deal pending in Boston, would she want him to whisper and beg her to stay? No, in this marriage she'd agreed to give him his own space and place. How could she complain the first time she wanted something. Instead she said, "Don't you need to pack an overnight bag?"

"Oh, I'll stop and buy a shirt along the way and pick up a toothbrush somewhere. It's like camping out."

She laughed. "Sure, and I'll bet you'll be camping at the Ritz Carlton."

"Right, dear. Talk to you later."

She put the phone down and looked at her watch. She had an idea. There was time. Time to be a loving wife. She'd pack a bag for Jimmy, get Karl, and race out to La Guardia. As Jimmy prepared to board the plane, she'd stand there like a stewardess and hand him a fully packed bag. Of course. She'd be a giving partner. Wouldn't he be surprised? And Rollo—Rollo, who always looked at her as if she were yesterday's newspaper—wouldn't he be amazed at Jimmy's thoughtful wife! The thought of doing something just for Jimmy delighted her. She reached up to the top shelf of the closet in the foyer, but his overnight bag wasn't there. It must be in his closet. His closet! She went to the bedroom and stood for several minutes in front of his closet. Should she? Shouldn't she? She'd promised him not to look in there. Well, just this once she'd open it and get his black bag. She'd only look for a minute. Fastidious Jimmy certainly wouldn't have a sloppy closet; it would be easy to find things. Surely he wouldn't be angry if she opened his closet just this once. She put her hand on the knob and withdrew it. Was she violating his privacy? Oh, how silly. Of course she wasn't. She put her hand firmly on the doorknob and pulled it open. The light went on, and she saw just what she expected to see. Hanging there awaiting the call to action was a row of perfectly tailored suits, all categorized by color. The blues here, the browns there, the grays in between. What a beautiful wardrobe. She touched the tuxedo he'd worn at their wedding. Couldn't a woman take a minute to be sentimental about the man she loved? Then she pinched herself back to her usual brisk maneuvers. She was in a hurry, after all. Up on the top shelf. That must be where he'd put the bag. It wasn't on the floor; a quick glance told her that. She took a chair from the kitchen, climbed up. Yes, the better to see the topmost shelf. Was it there? Push. Poke. She tugged, and the bag came down bringing with it a pile of magazines. They must have been under the bag. Oh damn. Should she take time to put them away? No, she'd do it when she got home. She opened the bag—why not?—why not add one of those magazines he obviously wants to read. She bent and picked one up. She frowned. What was this? A naked man on the cover. She opened the magazine. This was no ordinary sex magazine like the ones boys tittered over in drugstores. This wasn't like the magazines Dalton boys used to hide in their notebooks. No, this wasn't like any magazine Cassie had ever seen. Page after page of nude males. Close-ups of male sexual organs. Oh my god. This was a gay magazine. It was for homosexuals. Jimmy was—beautiful Jimmy was—

She stepped back from the closet as if it were on fire. So that was the secret. No wonder she wasn't allowed to see his closet. No wonder . . . no wonder . . . memories flooded her mind. It was too unbelievable. Could it really be? She looked at another magazine. The same sort of thing. She threw it on the floor and sat on the edge of her bed, but she didn't cry. Not a tear. Instead Cassie began to retch. She went into the bathroom and tried to vomit the ugliness out of her life. Twenty minutes later, weak and exhausted, she knew she needed to talk to someone. Someone who'd know, understand, explain. She needed to talk to Jimmy. All right. She'd wait for him. She'd wait right here. Cassie lay down on the bed. She would stay here, just like this, still and waiting. She wouldn't answer the door. She wouldn't answer the phone. She wouldn't eat. Cassie closed her eyes, and for the first time in her life she saw the black pit that Diane knew so well.

Saturday, the next day, at five-thirty Jimmy came into the darkened apartment. "Cass," he called. "Are you home, Cassie?"

She opened her eyes. They were dry. Dry as her stomach. Dry as her mouth. Dry as her heart. She was too dry to answer.

Jimmy walked into the bedroom, snapped the light switch and saw it all at once. Cassie, fully dressed, lying on top of the carefully made bed, and the closet—the forbidden closet open—and the magazines strewn on the floor.

"What a relief," he said. "You finally found out."

She raised herself on one elbow. "You contemptible sneak. You traitor. You villain."

Jimmy smiled benignly. "You sound like Ophelia."

"Do you expect me to use the kind of words in your dirty magazines?"

He sat on the edge of the bed and stroked her back.

"Don't touch me."

"But I love you."

"How can you possibly love me?"

"Cassie, darling, I always have. I told you from the beginning I would never love any woman the way I love you. I didn't say anything about men."

"Jimmy!"

"Don't be so shocked. You're such a kid. You must realize what the world's about. Cassie, the world is full of us. I'm not the only one. There's Rollo—"

"Rollo? He's a—a—" She couldn't bring herself to say the word homosexual.

"Like Robin Hood's merry men, there's a whole band of us. Sit up, Cassie. Sit up and listen to me."

She felt sick again. She rolled over and turned her back to him. He sighed.

Every thought had gone through her head during the past twenty-four hours. The betrayal, the deceit, the hypocrisy. Everything she hated was embodied in Jimmy. She had nothing to say to him.

"I don't want anything in our lives to change, Cassie. I think it's perfect."

"It was."

"It still can be," he promised.

"No, it can't, Jimmy. It's so hard to be open and honest in the world. I'm having so much trouble trying to be one thing in business and another to my grandfather that I just can't play any more parts, Jimmy. I don't want to pretend to be your wife and know you're sleeping with—"

"With someone you can't compete with," Jimmy said, completing her sentence.

"I think you'd better leave," she said.

"Cassie, I'd give you anything you want. I like this marriage. I like the whole sense of us. I'm delighted with you, and it's important for me to look as if I'm leading a completely straight life. You can have anything you want. Do you want a baby? I'm willing."

"Get out," she half-whispered. "Get out of my house and my life."

"Someday when you're less emotional, Cassie, think of me, and call me if you need me. I'll always be your best friend."

Cassie fell back on the pillow totally spent. She hoped she would never have to speak to Jimmy Brown again.

Cassie went through the motions of living.

Brush teeth. Go to office. Keep mind on work. Give it the old try. Ha ha. Hi. Hello. Fine, and how are you? Walk home. Back to bed and to sleep. Depressed, troubled sleep.

Marcia and Hilda wanted to take her to dinner. She turned them both down. She didn't feel like talking. No matter how much good they said talking would do, she didn't want to talk.

The pretty clothes she'd bought as Jimmy's girl and then as

Jimmy's wife stayed in the closet. She reached to the back for her old self, for the drab, long skirts and shapeless tops. Being attractive no longer seemed important.

For days Cassie walked around in a semistupor. She was determined to shut out the world. One morning, eight days later, she was brushing her teeth and looked into the mirror. She was shocked at what she saw. It was as if her pretty face had been touched by the wand of the wicked witch. The eyes were dull, the skin blotchy. Her cheeks were no longer full of color. She had lost weight, and the look of her was the look of despair and defeat.

Was this . . . could this be her mother: had Diane looked at herself once and seen these same things?

The thought sent a shudder through her body. No. She had to fight. She couldn't go into that pit. No. No, she wouldn't let it happen. She couldn't. It would be so easy: that was the escape. The escape into the pit when you didn't want to believe something. But Cassie was strong. She was stronger than Diane. She breathed deeply. She was feeling pity for herself when what she should have felt was anger toward him. Not anger for what he was. But anger for deceiving her. Yet shouldn't some of that anger be self-directed? All the clues had been there; she just hadn't read them right. It took time to learn the game. She gripped the sink. She'd be all right.

She would have liked Jimmy to disappear down the rabbit hole, but of course he didn't.

He called twice at the office, but she did not accept his calls.

The third time he called her at home at night, and she couldn't escape. "Cassie, I want to come back," he said.

The nerve of him. "No, I'm finished," she said angrily. "I can't live a lie."

"It's not a lie. I love you. I don't want any other woman."

"Jimmy, what do you mean? I don't care if you don't want any other woman. Don't discuss your sex life."

"This is more than sex, Cassie. It's the way I am. I don't want a relationship with anyone except you. I can get that other sexual satisfaction anywhere; it's quite easy in New York. But I want more. I like marriage. I like structure—"

"Jimmy, it's over."

"Please, Cassie, think about it."

"I have. The answer is no."

He sighed. "All right then. Cassie, if you won't let me come back, I'm going to leave New York. I don't want to face everyone."

"You don't have to be afraid, Jimmy. I didn't tell anyone the reason for our separation."

"Certainly your grandfather—"

"No, I didn't tell him."

"Thank you. That was very nice of you."

"I didn't do it for you; I did it for me. I don't want anybody's pity."

"I'm sure your friend Hilda knows. She'll figure it out."

Cassie said nothing. Of course Hilda knew. Hilda always knew things. Marcia probably knew, too. Only naive, trusting Cassie was in the dark.

"Maybe you're right," Cassie murmured. "Maybe you ought to leave the city."

"I have a chance to go to California. It's a deal with a new cable network. It's a great investment opportunity. I know you don't have any money now, but if you ever did and wanted to invest—"

"I don't want to invest," she said sadly. "I don't want anything to do with you, but—but—oh, Jimmy, I wish you well. I really do." She felt the sorrow welling in the depths of her heart. She had never felt such sadness. She was sorry for him. She was sorry for herself. She was sorry for every woman who ever believed a man. Only he wasn't a man. At least, not a—"

"If you ever need me, Cassie—"

"No, Jimmy, I'll never need you again."

Cassie walked out of the kitchen and into her bedroom. She opened the closet and took out a bright orange dress. She put it on and rummaged through her drawers for a lipstick to match. Then she called Hilda and went out to dinner.

And that night Cassie made the decision to file for divorce.

Everyone in the family handled the news differently.

Grandpa shrugged it off. "So who needs marriage anyway? Dummies and weaklings like your sister. That's who."

[148]

Her father shook his head grimly. "Too bad it's not Stephanie who's getting the divorce."

Diane bought seven pairs of shoes at Charles Jourdan.

Marcia was indignant. "Well, you finally found out," she said, kicking off her shoes in Cassie's living room. "The bastard. Why didn't he ever tell you himself? I always knew."

"Then why didn't you tell me?"

"I tried to once. Remember? You made some crack about my sex life, and I thought I'd better keep my mouth shut."

Cassie remembered with bitterness and shame. "But how would I ever dream he's bisexual?"

"Bisexual!" Marcia snorted. "Don't think that, Cassie. A bisexual is a man who tried it once and hated it. Let's put it this way. You were involved in a mixed marriage."

XVI

TRUE TO HIS WORD, Sam Cassman did give Cassie her own area of responsibility, the housekeeping end of the business.

It was Cassie's job to supervise the collecting of rents, answer service complaints of tenants in buildings, buy cleaning supplies, and supervise utility usage. Cassie was the one who was called when the air conditioners didn't work in August—and when they went full blast in February.

"I could learn this as a maid in my mother's house," Cassie told Grandpa time and again.

"Then that makes you the best-paid maid in New York," her grandfather said.

"But I'm not that well paid. I'd be making more money selling co-ops with Hilda."

"The opportunities aren't the same," her grandfather answered in his usual glib manner when he wanted to avoid further conversation. "You'll see. You'll get your chance."

Cassie's chance consisted of watching Grandpa at work. And Grandpa at work was a never-ending show. When a tenant who fought for each point in his lease finally agreed to sign a one-year lease and wearily picked up the pen, Grandpa held up his hand. "No, I want a three-year lease." When the tenant asked the reason, Grandpa looked in him the eye and said, "Because I'm seventy-seven years old now, and I want a three-year lease so you won't bug me again until I'm eighty."

She heard her grandfather called everything from good-hearted to downright despicable. He was a lot of people, all right.

At the end of three months, Grandpa called Cassie into his office. "Cassela, you're getting your chance."

"Yes, Grandpa?"

"You think you can do everything. Now I'll let you prove it. We've got a building on Park Avenue South. It's an office building, half-occupied. I think it should bring us a million dollars a year in rentals, but it's only bringing in around two hundred thousand. You go and rent that building. I'll give you two months. You rent it, and you'll get another assignment. An even bigger one. Now go rent."

She kissed her grandfather on the cheek. What an opportunity! Six months of soapsuds and now this!

Hilda stood in the middle of Park Avenue, squinted, and stood back to look. "So this is the building he gave you to rent?"

"Not bad, is it?" Cassie asked with hope in her voice.

"Not if people want it. But who wants this, Cassie? Owners are having trouble renting prime space on Third Avenue, and Sixth Avenue is going begging. This is Park Avenue South at Twenty-third Street. Not a good location and not a prime building. No leases even. Tenants are all there month to month."

"What do I do?"

"My advice is give the assignment back to S.C. You're headed for a sure loss with this."

Cassie set her mouth in a grim line. She'd never admit defeat with one impossible assignment.

Holt gave her the same advice as Hilda.

Marcia was the only one who had an idea. "Why don't we go into all the buildings around here, Cassie, and copy the names of the tenants from the lobby list. Then you can approach the people in the other buildings, and who knows? Maybe somebody'll be willing to move."

So the two young women, while building attendants looked at them suspiciously, copied names in lobbies.

Once Cassie was told by a policeman, "Keep moving, babe, and look for your johns on the street."

After a week, Cassie was armed with a list of two hundred names. She called office managers for appointments and was shocked to find she was as welcome as an insurance salesman. Her opening line was, "I'd like to talk to someone in your organization about office space."

One secretary said, "Renting is done by our parent company." Another said, "We just signed a five-year lease." One man laughed and said, "I'm not moving unless you give me a free trip to Europe."

This was nothing like the co-op market.

At the end of four weeks Samuel Cassman asked, "How are you doing with the building, Cassie?"

"Coming along," she said spiritedly.

Grandpa just smiled.

At the end of two months Cassie had not signed one tenant. Dejected, she went to see her grandfather. "Okay, Grandpa," she said. "You did it. You proved I don't know enough to sell leases in buildings that nobody wants. So tell me. How do you do it?"

Grandpa stood and pointed to a painting on his wall. "See that painting, Cassie? I bought it for two hundred dollars fifteen years ago. It's been hanging right in that spot ever since. Just the other day an art dealer came to see me, looked at it and said, 'Oh my God, that's by Roy Lichtenstein. It's worth thirty thousand dollars.' Now I didn't do anything to make the painting worth more. I didn't change the frame or put new lights on it. I didn't redraw Mr. Lichtenstein's work. I just sat with it. And that's how it is with real estate, Cassie. You can put in new lobbies and modernize the front. You can give the people six months' free rent and send their kids to private schools. But you know what makes a building worth money? Just sitting with it long enough."

Sam Cassman smiled. Then he turned and walked back to his desk. "Watch, Cassie. We'll just sit with that building, and someday somebody will come to us. I hope you learned a lesson from this. It all takes time. There are no instant answers, no quick ways. You're not going to go out and in ten minutes do it all better than I did, Cassie. Go slow. Learn a step at a time, and before you realize it, you'll have learned a lot. You see, there's a lot more to selling real estate in New York, Cassie, than finding co-ops for a bunch of rich Europeans."

"You seem down, Cassie," Hilda said one day. "I know what it's like to go through a divorce. What you need most is friends. I think you'd better be reminded you have a couple of good friends."

Cassie's eyes burned with love and gratitude for Hilda's concern. How observant of her. Only a good friend would see that under the red badge of Courrèges was a wounded woman.

"Cassie, I'll call Marcia and we'll have a nice, quiet lunch; the three of us."

"I'd like that," Cassie said.

"Oh, how do I reach Marcia now?"

"She's still at Macy's. But I've been so busy I haven't seen her for about three weeks. Believe it or not, it's five years this week since we graduated from Wellesley. I don't want to go to our reunion, but I do want to be with the two of you."

So Hilda made a reservation at Lutèce and took the two younger women to luncheon.

Marcia ordered a spritzer, Cassie a Lillet, and Hilda a double martini. "At noon?" Cassie asked her former employer.

"Only at noon," Hilda said. "By night I don't need it. I'm out of the office."

"A toast to us," Marcia said. "To the ladies."

"Now known as women," Cassie amended.

"Wellesley women," Marcia reminded her, "products of Wellesley College, the only seven sisters school that has had only women serve as president throughout its history. More than a hundred years of female presidency."

"A tradition Cassie will carry on at Cassman and Company," Hilda prophesied.

Cassie shook her head. "I don't know. First we have to get Grandpa to let me do something on my own."

"But he promised you—" Marcia began.

Hilda laughed. "We wouldn't count on a Sam Cassman promise."

Once Cassie would have sprung to Grandpa's defense after such a remark. Now she felt her heart twist, but she said nothing.

Marcia, however, turned to Hilda. "What a terrible thing to say. But look, Cass, even if things are bad at the office, at least you can say you've been married."

"I miss marriage," Hilda said. "I think women do need to be married. Maybe men don't, but we do."

"It's not as easy for us women as everyone likes to think, is it?" Marcia asked softly.

"Yes, it is," Hilda answered brightly. "It's easy, comparatively easy anyway. I'm older than you are, and I remember how hard it used to be for women. What if you had no choice?"

"But I've got a big choice to make now," Marcia said.

"Is Macy's moving you up again? Are you about to become store president?" That was Cassie's question.

Marcia looked at her former roommate. "That would be a simple choice. I'd say no."

Both women looked at her in surprise.

"I don't want a presidency to warm my feet in my old age."

"Then get an electric blanket," Hilda said.

"I've been offered a man."

"A man?"

"There's a really nice young guy at the store. His name is Steve Schwartz, and he works in my department. I've been seeing him, and—"

"Don't," Cassie said quickly. "For God's sake, don't. Don't marry him. Don't shut out all our chances. Oh, can't you see, Marsh? You've only got this time and this place to be young and alive and full of opportunity. It'll never happen again. What'll you do? Push baby carriages and give this up? This is the first real time for women. You've got to fulfill the destiny for our generation. Men will never give it to us again. We have to be good or we'll lose it for all women. I've had a husband—and—" she stopped.

"What do you think, Hilda?" Marcia asked.

"I think I'll have the Boston sole," she replied.

"Hilda, you're a cagey old girl." Cassie said. "There you sit, looking not a day over thirty, and I know you've got to be—well, over forty, anyway. Come on. Tell Marcia. Isn't it your career that keeps you looking so alive and vital?"

Hilda put her glass down and looked at her two companions. "My dears, up to the age of thirty, God is responsible for your face. After thirty, when you're in your thirties, forties, and fifties, you're responsible. It doesn't matter whether you're married or single, with or without a career. It all comes from how you feel about yourself. There are some people who've been disappointed and disillusioned and unhappy, and that's in their faces. And there are some people who haven't been—but think they have—and that's in their faces, too. Cosmetic surgery won't eliminate discontent, and a good job won't make a basically discontented person joyous."

"No matter what Hilda says, take your time about getting married, Marsh," Cassie advised. "He'll still be there after you've had time to think."

"To the men who'll still be there," Hilda said raising her glass once more.

"To our careers," Cassie answered.

"To a man," Marcia said.

Cassie sipped her drink and thought how easy she'd expected life to be. The best career. The best man. She'd promised herself both so naively, so blithely, five years ago. Now there seemed to be no end to the surprises life had in store.

Summer 1974

If you look at where a woman has been, and what her major goals have been in different ten-year segments of her life, you'll often find sudden discontinuities, surprises—and frequently astonishing ingenuity and invention!

Maggie Scarf
Unfinished Business

XVII

STEPHANIE WATCHED THE HEAT, the never-ending waves that cor-
rugated the landscape. This Las Vegas heat was a killer; nothing
could live in it. Not grass or flowers or love.

Inside the red-walled room with the heavy dark imitation oak
furniture Stephanie looked for the coolest spot. She walked to the
window and put her cheek there, comforted by blasts of air conditioning. Stephanie slowly raised her arm to look at her watch. She
moved listlessly these days. Ten minutes.

Ten minutes of that cold air was all she could have. If she didn't
shut it off, he'd wake up screaming, "Turn off the goddamned air
conditioning. What are you trying to do, you dumb broad? Want
to kill me? How can I sing if you freeze my pipes?" Oh yes, she
could recite his speech by heart. She'd heard it enough times. She
pressed her cheek harder against the window. At least the cool-
ness made her feel human. That man in the bed didn't.

She turned and looked at her sleeping husband, his naked body
spread across the bed, unmasking the sagging stomach, the wrin-
kled buttocks. Everything about him was old. Those old songs he
sang, the standards of another time; he could remember when
they were written, when they were introduced by the big singers.
Dick Haymes. Frank Sinatra. Tony Bennett. Nat "King" Cole.
Johnny Mathis. That remembering was all part of the act. It was
even named for the time. "I'm bringing back a whole era like the
big band sound," he said. His act was "Memories of a Crooner,"
and he sang his songs to the ladies with the grocery bags filled
with quarters and the ladies with the bouffant hairdos and the
ladies whose husbands and boyfriends were losing money in the
other room. But he wasn't in the big room. Sal Romano had been
moved in as a lounge singer two months ago. If you were young,
the lounge was where you stopped on the way up. If you were—
well, if you were Sal Romano, you came down to the lounge. Sal
had come down from the Romany Room, the main nightclub at
the Gypsy. It was one of the places on the Strip, and the ads had
said Romano at the Romany. But not now.

They'd moved him.

Sal never told Stephanie exactly who "they" were. But she knew that they were the ones who'd arranged the marriage. They were the ones who'd got him the job. They were the ones who'd put her in this tight, terrible room to live her life.

Sal hadn't even told her he'd been moved to the lounge. The captain had told her when she'd gone to sit at her corner table one night. When she asked Sal what had happened, all he said was, "I crapped out."

Then she'd asked why. But she couldn't remember his answer. That was the trouble. She couldn't remember much of anything. Maybe it was the heat. Besides, when she was growing up nobody had ever made her remember anything. She shook her head. Why couldn't she have stayed little? Hadn't Sal promised her she could? She'd be his adorable little girl, the way she was at first.

She looked around the room, the evidence of his career filling every corner. In the closet, the twenty-two tuxedos and eight pairs of patent-leather shoes were all neatly lined up. On the wall was a photograph of Frank and Dino with Sal. She remembered the night they took the picture. Sal had pushed himself in with the stars. They didn't know who he was. He could have been a waiter. But he'd had wallet-size pictures made, carried them around, and on the back was his name and the address of the Gypsy. She'd sent one to her mother, but she never had an answer. Cassie had written, "Who are those two punks with Sal Romano? Ha Ha." Sal had looked at Cassie's card. "That supposed to be some kind of smart remark?" he'd asked.

"My sister is smart," Stephanie assured him.

"I'll show you something smarter," Sal said. Then he'd opened his drawer, and under the pile of white-on-white shirts he pulled out a twenty-two revolver.

Stephanie had gasped.

"Don't get scared, honey," Sal had reassured her. "I just want you to know that I can handle smartasses. No matter what happens you got a real man who can take care of you. I don't want you takin' nothin' from nobody. You're my old lady, and don't you forget it. We're goin' to the top, baby. This is just our first stop."

[158]

She'd believed him.

Well, why not? Everybody had made a fuss over her when she first came to Las Vegas with Sal. Even Vince Filippo had told Sal she was some doll. When Irv Fingerman, Sal's agent, found she was a rich Jewish girl from New York, he had sat down with her to talk about Sal's career. She couldn't remember just what Irv had said either. It had all been kind of confusing. Irv wanted her to make decisions for Sal. She'd blinked her brown eyes slowly and pushed her hair back. Didn't Irv understand? That wasn't what this marriage was about. She didn't want to manage Sal. Sal was her daddy. Better than a daddy. Her own daddy only wanted to play golf. This daddy sang about how much he loved her.

Vince. Irv. They'd both talked to her, but more and more she heard less and less. It was nicer that way. If she didn't know stuff, how could she decide things? And why did they keep bothering her with what they both called "the plain truth?" Didn't they understand that what she loved about Sal wasn't the truth at all? It was the pretend part. She liked sitting in the club with everyone knowing the love songs belonged to her. She liked dressing up and being the one everyone pointed out. See? That's the society girl he married. She could hear them when they talked. The stories got bigger with each telling. Once she heard someone say she was a Rockefeller. She'd laughed. Her grandfathers would have liked that.

Sal stirred. The fat shifted. She made a face. Thank God she was dressed. She wouldn't have to get into bed and try to help him prove he was still a man. Being dressed was a good excuse. She'd used the one about her period last week. Sal was dumb, but he wasn't stupid. Once she'd used the period excuse two weeks in a row, and he'd remembered. He'd pushed her around a little. Nothing like that time before they were married—but still—

Her mouth twisted into a contemptuous smile. The revulsion was turning to hate. The crowds were gone now, and there was only—

She lifted her head slowly. Was that the telephone?

What the hell? What difference did it make? Let it ring. Wake him up. Serve him right.

"Get it," he mumbled.

[159]

"Sure," she said without taking a step.

He lifted his head. "Move, for Christ's sake."

"You're next to the phone. If you want it so much, answer it." Who cared if it rang six, seven, eleven times?

Sal reached over, took the phone and threw it across the room. "Hello. Hello. Hello." Stephanie could hear the unmistakable voice of—of—could it be?—it had to be—

For the first time in months she moved quickly. Cassie. Cassie was calling. She hadn't heard from her in ages. In a fraction of a second the joy was tempered. Oh God, was it about Mother? Always. Always there was the specter of Diane dead. An unexpected message from home, a late-night telephone call. Each call triggered the same first fear. Or was it hope? Diane dead would be a reason to go home. And she needed that kind of passport to get back to New York.

"Are things all right?" Stephanie asked. She wanted to hear the big news—even if was terrible news—first.

"Everything's fine."

Then why was Cassie calling? "It's not Mother?"

"She's fine."

"Daddy?"

"Fine, fine. But they miss you." Cassie didn't want to say any more about her parents. And she certainly didn't want to talk about Jimmy. The divorce would be final in just a few weeks.

There was a pause.

"And the grandfathers are fine, too," Cassie added, anticipating the question.

Another pause.

"Oh, Cassie I miss you so. I miss everybody. Even Grandpa."

"I miss you, too. I can't stand it without our talking and being together."

Stephanie's eyes filled with tears. It had been so long since anyone had missed her. In the beginning it had been hard for all the family. They hadn't wanted to meet Sal. Diane and Bill had ignored the marriage. The grandfathers damned it. Only Cassie called from time to time. And it had been so long now since Stephanie had heard from her sister. "I want to see you, Cassie," she said, her voice shaking with fear. What if Cassie didn't want to see her?

"I'm coming to visit you," Cassie said abruptly.

"You are? You're coming here? But I thought—I thought I'd—I mean—don't you want me to go to New York?"

"It would be terrible here." Cassie told her, but she didn't add that she wanted to get away, away from New York for a few days. "Look, if you came here you'd have to see everyone; we wouldn't have any time together. There'd be Mother, Daddy, the grandfathers, and then they'd run you around to see all the cousins. It would be awful."

Stephanie knew Cassie was right. But still she could hope. "You mean you're not—they're not—sending for me?" Stephanie asked wistfully.

"No. Instead I'm coming to see you, Stephanie. I'll fly out tomorrow and spend the weekend with you and Sal. Get me a room at the Gypsy, and we'll be together all the time. Let's just talk and have fun." Cassie didn't add the words "for a change." But she was tired; she ached with responsibility and cares and Grandpa's trickery. She was ready for fun. She wanted the peace of dealing with her uncomplicated, simple sister.

Stephanie didn't need a pencil. She'd remember this. The flight number. The time. "I'll meet you at the airport," she promised. There was a pause, and Stephanie cried out, "I love you, Cassie." The tears were streaming down her cheeks when she put the phone back on the night stand next to Sal. She half sobbed, choking on the words as she spoke to Sal. "M-m-my sister, she's coming tomorrow. You'd really better be nice to her."

"Oh, I'll try to eat with the right fork for the fancy relative," Sal said, extending his pinky.

She felt the anger move from her heart into her hands, her feet. She wanted to beat him. "You bastard," she screamed. "Bastard. You know that's not what I mean."

"Shut up, or you'll end up a nut like your mother," he snarled. Then he began to cough. "Turn off the goddamned air conditioning. What are you trying to do, you dumb broad? Want to kill me? How can I sing if you freeze my pipes?"

"Bastard. Bastard," she screamed again.

He sat up, his face twisted in an ugly snarl. "Who do you think you're calling a bastard?"

She looked at him for a minute, then lowered her eyes. Why

was she doing this? As bad as he was, who was better to her? This call from Cassie was her first contact in months with her family. Just because Cassie was coming it didn't mean anyone really cared anything about her. Besides, Cassie would stay a couple of days, then leave, and she'd be alone again. So what was the point of making Sal angry? Besides, Stephanie never forgot what was hidden under those white-on-white shirts.

She became contrite instantly. "I'm sorry, honey. You know how I get in this heat. I guess I just got excited because my family's finally going to discover me again."

Sal blinked. "I get it," he said; he looked up at her. Then, as if his brain were suddenly in contact with his face, Sal's expression changed. Cassie's coming could be just the ticket. He reached out for Stephanie and pulled her next to him on the bed. He put his arm around her; no pawing, just a nice, affectionate gesture. "Listen, baby, I think we're both getting a little crazy here. I think it's about time we blew this dump."

"Oh," she said. "You want to go to the Sands or Caesar's?"

"Naw. I think we ought to cut out of Vegas. I've been thinking. I'm ready for the big time."

Her heart raced. She hugged him tight. How happy she was to hear those words. She wished Cassie and Diane and Bill could hear Sal now. Make all that New York family sit at her feet for a change. Let those two grandfathers see what she could be. A star's wife! If Sal had a big career, that would be a gas. "I'm ready, too," she reassured him.

"Yeah," he agreed. "The only problem is how we take the next step."

"What do you mean?"

"Listen, honey, we can get out of this flea trap, get a date here, another date there, but the only way to go for good is to take the big step up. I have to get out of this club scene. I gotta go on and make it in the movies. I need a big record. That's where the business is today."

"Then let's do it," she said shrugging her shoulders, palms upraised.

"It's not so easy."

"You have the talent, sweetheart."

"You're a doll. You really think so?"

"You're the best. Nobody sings those songs like you do. Honest to God, Sal, it breaks my heart every time I hear you sing 'If I Loved You'!"

"Well, that's a biggie."

"You're really fantastic."

"So what good does it do? In this business you need a gold record. A movie deal. You think Frank or Dino could have made it without records and movies? No way. You see, you get yourself a hit record and a film deal or a TV movie, and then the saloons pay you the big bucks. But first you gotta have movies and records. That's what helps you sell tickets today."

Stephanie blinked. This was all pretty hard to follow. "Do you mean you need a new agent?"

"No, doll, I need new money."

"Money?"

"Yeah. Money. Irv's been talking to me about it. See, the boys will come in for a couple hundred thou if we raise that kind of dough. With that kind of stakes, we can get a piece of the action. See? Then we'll get to own part of a film company. Make our own deals. Do the same thing with records. All we have to do is make it. Pay the musicians, the session fees. The boys'll get it out for us. They got distribution connections."

She nodded as if she understood each word.

"Yeah," he said getting up from the bed, "the only thing between me and the big time is money."

He walked over to the dresser, opened the drawers where the shirts lay, reached underneath and pulled out the small revolver. He twirled it and pointed it at Stephanie.

She screamed.

"Scared you, didn't I? I wonder if it would scare your sister, too. She's got all the dough, and to tell you the truth, Stephanie, I'm a fuckin' good investment."

Sal threw his head back and laughed.

Then he put the gun back in the drawer. Stephanie realized that she was trembling from head to foot.

Sal always went down to the lounge before she did. He liked to walk among the gamblers and get a sense of the crowd. She didn't understand the reason. The crowd never changed, except that some nights the polyester pant suits were pink instead of blue, and some nights the men wore white shoes instead of tennis shoes. But always Sal was immaculate in the perfectly fitted tuxedo that hid the paunch, the gleaming white shirts that gave life to the swarthy skin.

She put her makeup on carefully. She wanted to please him tonight. Sal could be a charmer when things were going his way, and she wanted him to feel like a star so he'd be a doll tomorrow and make her sister realize that Sal Romano was some important guy here in Vegas.

For once, she was going to be the big sister.

Vince and Irv stood against the doorway as Sal began to sing. "The guy's still got good pipes," Irv said.

"Only to an agent," Vince answered, shifting the toothpick in his mouth.

"Come on. He's good enough for the Dyslexia Telethon."

"The Dyslexia Telethon? What's that?"

"You know, the disease special Charlie Gordon is doing from the hotel this weekend."

"Charlie Gordon? That jerk can't stand being out of the limelight, so he invents a disease."

"Naw, he didn't invent it. Dyslexia is about kids with reading problems. They read backwards."

"Everyday something new. They never had dyslexia where I grew up."

"Listen, Vince, where you grew up nobody could read forwards."

"Ha ha. Some comic you are."

"Better than Charlie Gordon. Listen, that guy's using this telethon for his comeback. Three whole years since he's been on the network."

"Hasn't he done some gigs since then, Irv?"

"Sure. Sure, he still plays a few dates. East Heartburn, Tennessee. Chopped Liver, Texas. But this guy needs an audience all the time. He's always on. For God's sake, when he sees the light in the Frigidaire, he does twenty minutes to a roast chicken."

"If things are that tough, I guess you're not his agent."

"Thank God, that's one I missed. But our office in L.A. handles him. That's how I got this spot for our boy."

"Just a guest shot?"

"What do you mean, *just* a guest shot? Sal's gonna sing. Those other clowns on the show are just gonna bring kids up on stage so the folks at home can have a good cry and send money."

"Perfect timing. It'll all happen when Stephanie's sister is here. And then she sees Sal in action."

"But can Sal put the squeeze on her?"

"You know Sal as well as I do. He can be Mr. Wonderful or he can be the number one bastard in the world."

"Well, tell him to play Mr. Wonderful if he wants to get out of this dump."

Irv smiled. "I will if you think anybody listens to an agent more than ten percent of the time."

Vince nodded. "Let's do it another way. Let's talk to Stephanie. We'll tell her about the telethon. Between us we can coach her good. I hear the sisters are very tight, and Grandpa gives everything to the other sister."

"Fine," Irv said. "Let's lay a couple of numbers on her, and see what she can memorize by morning."

Irv shoved Vince toward the gypsy tent where Stephanie sat. "Let's do it now before he screws it up and belts her one."

Stephanie flashed her best smile at Irv and Vince.

"I hear your sister's coming tomorrow," Irv said.

"Yes, isn't that great?" Stephanie seemed more alive than Irv could ever remember.

"Did Sal tell you what we been thinking about for him?" Vince asked.

She blinked. Then she nodded. During the time she'd been in Vegas, she'd learned the value of not appearing to know too much. Once Sal had slapped her because she'd told Irv her husband had made a pass at an airline stewardess. "You tell those guys nothing. They got the big connections," Sal had warned her. "Especially you never tell them business things." Stephanie couldn't imagine what business things she could talk about—but still, the sting of Sal's slaps lasted for days.

"Sal can make it in the big time," Irv said. "It'll take a little money, a little time."

"A lotta money," Vince added quickly.

Stephanie looked at them closely. So they were after her family's money. Why else would they mention Cassie's coming? And didn't she know deep in her heart that these two connectors were just waiting for her connections to work in their favor? Still, what Sal said made sense. It did take money to build a star. You read about it all the time. Look what Ann-Margret's act cost. Look how much the Beatles paid to produce their records—and they were stars.

"We were thinking that maybe you and your sister could have a little talk," Vince said. "You girls are close. No reason she shouldn't invest in—ha ha—the family, so to speak."

Stephanie turned her head slowly. Then her suspicions were right. "What am I supposed to do?" She'd keep playing slowly; she'd pretend to listen.

". . . so then you can say that your sister could get a piece of the action . . ." That was Vince.

Who was that woman moving to the ringside table?

". . . and you gotta remember what the union costs are today . . ." Irv was talking.

". . . but the best investment is still people . . ." Vince said.

"Shh," Stephanie whispered. "They're going to introduce him now."

"Ladies and gentlemen, the Gypsy proudly presents its own singing gypsy, Sal Romano."

A polite smattering of applause. The usual.

All except the ringside table. It was that woman, the one who looked familiar. She was standing, smiling right at Sal and leading the applause in the room. Stephanie felt those old chilling waves of jealousy. What right did this person have to smile like that at Sal Romano? The woman turned and faced the room, and then Stephanie knew who she was. She recognized the long red hair and the big green eyes. "Is that Tina Tracy?" she asked Irv.

"Yeah. Hottest singer this year. That kid from Tennessee is going to the top."

"She's pretty, isn't she?"

"Not as pretty as you are. You got no worries in that department. This one's a business deal. She'll be on the special with Sal," he said casually.

"What special?" She jumped on the words just as Irv knew she would.

"Oh, the boys are setting up one of those charity telethons. They're doing it from here this weekend, and just today I found out we can get a spot for Sal on the show. Terrific showcase. I'll have a few people watch. And who knows? With him appearing on the bill with Tina . . . you know, it looks good when a guy's who's been around is with the new talent. Well, you get the picture."

"You bet I do," Stephanie said sarcastically.

"Aw, kid, don't worry," Vince assured her.

Stephanie took a deep breath. Okay. So she wouldn't worry. She'd just sit back and listen. He was starting now. The Nat "King" Cole stuff came first. She liked this segment. He'd worked hard on it. Listened to all those old records. She had, too. Coached him on the lyrics when he forgot. That was her job. That was the best part of the marriage. It made her feel really wedded, a part of him and his life.

He finished the medley. Tina stood and applauded, and as she rose Stephanie's hatred of her grew. Stephanie hated the young body and the red hair. She hated the good voice, the promising career. Sal couldn't turn down young girls. Didn't Stephanie know that? Tina Tracy was not only a hot new singer; she liked Sal. It was a killing combination. Tina sat down, and the music started once again. This time Stephanie didn't watch the act. She watched Tina Tracy. Tina looked at Sal the way Stephanie looked at him when he was up there, and he looked at Tina . . .

Oh God. He was singing "If I Loved You." Her song, and he was looking at Tina Tracy.

"I don't want that bitch in this room," Stephanie said to Irv.

"She's no problem to you," Irv assured her.

Stephanie narrowed her eyes. No problem? Just like the waitress in the lounge across the street? And the hat check girl at the Sands? Or the girl in the topless show at—and what about this one and that one? What about? What about? Stephanie's head was throbbing. What did she have to do to make him stop? How could she get rid of these hungry women all pressing for her man? A record deal would do it. A movie deal would take him out of Vegas and that night-after-night adulation. For God's sake, wasn't it time she and Sal sat in front of a TV set every night like the rest of America?

Stephanie picked up her handbag and pushed back her chair. She stood. Sal was still singing "If I Loved You."

"Let's leave now," Stephanie said loudly. "I want you guys to tell me exactly what I have to say to my sister tomorrow."

XVIII

STEPHANIE CHANGED HER CLOTHES three times before she went to meet the plane. The jeans looked too California. The white cotton suit was too dressy to wear at noon. Finally she settled on a slim black linen skirt and silk shirt, the kind of thing she knew Cassie herself would wear. She kept wiping the perspiration from her face as she waited for the plane. Heat or nervousness?

When the flight arrived, Stephanie stood in the waiting area shaking with anticipation.

Finally Stephanie saw her. It was Cassie, wasn't it? Yes, oh yes. She felt a lump rise in her throat; her eyes filled with tears of relief. Cassie had actually come for her. The sisters rushed to embrace and clutched one another sobbing.

Finally they pulled apart. "Let me look at you," Cassie said. "Oh, what a grown-up you are. And wouldn't you know? You still look perfect."

Perfect? Oh sure. Perfect. Cassie was judging the outside just the way Diane always did. Broken hearts didn't show through silk shirts. Cassie herself was in jeans (wouldn't you know?) and carrying a duffel bag. "I've got a driver outside. Let's get your luggage," Stephanie said.

"A driver?" Cassie asked.

"That's how we treat visiting celebrities," Stephanie grinned. Already she was beginning to feel like the big sister. This was her territory. Here she was in command. For the moment she was glad not to be in New York, where Cassie automatically took charge.

"Where's Sal?" Cassie asked, her quick eyes darting about the lounge.

"Back at the hotel waiting to have lunch with us," Stephanie announced. She didn't add that Sal never got up before noon.

Cassie linked her arm through her sister's. "Come on, I'm starving, and I can't wait to see Sal."

Stephanie sighed. She could wait to see Sal, all right. She wondered if he'd be on his good behavior. Well, for sure he wouldn't slap her around in front of Cassie. And he had arranged for the car, hadn't he? Or had Vince done it? She couldn't quite remember.

Sal was in the VIP suite that Vince had reserved for Cassie. The living room had the heavy red-and-gold look of the room where Stephanie and Sal stayed, but this room had a large basket of red roses anchoring one end and a large basket of fruit on the other side.

"Oh . . . oh . . . it's . . . well, isn't it something," Cassie said. She'd never seen anything so gaudy in her life.

"Wait 'til you see the bathroom," Sal said after the perfunctory kiss and handshake.

Stephanie breathed a sigh of relief. Oh yes, this was sweet Sal they were getting. Stephanie could hear the squeals of surprise as Sal gave Cassie the bathroom tour: the sauna, the Jacuzzi, the sunken tub with telephone. "You look wonderful, Sal," Cassie said.

"That's what living with your beautiful sister does for me," he answered, walking over to Stephanie and giving her a little hug. She looked up at him, the love spilling from her eyes. This was the Sal she adored.

"I'll leave you guys alone," Sal said. "I know what it's like when you want to be alone and everybody's hanging around. I'll meet you in the lobby in half an hour, and we'll have lunch."

Cassie shook her head. "Look, Sal, I'm not really very hungry. Stephanie and I can order room service and well . . ."

Sal walked over to Cassie and put an arm around her. He gave

[169]

her a small squeeze. "That's not very thoughtful of me, is it? You girls haven't seen each other for a long time, and I should let you catch up."

Stephanie couldn't believe her ears. Sal? Her Sal, ingratiating himself with Cassie? She'd seen Sal at his best with fans in the club, but she'd never seen him really turn on the charm for anyone who mattered to her. She was fascinated. She wouldn't have to worry about this weekend at all. It was going to be terrific.

"Let's go to the casino," Stephanie said after Sal left. She was beginning to feel nervous; she didn't know just how to begin a conversation with Cassie. It would be easier against the hum of other people's voices, the interruption of slot machines.

"Sure. Sure."

When they got to the casino, Cassie blinked at the crowds. "It's only two o'clock," she said.

"It's like this all the time. Oh, maybe at four in the morning it's not quite as mobbed. But they all come here to get rich." She didn't add . . . *Like me. Like me, Cassie. I came here to get rich with love. Only problem is that the last five minutes is as close to love as I've been.*

"The people all look so—I don't know—so real. I guess I thought everybody in Las Vegas was going to look like a gorgeous showgirl or something out of *Guys and Dolls.*"

Stephanie nodded. Wait till she met Vince and Irv. She wondered. Would Cassie have to meet them? Couldn't she ask Cassie without them there? Wait. What had they said? Oh yes, she had to ask for the money. Abruptly Stephanie said, "Let's go across the street and have a drink."

"A drink?" Cassie didn't hide her surprise. "Isn't it a little early?"

"I thought we could talk if we had a drink."

Cassie nodded. "I understand. It's too hard to talk in here." She let Stephanie lead her across the street to the bar at the Cleopatra. The Cleopatra was the Roman Empire version of the Gypsy. Instead of reds and oranges in the public rooms, there were blacks and golds. But the same faces were there. Tucked, lifted, smoothed, bronzed, anxious.

The two young women sat at a tiny table. "Do you know those men?" Cassie asked. She turned, with that sense of being watched.

Stephanie waved to two men standing at the bar. "That's Vince and Irv. I'll introduce you. Irv is Sal's agent, and Vince is— well, Vince is sort of connected."

"Connected?"

"Yes. Here in Vegas connections are very important." Hadn't she heard that somewhere?

Cassie looked closely at her sister now, the first time she'd really studied her face. There was something different. She couldn't quite put her finger on it.

Stephanie pulled a cigarette from a silver case in her handbag. That was one difference, Stephanie hadn't stopped smoking since she'd met the plane. Stephanie had never smoked.

"Why do you smoke so much, Stephanie?"

"I'm not Daddy's perfect little girl anymore."

"Well, you probably could be if you wanted."

"Come on, Cass, you know I can't. Besides, Daddy's got his perfect big girls."

Cassie felt a chill along her spine. How did Stephanie know?

Stephanie sighed. Wasn't that what Irv and Vince had told her? Hadn't they said she should get the money out of Cassie before her father took it all for his girlfriends? Hadn't they spelled it all out? She couldn't remember all the numbers, but she remembered that.

"How do you know?" Cassie asked.

"You know everything out here. You think this is the desert, and you think I'm far from New York. Well, I hear all about all of you out here." She blinked back tears. It was all too emotional. She couldn't stand thinking about Daddy and those—those women.

"I found out about Daddy, too," Cassie said. "I'm still not sure I believe it."

"Oh, I believe it. That's what men are like."

"You sound like some unhappy housewife."

Stephanie fought the temptation to say . . . but I am. Instead she shrugged. That was easier than talking. She took a long drag on her cigarette. Then she remembered she hadn't asked about Cassie and Jimmy.

Cassie recognized the silence as an unasked question. Better to deal with it now. "No woman should stay in a bad marriage, Stephanie." She lowered her eyes. "I didn't."

"Was it other women?"

"No. Other men," Cassie said in a tone that would dismiss any further questioning.

Stephanie shrugged. "I'd have guessed as much."

"How would you know?"

"After living in Vegas, Cassie, nothing would ever surprise me again. I've seen them all. The transsexuals, the lesbians, the closet fags."

Cassie had to stop her. She didn't want to hear the stories. She wanted to say something nice, something upbeat. "Sal seems to be sweet to you."

"Yes." Then she paused. Vince had said to watch for the opening. Well, this was as good as she'd get. She tried hard to get the next words out, but they were stuck in her chest. Or was that her head? Where were the words she couldn't say?

"Does Sal want to stay in Las Vegas?"

Oh, thank you, Cassie. You're making it easier. The words are coming unglued now. Yes. I think I can say them. "Cassie . . ." her voice was unnaturally high.

Cassie sipped the iced tea she'd ordered. She looked up from the straw. What was all this awkwardness about? Maybe Stephanie needed to say something. Maybe that's why Stephanie was groping for words. "Look, Stephanie, I'm sure a million men all over the world are cheating at this very minute—"

"You're not kidding."

"And I suppose as long as there's some discretion, a woman can't ask for much more."

"But he's not discreet," Stephanie argued.

"I suppose not if you heard out here."

"Heard out here? It's under my nose. It's that waitress over there . . . she's this week's girl. Last week it was that redhead over there. Every week he has a different one, and in between those

[172]

women he pushes me around, takes me to bed." Stephanie paused for breath. That wasn't what she'd meant to say at all.

Cassie shook her head. "What are you talking about?"

"Sal," she said simply. "What did you think I was talking about?"

"I was talking about Daddy and Mrs. Fink."

Stephanie didn't have the names. She shrugged. "All men ever do is let you down, disappoint you. They're all the same."

Cassie's shoulders dropped. So that was it. That was the real sadness she'd sensed in Stephanie. Now she knew. Sal's love songs weren't for her. "That's awful. How can you stand it?"

"I can," Stephanie said. Then, like an actress who gets her cue and moves to her most important speech, she remembered the reason. "You see, Cassie, Sal is headed for the big time, and I want to be around for that."

"The big time?"

"Oh, for sure. He's going to be a big star."

"A star? Sal?" Cassie could remember his cornball singing at the bar mitzvah. Just the other day she'd heard a disc jockey talk about the acts in Las Vegas, and he'd said something about that old has-been, never-was Sal Romano. But it wasn't the kind of quote you repeated to your family.

"Oh yes," Stephanie said confidently. "Nothing between him and the big time except a few hundred thou."

"You mean a few hundred thou between what he makes here and what he'd make in the big time."

"No, you don't understand show biz, Cassie. You see, if you really want to make it big in the business today—you know, like Frank and Dino—then you have to have a hit record or a film deal or a TV movie."

"That's all it takes?"

"Well, we're going to start it all, get the ball rolling, get the show on the road"—Stephanie paused to lick her lips nervously— "and then, then . . ." She faltered. She couldn't quite remember the next part.

"How will you start it, Stephanie?"

The younger sister smiled. Of course. That was the next part, the part she almost forgot. "There's going to be a big telethon here this weekend. It starts tonight, and Irv—he's Sal's agent—well, Irv arranged for Sal to be on network TV on this telethon, and it could just be the big break for him."

"I hope so," Cassie said.

"And you have to invest a few hundred thou," she continued.

"Who has to invest?" Cassie asked.

"We do," Stephanie said softly.

"We do? Us? You and I?"

"Well, not I. I don't have any money. Grandpa didn't give it to me. You have it all. You work there."

"I don't really have anything yet." She wasn't ready now to tell Stephanie that joining Grandpa didn't mean instant wealth.

"That's not what I hear."

"No?"

"I hear there was just a big land deal in Florida, and Grandpa made a bundle, so that means you'll get your cut."

Cassie blinked. What was Stephanie talking about?

"I think the Cassman sisters are both kind of confused," Cassie said softly.

"No. No. This is an investment, Cassie. It's a business deal. Ask Irv and Vince. They know it, too."

"Look, Stephanie, I didn't come out here to invest in your husband's career. I'm in real estate, not show business."

Now Stephanie drew a breath and said the words she'd been so carefully taught. "Sal is better than a piece of land. He's a piece of talent. You invest, and you get your money back. In spades."

"Spades? What are you talking about?"

Stephanie pursed her lips. Had she said the wrong thing? Had she forgotten again?

"Come on, Cassie. This is really a good deal for you."

"Stop," Cassie said, making her voice as gentle as she could. "I get the picture. Sal is running around, and you want him out of this place, so you figure that he can make movies and records, and then the marriage will be fine."

"Not exactly," Stephanie said. "But out here if you're the wife of a big star, you really get the treatment."

"The treatment?"

"You know. Everybody's nice to you. But you really have to be somebody before they are. Otherwise it's rotten. You see, Sal got moved out of the big room at the Gypsy—it's the Romany Room—well, he got moved out of the Romany Room, and nobody at the hotel treats me the same."

"That's a pretty crummy bunch you pal around with," Cassie said, "and they don't seem too bright."

"No, they're not. It's such a relief."

"A relief?"

"It's kind of nice never having to read a book or talk about politics or care what happened in the Middle East or Russia. I suppose there are smart people out here, too, but I never have to see them. The kind of people I see are dumb like me. Nobody gives a damn about your conversation. All you have to do is look nice and keep on screwing."

"Don't you want more out of life than that?"

"Sure. I want Sal to be a star."

"You can't buy stardom, Stephanie."

"Look, Cassie, you may know the real estate business, but I know show business." She said the words triumphantly, then looked up to see if Vince and Irv were still watching. She wanted applause, curtain calls. She'd done it. She'd made her speech.

"I think you ought to get out of this place. Come back to New York with me."

"That's funny, Cassie. That's really funny. Yesterday I thought that's what I wanted to do, but after I talked to Vince and Irv, I realized New York isn't for me. What could I do there? I can't work. I don't have a New York kind of mind—you know, clever and everything—the way you do. I'm fine for Las Vegas. I don't want to be where you have to think all the time. I'd like California, too. They have people like me there. You know, out here I'm somebody. Who would I be in New York? At least here—even though Sal's lousy—I'm his wife. And he's got connections."

"Connections?"

"Uh-huh. That's the word, Cassie. Connections. You're my connection. Irv and Vince told me that. They told me that it takes connections to make Sal a star. They told me all these things to say to you because if I raise the money, they'll use their connec-

[175]

tions. You see, I don't have to raise all the money. If I put in two hundred thou, they'll match it. First we'll do the record, and then we'll buy a piece of a film production company. You see, you have to do that in order to control casting—"

"And you believe them?"

"Naturally. They know how it's done."

Cassie looked long at her little sister. "I wish I could help you, but I can't do it. I don't have the money. Not yet anyway."

"So you're saying no."

"For the moment. Maybe I can later."

"How much later, Cassie?"

"I don't know."

"I don't know if Sal and I can last, Cass."

"Try. Just try. You still feel something for him, don't you? Isn't there some love?"

"Love? I guess you're about the only person left for me to love, Cassie."

Cassie was silent. Poor, poor Stephanie.

"I can't help you now, Stephanie, but I will."

"Promise?"

"Sure. I promise."

"I suppose I shouldn't have married Sal," Stephanie said, "but who knew? I probably should have married somebody else. You know, somebody who comes from the same place. I keep thinking that if I'd married Cousin Alex, I'd have been all right."

XIX

"Two SELTZERS," Irv said to the bartender.

"Bromo or Alka?" the bartender asked.

"Very funny," Vince said, in a tone that indicated the question was anything but funny.

"You're on edge, Vince. Relax," Irv advised. "That's a new guy behind the bar. Ask for a coupla sodas. Maybe he'd understand that."

"Two sodas," Irv repeated dutifully.

"Look," Irv said in a half whisper, "I know why you're uptight. To tell you the truth, I'm sweating, too. That broad's zip in the brain department. Who'd believe she's S.C.'s granddaughter? Hey, look," Irv said as he punched Vince's arm, "she's actually talking. Maybe even a whole sentence."

"Dummy, you look. Look. Look," Vince said, excitement raising his normal hoarse tone. "The sister's touching her hand. Oh my God, Stephanie just kissed her. I bet she got the dough."

"Jesus, who would believe she could do it?" Irv wondered. "Turn your stool around quick, Vince. Don't let her know we see her. Don't kill the deal."

"It don't make any difference," Vince said. "She either got it or she didn't. That was the key time. I can tell. But between you and me, I'd lay you five to three she got it."

"To tell you the truth," Irv confided, "the only thing that worries me about this whole deal is that Sal will end up screwing the wrong sister. I just hope he doesn't make a play for the big one."

"The grandfather will kill him if he does."

"Sal said every time she sees him she makes a face like she's holding her nose."

"Maybe she smells our deal," Vince said. Then he laughed. "Or maybe she smells Sal."

"Come on. Sal's got talent."

"Irv, you may be his agent, but that guy's got one talent in the whole world. He can lay young broads."

"His old lady's not that young."

"No, not anymore. Christ, she got old just counting his girls. I can't figure how the hell he gets them. He must do things in bed that haven't even been invented."

"It's something else. I'm telling you, Vince, he can still sell a song like nobody else. He's got those chicks hanging on every note. Night after night they sit there, and believe me, even Sal can't screw 'em all. The guy's gotta have something."

"Irv, for God's sake, those chicks aren't such chicks now. Go look. His act's got too much schmaltz for young girls. That's not what they buy now. You know, ever since Elvis, the business is different. The young ones today like the screamers and the shakers. Even the old broads like it loud. Sal's still doing that soft shtick."

"It works for Frank and Dean," Irv countered.

"Don't give me that works-for-Frank-and-Dean crap. Frank's one of a kind. He owns show business. But still he's got his big records, plays dates all over the country. And then," he emphasized, his fist pounding the bar, "only then does Frank decide if and when he wants to play Vegas. How do you compare this kind of punk? You telling me they sing the same songs so that makes them twins? That's like me telling you I'm Onassis because once I went to a Greek restaurant."

"Stop already. So he's not Frank."

"Damn right. This is his last chance, and I laid it on the line to him. I only hope it sank in. You can be sure Stephanie doesn't know what's going on. I don't mean just about S.C., but she doesn't dream that Sal'll be out on his ass if she don't pull this deal together."

"Come on. You wouldn't take him out of the lounge," Irv said, but even as he spoke he knew the answer.

Vince smiled, but there was no humor in the smile. "You're a good agent, Irv. What are you doing with this punk?"

"He was my first client back in New York. I always figured he'd make it. I can remember back to a time when nobody would hire Sinatra. And finally, finally he sweated and got that part in *From Here to Eternity*. Took a pay cut. Did everything and acted his heart out. After that he was numero uno. Chairman of the board. Well, I always figured I could ride Sal the same way."

Vince shook his head. "I don't think the boys have the time to let you try. This is it. Get the dough now or Sal goes back to the pizza factory. Maybe even the glue factory."

"Poor guy. He's kinda sweet."

"Sweet? You call it sweet when he belts a broad because he has a bad roll at the crap table? I saw it with my own eyes. You call it sweet when he takes an alley cat, a honest-to-god alley cat, and throws it down an open stairwell? Sweet? The only thing sweet about that shmuck is the two pounds of candy he ate last week. And speaking of candy, Irv, you better tell Sal to watch it. His four hundred and fifty tuxedos are all beginning to look tight around the gut."

"Not four hundred and fifty. Only twenty-two."

Sal stood in front of the closet and looked at the lineup.

There was a story behind each tuxedo. Sometimes two stories. Stephanie watched him shuffle through the suits. She felt so good. She wasn't alone anymore. Hadn't Cassie promised to help? She hadn't said exactly when, but Cassie's word was as good as her marker.

Sal put his hands on his hips. This was important. Tonight was bigger than any broad. He had to be good. He needed a lucky suit. The Frank-and-Dino one. That would do it. He heard Stephanie's soft laugh. He turned. "Now what?"

"I bet I know what you're going to wear tonight. I bet I know which tux. The one you wore the night you had your picture taken with Frank and Dean."

If there was one thing he couldn't stand, it was a smartass broad. He hated her. He felt the anger, the annoyance, the disgust pressing in his chest. Smile, kid, he told himself. She's the ticket. Use her. Okay, he'd use her, but he didn't have to like it. He wanted to punch her. Damn it. That's what that broad needed. He looked down. His arm was raised, and he was moving toward her. God. He couldn't afford to screw up in front of the beady-eyed sister. He put his arm down slowly. If he'd stood it this long, he'd get through one more weekend. Then it would be over. No more crummy rooms in Las Vegas. No more Vince. Hello, Hollywood. I'm coming back, L.A. Yeah, he could taste the big time again. Hadn't Sal told him that if he got the money from Stephanie's family, the boys would get their hands on that record company? Sure. That's exactly what he'd said.

Sal whistled softly under his breath. He'd forgotten the part, the other part when Vince said, ". . . and if you don't get it, Sal, you'll be out on your ass."

Sal reached in the closet and took out the white gabardine tuxedo, the one piped in black satin. "I'm goin' formal tonight," he said to Stephanie. "Look out, America."

[179]

Stephanie took a step back and shuddered, but she said nothing. It wasn't worth a black-and-blue mark on her arm to say that when he wore that tuxedo he looked like a walking condolence card.

Cassie dialed the number, then leaned back against the pillows. "Mr. Cassman, please. It's Cassie."

The call went through and rang in his office immediately, just as she had known it would.

"Yes!" That was Grandpa. Not "Yes" with a question in his voice, but "Yes" with the assurance that comes when you never take no for an answer.

"How're things, Grandpa?" She'd play him slowly.

"Fine. You having a nice time? How're they treating you?"

"They?"

"Your sister and the bum."

"Okay, Grandpa. Quit playing your games. I know what's going on."

"What?" In his voice was astonishment, an open-toned astonishment that meant there was no surprise at all.

Cassie leaned forward. She was intent now. She had to make Grandpa understand that she not only knew the game but the players. "Grandpa, I saw Irv and Vince; I talked to Stephanie and now I've got a pretty good idea where the Florida money came from. I know how Sal got his job here, how Stephanie got married and why they're so happy to see me here."

Cassie was sure of one thing, was rolling on the other two, but after all, this was Las Vegas, and this was the moment to let Grandpa know that she didn't just see things. She understood them.

Grandpa chuckled. "You passed the test."

"What do you mean?"

"You think your father would have figured it out?"

Cassie was silent. Of course Bill never could have interpreted the signs.

"Or your mother?"

Cassie sighed. Diane would be shopping at the boutique at the

[180]

hotel. Poor Diane. If you couldn't charge it, she wouldn't understand it.

"It's like I always said, Cassie. You're me. You're the only one smart enough to run this business."

She knew he was right, yet she felt a loyalty, a devotion, a kind of love for both Bill and Diane. But coloring her positive feelings, underlying and giving them their true meaning, was Cassie's determination not to be like her parents in any way, not in thought, speech, looks, or action. And Grandpa had always known that.

"The boys want more money," Cassie said abruptly.

"Are you calling from the hotel?"

"Yes."

"Then I have nothing to say. Call me at eleven tomorrow morning—my time—from a pay phone. We'll work things out. Meanwhile don't say anything to Stephanie or the bum. Let him go on the telethon tonight—"

"You know about that, too?"

"I'll even watch, maybe send a donation."

"You're too much, Grandpa."

"Just give me time to look at the numbers. And one thing more, Cassie."

"Yes?"

"Don't call them 'the boys.' Otherwise you're doing just fine. You're learning. You see, facts you get from Wellesley. An education you get from life."

"You look beautiful, Cassie," Sal said, his white teeth flashing its own beauty signs. Well, why not say it? No woman ever disagreed with that line.

Cassie smiled appreciatively as she joined them in the lounge.

Sal shook his head. Dumb. Smart. Old. Young. You could get any broad with a smile and two sweet words about her looks. Too bad most guys never understood. Oh, well. It only made it easier for the guys who did.

"I think I'm gonna have one more drink before I go on," Sal said.

"What are you going to do on the telethon?" Cassie asked.

[181]

"Well, you know Charlie Gordon—the comic, Charlie Gordon. Charlie's been a friend of mine since, oh my God, ever since I was busting my butt in little clubs in New Jersey. We'd be on the same bill in those days—"

"You're as old as Charlie Gordon?" Cassie asked in surprise.

"Naw, naw. He's a good ten, twelve years older," Sal said quickly.

"Then how do you know him so well?" Stephanie asked.

"For Christ's sake, you think you have to show your birth certificate to play a club in New Jersey? I could sing. From the time my voice changed, I could sing. Now shut up."

Cassie shuddered. And she was supposed to help keep this marriage going?

Sal, realizing the harshness of his words, stood up, went over to Stephanie and kissed her.

"Listen, honey, I'm sorry. I didn't mean to blow up in front of the family and everything. But I'm nervous. I'm going into the Romany Room tonight, and I got my big chance on national television, and I don't want to blow it."

"I understand," Cassie said.

"Hey, look. Irv's bringing Charlie Gordon over here now. Let's all have a drink together," Sal shouted.

Then Sal stood up, opened his arms and embraced Charlie Gordon. Charlie was slimmer than Sal. His black hair was shinier. His tuxedo was more expensive. His smile was bigger, his manner more frenetic, his voice louder, and his laugh deeper. Everything about Charlie Gordon was larger than life. Cassie wondered how they'd ever contain Charlie in an eighteen-inch television screen.

"Charlie, you look like a million," Sal said, the admiration oozing from his pores.

"A million years or a million bucks?" Charlie asked.

Irv laughed dutifully.

Stephanie took her cue and laughed.

Cassie sat stone-faced.

"Hey, remember the good old days?" Sal asked.

Charlie snapped his fingers, broke into a small tap dance and sang tunelessly, "Everything about the good old days is bad, bad, baaad."

[182]

"Yeah, I guess they weren't so good," Sal agreed.

Charlie looked quickly around the room to make sure he had an audience for his routine at the table. Two people at the next table were talking together. Christ. Must be some honeymoon couple from Kansas. He'd get them. Charlie jumped up on Sal's chair. "Fire," he yelled.

"No, no," Irv screamed. "Charlie's kidding. It's a joke."

"Some joke," Cassie grumbled. "You could cause a riot."

"Cause a riot? I am a riot, a laugh riot," Charlie said. This time he was using his little-boy voice, folding his body in thirds and peering up over the edge of the table in an imitation of the Red Skelton mean-little-kid routine.

"You're a million laughs," Sal said, his body shaking with laughter.

Now Charlie stood up, glared at Sal, and said, "You got a very weird sense of humor, Sal. Good thing you can sing. You *can* sing, can't you?"

Sal was now laughing so hard the tears were coming down his cheeks. "Charlie, you never change."

Charlie walked over, grabbed Stephanie, threw her back and planted a long kiss on her lips. "Little girl," he said imitating Humphrey Bogart as he stood and lit a cigarette, "Little girl, you're the one who needs a change."

Then he hitched his pants with his forearms, in perfect pantomime of Bogart and walked off puffing his cigarette no hands.

"He breaks me up," Sal said.

"Why did you let him kiss Stephanie like that? Doesn't he know she's your wife?" Cassie asked.

"That's why he kissed me," Stephanie said. "He's just showing us that he thinks he can have anything he wants."

Irv looked at her in surprise. Maybe she wasn't as dumb as everybody said.

"Let's go over to the Romany Room," Irv said. "I booked a table. Sal, you'll be on in a few minutes. Girls, you just have time to go to the ladies' room. Hurry up, and meet us there. One thing I learned from women in clubs. They never go to the bathroom alone. Whatever it is they do, they gotta do it there together."

Irv laughed. "I think you're funnier than Charlie Gordon."

[183]

"That kind of talk will put me back in the unemployment lines," Sal said. Then Irv slapped Sal on the back. "You're on, kid. Go out and kill 'em."

Stephanie and Cassie edged through the tightly packed tables. For the first time Cassie understood the bleakness of her sister's Las Vegas life. She had to let Stephanie know help was coming. As they stood at the mirrors in the pink-lighted powder room, Cassie leaned to her sister and whispered, "I've got it, Stephanie. Whatever money you need."

Stephanie smiled and kept combing her hair. Cassie hadn't let her down. She wished she could kiss her sister now, but if she did, she was sure she'd burst into tears. And in Las Vegas the smart girls hid their tears.

Cassie slid into her seat as Charlie Gordon introduced Sal. Drinks appeared, and then "Sh sh!" Charlie Gordon was introducing Sal. There was a polite smattering of applause, the inevitable coughers and throat-clearers, and it began. First Charlie and Sal did a bit on the good old days. Ha ha. Remember when? She groaned inwardly. Remember, remember, remember? Then, after slapping him on the back and kissing his cheek, Charlie moved out of camera range to let Sal sing. The orchestra played the intro; Sal opened his mouth, and—Charlie ran back in, grabbed the mike and announced that Frank had just sent a contribution. "Come on," he said lovingly to the microphone, "Isn't that just like Frank, folks? Wouldn't you know the biggest stars have the biggest hearts? And now back to our show at the Romany Room and our dear friend, our old pal, that great singer—" Charlie pretended to forget Sal's name. He extended the bit by rummaging through his inside coat pocket, checking his cuff for notes. At last he ran over to Sal, whispered in his ear, Sal whispered back and then Charlie shouted, "Sal Romano."

For the first time Cassie sympathized with Sal. Poor fellow. He must be a basket case by now with that manic Charlie Gordon.

The orchestra played the intro, and Cassie sat forward to listen. She wanted to like him; she really wanted to like him. For her sister's sake. For his sake. For her sake. But his act was so, so

[184]

corny. Old. Tired. Sal clutched the mike like a young Sinatra. He drank while he sang. Just like a young Dean Martin. He sweated and tore off his tie like a young Tony Bennett. Cassie sat back. All he was was an old Sal Romano.

Old.

Everything about him was so old.

Even the songs. Oh no. Not that old tear jerker, "If I Loved You." She cast a sideways glance. How was Stephanie reacting? Mooning and adoring him? Was she blown away by it all? No. No, she wasn't. Cassie sat upright, the better to see Stephanie. Stephanie's eyes weren't on Sal at all; she was surveying the room. Tables front, tables back. Stephanie was checking them all until her eyes finally came to rest on a woman who was listening to Sal, looking at him and obviously adoring him. Who was she? Flashy-looking redhead. A hot number. And she looked familiar. Oh, now Cassie knew. That was Tina Tracy. The singer. The new Cher, they called her. And she never took her eyes off him. Cassie looked at Sal. Oh no. He was singing that song right to Tina. In front of his wife and everyone, Sal Romano was singing a love song to another woman.

The song ended. Charlie came out on stage, embraced Sal, kissed him—and Sal, his black hair catching the lights, made his way to—no, not to their table! He was going straight for Tina. Cassie could hear Stephanie's sharp intake of breath. A moment later she felt Stephanie brush past her. She sank lower in her chair. Oh no, she was going right to that table, too.

Stephanie knocked two glasses from a waiter's tray, but she didn't look back. She reached the table, put her hands on her hips and said in a loud voice, "Get over where you belong, Sal."

"Quiet," he commanded. "The TV's gonna pick up your voice."

"Move," she shouted.

"Okay, Okay," Sal said, feeling the sweat on his forehead. He put his arm around his wife, "I just wanted to say hello to my friends here."

Tina moved between Sal and Stephanie to kiss Sal. "Love the act," she crooned.

[185]

"I got a crazy wife," Sal said, "crazy for me. Ha ha."

Tina laughed. Sal pulled out a pen and wrote on a matchcover, "Here's my telephone number. Let's talk later."

Stephanie sucked her breath. He'd done it for the last time. She could stand it in front of the Las Vegas characters. But how could he do it tonight? How could he make a pass when her sister was in the room? She wrenched her arm from his grasp. "You just fucked up, Sal," she hissed. "Now I won't give you any money."

"You? Since when do you have money?"

"Since now. I've got it all, Sal. But you can't have it."

Sal grabbed her arm once more. This time he held it so she could feel the circulation to her hand stop. "Let's go upstairs and get this over with now," Sal said. "I sure as hell don't want to spill my guts on network TV."

He slammed the bedroom door behind them.

Sal was breathing hard now.

They were probably calling for him down there. Charlie probably wanted him to do a second number. But not now. He'd do it when he finished here.

He'd raced out of the Romany Room before the bitch could open her mouth again. On camera yet.

He hadn't even put his jacket on. Was it at Tina's table? Didn't matter. All that mattered was this dumb broad and the money he wanted.

What did she mean she had it?

His fingers were still digging in her thin arm; the sweat was running down his face. His shirt was soaked. And through the heavy smell of after-shave lotion, she could smell the juices of Sal Romano, the hot, stinking hatred dripping from his body.

He pushed her down on the bed and pulled his arm back—

"Not my face," she screamed. "Not my face."

"Then where do you want it?" he whispered hoarsely. Contempt for her was chilling him. He felt his temperature plummet. She put her hands over her face. Now the revulsion was choking him. This stupid bitch. She had the money, and she wouldn't give it to him. She wouldn't even look at him. Her eyes were covered.

He made a fist and punched her in the stomach. Hard. He laughed. That felt good.

Her hands flew from her face as she screamed.

He laughed again. "Well, it wasn't your face, Stephanie. Now, bitch, what was it you said downstairs? Sit up, and say it again."

She lay back and whimpered.

"Sit up and say it again, bitch."

She shook her head, sniffled and held her stomach.

"You tell me or I'll hit you so hard you'll be sterile for life."

She whimpered but said nothing.

"So you can't talk now. Cat got your tongue, baby? Or are you waiting for the second show?"

Stephanie moaned.

"You can't tell anyone about this, can you? Who'd believe you? Where are the black-and-blue marks? You know something? I got another hit in the gut for you." He raised his arm.

"No, no," she moaned. "No, I'll be good. I'll do anything."

"Anything? Since when are rich girls good for anything? You're no damned good, Stephanie. You're a lousy lay, and I ain't seen none of that Cassman money yet."

She sobbed.

"So that's why I was talking business with Tina. You see, Stephanie, I'm good. I can make it on my own. Didn't Charlie Gordon himself pick me for the Dyx—Dux—the telethon? Now Tina Tracy says she'll put me in her TV show. She's thinking about it. She really is. You thought I was banging her. You dumb broad. I was saving that for later. You don't even know the difference between a business fuck and pleasure." He laughed and moved toward the bureau drawer, the drawer where he kept the gun.

The pain was bearable now, but Stephanie couldn't let him know. She was scared. She had the money to give him. Wasn't that the real weapon? As good as a gun? She couldn't let him walk out now.

"You need money," Stephanie said in a little voice. "Be good to me, Sal, and I'll give it to you."

"Good to you? Why?"

"I can get the money."

[187]

"Says who?"

"Cassie."

"Cassie? Shit. I knew I was screwing the wrong sister."

"She doesn't like fucking. She's smart. You know, like the New York women."

"Never saw a woman who didn't want it," he said.

"She wants you to be good to me."

"Well, get this straight, Stephanie. Nobody's gonna tell Sal Romano nothin'."

"What about Vince and Irv?"

"What about 'em?"

She moved slowly. She had to get off the bed before he hit her—or worse—again.

Sal was opening the drawer.

"What are you doing?" she asked.

"Pullin' out. Go find yourself another boy. I've had it. I don't need you."

"But I have the money now."

"You're too late. Tina'll do it for me."

"Please . . . please."

"Get your hands off me. I'm through. Find yourself another paper doll. Go get another stud."

She stepped back. "Stud? If I waited for you to lay me, I'd be the only virgin in Las Vegas."

"I don't care if you're ballin' the entire band. I'm goin'." He walked to the closet and took out the Gucci luggage she'd bought for him.

"That's your trousseau luggage," she said.

"So what? I deserve it."

"When you married me, you had two pieces of Kleenex to your name. Now you walk out with monogrammed shirts in the Gucci luggage."

"So keep your fuckin' luggage," he screamed as he picked up a canvas case and threw it at her.

She ducked and stood up in time to see him take the twenty-two out of the drawer. He held it in the palm of his hand and looked at it lovingly. "I should have used this earlier," he muttered.

[188]

"What does that mean?" she asked.

"I might've gotten the dough."

"I'm the one who should've used it," she said, "and then you wouldn't be going anyplace."

"You can't keep me with guns or dough. I'm splittin'." He tossed the gun on top of his shirts.

"You're not going," she said softly.

"You can't stop me." He turned to get his shoes from the closet. He kept talking as he pulled them out. "I don't want you or your sister or your grandfather. All I want is out."

"No," she screamed and moved for the gun.

He was confused by her action. "What—what?"

She pointed the gun, the little darling, the honey, her savior, her lover. A little twenty-two would keep him.

"Put that down. You don't know what you're doing."

"Oh yes I do. For the first time Grandpa and Cassie and all those people can't run me. You stay or I pull the trigger."

Sal said nothing, but slowly—slowly—he edged toward her. She kept backing away.

Back.

One step back.

He followed.

Two steps back.

He was getting closer. He'd grab now. He'd get it. She saw him coming toward her, and she knew. She'd better scare him. Fast.

Stephanie took a breath and fired. Bang.

She laughed.

Was it really a shot? It sounded like a popgun. A firecracker.

She looked at the gun. Wasn't much, was it?

Then she looked up at Sal. Up. Sal? Sal?

Where was he? Where? Where?

She screamed. And then she ran.

Ran from their room.

Down the hall. The stairs. Take the stairs. Don't wait for the elevator.

Lounge. Get to the lounge. Race through the audience.

No. No. It wasn't the lounge.

[189]

The Romany Room. There. Go there.

"Cassie. Cassie." She cried her sister's name.

Because she knew. Stephanie knew.

She didn't have to look twice. She knew the moment she saw him lying there.

Sal Romano was dead.

Charlie Gordon was doing his Humphrey Bogart–Lauren Bacall on-camera scene. "—just pucker up and—"

There was a commotion at the back of the room. Charlie couldn't see what it was about. All he knew was that the camera with the red light, the camera that meant you were "on," wasn't on him. Jesus. Probably some show-off drunk in the audience upstaging him.

Slowly, slowly the camera panned the room.

And when it found Stephanie, it came in slow and tight. And the camera stayed on her.

On Stephanie. Shaking. Crying. But still holding tight.

Tight with the little twenty-two.

Forty million people watching a Saturday night telethon thought she was part of crazy Charlie's act.

But Sam Cassman, watching back in New York, knew instantly that this was no act.

Because standing next to the girl with the gun was another girl, a girl with cinnamon-colored hair and blue eyes, a girl who was looking into a TV camera and crying one word over and over, "Grandpa . . . Grandpa . . . Grandpa . . ."

April 1975

A continuing series of minor forays and adventures
can keep life interesting and sometimes exciting.
William Zeckendorf

XX

GRANDPA PUFFED ON his cigar and walked briskly up Fifth Avenue, his coat open to the fresh April air. Next to him Cassie wrapped her camel-hair polo coat tighter and took longer steps. She hadn't expected the April chill. But since when did events match expectations? It was almost eight months since that terrible night, months punctuated by flashing camera bulbs, TV newsmen and the thing she hated most: the flat, cold, deafening silence whenever she entered a meeting or a party. All her life Cassie had felt special: she was *his* granddaughter. Now she was special because she was *her* sister. And *she* was sitting out this pretrial time in a small house in Las Vegas, a bungalow that Papa Charles had bought for her at Diane's insistence.

"Did you talk to Stephanie today?" Grandpa asked.

"Yes."

"What'd she say?"

"Only that she's getting really good at needlepoint."

"Well, you have to be thankful for small things. Too bad she didn't try needlepoint before gunpoint."

Cassie cast a glance at Grandpa and shook her head.

"Listen, Cassie, you can't lose your marbles in a situation like this. You know, when I saw that on television . . . that, that gun . . . her face, you, all of it . . . the first thing I thought was, 'Why doesn't Cassie take the gun and hide her from the camera?' "

"That's what you would've done?"

"Absolutely. Stay cool. Don't panic. And protect the dummy. I'll tell you something else. That's what life is about. The strong protect the weak, and you don't ask what's fair."

"You think I'm weak, Grandpa?"

"Watch out, there's a big puddle there." He put a firm hand under her elbow and guided her across the water on the corner of East Sixty-third Street. "Now, what did you say about weak?"

"Forget it," she laughed.

"Cassie, did I tell you that Holt Hayward himself is going to be the courtroom lawyer for Stephanie?"

"Holt told me."

Grandpa shot a quick look at her. "He's not supposed to do that."

"Why not?"

"He's mine," Sam Cassman said, with some fierceness.

"What does that mean? And why do you say he's yours? Didn't I introduce you to Holt Hayward myself?"

"You were the conduit, Cassie. I was the big fish."

"Oh, pardon me, I'm just a nothing."

"To him, yes."

"Well, let me tell you something. I think you're wrong. Holt Hayward told me I'm the smartest woman he ever met—"

"That's always a good line, but you can only use it on women."

"What are you so cute about today?"

"Cassie, sometimes I get tired of teaching you the facts of life, but then I have to remember that you never had any parents to do it for you. Oh, what your father could have been. I don't know. Maybe Grandma and I were too easy on our children. When Bill was little, I'd look at him and say, 'Never, I promise he'll never have to work like I did.' So I did things. I gave him a convertible when he was sixteen, always handed him plenty of money. I don't know; maybe it was the times. He went to the war, and I felt guilty because he might die, and I'd only get richer. Whatever. I'm not sure I did him such a favor being so good. But at the time I thought it was right." Sam shrugged. "All right. Enough already. I want to talk about Holt and explain something. He's a user. But I'll tell you something else. I'm a bigger user. I know that Holt's a very unusual man."

"Unusual because he's good-looking and smart?"

"No, Cassie. That's the surface stuff. I always look below the surface. You won't meet many men like Holt. I'm a bit older than you are, and I can't think of too many fellows who have the kind of magic he has. Oh, back a few years ago Dan Topping had some of it. It's the kind of thing Howard Hughes has. You know what I'm saying?"

"I'm not sure."

"Holt is a lawyer in a big law firm. He's a partner. He's in a good position to see what's happening. He's into everything from real estate to the film business. He's a man's man. He even owns a piece of the New York Yankees."

"I didn't know that."

"Ah, but you see, I do. I manage to know about all the people I meet. Holt is the only man I ever knew who at forty years old didn't have everyone wondering why he wasn't married. In fact, with Holt they wouldn't understand if he got married, because"— Grandpa snapped his fingers—"that's how fast he can get a woman."

Cassie snapped her fingers in response. "Not this one." Was Grandpa making a sly allusion to Jimmy and the never-mentioned reason for their divorce?

"We'll see," Grandpa said. "Holt gets what Holt wants. That's why his firm is going to mastermind your sister's defense. I trust him."

"If you trust him so much, why didn't you want me to go into that Louisville building with him?"

Grandpa snorted. "That small potatoes deal? It's just as easy to learn with a big deal as a small one, and there's a lot more money in a big deal. And more people to learn from."

"A lot more fine and fancy people, I suppose," Cassie said, her voice insinuating they were anything but.

"So some of the people aren't so fine," Grandpa said, answering the tone.

"I'm glad you brought that up," Cassie said.

Grandpa nodded. "I see you've been carrying questions for months, but you held back."

"Yes, Grandpa, I did."

"That's commendable, Cassie. A lot of young people would think they have to start moralizing and reorganizing the company the minute they come in. I should be thankful you waited a few months."

"I'm serious. I just can't understand why you're so tied up with people like those Vegas characters—"

"That's how much you know. What business am I in?"

"Real estate. A little bit of everything."

"When you're in real estate, you're in touch with the world, all of it. There isn't a real estate man worth his salt who doesn't have strong alliances with the banks. The commercial banks, the contractors and the construction industry are all locked together because of strong deposit relationships. Those deposits make for fast friends. And those deposits are important to me. Deposits, not cash, because the one thing I never see is cash. Why do I need cash? I have access to money. Other people's money is always there when I want it. Now your Papa Charles always has cash. I used to envy him; he could put his hands on his own money. But that was before I learned that rich people *had* money, and richer people *used* money. So I learned my lessons well, Cassie. Don't worry about saving your own money; just go where the money is and get what you need. The money you need is waiting with investors. Now how do the investors make their money? I don't think it's polite to ask. Is there money in gambling? Sure. Don't ask me if those dollars go into prostitution or narcotics; that's not my business, but if those people want to take their gambling money and invest with me, why, honey, then it is my money. I just take the money and make more money with it."

"Grandpa, you never told me this before. I didn't really know where the money came from. I don't approve of what you're doing."

"Cassie, wait . . . watch out, there's another puddle. Listen, are you going to tell me how to stay out of deep water when you can't even stay out of shallow water?" Grandpa laughed at his own joke and tossed his cigar in the street.

"Grandpa, don't do that!"

"I invest my way—"

"No, no, don't throw your cigar in the street."

"Cassie, you're a typical young girl—"

"Woman," she interjected.

"To me you're still a girl. You've got all kinds of standards. Okay. Go ahead. You live by them and see where they get you. I've been around a long time. Where do you think my company would be if I didn't take every advantage? Maybe you think I should have said no thank you to the tax-loss carry-forward."

She shook her head. She couldn't remember the term.

"It means that when a company has a loss, it can ask for a tax allowance to help it recover. Meanwhile a nice, fat, profitable company can buy that losing company, merge the two and come up showing a loss, so the combined company can use the tax credits of the weak company and keep the profits of the strong company. Now that's what the clean, fine businessmen like your Papa Charles do. There are people who say he invented that tax-loss carry-forward to buy and sell companies. I don't think so; he's not that smart. But he sure used it. He took a tax loss, his daughter, and gave her to a profitable company, me."

"She's my mother," Cassie said in a quiet voice.

"Forget it already," Grandpa said with a wave of his hand. "We're almost there."

"Don't you think it's wrong to take gambling money and use it? Honestly, Grandpa, don't you?"

"Listen, Cassie, nobody knows the mother and father of a dollar. All you can do is run your own life honestly. I think I'm an honest man."

"But look where the money comes from."

"Look where any money comes from. What's so holy about money that comes from Chase National Bank? Everybody's in business for the dollar. Once I heard an astronaut on television, and somebody asked him to tell what made him most nervous, and he said, 'The fact that I'm riding in an aircraft with twenty thousand parts, all of which were supplied by the lowest bidder.' That's the society we live in."

Grandpa put his arm around her shoulder, increased his pace and guided her across Fifth Avenue. "I don't want to be late," he said.

"Where are we going?"

"One of my favorite places in New York. You'll see."

"It's funny, Grandpa, but I never would've expected you to ask me to walk up Fifth Avenue. Usually we take the car."

"It's a good thing to walk. You get a feeling of what this city's really like. Look, those beautiful apartments on that side of the street are for the rich, and on this side—Central Park—the most

[197]

expensive real estate in the world is for all the people. On one side of the street they rob to build on the land, and on the other side of the street they let you use the land for nothing. This is some country, Cassie."

They walked in silence. Finally Cassie asked, "Why didn't you ever move to Fifth Avenue, Grandpa?"

"I like my view. I like my apartment. And someday the West Side will make a big comeback. This is only a small island, only so many places to build." His voice trailed, and Cassie knew there was a story yet to tell.

"Grandpa, you're thinking of some other places in New York besides the West Side, aren't you?"

"You caught it, didn't you? You knew I wasn't telling everything. That's a good sign. Reading other people is a sign of a smart person. You know what's wrong with most of us?"

Cassie shook her head. Another Grandpa epigram.

"Most people talk to themselves instead of listening to others."

"Okay, Grandpa, you tried to throw me off the track. Now tell me. What's the next hot place to build in New York?"

He chuckled. "Not up here. The city won't go north. Not the building part of the city. It's going east."

"East? The East Side is jammed with buildings."

"East, across the river. East where all those warehouses are sitting. East, where they're building Roosevelt Island. That Roosevelt Island is a good idea, but it doesn't go far enough."

"What do you mean?"

"My dream isn't an island; it's a city. I want theaters and shopping areas and beautiful apartments and a private bridge into the city."

"A private bridge?"

"Sure. You can't add more traffic to the bridges we have. I want a small expressway that goes only to and from my city. I want to get that land on the other side of the East River, and I want to build a Little New York."

"And you can heat it with solar energy and really make it a terrific place ecologically," Cassie said, caught up in her grandfather's fervor.

"What kind of rubbish are you talking? I want a city that's

[198]

good to live in, where you can make money. I'm not writing James Reston's column."

"But Grandpa, here's a real opportunity to do something good for people."

"So who sits around and looks at solar energy? I want things that make people happy. Shows. Flowers. A good corned beef sandwich."

"Have you started buying land yet?"

"I'm not ready to answer. First I have to know how you feel about the idea."

"I love it."

"So does your friend Holt."

"How does he know about it?"

"Cassie, you're so naive. He knew about it before he ever came to the house in the country. Holt knew what he was doing when he met you; he even said that night that he'd come to Twelvetrees just to meet me. Holt is a very powerful man, and in my way, I am, too. So we had to meet. Meet or collide. That's the use of power. It was nice that we had you as neutral territory."

Cassie was annoyed. What right did they have to use her?

"Don't look at me like that. He wanted to meet me. So what harm is done?"

Cassie didn't know. She couldn't answer, but somehow she knew harm had been done. Her spirit sank a little. She was annoyed with herself for even caring.

"Some walk your Grandpa is taking you on today. You're learning a lot, aren't you?"

She cast a sidelong glance at him. Walking fast, faster, and still he showed no fatigue. She increased her speed.

"About Holt, Cassie. Don't get upset. He's tough, but he's good. I'm sure he's fair. We'll see."

"Are we taking a chance letting him handle Stephanie's trial?"

"No. Stephanie won't get the death sentence. I don't think she'll get a very heavy sentence if she even gets one at all."

"How do you know?"

"No, no, I didn't fix anything. I don't do things like that. All I do is hire the best professionals and let them do their job. Holt is the best professional, and we've discussed every part of the case.

He feels confident because of Stephanie herself. She's not going to go out into the world and murder people at random. She's not violent. She's just confused."

They walked wordlessly for a few minutes. Finally Cassie turned, "Grandpa, are you going to tell me where we're going? We just passed Seventy-ninth Street."

"I thought you'd guess by now."

"The only place I go when I'm this far uptown is the Metropolitan Museum—Grandpa!"

"That's where we're going."

"But you? In a museum?"

"Your grandpa has secrets you can't even imagine. I love the Metropolitan Museum."

"But it's so big."

"That's why I love' it. I don't love the Whitney. The Guggenheim makes me dizzy, and at the Modern they try to confuse me with all that new stuff. So I keep going to the Metropolitan."

"What is it that you like there?"

"Can't you guess? You don't think I want to see the Italian art, do you? Look at Pompeii. Those Italians couldn't build to last. You think maybe French? Not for me. They lost all their kings, not to mention the land. Me, I like the Egyptians. They built the only thing that lasted, the pyramids."

Cassie threw her head back and laughed. Just when you thought you knew everything about Sam Cassman, he threw a curve.

"Sure. The Egyptians built to last, and someday, Cassie," Grandpa said as they walked up the broad steps, "someday they'll talk about my city on the river the same way."

XXI

THEY SAT IN THE living room, a room the seasick green color of old hospitals and battleships. And, thought Cassie, the color of jails. But then, wasn't this little house in the desert a jail of sorts?

It was all so incongruous. Elegant Holt seated in—of all things—

an imitation leather chair; Cassie, her tense body sticking to the flowered slipcover of a couch that wouldn't have been deemed good enough for a maid's room in her mother's house, and Stephanie, trapped and birdlike, pacing the room.

Now Stephanie lifted the slats of the venetian blinds and shuddered. The groupies were still there. The newspaper groupies, the town groupies, the sightseers on the buses—all circling, sighting and waiting to land and trap their prey. "I thought this house was supposed to be so far from things that nobody'd care about me," Stephanie said loudly.

"Shh," Cassie cautioned. "You don't have to shout. I'm two feet away from you. Remember, in this house the walls are so thin that everyone out there can hear you."

"Vultures. Rotten, creepy bastards," Stephanie muttered. Then she raised the blind and shook her fist. "I hate you all," she screamed.

Holt jumped from the chair, and in one swift movement pushed Stephanie back and lowered the blind. "Sit," he commanded, "and we'll get on with this."

"I can't do it. I can't learn all these things," Stephanie moaned.

Holt grabbed her by both shoulders. "Do you want to live?"

She looked at him and slowly shook her head. "No. No, I don't. What for? You shouldn't even bother with me. I wish I'd killed myself instead of Sal."

"Don't talk like that," Cassie said quickly. "What's done is done. We've got to make the best of it. Look, Stephanie. Holt is here because he thinks—we think—all of us think that you're worth saving. You're my sister, and I love you. Now we've got to make sure that when you get on that witness stand, you do and say the right things."

"The right things are the honest things," Holt said gently. "I know how terrible this has been for you, Stephanie. It's terrible for everybody who loves you, too. Now let's just sit down, and let's quietly figure out the best way to make the trial short. Short but right."

"But why are these people always here? Why do all those strangers come to look at me?"

"My dear," Holt said, his voice as gentle as a woman's, "mur-

[201]

der among the rich is always interesting. It's a continuing story because it sells papers. That's why *they're* here. *I'm* here because I don't think you're guilty of premeditated murder. I think you were driven to an irrational act by a cruel, irresponsible man. Now let's talk about the trial and the way we're going to handle things."

"Everybody thinks I'm just some dumb rich girl who's going to buy her way out of this," Stephanie said as she slumped next to Cassie on the sofa.

Cassie put her arm around her sister and held her close.

"I wish that were true," Holt said. "Now look at me, Stephanie. Please understand something, dear. It's normal to feel guilt. Nobody expects you to go through something like this and not feel pangs of remorse, self-recrimination—oh, hell. Guilt. That's the only word for it. But go ahead. Let it out. Feel it. Cry it out. Scream it out. But get it out. Because that guilty feeling is the most valuable thing we have going for us. Look, dear, if you didn't feel some guilt we'd know you were a real psychopath. It's the antisocial person who can commit the vilest crimes and feel nothing. But you don't help anybody, least of all yourself, by the things you're saying now. You've learned something from all this. And the most important thing you should have learned is that you do have people who care deeply for you. Sal wasn't one of them. It's too late to help Sal, but it isn't too late to save you."

Cassie fumbled for a tissue and wiped her sister's tears. "I'm going to make some coffee. Go ahead, Holt. Tell Stephanie what we've been talking about."

"You're charged with second-degree murder," Holt said matter-of-factly.

Stephanie shuddered, but Holt ignored her reaction.

"Both first and second degree mean premeditation, but first degree is used if you kill a policeman, prison guard, correction officer, or official. That charge carries the heaviest possible conviction."

"I don't want to go to jail," Stephanie sobbed. "What if I get life?"

"You're talking about the sentence. I don't even want to get that far in this case. I'm only concerned with the charge. We

[202]

want to prove that you fired in self-defense, that you literally didn't know what you were doing."

"I didn't."

"Good. Keep remembering that." Then he intoned slowly, "You didn't know what you were doing. There's going to be a lot of unpleasant stuff, Stephanie. Photographs of the body. Coroner's report. They'll replay the tape of the Charlie Gordon telethon where you're holding the gun. It's tough, baby, but you'll get through it. Before any of that happens, though, we'll spend days selecting a jury."

"Jury?" Cassie walked in on the last word, carrying a tray filled with coffee mugs. "Why a jury?"

"Simple mathematics," Holt answered without taking his eyes off Stephanie. "We want twelve chances instead of one. When you get a jury, you know in advance that only two or three of them will have any real influence on the vote. But the rub is that you never know which two or three. The toughest thing for us will be to pick that jury. Appearances are deceiving."

"It sounds too risky to me. Let's get a judge," Cassie said.

"Stick to real estate," Holt countered. "I don't want a judge. Judges are tied in to prosecutors. Matter of fact, a lot of judges used to be prosecutors themselves, so that's where their sympathies are. Judges find it damned hard to get out the words 'not guilty,' and they take a lot of heat for letting people off. And one other thing. Judges are jaded. They've heard every story before. You get yourself a jury, and you've got yourself a bunch of people who love TV soap operas. They're eager beavers; they'll lap up the story we feed them."

"You sound so sure," Stephanie said, her eyes wide with wonder.

"With this trial I'll keep my batting average at one thousand," Holt smiled. "You're a cinch, kid. By the way, have you ever been to a shrink?"

Cassie laughed a hollow, no-happiness laugh. "Stephanie? She was the perfect one."

Holt made a note. "That figures."

"I wouldn't go near one," Stephanie said. "That was Mother's territory."

[203]

Holt made another note. "I'll talk to your mother's doctor, too. Good idea. Keep talking, both of you. Let's go back and pick up. Things that happened to you when you were little, when you were teenagers. Anything. Just anything. Go ahead. Start talking."

Both were silent.

Holt had seen this many times before, people who were eager to talk until the time came. He paused for a moment; he'd have to help them start the spool of memory. "Do you remember things when you were little, Stephanie?" Another pause, then, "Do you remember your grandfather's sixtieth birthday party at "21"?"

She gasped. So Cassie had told him.

That night . . .

That night of her first betrayal. "Oh, I remember," she said, the hostility and bitterness suffusing her once more in the relived moment. "Oh, I do remember. You do, too, Cassie. We'll never forget it. There was a dress Mommy wanted Cassie to wear. . . ." Now Stephanie lapsed back into the baby words and sounds of childhood remembered. " 'Member, Cass? 'Member?"

"I remember," Cassie whispered.

"It was a pretty dress. We had the same one, but Cassie didn't like hers." She giggled nervously. "Oh, no. Cassie didn't like it. She said it was a baby dress. That made me mad, but I didn't say anything. Besides, I thought it was pretty. Then Grandpa came and talked to Cassie, and pretty soon Cassie said she wouldn't go to the party. And Mommy—Mommy didn't go. I-I-I don't know why. But Daddy took me. Just me. Not Mommy or Cassie. He just took me. And we went to "21" together. And I was the mommy. I was pretty like Mommy, and I knew everybody would look at me. Usually they looked at Mommy first, then they'd look at me and pat me on the head and say, 'Oh, she's a little Diane.' But tonight everybody'd look at me because, ha ha, Mommy wasn't there. Mommy couldn't go. So I'd be Mommy. I walked into the restaurant just like Mommy and said 'hello' to the man at the desk, and then I said to Daddy, 'Be back in a minute,' and I went to the ladies' room. That's what Mommy always did when we went anyplace. She went to the ladies' room, and that's when I heard them talking. Two ladies. They were washing their hands in the little room where the toilets are, right next to the room where you comb your hair. And one of them said, 'Did you hear? Crazy Diane's staying home tonight, and Bill's stuck with one of the kids.' They didn't see me. They couldn't. I was so mad at them I just went out right away and looked for Daddy. I'd show them. Daddy'd be glad to take me. He wouldn't be stuck. He'd show me off the way he always showed Mommy off. But I looked and looked, and I couldn't find him. Then I saw him, and he was at the bar with Mrs. Brooks. You remember Mrs. Brooks, Cassie. She was Daddy's friend when we were little. She wasn't ever Mommy's friend. Daddy played golf with her . . .''

Cassie nodded. So Stephanie remembered Mrs. Brooks. Silently now Cassie catalogued them. Mrs. Brooks. Mrs. Faber. Mrs. Gelson. Of course. That's who they all were. Daddy's friends. Why hadn't she realized then? But who ever thought her own daddy had girlfriends? Certainly not a daughter.

"I wanted Daddy to dance with me at the party. Isn't that funny?" Stephanie leaned back, and there was a faraway look in her eyes. Now she was a grown-up Stephanie once more, her eyes blinking as if she were screening the years from then until now. Her voice changed back; the little-girl sound vanished, and the quiet, sad tones of adulthood returned. "But why would he want to dance with me? Why would he pay attention to me? I was the pretty one, but not as pretty as Mother. I wasn't smart like Cassie, so Grandpa loved her better. And Papa Charles never saw me unless I was being dragged someplace with Mother. Until that minute when I looked around and really couldn't find Daddy, I didn't realize he wouldn't dance with me or talk to me. I just didn't know that at all. But once I did I couldn't look at those people. They were all taking my daddy from me. So I went back to the ladies' room and hid in one of those stalls. Nobody—especially Daddy—even knew I was gone. I kept waiting and waiting in that bathroom for somebody to come to find me. But the ladies went in and out, and nobody even noticed I was there. I cried a lot. I remember that, and finally I went out again, and I knew Daddy would say he'd been looking everywhere for me. And it was true. He was looking for me. 'Get the kid. Fast.' That's what he said. He was talking to Mrs. Brooks, and he said, 'Get the kid.'

[205]

Not another word. He grabbed me by the arm, and we didn't even say goodnight to Grandpa or Uncle Dick or anyone. He seemed so strange. Daddy was just weird, I thought, and I was scared. We got in the car, and Karl drove us straight home. I got out of the car when Karl opened the door, and Daddy didn't say a word to me. All he said to Karl was, 'Keep going.' My legs were so stiff with fear I could scarcely walk up to the front door. What had I done? Why did Daddy hate me so? I rang the bell, and Bridget, the maid came to the door. Cassie, you weren't there. You were upstairs. Bridget told me Mommy was real sick and in the hospital, and I thought, 'Good, good, it serves them right. Maybe she'll die, and I don't care, and then I won't talk to him either. And see how he likes that.' "

Stephanie fell back against the cushions, her breath caught in the tide of her emotions. She shook her head slowly. "I understand now. I really do. They didn't mean they didn't love us. I mean, it was nothing personal. You know, it was different with Sal. That was personal. He personally had no use for me. I don't mean that exactly. He liked the money and showing me off. That kind of stuff. But with Sal, I was a thing. It was my mother in some ways, my mother—the worst part of her—all over again. Stand straight. Your shoes aren't clean. Comb your hair. Don't say that to Vince. Don't look at that man that way; he'll think you don't get any at home. He did it like that. Only he hit me when he didn't like what I did. Mommy never hit me. Never once ever."

Cassie put her head down, and the tears spilled on her skirt. Holt felt his eyes misting. What was it about these sisters that touched some part of him? Was it the coincidence of suicidal parents? Hadn't his own father killed himself during the Depression? Still, it was more than that. He looked at the sisters seated side by side. Poor Stephanie, in such pain.

Cassie, too, was pained, hurting from old memories, but there was a tough side to Cassie's pain. It was almost as if Cassie were defying the gods to bring it on; she'd take all comers. She was like Sugar Ray or Ali, Holt decided. She'd take a few bumps along the way, but she'd fight back.

The thought braced him. He didn't feel nearly so sorry for Cassie.

For three days Holt worked with Cassie and Stephanie reweaving the fabric of their lives.

At the end of the second day Holt had an idea he hoped would comfort Stephanie. He asked Cassie to call her mother and arrange to send Bridget, their maid, to stay at the house with Stephanie.

"I don't want her alone," Holt said to Cassie, "and you have to get out of here. You're beginning to look as frightened as she."

Bridget came the following day.

The morning of the third day Cassie checked into Memory Lane, a small motel outside town, where Holt was also staying.

Later that afternoon the sisters and Holt sat once again in the little living room of the house, to which the press and the public were laying siege.

"Can't those people hovering out there see we're not talking? At least not to them," Cassie said.

"We may need the press. Let's not alienate them," Holt warned. "Remember, we've yet to pick our jury, and we want to be sure that anything any prospective juror reads about this case doesn't produce prejudice against Stephanie. Bridget's coming was a good move and duly noted by the press. I do think, though, I'm going to ask to have the jury sequestered. I don't want those twelve people picking up the papers every day or turning on TV and finding some kind of story about Sam or any one of us that can make them think we've got too much money or too much influence."

Cassie nodded.

Stephanie, her mind wandering amid the ruins of her past, said nothing. She no longer noticed the people outside; she scarcely noticed the people inside with her. Even for Bridget she'd produced only the most distant hello.

"Stephanie, I want to talk a little more about Sal," Holt said softly. "Just once more, dear. Then Cassie and I will leave you alone."

Stephanie looked up but did not speak.

"Tell me what happened that night. Tell me why you were afraid. What started it?"

Stephanie began speaking rapidly. "There was a party at Véronique, and Mother wanted me to go with some cousin of ours. When I told Sal I couldn't be with him, he said I was ashamed of him. I wouldn't take him to a big party. He was some no-good singer, and my family was too fancy." She paused. "If you only knew how I hated my mother and father and grandfathers at that minute. I even hated you, Cassie. You were all the ones who made us rich. I hated being a Cassman and a Winters. I wanted him to know I wasn't too good for him. He was going to be wonderful to me. He'd dance with me. Not like Daddy. He'd know when I wasn't there. He wanted me around all the time. Nobody else ever had. I had to let him know I'd do anything for him. So I got down on my knees to kiss his shoes. That's what I wanted to do. Kiss his shoes. Oh my God. I wanted to kiss his shoes so he wouldn't leave me. And that, that, that was when he did it. Just when I loved him most." She sobbed in great, gulping sounds, but her story never stopped. "I loved him so much when he did it. He kicked me in the head, and then he stepped on me. He just stepped on me. I heard the bones in my cheek crunch."

Cassie gasped.

"Go on," Holt said, paying no attention to Cassie's involuntary reaction.

"I went to Cassie's house that night. She took me in. But I went back to him the next day after I went to the doctor."

"Why?" Holt asked.

"Because he wanted me. Nobody'd ever wanted me like that. He wanted me all the time. He loved me so much he got mad when I didn't do good things. And even when he was bad to me, he wanted me."

"Did he ever hit you again?"

"Never in the face," Stephanie said proudly.

"God help us," Cassie murmured.

"Where did he hit you?" Holt asked, ignoring Cassie.

Stephanie pointed to her arms, her thighs, her stomach.

"Never there?" Holt pointed to her groin.

[208]

"No, he said maybe someday he'd want a baby, and he wanted to keep the oven working."

"How would you tell when he was going to hit you?"

"Oh, I always knew. First he'd smile. Then he'd raise his arm and start to laugh. And then he'd begin to hit me, and all the time there was the crazy, wild laughing."

Holt rose quickly, smiled, raised his arm toward Stephanie and began to laugh.

Stephanie screamed. "No, Sal. No. Don't do it. Please. Not again."

Just as quickly as he moved toward her, Holt sank back in his chair. "I'm sorry, Stephanie. It's all right. But that does it. We'll plead self-defense. That's our case. You didn't know what you were doing. You were driven to a state of hysteria. The thought of his touching you was so frightening. You feared him with all your heart and soul and body. He was killing you by inches. You had to save your life. That's it." He snapped his pen shut, closed his notebook, and stood up.

"Tell Bridget to come in, Cassie. We'll give Stephanie a tranquilizer and put her to bed. We're going now, Cassie. Our homework's done."

XXII

"WE'LL BRING YOUR PARENTS out, dress them conservatively, and put them in the courtroom, Cassie. That always adds a good touch," Holt said as the rented Mercedes thrummed down the highway.

"Will a jury acquit her?" Cassie asked.

"*I* can get an acquittal."

"*You* can?"

"M-m-m."

"I thought you weren't trying this."

"I'm not."

"So?"

"I'm calling all the shots."

"*All* the shots?"

"All."

"Such as?"

"Picking the psychiatrist she'll use, the one who'll testify."

"Oh. And just who is that?"

"Dr. Herman Rosefield."

"At least he sounds like a Park Avenue shrink."

"He's not from New York."

"No?"

"No. I don't want the stigma of New York attached to this trial."

"Where's he from?"

"Santa Fe."

"And that's better?"

"Infinitely."

"How do you know this doctor?"

"I've used him before."

"Another case?"

"Not exactly."

A pause filled with her unasked questions.

"Mysterious, aren't you, Holt?"

"The doctor's wife was someone I knew."

She backed down quickly. "Oh, I'm sorry. I didn't realize. I don't want you to violate the lawyer-client relationship."

"It wasn't a lawyer-client relationship."

"Oh."

"It was a relationship."

"I see."

"It's what we in the East popularly call 'seeing one another.' "

"Ah, before her marriage you knew her?"

"No. During."

Cassie folded and unfolded her hands. She didn't look at him. She just looked straight at the road ahead. "I guess a lot of women turn to you."

"A lot."

"You don't have an inferiority complex, do you?"

"Why should I? It's just fact."

"Well, men are attracted to me, too."

[210]

He laughed. "Zingo. Who said they weren't?"

"Let's get back to the case. What's the shrink supposed to do?"

"Examine Stephanie, and then stand ready to testify."

"And say what?"

"He'll probably say that as a result of the beatings she was reduced to a psychotic state of fear and trembling. Even if the act was premeditated—and I don't for a moment believe it was—the doctor can trigger some of the insanity she must have felt, and we want that insanity to flower in court."

"But my mother—"

"What about her?"

"It'll kill her."

"Then it's her life or Stephanie's. Take your choice."

"You sound like a doctor. Save the mother or the child."

"I say save the child, but then I'm the lawyer. You're the daughter and the sister."

"You're tough, aren't you?"

"In some ways, yes."

Cassie's eyes filled.

"Save the tears for the jurors. I'm counting on you and your parents to act grief-stricken."

"You can count on that. We are."

"I just wish I knew the composition of the jury. I'm going to go for women on this jury."

"Why?"

"Because women all relate. Even if they haven't been kicked around by some guy, they'll hate the idea. Young women. That's what we need. They'll be outraged. Young guys could do it, too. Jesus," he said as he slapped the wheel, "the more I think about it, this case cries out for a young jury."

"Then pick it," she said coldly.

He laughed. "And hold the mayo? I wish I could order a jury from the deli. The luck of the draw is simply incredible. You use up all your challenges, and then see what's still there, and you panic. You're down to an old guy and a young black woman. What do you take? The young black woman, of course. But it just so happens that he's an old leftie from the thirties, while she's married to a cop and has a total cop mentality. My biggest fear is

[211]

that some rigid-assed man who thinks it's perfectly all right for a guy to kick a woman around will get on the jury."

"I'm sure that since you know everything you'll keep out all rigid-assed men," she said coldly.

He laughed and pulled into the motel courtyard.

"Good evening, Mr. Hayward," the doorman said solicitously. ". . . and yet another beautiful lady."

"Another?" Cassie asked Holt.

"I never promised you a monk."

"Monk, no. Respectable attorney, yes."

He laughed once more. "What's one got to do with the other? Besides, your generation invented sex."

"Not all of us are mattress testers," she snapped.

"Maybe you ought to be."

"What's that? A reverse invitation?"

"No. Just an invitation. No reverse."

"How do we know I can satisfy the great Holt Hayward?"

"We'll never know until we try."

"I don't think you're kidding."

"I'm not."

She felt her cheeks burn. So Holt really had wanted her. She let out a deep breath.

"What's that supposed to mean?"

"That I'm surprised."

"I care for you, Cassie. I'm not making a pass at just some woman. You're very special, and I want to treat you in a special way."

He leaned over and kissed her on the cheek.

And she felt the coldness in her melt. Maybe at last she'd find some warmth and tenderness, the things she'd been missing for so long.

She bit her lip, fumbled in her handbag, and handed him her key.

Almost from the day she'd met Holt, she'd imagined what it would be like to go to bed with him.

Now, lying next to him, she was finding out.

There had been a flurry of undressing, unfastening here, opening there, and this—this now. Sliding under the sheets in a motel that was far from the prettiness where you wanted all this to happen. Still—she closed her eyes. There. That made it better.

He was kissing her now, kissing her with kindness. A grown man kissing her as if—how strange—as if she were a little girl.

Suddenly she felt safe in his arms, safer even than Jimmy had ever made her feel.

She felt her body pulsating to this kindness, this generosity, this other side of Holt, a side she hadn't suspected but suddenly wanted desperately. She held him tightly. Yet affectionate as he was, there was a curious remoteness. It was almost as if he were watching them from a chair in the corner. The smell of him was nice—fresh and tweedy. Whatever that fragrance was, she liked it. She wondered if she were as pleasing to him.

"Is everything all right?" she asked. She didn't know what else to say.

"Yes," he said softly, and then he expertly began to make love to her.

Cassie felt she was floating outside herself. She was so, so sort of helpless. Not the way she usually thought of herself at all. This must be it, she thought. This must be what it was all about. "I love you," she whispered.

"Thank you," he said.

She felt flat. No "I love you" in return. Just a polite thank-you. Where was he? Where was the heart of him? Didn't he know what was happening? Couldn't he tell?

The early euphoria ended before the climactic lovemaking began. The little girl floating outside herself returned to the heart of her. All right. If he were going to be a professional lovemaker, so would she. She concentrated on him now, not on herself. It didn't take very long. Five minutes. Ten minutes at the most. Then . . . over.

Still, it had been surprisingly good. At least it was for her. She wanted to tell him, but he rolled over and said nothing.

She felt a sexual frustration that didn't match the events of the minutes before. How dare he do this to her? He had to tell her something. She rolled toward him. "How was it?"

"Okay."

Only okay? What did he expect?

He laughed. "I've had worse."

So it was a joke. Damn him. Now she was annoyed. "Did you ever have better?"

"I think so."

"Then let's try again. Maybe if we combine the score of two, I can meet your standards." The minute the words were said she hated herself. What kind of competition was this?

"It's not a question of standards, dear," he said. "It's goals. And who understands goals better than you?"

She felt her arms stiffen. At the moment she didn't know who she disliked more, herself or Holt. "Do you think you—this—was a goal I wanted to set for myself?"

"Not consciously. It sort of turned out that way. But then, we both wanted this. What were we trying to prove? Who knows? Maybe that we could get one another to—well, to bend—almost as if it were against our wills."

"So we dueled to a draw?"

"Looks that way. Oh, come on, dear"—he sensed her need for a sweet word; *dear* would do—"you've been a goal of mine since the day we met. I set out to woo and win. That was my goal, but then what's wrong with goals? Your grandfather knows you have goals. That's why he's been your champion."

She said nothing. No one knew their family now quite the way Holt did. The outsider looking in. And now he was describing what he saw, what he thought. After a moment or two Holt spoke again. "Listening to your sister tonight made me understand a lot of things. I'm putting the pieces together and watching the way S.C. plays you all. He's the master chess player in your family, isn't he?"

"You think we're all pawns?"

"Oh, let's not carry metaphors to silly conclusions. All that I'm trying to say to you is that Stephanie's story touched me. You can put all the parts of her together just by listening to that one sad tale."

She bit her lip. "Could you do the same with me?"

"Meaning?"

"If I told you what that night of my grandfather's party meant to me, would you be able to put me together?"

"Better than all the king's horses and all the king's men, my dear Humpty Dumpty." He drew her close and kissed her.

[214]

She hesitated. Could she trust him to be the first to hear the story? She sighed. Yes, yes she could. Not only would she tell, she must. Or Holt would think that night belonged only to Stephanie. But it didn't. No, it was Cassie's night, too. She began to speak.

"Holt."

"Uh-huh."

She cleared her throat. "I guess I was—no, no, I really was—I was mad that night, mad at them all. I didn't really want to stay home. I wanted to be at that party, but I couldn't go because of her."

"Her?"

"Mommy. It was her fault. Everything was her fault. This was going to be a big party. And Mommy designed dresses for us for the party that were beautiful. I could hardly wait to wear mine. I stood in my room and put it on at six. We weren't leaving till seven. I twirled. I preened. For once I was going to be as pretty as Stephanie. Not as pretty as Mommy, of course. But pretty . . . just like Stephanie. I was so proud of myself. I was really pretty. I ran to Mommy's room to show her. See, Mommy? That's what I wanted to say. But when I got to the door of Mommy's room, I heard her on the phone. We weren't ever allowed to go into Mommy's room when she was on the phone. We had to stand at the door and wait. So I stood there. First on one foot and then the other. Hurry, Mommy, hurry . . . that's what I kept saying to myself. Hurry and see me. Then I leaned against the door, and I heard her. She was talking to one of her friends, and she was saying, 'Oh, the girls' dresses are lovely, but it will be terrible to see them together. You know what happens. Stephanie always looks beautiful, and no matter how I dress Cassie, she always looks like a little bulldog, just like S.C.'

"A bulldog. That's all I was to her. A bulldog. I ran to my room, but I wouldn't cry. No. She'd never see me cry. I took the dress off. I can still see it. I tore two buttons, and I stood in front of the mirror . . . and oh Jesus, I growled. G-r-r-r. G-r-r-r. I was a bulldog, was I? Damned right I was a bulldog. Just like S.C.

"It must have been just a few minutes later that my mother came in and saw me. But you know how my mother saw me? She saw what she wanted to see—a little girl sitting on the floor who wouldn't get dressed. She didn't know I was animal growling in

[215]

terror and anger. No, I was just a little girl who wouldn't obey her mommy. I'd never obey her again. And I'd never tell her why. She told me to get dressed, and all I said was that I wouldn't wear the dress because it was a baby dress. I couldn't tell her I'd heard her on the phone. No. I couldn't . . . I wouldn't tell her anything. Then Grandpa came, and he acted as if it were a good thing that I wouldn't go to the party. That's Grandpa every time. He can find a reason bad is good. So my bulldog Grandpa said it was all right . . . no, more than all right . . . it was good for me to stay home, and gave me a speech about walking away. I understood him. I knew what he was saying. I never forgot any of it. But, oh, how I wanted to be at the party. When Daddy and Stephanie left, I sneaked downstairs, stood at the tall window in the living room, and hoped maybe they'd come back for me. But they didn't. So I went upstairs . . . maybe . . . just maybe Mommy would see me and ask me . . . no, make me . . . go to the party. I opened the door to her room and saw her lying there, just lying. Sort of flat and white. I screamed and screamed. I was screaming because I was so mad at her. I wasn't afraid she was dead, I was mad she was dead. Now she couldn't make me go to the party. And I knew I could never trust her with any part of me. I'd never trust anyone. I'd have to be strong. Just the way Grandpa was. I'd be a bulldog. Wasn't that what she'd said I was?"

Cassie lay on her back and looked at the ceiling.

Holt ran his hand gently through Cassie's curly hair. For a few minutes he said nothing. He shook his head in wonder at the whole mystery of life. Why was it that the night that had made one sister weak for life had made the other sister strong?

Finally Cassie asked, "Aren't you going to say anything?"

He sighed deeply and reached for her.

XXIII

Vince paced the small area at the airfield. Of course they'd come by private jet. S.C. wouldn't want any more publicity. God knows he'd had enough already. Next thing you know somebody'd poke around and blow the cover on everything out here.

Vince blew the sweat from his upper lip. Sure was hot in this place.

He lit a cigarette, then killed it.

Even smoking didn't help.

That broad. That dumb broad. Why did she have to pull the trigger and screw up his life?

He'd had such a good thing going. He was her nursemaid. That's what the monthly checks from S.C. were all about. And that S.C. was some guy. No complaining. No questioning. All he ever said was, "Keep an eye on the kid, and make sure he doesn't beat her up."

Nobody'd ever said anything about murder.

Christ. He'd probably have to get a job now. And nobody'd put him at the tables today. No, the new guys all looked sharp. Not Vince's kind of sharp, but that college-kid kind of sharp. They were all so young now. Jeez. Things sure were changing.

"Hey, hello, Mr. Cassman. Hello, Mrs. Cassman. I'm Vince. I'm gonna take you to your hotel. Your daughter will be very happy to see you."

Diane stood in front of the closet.

Which shoes should she wear?

It was the third day of this nightmare and still they were waiting outside, all those reporters. She'd have to look her best. Again, once again. Just like yesterday and the day before. What was it that man Mr. Hayworth? Hawgood? oh well, that man had told her? What was it again? Oh, yes. Yes. Wear something simple. What did he mean by that? Did that mean a simple little black dress? No. No. That wouldn't be right. She'd look as if she were in mourning. What was Stephanie going to wear again? What was it? Oh, right. A little gray dress with a white collar. She smiled. When Stephanie was six, she'd had a gray dress just like it. That little French schoolgirl look was so good on Stephanie. Poor Cassie. The matching one had made her look even more like a bulldog. But the moment Diane saw the dress she'd known—she and Bill were in Paris, and the dress was in a shop window on the Rue St.-Honoré. They'd just come from Dior, where she'd ordered that pink satin ballgown, the one with the voluminous skirt. She'd worn it to the April in Paris Ball that year, and it was *the* dress. Everybody had looked at it. Everybody had looked at her. Oh, how they'd photographed her in that. *The New York Times. Women's Wear Daily.* All of them. Diane Cassman in the best dress. And now they wanted to photograph her again. What to wear? Yesterday when she'd arrived with Bill, she couldn't believe how many reporters were waiting. And all those TV cameras. Pop. Flash. This way, please. Just one more. Turn. Turn to—oh, the closet. Yes, the closet. Must get back to the closet. Closet. Wear? What do I wear? Look at that dress. Isn't that funny? It didn't always look black. It used to be green. Why is it black? Black? I only see black. Oh no, I'm back down. Down in the pit. So dark in here. So dark. I have to crawl up. I have to get out. Out. I want to get out. Bill, you're wrong. See? It's not up to me. I am trying. I really am trying. I can't climb up. No. No. I can't do it. Wait. Stop. Now look. In the closet. Here. The closet. Look again. I wish I could breathe better. It's so—God, I'm suffocating in here. What happened to the air? What did I want? Wear? Wear something. Shoes. Which shoes? Tell your father he can pay the bill. I don't care if Gucci keeps calling. Don't tell my father. What good is that? He doesn't see the pit. Your father. Tell your father he can pay the bill. Your father knows. Stop asking me. Just leave me alone. How do I know why I need all those shoes? Daddy Long Legs. I want to wear them. No, you're right. I won't wear them. It's just . . . oh, don't you see? I can't make up my mind. And it's so black down here . . . so black . . . so . . . black . . . black. Stop, Bill. Don't tell me. I'm sorry . . . you'll be sorry, too . . . really sorry . . . reporters? No. No flashes. No more pictures. I don't know what to wear. Maybe if . . . a pill . . . a little pill . . . pills . . . and a nice hot bath and then . . . maybe . . . maybe . . . when you come back, Bill. . . .

Outside the reporters waited, unaware.

Later, when Bill and Holt returned to the suite, Bill put a key in the door, entered the living room and called, "Diane. Diane, Holt would like to talk to you. Diane! Diane! I suppose she went out." Where would she go? . . . now the fear, the old clutching fear. "Diane," he called sharply, "where are you?" Anger was always the best mask.

He walked toward the bathroom.

Why did he feel so frightened?

Later he said it was a premonition.

He walked slowly back into the living room and poured himself a scotch, his hands trembling. "This time she did it," he said quietly.

The jury had been selected and sequestered, so the news of Diane's death never reached them.

Eight days later, the verdict was, as Holt predicted, an easy decision for the jury of eight women and four men (no blacks; average age, thirty-eight). They all voted for acquittal, even the ex-Marine Holt had tried to keep off the jury. It turned out the marine's mother was herself a battered wife, and the leatherneck had been waiting all his life for a chance to get even with his old man.

November 1976

For those men who have the rare fortune to love what they do, the final shipwreck will take the form of small worries, and therefore appear less frightening as it approaches.

Jean-Paul Sartre
Situations

XXIV

SEATED IN FRONT OF the mirror, mascara wand in hand, Cassie focused on her wide-open eyes, lifted the wand to the lashes, and reflected on the *flick-flick* past four years.

One and a half *flick* years since Diane had done it. Amazing, wasn't it? You could know it and not cry or feel guilty or fall apart or—or—or what? She missed the lash and poked her eye. *Shit.* It never got better. It only gets ordinary.

Ordinary.

Wasn't that what adjustment was all about?

Not long after it happened, Cassie had been playing golf with Bill, and she'd brought it up. "Do you miss her, Daddy?" And Bill, his head bent over the ball, stopped and looked at his daughter. "Yes. Yes, I do. Isn't that strange? I used to wish she'd die, and now that she's dead, I can't live with myself."

Still, he was living with himself, living a life that used itself up in a series of self-destructive maneuvers. Within weeks of Diane's death, Bill was involved with a woman twenty years younger than himself. He would disappear for days at a time, then surface long enough to pick up his salary check at Cassman Realty, play some golf, and go to the fights, the hockey matches, the Giants games—and, in between, have a few drinks with the boys. The boys and the girls. They were the characters in Bill's act, and each played the same role: make Bill forget. The model twenty years younger was replaced by the secretary, who was replaced by the ex-hooker, who was replaced by the present hooker. There were never quite enough women, quite enough drinks to blot all memory. A year ago the golf games had stopped, and now Bill's salary check was mailed to him each time he neglected to pick it up.

Weak as she was, Diane was still some kind of control in a life made of Silly Putty.

For Cassie, adjustment was different.

Cassie had done well with Grandpa if you looked at the figures. There was the shopping center on Long Island, the developments on the east and west coasts of Florida. They'd even bought and sold the Empire State Building in the last twenty-four months.

They?

Who was she kidding?

It was Grandpa.

Always Grandpa.

Always and forever the great S.C., and trailing just behind was Cassie.

Darling Cassie.

Isn't that sweet the way that little Cassman girl—oh, she doesn't even use the Cassman name—isn't it adorable the way she just *worships* her grandfather?

Worshipped.

It wasn't the same anymore. It hadn't been the same since the day Cassie learned how Stephanie had gotten to Las Vegas. Grandpa may have had pure motives, but from that moment she knew he didn't have clean hands.

And Stephanie was paying the price.

But would life have really been different for her if Grandpa hadn't stepped in?

It's just that when your sister's a murderer and your mother is a suicide, you have a lot of baggage for the rest of your life. In all fairness, Stephanie did seem to be coping, if you could call running a needlepoint shop in Las Vegas coping. Well, did they expect her to discover the secrets of DNA? Of course not. Stephanie had never been the smart one. No, this face that looked back in anger, fear, and wonder, this face in the mirror was the smart one.

"How are you doing on that new Hausman deal, Cassie?" Grandpa asked as he picked up his toast. "Where did those dummies put the butter?" he growled, looking about the table.

"Waiter!" he bellowed.

Only two other diners at nearby tables in the Garden Room of the Charlemagne Hotel noticed the call.

"They're probably holding it somewhere with my raise," Cassie muttered in return.

"What'd you say?"

"Nothing. Nothing."

But she'd surprised herself just then. Outwardly she had pretended that all was well, but increasing exposure to Grandpa's flaws had made her understand their relationship in still another way. Grandpa was using her, using her to feel important just as he'd used the Vinces and the Mr. Hawkinses and God knows who else.

After their aerobic dance class one day even Hilda said, in the dressing room, "Cassie, isn't it about time you did something on your own? Get out of the housekeeping end of the business already. Somebody else can buy the toilet tissue for your buildings."

Cassie'd blushed; she had little interest or patience with collecting rents, handling service complaints, or buying supplies, but that's where Grandpa kept her.

"Waiter!" Sam bellowed.

Cassie jumped. Had to stop that wandering mind when you sat with Sam Cassman, or who knew where you'd end up?

"I think we're going to get the building," she said, in answer to his question about the Hausman deal. She decided to pay no attention to his breakfast request.

"Well, I'd say you've come a long way since you tried to rent the building on Park Avenue."

"So have you," she said, her smile taking the cutting edge from her words. "You've come all the way to breakfast at the Charlemagne on Central Park South."

"Not only are you smarter, you even look better."

"I didn't think you noticed that kind of thing."

But that wasn't quite true, and Cassie knew it. There was a difference to her look, and everyone noticed. Growing up and growing out of her early self had done it. So had Kenneth, with a becoming new haircut and the petite—but not junior-ish—clothes she was buying in Madison Avenue boutiques.

"You used to look too much like me," Grandpa mused.

She laughed. "I still do."

"No. Your face always had character, but now . . . I don't know? Do you wear pancake makeup or something? Pancake. Speaking of pancakes, where's the waiter?"

"Pancake makeup? Grandpa, that's about as modern as the Third Avenue El."

"So I don't know the right words, but I always had an eye for a pretty lady."

"So I've noticed. Who's the current winner of the Widow of the Week Club?"

"Don't laugh. I've got one now who's made it into the second month."

"What's her name?"

Grandpa paused, raised his eyes to the ceiling. "Let me see. What did she say it was?" Then he laughed at his own humor. "Her name is Ruth Granitz."

"Wasn't her husband—"

"Yes. He owned Granitz Steel. First woman in my life who's ever had more money than I."

"Good, so she can love you for your yellow hair."

"What's that mean?"

"Nothing. Just a paraphrase of Yeats."

"Stop all the fancy talk, Cassie. Real estate is dollars and cents—"

"Oh, Grandpa, don't you think I know that by now? Haven't I looked at enough figures and estimates? Grandpa, let's talk about something serious."

"What?"

"Me, Grandpa. Where am I going? I can't sit in that little office and put numbers together. Once, just once, let me handle a deal by myself."

"I think you need a little more training, Cassie."

"Grandpa, I'm going to be the most overtrained real estate person in New York, not to mention"—she gulped before she said the word—"underpaid."

"Underpaid? Twenty-five thousand dollars for a girl who isn't even thirty. When I was your age—"

"When you were my age, you paid a nickel for the subway and two cents for a newspaper. You ate at the Ritz for four dollars. Things are different now. You'll pay fifteen dollars for our breakfast."

Sam Cassman smiled. So she did have his fire, after all.

"And another thing, Grandpa. I know how much I'd make if I didn't work for you. I don't think I should be overpaid for being your granddaughter, but I shouldn't be underpaid either. Look, I did the entire rental of that building on Third Avenue. If an agent had done that, you'd have paid sixty thousand dollars in commissions. I get twenty-five thousand dollars a year. I think that's disgraceful."

"But who am I leaving everything to?"

"Grandpa. I don't want to sit around and count the days till you die—"

"I think that's what this waiter is doing. Where's the waiter?"

She was angry now, angry and frustrated. Why wouldn't he listen to her? "I'm talking about my life, and you're looking for some goddamned butter—"

Sam Cassman raised one eyebrow in amusement.

That action infuriated Cassie. She threw her napkin on the table. "Why don't you just buy the hotel and put your own butter on the tables?"

Sam threw out his arms. "Now you're talking my language."

"What?"

Sam shrugged, "Aaah, what am I saying? Who'd want to own this hotel?"

Cassie felt her temperature going down, her mind coming back into focus . . . own this hotel . . . wasn't that what he'd said?

Click.

Chance remark, S.C.

But click.

Oh joy. Now. Now was the time to say it. Now when she was still burning with the fire of ambition, when she'd finally gathered the courage to fight the bull.

"Grandpa!" Her eyes opened wide. "Grandpa, I have an idea."

"You want to steal the butter from another table."

"Grandpa, how would you like to put a tower over this hotel and create the most fantastic office space in New York?"

"That's crazy. Hotel Charlemagne is a landmark. It would take a lot of doing. Besides—" he stroked his chin.

"Think of it! You don't get rid of the landmark. You keep the Charlemagne just the way it is, and you put up a fifty-, sixty-,

[227]

seventy-story office building with commanding views of the entire city. Oh, I can see the prospectus now. It would be a dream come true—let me do it, Grandpa. Let me do it. It could be my—"

"Pyramids. Your pyramids," Sam Cassman said, his face breaking into a slow smile. "And at one hundred dollars a square foot."

"Come on, Grandpa. Let's do it."

"I'm not sure what we're doing."

"Grandpa, go with your gut instinct. You know this one is right."

"But what about *my* pyramids?"

"You go ahead and work on it. But let me work on this. I need your backing. The banks won't talk to me unless you're involved. But please, oh please, give me this one. Grandpa, think of it—Cassman Towers."

"I thought you were the hotshot lady who could make more money someplace else."

"I'll stay with you. You don't even have to give me a raise. Just give me a bigger office so I can talk to people, and hire somebody to do the work I do. I want to work on this."

"I don't know if you can do it, Cassie."

She smiled a broad smile and looked at him with the same blue eyes that were studying her. "But if I get into trouble, I always know where I can go."

"I don't know," Sam said slowly. "There'll be a lot of disappointments."

"But they'll be my disappointments. Just let me try."

Sam extended his hand. "Shake, partner. You just got yourself a deal. But remember one thing."

"Yes?"

"No raise."

"That's all right. I'll take it in my percentage."

"Your percentage?"

"Of course. My cut of the building."

"And what do you deserve, Miss Moneybags?"

"Fifty percent of the profit."

"Don't be ridiculous. Ten."

"I'm not ridiculous; I just want an honorable deal. Tell you what, Grandpa. I'll settle for twenty-five."

"Don't make me laugh."

Cassie stood. "Who's laughing?"

"Sit down. Twelve and a half. Take it or leave it."

Cassie sat down and said nothing.

"Take it or leave it," he repeated.

"Take it." She leaned back and smiled. She hadn't spent four years at Sam's knee for nothing.

S.C. grinned.

She should have asked for fifteen.

The first time Cassie wore black and ruffles to a charity ball, Holt looked at her with new eyes. Or was it old eyes and new appreciation? "You're very—oh, forget it. I just never realized how beautiful you are."

"Now that you know, don't forget again," she laughed. Funny that such a little thing could make her feel so good. But was it little? She was learning that no matter how liberated you are, there is no college course, no sale to equal the confidence that comes when a man who matters compliments you on your looks. Did that make her a traitor to all the women in the world? Cassie hoped not; she'd spent so many years hating her looks and feeling awful that she treasured the newly-won compliments and the way they made her feel about herself.

Even her father lifted his head from his vodka glass long enough one day to observe, "Success has gone to your face."

She'd laughed, but not with the same kind of lighthearted animation that she'd had for Holt's compliment. There was bittersweet praise in Bill's words, for as her closeness to S.C. seemed to grow, her relationship with Bill withered and faded.

Despite the general appreciation of her newfound looks, Cassie still tended to disbelieve most of the compliments. She was learning that a lot of men used "dear" and "darling" and "hey, beautiful" the way she used "hello."

Several times she and Holt had gone to parties where she was more noticed than Holt, a sharp contrast to their early dating days, when he had been the celebrity. While she sensed that this heightened awareness of her and her exploits did nothing to endear her to Holt, celebrity did make her more necessary. Holt certainly didn't want to be with a nobody; on the other hand, he didn't want to be eclipsed by a woman. Such a delicate balance to maintain.

Several times Holt had suggested that they live together, but Cassie was hesitant. "What's wrong with what we have?" she asked.

"Convenience without commitment," Holt said.

She nodded. She'd tried commitment once, and it hadn't worked. She wasn't ready to lay her life on the line once more. Or was it Holt himself who made her hesitate? There was a system of warning bells in Cassie's head, and they rang each time he suggested a semipermanent arrangement.

They talked little about their relationship, but they did talk long hours about business, and Holt, like Grandpa, told Cassie of great deals, both made and unmade. Holt was probably her best friend, but Hilda still had an important place in her life. Once a week they met for lunch at the Woman's Exchange. (Cheap and respectable, Hilda called it.) Between the two friends Cassie maintained a wholeness to her life. Marcia, for the moment, had drifted out of her daily life. To Holt Cassie reported successes, to Hilda, frustrations. Sexual politics, she called it, this division of talk.

Each week Hilda asked about the progress with the Charlemagne. "Have you picked an architect for the Charlemagne?" Hilda asked one noon.

Cassie shook her head. "I know you think we need a gifted architect, and I couldn't agree with you more—"

"Then call Calvin Gardiner. He's the next I.M. Pei."

"I don't think I'm ready for the next I.M. Pei."

"You'd better be, Cassie, or you'll never get your tower built."

"It's not that I don't think we should have someone good; I just don't have the confidence to hire an architect until we really have some idea that we can build this—"

"—and you'll never build it without a plan."

"But I have to get approval for the idea, and that's where I'm stopped."

"Why?"

"Hilda, I'm not getting anywhere with the landmarks commission. It's six months now since Grandpa and I first talked about the tower over the Charlemagne, and I haven't taken any important step forward. I can't get anyone to see me, much less make a decision."

"That's what real estate is really about. You wait for a bunch of jerks to decide things that aren't as important as you or me."

"And that's what makes them jerks?"

"That and the fact that they're elected by bigger jerks—us."

"But the landmarks commission isn't elected."

"The mayor is."

"The mayor! Hilda, you know as well as I do that if any proposal in this city doesn't favor blacks or Hispanics, the mayor won't look at it. He's only interested in the politics of the poor."

"Of course. The mayor can think that way because he's neither black nor Hispanic. He's just a well-meaning WASP who went to Princeton and Yale and has been apologizing for it ever since." She yawned broadly.

"I suppose you're right. You have so much political savvy; I wish I did. I think you have to have that in our business."

"You sure do. That's why we all play both sides of the street in election years. You never know who'll win. But I love it. Look, politics is a lot more fun than bridge."

"Okay. If you know so much, can you help me get to the right people? Why won't anyone on the landmarks commission call me? I make telephone calls nobody returns. I send letters nobody answers. I suppose I could tell Holt and ask him to help, but there's something in me—oh, I don't know—pride. Or foolishness. I just can't use his influence."

"I can understand that. You have to be careful of the favors you ask your friends; most of them stay friends because of the things you don't ask."

Cassie smiled. Hilda, in her own way, had just told Cassie she didn't want to be used in arranging the deal.

Hilda knew Cassie was drawing her own conclusions from that remark. She laid a hand on Cassie's arm. "I didn't say I'd never help. I will when I'm the only one you can count on. Get it?"

"I'm not sure. What do I do? Go to the mayor myself? Get the architect?"

[231]

Hilda sighed, "I hate to tell you this, Cassie, because it's exactly what you don't want to do."

Now Cassie understood. She knew what the answer would be. Together the two women said the words, "Get S.C. to see the mayor."

XXV

PORTER WINFIELD AND Samuel Cassman were standing in the reception room of Cassman Realty when Cassie came back from lunch. Cassie recognized the distinguished Winfield from his pictures. President of National Bank, head of this committee, member of that board. She shook her head. Grandpa sure knew 'em all. And they called on him. He didn't have to go to their offices. They all came to him. Pretty impressive.

"Porter, say hello to my granddaughter, Cassie Brown."

Mr. Winfield smiled. "Quite a grandfather you have, young lady."

Cassie smiled faintly. Now what?

"Your grandfather says you're very smart; you could even run this business."

"Someday. I said someday," Sam interrupted.

"And didn't he add 'maybe'?" Cassie asked, her laughing eyes letting Winfield know she was in on the joke.

"Come to think of it, he did," Mr. Winfield admitted.

S.C. put an arm around his granddaughter. "So who knows when 'someday' and 'maybe' will come? Right, Porter?"

The banker nodded. "Must be far off, Sam, because frankly, you look like a million dollars."

Sam laughed. "Good thing I look like a million because I owe you six million."

Cassie shook her head. That was what she was recognizing as Grandpa humor. Mr. Winfield shook hands soberly and left.

"What was he doing here?" Cassie asked.

"Come into my office," Sam said in a conspiratorial tone. "The walls have ears."

Cassie followed S.C. down the hall. Over the years the offices had remained true to Sam Cassman's philosophy that his own offices must contribute a profit. Early on S.C. told Cassie, "Nobody comes here to buy my offices; they only come to build theirs." So while Cassie would have liked an office with character, one that was more her style—which was turning out to be contemporary and sleek—S.C. kept the offices spare. Metal desks. Fluorescent lights. Naugahyde chairs. The first month on the job Cassie bought a giant ficus tree for her office. Grandpa walked in, took one look at the greenery and began to sneeze. "Plants give you diseases. Get that out of here," he'd said. After that disastrous attempt at humanizing her environment, Cassie had resigned herself to the tiny office with one window, and when she was finally elevated to an office with a corner window she felt greatly rewarded. "The executive touch is more windows," Grandpa had said. Cassie'd kept quiet. Wait. Just wait. Someday she'd show Grandpa what executive really was. She'd have a glamorous office like Holt Hayward's, an office planned by the newest architect, designed by someone marvelous. Meanwhile she enjoyed the larger space and secretly deplored the battleship-colored walls.

Cassie walked past her own office and entered Grandpa's to repeat her question, "Why did Porter Winfield come here?"

"He's an old friend," Sam said. "Met him when he was a young fellow appraising properties for National. I knew he was a comer."

"That's not why he was here."

Grandpa reached over and tousled Cassie's hair. "What's a pretty little girl like you worried about bankers for?"

"Stop that, Grandpa," she said indignantly. "Don't treat me like a little girl. Is there anything wrong? Anything I should know?"

"How can there be anything wrong with Cassman Realty?" Grandpa asked, his eyes growing larger with each word.

Cassie waved her hand. Evidently it was nothing. Just Grandpa playing another of his cat-and-mouse games. She'd have to learn to do that. Whatever she wanted she just blurted out at the first chance—just the way she wanted to do now. Well, maybe she'd take a cue from Grandpa. She cleared her throat. "Grandpa, do you ever get involved in politics?"

"Sure. I vote."

"Come on. Really involved."

"A little here. A little there."

"Did you support the mayor when he ran?"

"Sure I did. You know why?"

"Why?"

"I thought he'd win."

"Okay, but don't you believe in his philosophies?"

"You mean do I love the poor?" Grandpa laughed as he said it. "You know, there's an old saying, 'God must have loved the poor; He made so many of them.' As for me, no, I don't love the poor. They never rent in my buildings."

"So why did you vote for the mayor?"

"Who said I voted for him? I supported him. That means I gave him money."

"Why didn't you vote for him?"

"I liked the other fellow better."

"Who ran against him?"

"Who can remember losers?"

"Does the mayor know you didn't vote for him?"

"Of course not. Every winner thinks you voted for him."

"Well, Grandpa, I really did vote for him, and I'd like to meet him and tell him that I'm committed to his poverty program and his jobs program and—"

"So go meet."

"Go meet. Terrific. You can say that. But he wouldn't see me. You're the hot number in this family."

"Cassie, why don't you come out and say what you want?"

"What do you mean?"

"I mean why don't you just come and out and say that you want me to see the mayor for you because you want to build a tower over the Charlemagne Hotel and you can't get anywhere, so you think you better get His Honor's help. The mayor won't help you; he will help me, so you want me to go. Right?"

"Not quite. I want to go with you."

"So you want me to take you to see the mayor. Right now?"

"Right now."

"Then why didn't you say that in the first place?"

*　　*　　*

[234]

Hennessey, the mayor's appointments secretary, was a bearded male activist, someone who'd sat in, stood in, marched in, and now was "in." In the power office, close to the decision maker and part of the political process he'd deplored just a few years earlier. Still, Mayor Hank Crowell was the closest Hennessey could get to Kennedy. So Hennessey had hitched his star to the mayor and tried to shape him for the city. Hennessey had to admit that Hank was a pretty good guy. No question that women loved him, but—wise fellow!—he didn't give any of those political groupies a tumble. The mayor was married, a good family man, and if he did have a girlfriend, he kept it quiet, which was good. And one thing more about this mayor that Hennessey knew: Hank Crowell knew how to play his politics and fill his day. Two union heads to see in the office, a visiting movie star coming back home to plug her new flick (that would be good for the six o'clock news), dedication of a playground (even better), a luncheon speech for a Hadassah group and a dinner at the cardinal's request. Not a bad day for a WASP. Still, the mayor insisted that Hennessey sandwich in the next appointment. Seemed no one in town said no to Sam Cassman. Hennessey looked up. There they were. Sam Cassman, the real estate maven, and his—oh ho, his granddaughter. Not bad for an heiress. He'd have to check that one out. Another perk with this job. You got to meet a hell of a lot of rich women. And they all loved being close to power.

"Hello," Sam Cassman boomed. "Cassman here."

"I'd know that, sir," Hennessey grinned, "And this must be Miss Cassman."

"Ms. Brown," she said.

"But I thought—"

"She's independent," Sam shrugged. "What's the matter? You don't know about women nowadays?"

"Please be seated," Hennessey said. He went back to his work.

A minute later Sam asked, "Aren't you taking us in to see the boss?"

"Very shortly. Sorry to keep you waiting, but he has the head of the carpenters union in there right now."

That was a union Sam Cassman needed. "Let him stay as long as he wants," S.C. said generously.

[235]

Cassie crossed and uncrossed her legs. Her stomach felt like a homing pad for a thousand butterflies. Her palms were icy, and her face was hot. Who had ever said real estate was an easy business? She'd never been so scared in her life.

"You may go in now," Hennessey said six or seven minutes later.

"Where's the man from the carpenters union?" Cassie asked. "I didn't see him leave."

"We're like kings of old, Ms. Brown. We bring the new victims in one door, send the old ones out another."

The mayor was standing at the window when Sam and Cassie came in. "Sam, how wonderful to see you. You look like a million dollars."

"I should hope so. He owes the banks six million," Cassie said.

The mayor laughed. "You're picking up on your grandfather's cues, aren't you?"

Cassie nodded. "It runs in the family." She blushed. Should she have said that? What must the mayor think of her? Now she was flushed with embarrassment. But the mayor seemed not to notice anything. His hand was extended now. Oh God. Grandpa must have been introducing them, and she hadn't even heard. The mayor motioned them to a small sitting area. "Would you like some coffee, Ms. Brown?"

"No, thank you, Mr. Mayor." She was too nervous to hold a coffee cup.

"I'll take some," Sam interrupted. "Cream and two sugars."

"Two sugars still won't sweeten you, S.C.," the mayor teased.

Now the mayor sat back and looked at his guests. Let the coffee come. Let the day go. It was fun to watch these cat-and-mouse games, the games of people pursuing him for their own gain. All right. What did Sam Cassman want now? A speech for a group? A special license plate? A permit for a street fair? Sam Cassman's requests were usually easy to fill. A lot easier than those of some other real estate fellows.

"What can I do for you, Sam?"

S.C. smiled. He liked forthrightness. No beating about the bush with this mayor.

"I'm interested in making a major improvement in the city."

"Me, too," the mayor said.

"I have a plan," Sam said.

Now the mayor dropped the bantering tone. Sam was serious, and you didn't fool around with the serious ones.

"We—Cassman Realty—want to improve the skyline of New York."

The mayor smiled. "I didn't notice it needed improving."

"That's because you're not looking critically. I want more people to enjoy the view of New York, appreciate the park—" Sam stopped abruptly.

The mayor leaned forward. "Yes?"

Sam leaned back in his chair. Well, he had the mayor's attention. Fine. This was just the way he wanted things. The mayor on the edge of his seat. Sam relaxed. And Cassie? She was saying and doing nothing. Good. Let her watch and see how they do things uptown. S.C. reached into his pocket and took out a cigar. "Smoke, mayor?"

The mayor shook his head.

"I don't think you should pass these up, Mr. Mayor. Good Havana stuff. The real thing."

"I don't smoke," the mayor said.

"No cigarettes for me," Sam confided. "I always believed the surgeon general's report. But I like a good cigar." Sam made a Japanese tea ceremony out of the lighting of the cigar.

The mayor was getting restless. He leaned back, but he looked ill at ease.

Cassie was speechless. In just a few minutes Grandpa had turned the mayor's office into his. The mayor was now the supplicant and Sam the one controlling the timing, the one who might deign to grant Mayor Crowell an almighty favor.

The mayor made a stab at bringing the meeting back onto his terms. "Sam, I have a busy morning. Let's get back to the skyline of New York. I assume you had some reason for bringing that into the conversation."

"Fascinating subject, isn't it?" Sam asked. "You know, the New York skyline is an accident. That's what makes it so marvelous. No one could have planned it."

"Well, you've done some changing along the way," the mayor said.

"Not only in this city," Grandpa agreed. "We've built all over the United States. Texas. Denver. California. But I'm proudest of what I've done in New York. This is my home, and I want to leave a good city for the people. We've had some great real estate developers in this city, Mr. Mayor. I want to follow in their tradition. Fred French. Bill Zeckendorf."

"Yes, yes," the mayor agreed.

"I'm a builder, same way they were. So is my granddaughter. We want to build something of value in the city."

"Yes?"

Sam wet the end of his cigar, studied it, then looked at the mayor. "A tower over the Charlemagne Hotel."

The mayor choked. "Wh-what?"

"An office tower with room for multinationals and American-based companies. The most beautiful office space in town. Views of the rivers. Views of downtown, uptown, the park."

"That's ridiculous. The Charlemagne Hotel is a landmark. You can't ruin it. I won't let you."

Cassie swallowed her fear in one gulp. "We don't want to ruin it," she said. "We just want to keep it the way it is and build our tower over the present hotel so even more people can enjoy our city."

The mayor paused. "Do you have a plan?"

Cassie couldn't stop now. What to say? Of course. The name. Dredge the name of that architect from the memory bank where Hilda deposited it. "Calvin Gardiner . . . yes, Calvin Gardiner is working on it," Cassie said before Grandpa could answer.

"You've got taste," the mayor said. "He's the next I.M. Pei."

Cassie smiled. So that's what the world is about; getting everyone to repeat one stock phrase about you until it becomes the truth, gospel. Calvin Gardiner was the next I.M. Pei. Must be so. Even the mayor was mouthing the conventional wisdom.

"I assume you're going to buy the Charlemagne," the mayor said, "and I suppose no one knows what you have in mind."

Sam smiled. "Oh, sort of. You know, Mr. Mayor, these things get very complicated. Buying the Charlemagne is something we want to do. Quietly, of course. Very quietly. You know, General Oil bought the hotel six years ago. They've had a few failures in drilling, and they need a cash cow, not another loser. I've got

[238]

thirty days to buy the hotel in order to impact their current fiscal. The chairman of General is holding his job, depending on his figures for this year. Frankly, selling the Charlemagne is the only way they can look good."

"But who needs a one-time profit?" the mayor asked.

"The chairman of General Oil," Grandpa said easily. "He'll worry about next year's miracle later. You see, this is what buying and selling is all about."

"And I guess that's your business, S.C."

"No, not really. You see, Mr. Mayor, there are some fellows who never build. They don't want to. They just want to buy and sell. I call them traders, but I'm not one of them. I don't want to go out and buy the Charlemagne Hotel and fix up the rooms and paint the lobby and sell it for twice what I paid. I want to take the Charlemagne and keep its grandeur and make it a place for the 1980s, a vital office complex for the city. We are getting more people to come to New York to live and work. Why shouldn't everyone get the best of what we are? Do we want them all to work in buildings like that telephone company building on Ninth Avenue that has no doors or windows, just concrete walls?"

"Stop exaggerating, Mr. Cassman," the mayor said. "You know that people don't work in that building. It's just for equipment."

"So what's the difference?" Sam bellowed. "You get the point."

"I'd like to help you, both you, S.C., and you, Ms. Brown—"

"Cassie," she interjected.

"All right, I'd even like to help Cassie, but I don't think it's proper for me to get involved in this. People will say—"

Sam laughed.

"What's the joke, S.C.?"

"Mr. Mayor, what are your goals?"

Mayor Hank Crowell reddened.

"Just as I thought," Sam said. "You've got your eye on Albany. Well, why not? Ambition is nothing a man should be ashamed of. What you should be ashamed of is dreams you don't pursue. Hank—you don't mind if I call you Hank—after all, I've known

[239]

you since you were a councilman, and I'm old enough to be your father—"

Hank did not smile or look at Grandpa. Instead he now stared at the floor.

"Look, Hank, my plan is good for you—"

Cassie felt the hairs on the back of her neck prickle. Since when had this become S.C.'s plan?

"You've got a few roads to Albany. Let's look at things sensibly. After all, this is a private meeting. Kind of family, so to speak. You want to be the governor, and that takes money. I'm willing now to commit money to your campaign, and what I do the real estate industry does. You know that."

Still the mayor kept his eyes down and said nothing.

"Hank, a lot of the real estate fellows don't like you. What's to like? You're a reformer. Who needs a reformer? You don't win elections with charm and ideals or goals, and you don't win because you're tall and have a good wardrobe and a nice smile and a friendly wife. John Lindsay will tell you it takes more than that. What it takes today, Hank, is money. Money to buy the TV time. Money to get the word out. You win because someone commits four million dollars so you can get an eighty-thousand-a-year job. I'm willing to commit, Hank. I'll head your finance committee so you can make the run. Who else will do that for you? The blacks and Puerto Ricans? Come on, they don't have the power. Most of them forget to vote. With my guys, even if they don't vote, their money casts a ballot. You got two choices the way I see it, Hank. You go with us or—well, I guess you could end up practicing law. Maybe even be a senior partner. But not in one of our top firms. They're not too crazy about flaming liberals in those places. You know, they believe in the buck. Confidentially, everybody does, Hank. Even the blacks and Puerto Ricans. Go out and walk the streets, and ask them. They'll tell you. They'd rather be rich."

Hank Crowell looked up at last. This was what politics came down to every time. You started with the dream. You began with the ideals. But nobody ever taught you that you had to buy the dream and sell the ideals.

[240]

Hennessey cracked open the door.

"That's the signal," Hank Crowell said. "The next appointment's here."

"Well, do we have a deal?" S.C. asked as he stood.

"We'll see, Sam. We'll see."

As they left Gracie Mansion S.C. turned to Cassie. "Call your architect," he said gruffly.

"You mean we have a deal?"

"Sure."

"How can you tell, Grandpa?"

"He called me Sam, didn't he? Nobody calls me Sam unless they're buying."

XXVI

"Cassie, most people don't get the kind of chance you're getting," Grandpa said as he settled back in the limousine.

"Yes, I know," she said in an almost inaudible voice. It certainly did get boring having to thank Samuel Cassman every time you took a deep breath. Maybe that's why her father had checked out early in the business world.

"Take us to the office, Karl," S.C. said. Then he turned to his granddaughter. "What are you so glum about? You just walked out of the mayor's office and you're headed for a big project on your own, yet you look like you just lost your best friend."

"M-m-m, yes, I guess so."

Grandpa laughed. "Cassie, you're no different from any other kid who inherited money. You're all the same. You want the money. You want the fame. You want the glory. And you hate all us bastards who made it easy for you in the first place. Your parents were like that, but I—well, I kind of hoped you were different. Listen to me. I'm no kid anymore, but I can remember what it feels like. I knew them all, all the rich ones in this town. You know, you remind me of Vincent Astor."

[241]

"Vincent Astor?"

"He was before your time, long before your time, but he wanted to be a genius even though he was an Astor."

"How did you know him, Grandpa?"

"High-flying folks meet high-flying folks." S.C. smiled mischievously. "Cassie, I was called in on every big real estate deal in this town long before you were born. Karl was just a kid then, but he was already driving me. Remember, Karl?" The chauffeur nodded. "But Vincent Astor was really something. That was the oldes money I ever met. His great-grandfather came to this country from Germany in 1784."

"Was he the one who started the fur business?"

Grandpa slapped her knee affectionately. "You know your history. That's right. He made his first fortune in the fur business, but what the history books don't tell you is that he made a second fortune in the China trade and a third and most lasting one in New York real estate. When he died in 1848 he was the richest man in America. After his death, they were a family divided. Some of them went to England, and some of them stayed right here in America. By 1942 Vincent Astor was the holder of fifty million dollars in diversified New York real estate holdings. Today that doesn't sound like a lot. In those days, believe me, dolly, it was. Vincent owned the St. Regis Hotel on Fifth Avenue, some apartments and brownstones in midtown, downtown lofts and office buildings, Bowery tenements, meat markets, and even some rundown houses on the West Side. Well, when Vincent Astor went into the Navy in 1942, he decided to put his properties into the hands of a management company. He finally picked one, a good one, and the company sold some things off and acquired others. Well, by 1945, when Astor returned from the war, he was richer than ever because the value of his holdings had increased. A lot of us tried to interest Vincent in creative properties—building new kinds of developments, gambling on the future—but no, not Vincent. He had to prove that he was the financial genius, so he couldn't take any risk. For God's sake, his fancy friends might think for a minute he didn't do it."

"But I want to take risks," Cassie argued.

"Sure you do, but you want to be sure you get the byline. Just like he did. Cassie, you don't do anything in the world alone, except for coming in and going out. Those things you do alone. But even there you need some help."

Cassie said nothing. But her silence let Grandpa know that she understood his message.

Grandpa continued. "Vincent was such a snob. I can still see him sitting on his yacht drinking his martinis. And I'd talk to him. 'Vincent, I'd say, be an innovator. Don't be a trader.'" Grandpa turned in the car and poked Cassie in the shoulder. "That's still true. Whatever you do in this business, Cassie, don't be a trader. This city now is full of real estate people who turn around and sell their buildings to each other like someone selling quilts at a county fair. Remember something. The acquisition of sizable amounts of property calls for sizable amounts of money and a helluva lot of courage. You can get first or second mortgage money from the banks or you can finance through syndications. But no matter how creative the financing, it's what you do that counts. Make sure you build something worth building. We have enough cheese boxes in this town. Build buildings your grand-children will be proud of. If you do the Charlemagne, do it right. This whole city happened because a few men dared to dream, and you know something? Everybody thought they were crazy. I can remember when we had a string of slaughterhouses on First Ave-nue. Oh my God, the smell of those slaughterhouses! You know, there's a whole section of Tudor City that backs onto First Ave-nue, and to this day there are no windows in the buildings that face First because people couldn't deal with that smell. And then along came a man who turned the smell into a deal." Grandpa winked and laughed at his humor. "And it wasn't so long ago. It was the year before you were born. 1946. Right after the war, the United Nations was about to make Philadelphia its headquarters, and a smart real estate fellow named William Zeckendorf thought it was wrong for the UN to be in Philadelphia. He read about it in the paper, and he knew that the UN belonged in New York. So he picked up the phone, and he got the help of Mayor William O'Dwyer and Robert Moses, New York's commissioner of parks, and a brilliant young man named Nelson Rockefeller, and then Zeckendorf put a package together so that the Rockefellers bought that land where the slaughterhouses were—"

"How much did they pay for it?" Cassie asked.

"Eight and a half million dollars."

"The bargain of a lifetime, wasn't it?"

"In every way. Look what New York got for that. The best part, though, was that fine architects were hired, Wallace Harrison and Le Corbusier. But it all began with a real estate man's dream. And that's what I love about this business, Cassie. You can have a dream and make it happen. You don't need a lot of factories and a worldwide empire. All you need is the imagination of one person and talent. And one person who isn't afraid to try something new can make everyone live better. That's how we get buildings like the UN in New York. We don't get them from the Vincent Astors sitting on their yachts trying not to disappoint their ancestors and not giving a damn for the next generation."

"Do you give a damn for the next generation, Grandpa?"

S.C. looked out the window. "We're at the office," he said abruptly.

Cassie laid her hand gently on Grandpa's arm. "You didn't answer me."

Samuel Cassman turned and faced his granddaughter. "Don't you understand that if I didn't give a damn, I wouldn't talk to you like this? There's a moral in all the things I tell you, Cassie."

"Yes?"

"Make sure the dream is worth the mortgage."

She leaned over and kissed her grandfather. "Thanks for the mortgage."

Sam Cassman smiled. "That's more like it. I'll take my percentage in gratitude."

Cassie walked into her office and picked up the pink telephone-message slips. She frowned. *Mr. Brown.* Could it be? She turned the slip over. No. No more information. Was Jimmy back? And was he calling? It was years since she'd heard from him. What was he going to say? Was he married? Did he want her back? Did she want him? Was there—yes, there was a number. Her hands were clammy. She was still wearing her coat. And under her coat she was trembling. What could he possibly want? She had to call him. Now. Now. As fast as possible. She dialed. Three—oops, it should have been two. Too much of a hurry. Wrong digit. She pushed the receiver. Take a breath. Refocus. Dial again. There.

"Cassie!" Still the same happy boyish sound when he heard her voice.

"How are you, Jimmy?" She cupped her hand around the phone, cradling it as she'd once cradled him.

"It's great to be back in New York. California sucks."

The words didn't match her mood. "I think so, too," she answered.

"I couldn't get used to the freeways and that whole patio kind of life with the barbecues and salads. Give me New York dirt, and they can keep their smog and—"

Now she knew. She knew from the false cheeriness and easy denunciation of California life. "The job folded?"

"Well, not exactly. I can still do the same thing here in New York. Hey, Cass, I'd really like to see you. I know we're not married, but there's no law against having dinner with an ex-husband, is there? Besides, I want to tell you about this deal. It could be a great investment for you, and—"

She held the phone away from her ear, and still his voice, his boyish eager voice kept spinning another dream. Another soggy dream. So that's why he'd called. Not because he'd changed. Not because he understood what marriages were made of. No, he called because ". . . since your mother died."

So Jimmy was coming back in case there was anything left on the table. She slid out of her coat, let it fall to the floor, and slumped into her chair.

He was still talking. ". . . and so how about it, Cass?"

She sighed. How about it? How about what?

"No, Jimmy. No thanks. But good luck."

"You really won't come in on this? Or even listen?"

"No, Jimmy, no." She put the receiver back in place. She felt more alone than she had even at their parting. Why couldn't she help Jimmy?

All the emotion she had felt about the end of the marriage

rolled back in lonely waves now. The anger, the anxious feelings, and mostly, the horrifying, engulfing sadness of it all. Her heart remembered how it felt. Oh, the utter falseness, the desperate shabbiness of a relationship that had begun in glory and then whispered to a whimpering close. The pain could still be recast with a phone call. Who was it who said you couldn't relive pain? Oh yes, you could. Oh yes, all you doubters. Yes, I can. Yes, I can. All it takes is a phone call. One phone call and then you know. No matter when it happens, it hurts. And the guilt never goes away.

There is no good time to leave a man.

XXVII

HE HADN'T WANTED TO meet her. He'd seen her twice, but no one had introduced them either time. Once she'd been at lunch with Holt Hayward, and in the clubby atmosphere of The Four Seasons they hadn't known the same people, so they hadn't met that day. The next time they didn't meet she was walking along Fifth Avenue with her grandfather. You didn't have to know S.C. to recognize S.C. He was like the Chrysler Building or St. Patrick's Cathedral. A New York landmark.

And now here she was. Chic little suit. Corner table at Le Cirque. A spritzer in front of her. Sitting there studying the menu, she might have been any Upper East Side young matron at lunch. How many people here knew she was the heiress to the Samuel Cassman real estate empire? Oh, wait a minute. In Le Cirque they probably knew. Certainly the staff knew.

And he knew. He'd been briefed by the best briefer in town. Hilda Taylor.

Calvin Gardiner extended his hand. "Ms. Brown, how nice to meet you."

The captain rushed to the table. "A drink?" Calvin Gardiner shook his head no.

"Thank you for coming, Mr. Gardiner," Cassie said.

"I wouldn't have missed it for the world. You're getting yourself quite a reputation, Ms. Brown."

"Not quite the reputation you have, Mr. Gardiner. They say you're the next I.M. Pei."

"Wrong, Ms. Brown. I am better than I.M. Pei."

Cassie sat back and looked at him, really looked at him. Behind the brown eyes there was—what was it?—perhaps fear masked by bravado. Or maybe there really was a superior attitude, an attitude based on enormous confidence in his own work. "If you really are better, Mr. Gardiner, I hope we'll do business. I always approve of going one better."

"One better isn't enough for me."

"You sound like a young man in a hurry."

"My grandfather didn't take me into his empire. I have to hurry to catch up to you, Ms. Brown."

Cassie bristled. Is that how people had talked to Vincent Astor, too? No wonder he never wanted to do anything. "That's a rotten thing to say, Mr. Gardiner."

"Since we're going to trade insults, my name is Calvin."

"Don't your friends call you Cal?"

"Yes, but we're not friends, are we? Calvin will do."

Cassie wanted to get up and leave, but what would that prove? Only that she couldn't handle brash young men.

Cassie motioned to the captain.

"This is my lunch," he said as the captain arrived.

"But I invited you."

"I'm a New Englander. Our women don't take us to lunch."

"I'm not your woman, and I did the inviting, so I'll pay."

Calvin Gardiner glanced at the menu, then threw his head back and laughed. "You win. I just saw the prices."

Cassie looked at him coldly. He did look better laughing. Less angry, of course, but also less contemptuous of young heiresses. She wanted to tell him that she was a twenty-five-thousand-a-year heiress who still had no idea if—or when—she'd inherit the earth, the real estate, or anything besides the few pieces of jewelry her mother had left. "Is money the equalizer in everything you do?" Cassie asked.

"No. People, jobs, and ideas are what matter, but somehow it all goes back to money."

Cassie said nothing, her eyes fixed on the menu she knew very well.

The headwaiter, his hands folded and his smile in place, recited the *specialités du jour*. Calvin handed the menu to the captain.

"What are you having?" Cassie asked, fighting to keep her annoyance with this man from her voice.

"Scrambled eggs, sliced tomatoes and black coffee."

"But this is Le Cirque," she said. "Have something else."

"It's your lunch, not mine. I don't want to bring the Cassman empire to its knees with my luncheon check."

She cast a sidelong glance at him. What made him so prickly? Certainly he was nice looking enough. Plain but clean-cut.

"And what will you have, Miss Brown?" The captain was bowing deferentially.

"Grilled sole. But first, *asperge*. Wouldn't you like some asparagus first?" she asked Calvin Gardiner.

"Where I come from, we eat it with the lunch," he said.

She sighed. How could she work with someone like this? It would be a constant battle. Hilda must be crazy putting them together. Or else Hilda was trying to get even with him—or her.

"Why did you want to see me, Ms. Brown?"

"Stop this Ms. Brown business. No one calls me Ms. Brown. Absolutely no one. I'm called Cassie."

"That's a funny name."

"My real name is Alexandra."

"It doesn't suit you. Alexandra belongs to tall women; you're too short."

"How can you tell? I'm sitting down. When I am in my office, I can be very tall."

"I like my buildings tall."

"And you've designed a lot of buildings?"

"Hundreds."

"How many have you built?"

"None."

She choked on her drink, and she blurted, "Then why are we seeing each other?"

"You're asking me why? As I recall, you're the one who asked to see me."

She put her glass down firmly. "Let's stop this fencing and playacting. I'm not good at it." She turned slightly in her banquette seat and faced him. Now she saw his whole face. He had a

[248]

square, tough face. She wondered vaguely if he'd ever been a boxer. There was something about his looks. Keen brown eyes, the hint of lines in the corners. He didn't have Jimmy's dazzling good looks, nor did he have Holt's aesthetic appeal.

"You're staring, Cassie."

She blushed. "I didn't mean to."

"What do you see?"

"I'm not sure. You don't look like an architect."

"What's an architect supposed to look like?"

"I thought you'd be handsome," she said bluntly.

"And I'm not?"

"Not in the movie-star way."

"Did you want to hire someone handsome?"

"I don't really care what you look like, Calvin. I care what the things you design look like."

"Then ask me about them. Ask me about my philosophy. Tell me what you want."

She inhaled deeply. "I want to build the best office building in New York."

He shook his head. "I'm not sure I do. That is, I'm not sure you and I would necessarily agree on what we mean by 'best.'"

"I want a building that brings something new to the city. There's a site, a place to build where no one has been able to build, and I want to create—"

"You just said the magic word. I want to create, too."

She felt relief. Finally they'd agreed on something.

Now, swiftly, she told the story. He ate his lunch, nodded, and listened while she laid out the plan. The Charlemagne Hotel. The owners had to sell; the price would be two hundred million if it were just a hotel deal, but Sam would pay them a preemptive price of four hundred million. Then they had to get the air rights. The mayor was involved. He'd do it. Finally, they wanted to build over the Charlemagne and sell the space for one hundred a square foot.

Calvin Gardiner pushed his plate back. Her food was untouched, he noticed. "I think the numbers are beyond my wildest imagination. But I want to give you a building beyond your wildest imagination."

"I'm willing," she said.

"I'm not sure you are. It's easy to say you want beauty. And you could probablv take me to your home or your grandfather's, and you'd show me the art on the walls and the statuary and the furniture, and you'd think that because you live surrounded by beautiful things, I'd believe you'll build a beautiful building. But the two don't always go together."

"Why?"

"I'll tell you if you'll pay the check now and take a walk with me. Let's sit on a bench in the park, and look at the Charlemagne, and then let's talk about what I want to do and what you really want."

Cassie retrieved her stormcoat from the checkroom, and Calvin Gardiner helped her put it on. "Mink?" he asked when he saw the lining.

She nodded; she didn't bother to explain that she'd taken Diane's old mink coat and had her old raincoat lined with it. Wasn't it Henry Ford who'd said, "Never explain, never complain"? Let him think whatever he wanted.

As they walked out of the restaurant he asked, "Do you always eat like this?"

She shook her head. "Most of the time I have a sandwich at my desk."

"That's not a beautiful thing to do. Most of the time I leave my office, take a walk, look at the buildings, and then I think how I'd like the world to look."

"You're a dreamer."

"I prefer saying I'm an idealist whose time has come. You see, Cassie, I understand that we all have to build something that makes sense economically, but I believe buildings can also be beautiful and functional. I keep remembering that it's people who are going to work in those hundred-dollar-a-square-foot offices. Come on, walk a little faster. I have my own bench, and I don't want the pigeons to beat me to it. It's a wonderful day, isn't it?"

She looked at him. "I think it's cold and gray."

"Oh, but that light. Look at that wonderful light. No city in the world looks as good as New York in that light."

She looked again. He was right, of course. They walked up Sixty-fifth Street, and she watched her breath make small puffs in

[250]

the air. "My grandfather used to tell me I could blow smoke rings just the way he did," she laughed.

"Your grandfather loves the city, doesn't he?"

"Very much. He wants to build the pyramids before he dies."

"Maybe he will."

"The Charlemagne is my pyramids."

"Let me think about that," he said. Then Calvin Gardiner tucked his arm under Cassie's and walked briskly toward the park entrance. The day was deceptively mild for January, the kind of day that promises spring but still delivers winter. Black slush lined the curbs, and people moved with the slowness of winter clothes and January habit. The jaunty spring walk was not yet the tempo of New York.

"I like the winter," Calvin said as he guided her to a bench.

"This is your bench?" she asked.

"It has my name on it, and it has a very good view of the Charlemagne, almost as if I knew."

"Knew?"

"Knew that I'd meet a fair heiress who'd let me build a palace for her."

She looked at him in surprise. Was he two people or had she misinterpreted him earlier?

"Cassie, let's talk something out. You're a speculative builder, or let's assume you will be once you get the property. Do you really have the courage to do something out of the ordinary?"

"It depends what you call out of the ordinary."

"I don't want to build blank space."

"And I can't afford to."

"What I mean is I want to create something besides square footage. I've never built a building because at the last minute somebody always chickens out and won't follow my design. To most builders the important thing is to design as cheaply as possible, then borrow as much as possible, then put in as little as possible, and finally rent for as much as possible. Got the picture? Put in as little as you can, but get as much out as you can."

"I want to put in and take out equally."

"Can you convince bankers?"

"I think I can get my grandfather to help convince them."

"Can he really help you with the lending institutions who look at your plan and then say, 'It's very nice, but who needs it?' or 'I don't want to build a building that gets raves from the architecture editor of *The New York Times* and goes begging for tenants.' "

"I think we can handle that."

"I'm not sure. I know a lot about the economics of real estate today. You have to know your history, and I'm sure you do. New York was overbuilt in the twenties and underoccupied in the forties. Whole floors in modern office buildings were used as employee recreation areas at one time. Even after the war, in 1946, Rockefeller Center was forty-four percent unoccupied. And five years ago you couldn't give away office space in this town. I think we're turning around now. I think the day of the big office rental is coming."

"I'm gambling that it is," Cassie said.

"Then if you are, will you gamble on beauty, too?"

"I keep telling you I will."

"Cassie, I have a building idea for New York, something no one has ever done before."

Her eyes grew wide.

He leaned back against the bench and opened his coat. The heat of his ideas was warming him. "I want to build an office complex designed for people. I want galleries and a theater, a whole arts center, great shops. I want to build a little New York that opens out to the city and has a whole philosophy of living in one vertical unit. Could you sell that concept, Cassie? Could you?" Now his face was close to hers, and she took a deep breath. She'd show him. Yes, she could dream as big as he. Yes. Yes yes yes. She could meet the challenge.

"You'll have to fight your grandfather," he said.

"Oh no, I won't," she promised. "He'll love this."

Calvin stood and smiled. "Fine, Cassie, but I think optimism is one of those things only the rich can afford."

"Grandpa, I must see you," she said. Her coat was still on, her cheeks rosy, her eyes bright.

"Not now," he said, his hand cupping the mouthpiece of the telephone.

She started to plead her case, but Grandpa turned in his chair.

[252]

His back was to her, his conversation earnest, and she knew it was no time to interrupt.

Cassie went back to her office and sat staring out the window. Calvin Gardiner. He was different. At least he wasn't like anyone else in her life.

The phone must have rung two or three times before Cassie was aware of it. "Yes," she answered absentmindedly instead of with her customary brisk hello.

"So it's yes, is it?" the voice asked.

She laughed. It was Calvin Gardiner. "I don't know. I haven't seen him yet."

"Oh, you mean your grandfather?"

"Of course."

"I was hoping you'd say yes to me, Cassie. I want you to come away with me this weekend."

Her heart sank. So she'd misjudged him totally. Nice and polite, she'd thought. But now he was asking her to go away for a weekend, and he hadn't even known her for three hours. She was outraged.

"No," she barked. "No, I just met you, and I'm not running off with you. What do you think I am? And just what kind of man are you to ask me that—"

"Whoa," he laughed. "You're jumping the gun. I'd really like to talk to you about the Charlemagne, and I not only own a bench in Central Park, I own a whole beach on Martha's Vineyard. My parents live on the Vineyard about a five-minute walk from one of the world's most beautiful beaches. I thought maybe you'd go up there with me and stay with them."

"Well, that's a fast recovery," she said in total disbelief.

"Stop being the virgin queen," he chided. "Every man you meet isn't out to bed you, Cassie. Every once in a while you can trust one of us."

She felt a curious mixture of guilt and suspicion. Was he really telling the truth? Maybe he was. Maybe women like Hilda and Marcia and men like Holt, people who seemed to think sex was as available as hamburgers, confused her. Was Calvin really as guileless as he sounded? "Maybe I've lived in the city too long," she said in a half-apologetic tone.

"Well, when you want to get out of the city and breathe real air and see real people, call me, and I'll take you up to see my parents. You'll stay in the guestroom, next to my grandmother—"

"Stop," she laughed. "I believe you, Calvin. I believe you."

"Then will you come?"

"I'm seeing someone."

"That doesn't matter. This is business."

"Holt—I mean, he wouldn't like it."

"And you call yourself an independent woman," he said and hung up.

She sat immobile, her hand not leaving the phone. Somehow the hand on the receiver kept the connection between Calvin and her.

"Cassie. Cassie."

She looked up. How long had he been calling her?

"Oh yes, Grandpa." Her eyes were misted.

"Cassie, stand up and give your grandpa a kiss. I'm getting married tomorrow."

XXVIII

IT WAS SEVEN A.M., and the first light was filling the room. Cassie opened her eyes and sat up. Holt was already awake and reading. She fell back against the pillows. "I still can't believe it," she murmured.

"Relax, sweet," Holt said. "Your grandfather was bitten by the lovebug."

"Really!"

"Well, Cassie, it's not that he isn't old enough."

"Holt!" Now she was annoyed. What a dreary way to start the day. She wasn't looking for smart answers now, just helpful ones.

"Cassie," Holt said, with the age-old resignation of a man acceding to a woman's wishes, "I will put down *The New York Times,* hold you, and talk. Now would that be helpful?"

"Very."

Holt slowly and deliberately took off his reading glasses, placed them neatly in the case next to his bed, turned toward Cassie, put an arm around her, held her for a moment, then said, "What's bothering you about S.C.'s marriage? Don't you like your new step-grandmama?"

"It's not that. She's a perfectly lovely lady. I mean Ruth Granitz—"

"Oops—Cassman," he reminded her.

"Ruth," she said deliberately, "is a type. Facelift, nice clothes—"

"And rich. So your inheritance is safe. She did sign a prenuptial agreement."

"But why did he have to marry her?"

"Well, I don't imagine she was pregnant."

"Come on, Holt."

"Just because we think marriage is outmoded, should he?"

Another smartass answer. Cassie pulled away and slunk deep under the covers. Who said she thought marriage was outdated? Those were Holt's words, not hers. She thought marriage was a fine idea; it was just that no one ever promised you that every fine idea worked. Wasn't the tower over the Charlemagne a fine idea? Yet the plan was still far from completed. But—her thoughts drifted to Calvin Gardiner—the Charlemagne was on its way. In two days Cassman Realty would own it. Let that fact sink in, America. In two months Cassman & Co. would announce plans for the tower. Or three or four months. Whatever it took. It would be up to the architect. Up to Calvin. She felt confident. Calvin Gardiner didn't seem like a man who trafficked in defeat.

"Penny for your thoughts."

She was startled to hear Holt's voice. She didn't want to let him into her Calvin thoughts. She pulled up from under the covers. "Just thinking about the wedding. It was kind of sweet in its way, wasn't it?"

"That's better, Cassie. Yes, they certainly looked happy."

"I'm glad they were married at Grandpa's house. Somehow I wouldn't have wanted it at her house."

"Why?"

"Well, she's coming into our family, so it seems proper for us to have the wedding."

"That's what I call Cassie wisdom," Holt said. "It's wisdom that makes no sense to anyone but Cassie."

[255]

"Ha ha."

"Hey, little girl, I thought it was very nice of S.C. to include me in that family group at the wedding."

"It was, wasn't it? He didn't even have the Horribles."

"The Horribles?"

"Our cousins. That's what Stephanie and I used to call them."

"Well, it's always nice to be a stand-in for a Horrible."

"Too bad Ruth didn't have stand-ins for her children."

"Come on, Cass, they're all successful, aren't they?"

"You mean 'my son the doctor' and 'my son the dentist' and 'my daughter the wife of the professor.' Oh, God. That son the doctor is one step removed from the title of New York's permanent playboy—"

"Careful, Cassie. That could also sound like your father."

"Don't say that, Holt."

"Then for heaven's sake, don't be so tough on the rest of the world. Give your ironclad standards a rest. Don't be a snob."

"Oh, and I suppose you're not enamored of *Burke's Peerage* yourself?"

He flushed. So he'd had a fling with a countess or two. Did she always have to make those personal jabs? But then wasn't he making them, too? "Truce, truce," he said holding up his arm, then dropping it lightly across her body.

"No," she snapped. Grandpa's wedding was making her belligerent. "Let's get some of this stuff out in the open."

"Such as?"

She was silent. She didn't know what to say because she really didn't know what she wanted. All she knew was that something in her life was vaguely wrong.

"Cassie, I think that what's really troubling you isn't the marriage itself. It's what it means. Now Grandpa has a relationship in his life that threatens his feelings for you."

"That's a terrible thing to say, Holt."

"Well, I've thought it enough. If I were ever to be more important in your life—"

"More important? My life only centers around you."

"It does not, Cassie, and we both know it. Your life centers around S.C., and his around you. But somebody—one of you—had to break that chain, and he did it."

[256]

"Are you saying Grandpa got married to get me off his back?"

"Oh, you do have a way with words, Cassie Brown."

"Isn't that true?"

"I'm saying your grandfather now has a relationship—"

She drew herself up on one arm and turned toward him. "Men don't need a relationship; they need an audience."

"Oh, my God. Seven-thirty in the morning, and Ms. Brown is sounding like Oscar Wilde."

"Well, it's true."

"In that case, S.C. is going to have plenty of time to entertain his audience. A honeymoon on the QE 2. What could be better for complete isolation? The lady can't go off to Bergdorf's when things get dull."

Cassie was silent once more. That was a funny kind of wedding trip for Grandpa. Not characteristic at all. Grandpa isolated on an ocean liner for two weeks? Grandpa so far away he couldn't stop in "in case you need me"?

"How will you cope without S.C. for two weeks?"

"He won't really be out of touch that long," Cassie said quickly. "They get to ports all along the way, so I can reach him if I must. And, of course, I can always call the ship."

"But you won't, will you, Cassie?"

There was a strange, almost conspiratorial, sound in his voice. It was practically a challenge. Had S.C. put him up to it? Was this to be a test?

She slid down in the bed and looked intently at the ceiling. "No, I won't. I won't call. The option on the Charlemagne deal expires day after tomorrow, and I've got all the money in place, so that's no problem. Grandpa's friend, Porter Winfield of the National Bank, did that for us. There's really nothing that could go wrong. It's just funny not having Grandpa here when the biggest thing in my life is about to happen. But you know something, Holt? The world could turn upside down, and I wouldn't call S.C. This is the first time in my business life that he's ever left me alone in that office, and I'm going to handle anything that happens. Anything. You know that, don't you?"

"I'd put money on it," he said softly.

She said nothing. Maybe this marriage of Grandpa's would be a good thing. Something in this conversation was leading her to the

[257]

realization that S.C.'s marriage would make it easier for her to live her own life. Yes, that was it. Grandpa had married Ruth for Cassie's good. Of course. Wouldn't that be just like S.C.?

Holt, not understanding her silence, stroked her hair. "I guess there's something to be said for mature love, but the poets always burden us with young love."

She turned toward him. "Mature? Don't kid yourself. He thinks of himself as—oh, maybe a little older than you. But *old?* Grandpa's not *old*. Not old like those men on the park benches and old like the men on the newscasts, the ones you see when entertainers go to old people's homes. In his mind Grandpa's still a shiny dollar."

"Maybe he doesn't think so anymore, Cass. Maybe he thinks he's getting older, and he'd like a woman around. Maybe he finally got lonesome."

"Don't you think young people get lonesome, too?"

"Cassie, you're starting a very deep discussion at a very early hour." She felt his leg touch hers. Strange, but even after all their time together, lying here in the bedroom of his apartment for the hundredth time, she still felt small sparks go through her at the touch of him. She wondered if that happened to Grandpa, too.

"Like I said before, Cass. Penny for your thoughts."

"I think I'll brush my teeth."

"I already have."

That was her cue. She went to the bathroom.

Toothbrush in hand, she looked at the face in the mirror. Except for the foam around the mouth, it wasn't a bad face. She rinsed. Then she looked again. No, it wasn't a bad face at all. You didn't have to be afraid to give a face like that to a man. She walked quickly back into the bedroom and slid under the covers, her face and eyes smiling a welcome. Holt was reading the paper once more. She crawled across the big bed toward him, took off his glasses, put them on the table, brushed the papers aside and said softly, "Is there anything in *The New York Times* as newsworthy as this?"

He smiled. "No. And there never will be."

Cassie flashed a brighter-than-usual smile at the elevator man. Up elevator. Up mood.

Heigh ho
Heigh ho
It's off to work we go
No Grandpa in the way
It's a bright new day
Heigh ho
Heigh ho
Smile to the left. Smile to the right. I am Cassie Brown, woman on the way up. Woman in control. Going to burn my bridges. Ta ta, Grandpa.

She was whistling out loud by the time the elevator stopped at her office floor. The doors opened and—she took a step back. There was a crowd of people. Cameras. TV lights.

Pop!

Flash!

"Hold it!"

"There she is!"

Cassie looked around wildly. It must be the wrong floor. She'd just walked into someone else's life. But no, no—

"Cassie, over here."

"One shot, just one, Cassie."

She began to gag. It was Stephanie and the murder trial. It was Diane. It was—oh my God. It was Grandpa. It had to be. She let out a scream—

Flash!

Roll it!

—and ran down the hall.

The voices of the reporters were an insistent chorus: "What do you think about it, Cassie?" "Is it true?"

She was sobbing now. What was this? What had happened? The door to Cassman Realty was closed. Locked! She pounded on the door.

"It's me. It's Cassie. It's me," she screamed. Answer me. Somebody. Anybody. She never even thought of looking for her keys.

The door opened a crack. It was Wanda, the oldest office secretary. Cassie slid through the partly open door, and then she saw them. Both of them. Hilda and Daddy.

Later she was to remember the look on Hilda's face, the sharply penciled eyebrows drawn tightly together, the thin lips pursed, the body tensed and thrust forward as if she were walking against a fierce wind. And Bill's face. She saw Bill's face frozen in that same absent expression that she had last seen on the day Diane died.

Cassie's heart turned slowly. Her stomach churned. "Grandpa," she said in a choked voice. "It's Grandpa."

"Yes." Hilda said and came toward Cassie, her arms out-stretched.

"When? How?" Cassie gasped.

"We were going to call you at home when we saw the *Times,*" Hilda said. "I knew about the story last night around eleven; I saw the early edition of the paper. I called, but I guess you were out. Then I figured, 'Well, give her one good night's sleep. She won't have any more.' "

Cassie looked at them. She was outside these people. What were they talking about? This was a whirlpool, and she was a small ship. A tiny vessel being pulled. Sucked in by—by what? But she knew. She knew without asking. She felt her pulse stop, her heart quit.

"Grandpa's dead," Cassie said flatly.

"Oh, not S.C.," Hilda said. She moved back. "You can't count him out. S.C. can always make a comeback."

"A comeback? You're telling me Grandpa's dead, and he'll make a comeback?"

"Dead? Oh, Lord, he's not dead, Cassie. Did you or did you not see *The New York Times* this morning?"

"The *Times?* No, I—" She stopped. No, she hadn't read the paper; she'd made love. But this was no time to announce that.

Bill thrust the paper in front of Cassie. There on page one she saw it. The headlines that were bigger than death, worse than any dying. Death was an end. This was a beginning. Cassie leaned against the wall and read the headline: *Vegas Money in New York, Part I.*

She swallowed hard. Her eyes darted to the next line: "Samuel Cassman Reportedly Key New York Realtor in Mob Holdings."

So that's why they were there. The vultures, the press vultures, gathering to pick the bones. Her bones.

It was a long story. A very long story. *Continued on page 24.* With pictures. Pictures of Bill. Pictures of Diane and a cryptic account of her suicide. Pictures of Stephanie and a rehash of the murder story. And a picture of Cassie. Yes, there she was. "Favorite grandchild Alexandra Cassman Brown is rumored heiress to the empire." She shuddered.

"It's a bitch," Hilda said.

"Now we know why Dad was in such a hurry to get married and skip the country," Bill said, his mouth pulled down. Good old sanctimonious Dad, he thought. Getting his at last. The only rub was, would the money stop. Well, let it go. It was worth the price to see Daddy dear smeared.

"I can't stand reading this," Cassie whispered. "It's not true. It can't be. It's a pack of lies. Isn't it? Come on, Hilda, isn't it?"

Hilda said nothing.

Bill sneered. "Oh, of course. That would be Cassie's first reaction. How could Grandpa do anything that wasn't perfect? Only your parents were imperfect, my dear. Your grandfather is Mr. Clean."

Cassie didn't answer. But she knew that her pulse had come back, her heart was beating once again. She didn't want to listen to her father. "Hilda, please come with me."

The two women left Bill standing in the reception room and went down the hall to the sparsely furnished office where Cassie worked.

Hilda looked around. "Not exactly plush, is it?"

Cassie shook her head. "Doesn't matter."

"No, I guess it doesn't. Not now."

Wanda followed them and stood at the door. "Want some coffee?" Cassie looked at her and saw the empty, weary look on the woman's face. S.C. was Wanda's life, too. Cassie didn't want coffee, but instinctively she knew Wanda needed to be needed. "Two cups, both black. Then close the door and take my calls," she said. "Please," she added as Wanda left.

Moments later she was holding the mug between her hands and feeling her circulation start once more. She must have been chilled, but she'd been so numb she hadn't realized. Now she had to begin to make some sense of this. "What does it mean, Hilda?"

"You read the story," Hilda said.

"I didn't," Cassie answered shaking her head. "I couldn't bear to read it. You tell me. What did it say?"

"Basically that S.C. himself has no investments in Vegas, but Vegas people put money into all of S.C.'s projects. He—your grandfather—bought all his buildings and his land with money he got from—from—"

"It all figures," Cassie said. "I knew it, but I didn't really know it. Maybe I didn't want to know. But what about you? You figured he was mixed up with Vegas deals, didn't you?"

Hilda didn't answer.

"You're not talking much today, are you?" Cassie slumped in her chair. Neither woman said anything. "You figured it all out. Of course you did. You're no fool, but you never told me. When did you first know, Hilda?"

"When your sister went to Las Vegas with that broken-down singer. Nobody, Cassie, believe me, nobody except somebody with big connections could have gotten that guy a job as anything but an attendant in a men's room. When he went out there with a singing job, I knew he had contacts. And who but S.C. would have those contacts?"

"Of course. Why didn't I figure that out? Why else would Vince—"

"Who's Vince?"

"A kind of bodyguard, who was always with Stephanie. Wherever Stephanie went there was Vince with Irv, Sal's agent. It was all a favor for Grandpa. I can imagine Grandpa telling them, 'Watch the kid. Keep her out of trouble. Keep her out of here.' Poor Stephanie. We threw her life away."

"She did a pretty good job by herself," Hilda answered in her matter-of-fact tone.

"What should I do, Hilda?"

Hilda shrugged. "Go into hiding. Take poison. Or just do what your grandfather did. Get married and disappear."

Cassie looked at her. She said nothing, but she felt as if she'd suddenly been set adrift in a sea full of sharks.

Hilda spoke again. "You might as well know it all, Cassie. The story means the end for you. Cassman Realty is finished as of today. The *Times* calls your grandfather 'Sam the Laundryman' because he supposedly washed the Vegas money, put their money into clean deals. Tomorrow's story promises details of all the banks S.C.'s been in bed with. There isn't one banker in this town who'll talk to you after that breaks."

Cassie drew her breath sharply. She lifted her head. "Yes, there is one banker. Just one."

"Who's that?"

Cassie smiled—a small, wary smile. "You'll see." She thumbed through the telephone book, and now the small smile became a triumphant grin. For the first time she could breathe deeply. Help was on the way. She knew it. She felt it in her bones. She dialed. Ah, there was a secretary on the other end. Cassie said the name as portentously as if trumpets were sounding. "Mr. Porter Winfield, please. This is Alexandra Brown." She turned and looked at Hilda, gave her a quick, assertive nod.

"Oh, no," Hilda murmured.

But Cassie did not hear. She was smiling as if he were in the room. "Mr. Winfield," she said sweetly.

"Ye-e-e-es."

"This is Cassie Brown."

"Cassie Brown?"

"Samuel Cassman's granddaughter." Didn't he remember?

"Oh."

"I'd like to see you, Mr. Winfield. It's terribly important. I need to see you now."

"Oh. Oh yes, Ms. Brown. I remember. Your grandfather introduced us. As a matter of fact, I think it's rather a good idea to see you because—"

"Grandpa thinks you're a very special man, Mr. Winfield, and I need a very special man right now."

"I'm sure you do, Ms. Brown."

"Please call me Cassie."

"Yes. Um, yes. Cassie. Why don't you come over here now?"

"I'll be there in ten minutes."

"Good. Yes, that's very good, Ms. Brown."

"Cassie," she reminded him.

"Er, um. Yes. Yes."

[263]

Cassie put the receiver back, stood and clapped her hands. "All right, Hilda Know Everything. Mr. Porter Winfield will see me at once."

"Want me to go with you?"

Cassie stretched her body to its tallest. "I think I should do this alone."

Hilda shrugged. "I'll be here when you get back. And I'll have my first-aid kit ready."

Porter Winfield's office on Park Avenue occupied the top floor of a forty-eight–story skyscraper. The moment Cassie got off the elevator she knew she was visiting Old Money. Only Old Money furnished its offices in English antiques. Only Old Money had a receptionist on a floor that was untitled. "You must be Miss Brown," the woman at the desk said. Only Old Money was so secure it knew who was coming and didn't ask your name.

For the first time Cassie felt frightened. Was Big Brother watching? Who had told her name to this stony-faced woman?

"And you're here to see Mr. Winfield?" The Face knew everything.

Cassie nodded. You couldn't speak in hallowed halls like these.

"They're waiting," the face said.

Cassie followed the grim, black-clad figure down the long corridor. What did these people hang on their walls? She looked. Wow. Old masters. Or at least they looked like old masters. Tiny oils. Probably cost . . . forget what they cost. Who had walked down this path before? Which Rockefellers? Which chairmen of IBM? Which presidents of the United States? She felt her face burning. Her hands were like ice. She was still wearing her coat.

It was all so perfect Cassie wanted to scream. Where was the smell of Grandpa's cigar? Where were the shrill telephones? Where were the deal makers?

They were walking fast now. Faster. Cassie was on the receptionist's heels. Then, quick stop. Cassie almost stumbled over Miss Face. "Mr. Winfield is waiting for you," The Face announced.

Cassie nodded; she couldn't speak. She walked through the double doors into a high-ceilinged Georgian room. On the right were two low sofas arranged so that ten people could sit facing each other. Like a plush Amtrak waiting room. On the left was a conference table. There was no desk. She looked again. Where was Mr. Winfield?

A small door she hadn't noticed now opened silently, and through the doors came a gray-faced Porter Winfield. "Ms. Brown," he said, extending his hand. The room was so big it took him almost thirty seconds to cross it. Or did it just seem so long? Cassie felt the smile jell on her face. Frozen face. But legs like rubber bands. Ping.

Mr. Winfield pointed to the chair. Was there a chair behind her? No, it was the sofa. She stepped around the coffee table and sat on the edge of the long sofa. He sat across from her. He sat back. She sat further forward. You had to live here to sit back in the furniture. Cassie knew that without being told.

"Ms. Brown, I want to extend my sympathies. That was a most unfortunate story in the newspapers this morning."

Cassie nodded. Well, the man didn't waste time.

"Your grandfather must be very upset by this."

"He doesn't know."

"Oh, my dear, what do you mean?"

"Grandpa got married yesterday; he's on the QE 2."

Mr. Winfield raised one patrician eyebrow.

"That's why I'm here," Cassie said quickly. "I want you to know that I still want to do business with the National Bank."

"You do?" Mr. Winfield's voice was raised in disbelief.

"I still believe in your bank."

"You what?"

"I still believe in your bank."

"I thought that's what you said. You are incredibly naive, Ms. Brown. Or else you are exceedingly brash. You're Samuel Cassman's granddaughter. We cannot possibly do business with you."

"But Grandpa's been your customer—"

"Precisely. And it's been a very nice association—until today."

She felt the anger rising. "What are you trying to say to me?"

"Simply that I am calling a halt to a long and pleasant association, and it is with great regret—"

"Great regret," she parroted at the top of her voice.

[265]

"Please Ms. Brown, don't get hysterical."

"I'm not hysterical," she screamed.

"Ms. Brown, please relax. I told your grandfather I'd finance your purchase of the Charlemagne Hotel. Obviously under these circumstances I can no longer do that."

"Why not?"

"Because our big depositors certainly won't enjoy or appreciate the idea of their bank being mixed up with, um . . . shall we say . . . unsavory characters?"

"Oh, they won't?" Cassie asked, sarcasm edging the words. "Too bad." Now she moved further back on the sofa. "And why won't they like it, Mr. Winfield?"

"Oh come now, you know what some of these old-line companies are like."

"No, no, I really don't. I think you'd better tell me."

"Well, they're particular about the people with whom they do business. And we don't want the taint of the rackets."

"Mr. Winfield, may I ask you a personal question?"

"I'm not certain."

"Good. I'll ask anyway. Mr. Winfield, do you ask to see the mothers and fathers of all your dollars?"

"I don't know what you're trying to say."

"I'm saying that you have the deposits of the Bonchese Corporation, and its executives were indicted for the bribing of government officials in the Far East. Did you make them take their money away?"

"I-I don't know."

"But I do know. Because I can remember when it happened, and my grandfather said that on a day like that banks closed their eyes. I'm telling you I want you to close your eyes again today."

"Impossible."

"Of course it's not impossible. Look at the business we do with you."

"No, Ms. Brown. You no longer do business with us. That's why I wanted to see you when you phoned. I wanted to tell you in person we're calling your loans."

"Calling my loans? But they're my grandfather's."

"Not if he isn't here. Who's authorized in your business to speak for S.C.?"

She paused. Of course no one could speak for Grandpa. Not ever.

"Why are you doing this, Mr. Winfield?"

"Because we have depositors who—"

"Bullshit, Mr. Winfield."

He gasped.

"All right then. Poppycock."

He choked briefly.

"I'll tell you why you're calling these loans, Mr. Winfield, and then you'll really have something to cough about. You think I'm afraid of you. You think this story will make me panic and run away. And then in forty-eight hours when my option expires you'll hop right in there, pick up the Charlemagne and the rest of our properties, and within days you'll control the Cassman holdings. But it's not really going to work that way for you. Tomorrow the newspapers will have your name on the front page, and then let's see how you'll like having the reporters on your doorstep hounding you. Let's see what skeletons are rattling in that blue-blooded closet of yours."

"Ms. Brown, the only reason for my doing this is that my depositors have been calling all morning. They object to—"

"Isn't it funny that when the Vegas deals came crawling through the transom yesterday nobody bothered to smell the money? Now all of a sudden, deals hit the newspapers, and you're worried about what your luncheon club will think."

"I have a responsibility—"

She stood. "That's lovely. Just lovely. But you won't get rid of me so easily. Nobody will. You see, you're not playing fair with me. Mr. Winfield. What you don't realize is that I'm me. I'm not Sam Cassman." She drew her breath sharply. She'd never realized that until now.

"What I do I'll do in my own name," she said her voice growing stronger. "I want to be somebody in this town, and I will be. And not with 'tainted money.' My money will be cleaner than any money in this bank. I don't have anything to do with those

[267]

Vegas characters, but you don't seem to be interested in that, do you? But it's true. I don't have funny money. Nobody's paying me off. Nobody's financing me. Not anybody. I'm clean. One hundred percent clean. I'm not going to let your filthy story and innuendos stop me. I'm going to build that Charlemagne Tower. And nobody's going to stop me. Not *The New York Times* and not the National Bank. And not—and not—" now her voice broke, "not even Samuel Cassman."

The tears spilled down her cheeks. She hadn't meant to cry, but this was a different kind of crying. Not weak, but proud and strong.

Porter Winfield shifted uneasily in his seat.

"Ms. Brown, I admire your spirit—"

"That isn't all you'll admire about me, Mr. Winfield. Just you wait."

Then Cassie strode out the door. Long purposeful strides. Past the old masters. Over the thick carpet. Out the double doors. Down the high speed elevator.

Once outside Cassie hailed a cab, gave the address of her office and put her head in her hands. She was breathing hard. But she wouldn't cry now. No, the crying was over. Damn them all. You don't cry when the fish don't bite. You think. Think hard.

It was a full five minutes before Cassie raised her head. Her eyes were clear. She breathed deeply. She smiled. In those minutes all the words and epithets had been erased. The blackboard was clean once more. So Grandpa had failed her. It was a fact of life, and she had to face it. and fight. She couldn't bemoan Grandpa's desertion, curse Vince and cry for Stephanie. No. Here in her hands was the future. Two days from now she had to take control of the Charlemagne Hotel. She had to get the money. That was Step One.

Hilda was still sitting in Cassie's office when she came back.

"I saw Porter Winfield. You were right. He won't go along with me."

Hilda put her hands up. "Hello, Cassie, and welcome to the world."

Cassie sat at her desk, still wearing her coat. "What happened while I was out?"

"Every TV station, newspaper, and business magazine is calling. I just said you were out."

"Well, I'm not," Cassie said briskly. She buzzed for Wanda. "Let's issue a statement," she said to the secretary. "We'll announce that Alexandra Cassman has taken control of Cassman Realty until further notice."

"Good for you, kid," Hilda said.

"I'm not sure your grandfather would approve," Wanda said.

"If he were here, we'd ask him," Cassie snapped. "He's not so I'm making all the decisions. Now, let's get on with it. Any messages while I was out?"

"Besides the newspapers?"

"Yes."

"Well, your friend Marcia called to say she's thinking of you."

Cassie smiled for the first time. "Old friends are the best friends. Like you, Hilda. And the other message?"

"Mr. Calvin Gardiner."

"I suppose he's backing out," Cassie muttered.

"The message is," now she read her notes carefully. " 'Count on me for the plan. I will not call again until you're ready to take the room next to my grandmother. When you are, call me any time of day or night.' "

Cassie nodded. New friends could be good, too.

"What does that mean?" Hilda asked.

"Private message, Hilda. But knowing Calvin is with me is a plus. It'll help with my first step, and my first step is to get the money." Then Cassie turned and looked at Hilda, Cassie's eyes as old as the winter day. "There's just one thing I'm not sure about."

"What's that?"

"The name of the son of a bitch who ratted to the *Times.*"

"It probably wasn't one person."

"Sure it was. One rotten person who wants to see this deal fall apart. Think a minute. Think. Who? Who would want S.C. dead financially?"

"Well, Cassie, ask yourself, 'Who are S.C.'s enemies?'."

"That's easy," she grinned. "Practically everybody. No, that's a joke. Forgive me, Hilda. I'm a little bananas by now. In the cab, though, I was thinking about who would do a thing like this. It could have been Porter Winfield, except that he'll get his name smeared in this. So I ruled him out. We have to think of someone who wouldn't get smeared. Come on, help me. Who comes out smelling like a rose?"

"Your other grandfather," Hilda said.

"Of course," Cassie whispered. "Of course."

"Oh, Cassie, I was kidding."

"I'm not. Sure. Papa Charles had every reason. Why don't I ever see what's going on all around me?"

"Cassie, really. Diane was Charles's daughter."

"She's dead now, and Papa Charles has a real motive for sinking Grandpa. Look, he never thought I should have gone to work for Cassman Realty. And if Cassman Realty fails, Charles figures I'll have to go to him and beg for money and a job—"

"Will you?"

"No. Damn it. No, I'll go everyplace else first."

"Well, that's mighty interesting, Alexandra Cassman Brown. Because if you can't get this grandfather's money and you won't take that grandfather's money, and no one will give you bank money, what's your choice?"

Cassie thought for a minute. "There's only one person in this world who'll give me anything I want."

"Who's that?"

"Holt, of course."

XXIX

FROM THE MOMENT SHE said his name Cassie felt a warming sense of relief. Responsibility weighed on her shoulders. Now there'd be someone to share the load. A man. A caring man. Equal pay for equal work wasn't enough, and it never would be for a woman like her. She wanted—no, she needed—a man who loved her enough to listen and advise. There were always problems to be solved (how do you figure the multiple of a building sale?), but somehow Cassie felt safer when a man gave the answers. Not that men had *all* the answers (the multiple varies depending on . . .). No, men could back down, and did all the time. Nonetheless, there *was* a difference between men and women. A powerful difference. Men were still the bank presidents and the heads of networks and the chief executive officers of all the big real estate companies. True, a woman like Leona Helmsley wielded great power in real estate—she was the president—but her husband, Harry, was even more powerful. He was the chairman. Hilda said things were getting better for women. Yet, if she really believed that, why did Hilda keep her oar in the co-op market and not swim with the big fish in commercial properties? Either she was too old or too afraid. Maybe the timing was off for Hilda. Well, it wasn't for Cassie. And she was just coming into her own. There were signs of it everywhere. Wasn't she speaking up without that old fear? She'd told Grandpa, she had, that she wouldn't do women's work—oh no, definitely not—hadn't she told Grandpa she wanted to end her housekeeping role in the company? Grudgingly, he'd agreed. But of course, that was the duality, the dichotomy, of women today; you wanted men's roles, but you had to do women's work to get them. Secretary. Purchasing. Details. Smile at a man and move up. Always get a man to like you, to approve. Nobody feels secure without a man's approbation. Women can start old-girl networks with you, but men promote you. An ally like Hilda doesn't make you believe that all problems can be solved.

But an ally like Holt?

Yes.

Just the sound of his name—Holt!—was a presence.

And when she went to his apartment, he held her close and said the magic words, "No problem, love."

Her blue eyes widened. "No problem? I've just been through the most horrendous day of my life, and you say 'no problem'?"

"Come on, Cassie, come into the bedroom. Relax. We'll talk. This is just a newspaper story. It'll all blow over, and you'll be that much stronger for surviving it."

Cassie fell into one of the overstuffed chairs. She looked around. Was this the same place where she'd known such happiness just hours before? Yes. There were the same brass reading lamps on either side of the bed, the same telephone on his side, the same TV set on hers, the same captain's desk in the corner, the same armoire. But she wasn't the same Cassie, and he seemed a different Holt.

"Don't look at me like that, Cass. I can't bear to see how miserable you are." He knelt next to the chair and put an arm around her.

He felt so safe. "Holt, I want my building, my dream. I was within hours of getting the money so that I could buy the hotel. And now this has happened. I can't figure it all out."

He smoothed her curly hair. "Don't try. Don't even try," he crooned.

"I have to. I feel as if somebody had hit me in the stomach. There's some kind of conspiracy."

He laughed sympathetically. "Call it Cassiegate."

"I told you it wasn't like Grandpa to go off on a honeymoon where he couldn't be reached. Maybe I should call him. I can always put in a call to the ship—"

"But you said you wouldn't," Holt broke in.

"I know, but that was before I knew all his loans would be called."

"What?"

"That's what Porter Winfield said. Holt, let's run this down once more. Listen to what's going on, and see if you can help me sort it all out."

"Shoot."

"It started when Grandpa suddenly decided to get married and left on his honeymoon. The very next morning—today—*The New York Times* breaks a story about Sam the Laundryman and his connections in Vegas. All right, those are the facts. The results are that, number one, we have all become a media event, and number two, which is really number one—Porter Winfield, chairman of the National Bank, Grandpa's number one bank and maybe one of the most prestigious banks in the United States, won't lend me the money to buy the Charlemagne. Instead Mr. Winfield has threatened to call in all S.C.'s loans, and if he does, that will wipe out Cassman Realty."

"It's tough, Cassie, but we'll figure a way out."

What a relief to hear him say those words. Pat words picked up from some old television show. Yet one particular word mattered. *We.*

She clung to the word, wrapped it around the fears she felt, but a moment later the sense of distrust and fear surfaced again.

Holt lifted her slowly to her feet and held her as he moved her toward the bed.

Bed?

Was bed supposed to solve everything in a woman's life?

Was that the way out?

And if it was, why was she giving way to a deeper anguish?

The next thing she realized that he was there, next to her. In bed.

Shoes? Were her shoes on? She didn't know. Last time they weren't. Last time. There was something nagging her about last time.

"Holt. How did you find out about the story in the *Times?*"

"What's the difference?"

"I'm just wondering. I'll tell you how I learned about it. I got to the office and saw reporters and cameramen on our floor. It was so awful, just like the murder. Only this time I knew what to do. I covered my face so they couldn't get pictures, and I didn't stop to talk to anyone. See? Something good came out of all of that," she added wryly. She took a breath. She was better now. Talking helped. She was more in control of her emotions.

"Hilda thinks Papa Charles gave the story to the *Times.*"

She felt his body tense.

Suddenly she knew that she had to lie to get the truth. "But I think Hilda told the *Times.* What do you think, Holt?"

He was unbuttoning her blouse now. Top button. Fumble. Fumble. Second button.

"What do you think, Holt?"

"I've got other things on my mind."

"And nothing's more important than this?"

"No. And nothing ever will be."

No. And nothing ever will be.

The words rang in her mind. Resounded. Someone had rung

those bells before. Holt had said those words. Back. Go back. Back to—to—oh god.

Is there anything in The New York Times *as newsworthy as this?* That was the question she'd asked.

No. And there never will be. That's how he'd answered her.

The New York Times? Anything in The New York Times? She'd asked specifically because he'd been, he'd been . . . reading the paper.

He had been reading the *Times.*

Hadn't she taken his glasses from him?

She knew now. She knew. She reached for the top of her blouse and clutched it closed. She was already naked enough.

Cassie pulled away and sat at the edge of the bed, her back to Holt. She couldn't look at him. No, she couldn't face him when she said what she had to say. "Holt, you read the story before you left the house this morning. You read it, but you didn't tell me. Instead you—you made love, and you thought that made things right. That's all women need, isn't it? Anything wrong in a woman's life, and just give her the one thing she doesn't have. That didn't make things right for me." Now that she said it, she could turn and face him.

His eyes were lowered. "I didn't want to see the hurt on your face, Cassie, when you found out."

"No, of course not. It was much kinder to let me find out in a crowd of screaming meemies. You're all heart."

"Cassie, don't be sarcastic with me."

"Sarcastic? Holt, how could you be so—so unaware of me? You knew the most cataclysmic thing in my life, and instead of telling me and helping me understand it, you hid it under the bed."

"I thought I was doing the right thing, Cass."

Now she lifted her chin, threw back her head. "Right for whom? All that talk about you and me. When it comes right down to it, it's you and you."

She stood and gathered her belongings.

"I didn't mean to hurt you, Cassie. I didn't realize they'd play the story today. I thought they'd wait a few—"

He stopped. There could be no pretending now.

She knew.

She knew it all.

She turned and faced Holt. *"You* thought they'd wait? Oh my God, it was you. It really was. You were the one who told the *Times.* But how? What? You didn't hear it from me. I didn't know anything. It . . . wait . . . of course . . . Vince didn't have any job in Vegas after Stephanie. And he knew everything. Knew it all. You talked to him when we were out there. Sure you did. I used to see you with him. In the coffee shop. At the pool. He was the one who put the facts in place. Of course. No wonder you spent all that time with him. It wasn't just Stephanie. You found out how S.C. got Sal Romano a job in the lounge. Sure. Even Hilda said he couldn't have been a men's room attendant if it hadn't been for Grandpa. And you knew somebody had to have something on S.C. for Sal to be hired. So you asked around. Vince would be the logical one to squeal. He always had his hand out. But why did you do it? Because . . . because . . . you're like a fireman standing there with a net. You're going to catch the falling buildings. And as for me? Oh, I'm just the kid you're screwing on your way to the grownups you're screwing." Her voice was barely audible.

"Cassie, don't be mad," Holt said.

She shook her head in disbelief, gathered her belongings, and as she did she said, "You took all the things that made me vulnerable, my youth and inexperience and the terrible things that were happening in my family, and you used all my weakness to make yourself strong. But that's not going to make me mad, Holt. Hurt? Yes. Deeply hurt. And that hurt," she said, her fist clenched and raised, "is going to make me the toughest s.o.b. in New York."

Then Alexandra Cassman Brown walked out on Holt Hayward, and as she walked into the elevator she knew she'd never again feel safe just because a man gave her the answers.

XXX

HER COAT WAS OPEN even though there was a brisk wind coming from the west. Ordinarily Cassie would have had her coat clutched tight about her, the collar rolled high to keep her ears and cheeks warm. Tonight the rage that consumed her warmed not only the exposed nose and fingers but the hidden heart. Crossing Fifty-seventh Street Cassie broke into a run. Run. Race. Feet faster. Legs go. Move. Get on with it. She wanted to get as far away from *him* as she could.

Run. Leave Holt behind. Far behind. She was sobbing now. Sobbing. Racing.

Her feet came down—thunk—and she splashed slush on a mink-clad, blue-haired woman.

"Crazy jogger," the woman screamed after her.

Crazy. That's what she was for sure. Crazy with hate. Crazy with fear. Crazy with—what was there to do?

Do? Do? What could she do?

There was no Grandpa to turn to. Hilda'd been as good as a friend could be. Other family? What other family? Her own father didn't give a damn; he was no help. Stephanie wasn't just helpless; she was hopeless.

And every time she thought of Papa Charles her stomach churned. But she had to try. He was the only one with the money and the power to help. He was her last chance.

Charles Winters lived in baronial splendor in one of the few private houses left on Fifth Avenue. The others, like the Frick home, had become museums or embassies; still others had been razed to make room for glass monoliths divided into cooperative apartments that Cassie herself had sold *(lr, dr, wbf, pk vu)*.

The Winters home had been occupied by a member of the Winters family ever since Selig Winters had built the house in 1872. The land alone was worth millions. And the house? It couldn't be duplicated in today's world. A Venetian marble foyer, a library with panels sent from England, great stone fireplaces, hand-painted silk walls. Rumor had it that when Charles died the house would go to one of the major Jewish charities. Cassie had wondered long ago why Charles continued to live there. Crippled by that taxi accident in 1960, he was virtually confined to his bedroom. Before the accident there had been parties (that's what Diane had said, parties for birthdays and holidays, the only times her widowed father came to visit). But since the accident, Papa

[276]

Charles had been transported to his Wall Street office each day and brought home each night; he dined alone from a tray in his bedroom suite. The rest of the thirty-six-room house went unused. Or did the servants disco there? Maybe even bed down? Why not? It seemed senseless to let the whole house stand guard over one man. Of course, not just one man lived there if you counted the staff. Thirteen in all. Fifteen including the security force Papa Charles kept on twenty-four-hour duty.

"He thinks he's King Charles," Bill had said of his father-in-law, "which really makes my wife the world's only authentic Jewish princess."

Diane hadn't laughed at the joke; she was too much in awe of her father, the shadowy figure who occupied her thoughts, but rarely her home.

It was eleven P.M. when Cassie reached the corner of Seventy-second and Madison. She turned towards Fifth Avenue. He'd be in bed, but no matter.

She blinked rapidly. Was he awake? Asleep? Would he be pleased to see her? Proud that his only daughter's daughter turned to him? Angry? She didn't know any of the answers, but she soon would, for now she was ready, ready out of an all-consuming fear to go before her grandfather and beg and plead her case.

She walked up to the double oak doors and rang the bell. She sensed she was being watched. Maybe it was just nerves. She looked around. Oh God, a man in a dark coat with a German shepherd dog at his heels came forward and flashed a badge. Or was it lightning? No, a badge. "Who are you?" he asked sharply.

"M-M-Mr. Winter's granddaughter," she said in a voice that didn't seem to belong to her.

"Identification, please."

She fumbled in her shoulder bag. Why did everything drop to the bottom in those bags? Please let her find something before he shot her or the dogs bit. She was shaking. "I'm Alexandra Cassman Brown," she explained.

The man did not smile.

"I really am Mr. Winters's granddaughter. My mother—"

"Do you have identification? I can't let you in without it. We don't have your name as an authorized visitor tonight."

Just like the Kremlin she thought.

She found her driver's license and showed it to him, and then he smiled, "You're getting a little publicity these days, aren't you?"

She wanted to hit him, but what good would that do? It would only delay seeing Papa Charles. Instead she said with honest fervor, "I desperately want to see him now."

He nodded and lifted a panel in the door. There was a series of buttons; he punched them and seconds later the door opened.

"Andrew!" she shouted. For the moment delight overtook fear. So Papa Charles' longtime valet was still with him!

Andrew was wearing a dressing gown rather than a black suit. That must be the signal that visiting hours—if ever they had begun—were now ended. "Miss Alexandra, what are you doing here at this hour?"

She touched his arm, pulled at the silk of the robe. "I need to see my grandfather. It's very important." Her eyes followed the marble balustrade that marked the curve of the staircase. "Let me go to see him. Please."

"Let me tell him you're here," he said as he ushered her into the house.

Cassie sat on the edge of a brocade chair staring at the Turner on the opposite wall. She was so lost in thought, thoughts of Diane and the little-girl days, that she jumped in surprise when Andrew, a few minutes later, announced, "He's in bed, but he'll see you, Miss Alexandra."

"I don't know why you came here, Alexandra." The patrician face was etched sharply against the pillows. "And I particularly wonder why you had to awaken me."

"Because, Papa Charles, I have no other place to turn."

"It seems to me that in the past whenever you've needed a place to turn, you've found your other grandfather a willing listener. Go and talk to him now."

"I can't, and you know it."

"All I know, Alexandra, is that Sam Cassman ruined the Winters' family reputation with his scheming and conniving, and it culminated in that smut story today. I wouldn't lift a finger to help him."

"But it's not him; it's me. You'd be helping me."

"I don't see any difference. You made your bed, now lie in it."

Cassie bent her head, folded and unfolded her hands. She needed the right words to move this unmoving man. "Were you always this cold, Papa Charles?"

"What?"

"I mean, before the accident, were you like this? I was thirteen when you were hit by that taxicab, but somehow I don't remember you very much before then. All I know is that on the high holy days we had dinner together, and the rest of the time you were someplace else. You were always traveling then. We never saw you. Stephanie and I hardly knew you, and Mommy never talked about you."

"Talk about me? Why would she talk about me? Your mother was given the best possible education," he said sadly. Then Charles Winters paused and turned his head toward the windows. Cassie knew there were tears in his eyes.

She stood and walked to the bed. She touched the gray coverlet, a pale gray silk banded in deeper gray satin and monogrammed with the familiar looking "W," the quasi-crest that had been designed for the Winters family generations ago as a sop to the titled, crested Anglo-Saxons who had come to the United States even after the Winters. The Anglo-Saxons were not quite so bright as the first Winters, but they were much more social, since they did not have the stigma of Judaism in a city that tolerated but never embraced its Jews.

"Papa Charles, I need you. I really need you. Please help me. I don't want to lose the Charlemagne Hotel. I think that what I want to do would be marvelous for the city, but most of all it's my start in the business."

"Business? What do you need that business for? It's hard enough being a Jew; we didn't need Sam Cassman's dirty laundry. Sam the Laundryman. Some fine title."

"I can't talk to you about him. I want to talk about me, my chance. I know I'm smart, and I want to do good things. I'm different from my grandfather."

"I always thought you sprang straight from him. I never saw any Winters blood in you."

"Oh, Papa Charles, I'm my mother's daughter, too. My mother wasn't very smart. Look, I know that. It's not easy to say, but smart or not, we loved her. You and I really loved her. And, you know, as I get older I love her even more. I understand so much more. I realize now why she did the dumb things she did. You see it, too. My father was no husband, no father, no son. He still isn't. I know that, and it hurts me. It's hard to have a relationship when you do ninety-five percent of the giving. I think I'm better at that kind of thing than my mother was. But I'm sure of one thing. My mother adored you, Papa Charles. She really adored you . . ." Her eyes filled, her throat tightened. It hurt so much to talk about Diane. "My mother wanted love. That's what she wanted and needed so much, and she just didn't know how to get it. She dressed Stephanie and me in little designer dresses because she wanted to be a perfect Winters woman and make you proud. You weren't here to see, but she did it anyway. She's not here now, but for her, for me, please—oh please help me."

Papa Charles turned back and faced Cassie. His eyes were dry now. "This is all rather tiresome, Alexandra. Why should I help you?"

"Because I have the chance to build an important business, and I can't fail now. Don't you see? If I fail, I'll never get another chance. Everyone will say the granddaughter couldn't cut it. If I were a man, they'd say, oh well, give him another chance. Don't you see, Papa Charles? We're just not equal. I mean men and women just aren't equal. Because I don't have the freedom to fail. That's a male prerogative. If I don't put this deal together, I'm ruined. Nobody'll ever give me a chance again. It's different with men. They can lose one continent and come back and conquer the world because the world is still run by men, and they still help each other. If a woman succeeds, she has to be better than a man would be. There's no leeway for failure. You see, if we women do muck up, we haven't a place to turn because there just aren't enough women around to help one another. When we succeed, it's because we're better and then men call us equals. But when we fail, we fail as women, and we don't get another chance. Only strong men can help us. You're a strong man, Papa Charles. You have to help."

"I don't have to do anything, Alexandra. Understand that. I

make all my own decisions. And I think you just touched on the reason I won't help. I don't think women belong in business. What right do you have to run a company? You don't have the strength, you don't have the emotional stamina to get up and kick the stuffing out of an enemy."

"And that's a virtue?"

"It is in business. You stand here with the tears running down your face talking about your mother. That's weakness, Alexandra. It's the same kind of weakness I saw in your mother. My son, Dick, isn't bright, but at least he's not weak. He doesn't cry. I don't like anyone playing on my sympathies, twisting my emotions. Business is business, and family is family, and just because they sometimes intertwine doesn't mean I ever forget about the rudiments of business. Business is systems and order and tradition. You see, Alexandra, if you were a man, I'd probably help you. But I don't want to see another woman trying to replace us in business. You all think you're the new minority, and the world owes you a living."

"You don't understand a word I've said, do you?"

"On the contrary, Alexandra, you don't understand anything I've said. I'm telling you I don't think women belong in business. They belong in the home. Forget all this stuff. Don't get mixed up in the garbage your grandfather created. Take a trip. Go away. Maybe you'll meet a nice man somewhere along the way, and then, when you do, Alexandra, marry him. Marry him and stay home and raise your children."

Cassie picked up her shoulder bag from the floor, slung it over her shoulder and walked to the doorway. She paused and turned back to her grandfather. "You're wrong, Papa Charles. You don't really know me. I'm not Alexandra. I'm Cassie. I know what I need better than you do, and what I need is a strong man to help me, not a husband to support me. You see, a husband isn't the solution for me any more than it was for my mother."

It was midnight when she hailed a cab on Fifth Avenue and went back to her apartment. Her heart was so heavy she could scarcely breathe. She nodded to the doorman. "Miss Brown, there's a cablegram here for you," he said.

She grabbed the wire and tore it open. Her eyes dropped to the bottom of the page. It was from Grandpa. Her eyes filled. The words dimmed. Don't cry. Read it. Read it. She tried to make her eyes focus. Tears. Nerves. Fatigue. Bad light here in the foyer. Wait—now the words were readable. Her hand shook. She read it again. She squeezed her eyes shut. She didn't have to read it a third time. She'd memorized it during the second reading: HAVE SEEN PAPERS STOP REPORTS EXAGGERATED STOP WILL FLY HOME AS SOON AS BOAT DOCKS STOP I LOVE YOU STOP GRANDPA

XXXI

CASSIE LET THE CABLE flutter to the floor.

There were no reassurances in those few words.

One by one they were letting her down. First Holt with his treachery and soft words. Now Grandpa. They thought they could tell her anything. She was still their naive little girl, the perennial student.

Student . . . student.

Her mind came to attention.

Students read books. Real estate books. Law books. She'd studied for years; she knew every paragraph in the proposed Charlemagne deal. Every word. Every *whereas* and semicolon. She knew it all. She'd memorized it. She raised her head and looked outside. Somewhere in the proposal had to be a word, a phrase, a clue. Oh, if she were only on some faraway island now. Maybe Hawaii . . .

Hawaii. Of course.

The Zeckendorf scheme.

Why hadn't she thought of it before?

There was a door out of this after all. She wasn't sealed in an airless room. She gulped deep breaths. How fast could she move before someone bolted that door shut?

She looked at her watch.

She looked around the familiar lobby of her building. The doorman, now doubling as elevator man on the late shift, was holding the elevator doors open. He tugged at his mustache anxiously and looked at the ceiling. Jeez, was she just going to stand there all night looking out the door? Get a move on, lady. Get on the elevator already. He yawned and heard the front door open, looked up and saw Cassie rush pell-mell back into the cold night. "Dumb broad," he muttered.

The moon was full. That had to be a good omen. She shook her curly head. Get it all in order now. One more time. It was incredible how good she felt. How long was it since she'd been depressed and scared? Five minutes. Maybe six. In those minutes fortunes changed. The balance shifted . . .

And now she knew.

Step one.

Step two.

A plan.

A scheme.

It was all taking place in her head.

At last she had a scenario.

Now if all the actors came in on cue . . .

He was sitting in the big chair. The television was turned to the Carson show, but he wasn't. He was turned to the city below. Someplace in that city she was running. Running from him, to someone—he couldn't guess. But one thing was certain. He couldn't have played it any differently. Not he. Not Holt Hayward. She'd have to learn that one basic fact about him, the fact that there wasn't a woman he thought as seductive as business. Maybe she did know that. Maybe that's why she thought he'd betrayed her. But he hadn't. Well, not exactly in the way she thought. All he'd done was corroborate the story the *Times* had already had. Hell. Who could afford to lie to the most influential paper in the city? Could he have killed the story? He stroked his chin. Maybe. Maybe if he hadn't said, "Yes, it's true. Yes, I saw . . . yes, I did . . . yes, I was there." If only he'd maybe'd his way through instead of saying yes. Well, so what? He hadn't, and now she was gone. Another one gone. Another fact of life. People always wondered how he stayed a bachelor. He smiled to himself. It wasn't difficult when you knew what you wanted, when you

[283]

had priorities. He knew his priorities; his women knew them, too. It was just that women could never accept them. Women always wanted to be first on the list, but that wasn't the structure of his life. Business came first with him. Always would. He smiled a bemused smile. Still . . . she was something special. Alexandra Cassman Brown. A different woman. Curious, eager, straining to be better. This story would slow her down, maybe even stop her. But again, she might in time survive this kind of publicity. Oh well, it would test her toughness. He could almost see her . . . he closed his eyes . . . for a minute, ten minutes . . .

Something awakened him. He opened his eyes, looked up and froze.

She was standing there. Clear-eyed. Serious. Gone was the high emotion of earlier, when she'd left. Now she was back. Still in the same clothes. So. His mind worked fast. Probably hadn't been with another man. Then why was she here? A terrible thought struck. What if she had a gun? Her sister had had one. His mouth was dry. He wanted to speak, but he couldn't. And he knew he was afraid of her.

Facing him, Cassie tried to hide her trembling. Her whole life depended on the next moment. Don't show him you're scared. Don't make him suspicious. Don't get him angry. She dug her nails into the palms of her hands. "Hi." Her voice sounded feeble.

He looked at her in total surprise, then relief. So she wasn't going to kill him. She was frightened, too. Good. That put him in command. He began to unbend. "You're back," he said.

"Yes."

"I didn't expect to see you again. I thought—"

"Well, I'm here."

He felt a twinge of pity. Poor kid. She probably had no place to go. No one who'd take her in and give her love. Certainly not that father of hers—more interested in sleeping with girls his daughter's age than in his daughter. And there were no other men in her life. Not loving men. Men to love back. Holt's emotions were almost too much for him. He wanted to protect her. She needed him for his strength, his sureness. He stood.

He put his arms around her and held her. He felt her thin body tremble under his touch. He'd never felt so close to her. Not the times in bed, not the times they'd talked about their hates and hopes. But now. Now that she'd returned. Now that he'd betrayed her and she'd forgiven him—the return was the sign of forgiveness—now he could afford to show her tenderness. Warmth even. This return was his turn-on; he'd abused her, and still she adored him.

Treachery as foreplay.

He laughed, and she felt the laughter shaking his body.

"What's so funny?"

"Life, Cassie. Life." Now that he had broken her, he was ready to love her.

She unlocked their tangle of arms, took off her coat, and threw it on the sofa. Her handbag followed and landed under the coffee table. She flung her arms outward. "I guess I'm back because I'm addicted to you." She looked at him sideways. Would he believe that?

He squirmed. "Addictions are dangerous."

"I guess I'm ready to play with danger." It was like a bad movie. She smiled to herself. If only he knew what that line really meant.

Cassie walked to the window, her back to Holt. He suspected nothing. Men were always ready to believe the best about themselves. She'd defused him, but not dishonestly. She did love him; she loved him in a way she'd never love again, but love alone wouldn't have brought her back, because loving Holt was too dangerous, a one-way street to self-destruction. Holt was a dreamer; he'd kill for the dream, but only if the dream had his initials on it.

He stood next to her. "I'm glad you came back."

She pressed his arm and put her head against his shoulder. He brushed her hair with his lips.

"I was very frightened when I left here tonight. It's scary out there alone," Cassie said.

"Where did you go?"

"Couple of places."

"Couple of places?" He seemed skeptical.

She hurried to erase his doubts. "Oh, I'll tell you. I went to the office."

"The office?"

"And one other place."

Pause.

Silence.

She took a step back, looked at him, and breathed deeply. This was the time. Now. Do it now. It was the magic moment, the minute when something had to happen or nothing ever would. Go! Charge! Flags high! Now!

She rehearsed the line in her head one more time. Then she said it, "Holt, have you ever heard of the Hawaiian technique?"

He shook his head.

"It's something I learned from Grandpa, but it's a technique everybody uses. Grandpa knows about it from Bill Zeckendorf."

"Well, Zeckendorf invented plenty of them. What's this one again?"

"A system used by buyers to mortgage the ground separately from the building on it."

"Of course," Holt said easily. "I remember now. It's used a lot because it's good for the developer. The ground rent has to be paid before any other expenses, so it's the safest of all possible incomes to the property." He stopped. If she knew, why was he telling her?

She said nothing.

Unable to contain his curiosity, Holt broke the silence. "Why are you thinking about the Hawaiian technique?"

"I want to mortgage the ground under the Charlemagne." Could he detect the quiver in her voice?

"What?" Ridiculous to think she could do it. A kid.

She swallowed and said in a level tone, "Paragraph thirty-two in the option agreement says I can mortgage the ground under the Charlemagne."

Test her. She's fishing for information. "Are you sure?"

She wanted to say, "No, no, I'm not sure," but this was not the time to look uncertain. Instead she said boldly, "I have the contract with me. I told you I just came from the office."

He frowned. "Why bother with something like this?" He ran his fingers through her hair. "It's awfully complex, sweetheart."

"I know."

"I—well, frankly, I don't think it can be worked out, Cass."
The frown was deepening. He pulled away from her and walked
to the sofa. He looked about the room, then sat down. She followed him. Neither spoke.

So. He was getting worried. That meant it could work.
Now she timed the wait—beat, beat, beat—and then she spoke.
"They're asking one hundred million for the Charlemagne as it is.
Without the office space we'll build, the hotel generates ten million dollars income in a year. I could sell the land outright, but I
think it may make more sense to get an insurance company or
pension fund to take an eight percent return on a ground mortgage. I figure I could sell a ground mortgage for thirty million,
and that would eat up two million four hundred thousand of the
land's total income. The remaining seven million six hundred
thousand of income capitalized at the rate of thirteen percent—"

"Cassie, get to the bottom line."

She fumbled through the handbag she'd tossed under the coffee
table. She pulled out two American Express receipts and a dry
cleaning ticket.

"Cassie, for God's sake!"

That was annoyance in his voice. Good.

"Cassie, where do you have this written? On the back of an
envelope?"

"As a matter of fact, I do," she said, a small, smug smile on her
face. "Oh, here it is." She pulled the crumpled envelope from the
bag and began to read her notes.

"Well, what is it?" Now his impatience was compounded by
the disturbing notion that she might be right.

Oh God, let him believe her. "It's rather complicated, Holt.
What it comes down to is this. I can arrange to sell and mortgage
an inner lease to someone who would in effect own the building.
Next I'll sell an operating lease to a major hotel chain. I figure I
can sell the inner lease for sixty-five million and the operating
lease for thirty-five million. So I can get a hundred and fifty
million for the one-hundred-million-dollar purchase and have the
money to put up my tower."

"I don't believe this," Holt choked. "I don't believe it. You
think you can take the Charlemagne and transform that one-

[287]

hundred-million-dollar ugly-duckling deal into some kind of swan."

"Yes."

He leaned back. Of course she couldn't do it. No way. Absolutely impossible. Pipe dream. He smiled indulgently. "And who is the big daddy who'll buy the land and move this along?"

"Oh, it's all taken care of." Could he tell it really wasn't?

"M-m-m. Anyone I know?"

"Sort of." Her palms were wet once more.

"And who is this special person who thinks so much of you he'd put millions of dollars into any venture with your name— especially after that *Times* story today?" Low blow, but he had to say it. "Just who would do that?"

"Papa Charles." There. She'd named him. Out at last.

The big lie.

"Papa who?"

"Oh, come on, Holt. You know, I'm sure, that I'm not only S.C.'s granddaughter. I have two grandfathers. And the other is Charles Winters."

"He wouldn't—"

"Oh, but he would. You see, Papa Charles loves the *Times*. They really stuck it to Grandpa. Papa Charles read the paper, and he couldn't wait to rush and help me." Cassie coughed. Even she had to choke on that phony line. Holt, his eyes riveted on her, waited for the next words. "Well, when Papa Charles called, he didn't reach me. I was out. So he left word to call him anytime today or tonight that I needed him. That story left him gloating. When I went to see him tonight, he was grinning like a Cheshire cat. He knew he finally had me in the Winters family. Oh, one more thing. He thinks I may take over his business one day."

Holt's eyes widened. "That whole brokerage house?"

She shrugged and lifted her hands helplessly. "Only time will tell." It was all playing so well she couldn't resist the colorful embellishments.

"But you—you hate Papa Charles, Cassie."

"That was then. He was very good to me tonight, and I'm sure you understand that blood is thicker than water."

[288]

Holt felt his pressure rising. This kid. This child woman. Running a major Wall Street house? Preposterous.

"Holt, I came back to tell you all this because I thought you'd be pleased to know that I found a way to save the Charlemagne and put the deal together. I thought you'd be proud of me."

"Of course. Sure. Naturally. But—"

"But what?"

Bitch. How dare she play it alone?

"I'd really like to be a part of that deal, too, Cassie. I think I can make some very good contributions. I know you're mad or at least you were earlier, because you think I gave the *Times* the story about S.C., but they had it without me. I swear, as God is my witness, I never called the *Times*."

"Holt, I know you wouldn't lie to me any more than I would lie to you." She could barely keep a straight face. "It was like this, Holt. S.C. sent me a telex and asked me to come to see you because he wants to be sure you'll continue to represent me in the deal. So, represent me. That puts you in."

"Not the way I want to be. I want to be a partner."

"I don't see how we can take you. Papa Charles is just so anxious to put one over on Grandpa."

"Cassie. Cassie, that's it. Don't you see?" He jumped up and waved his fist in her face. "How can you let Mr. Winters do that to S.C.?"

"I don't think I have a choice." She lowered her head and folded her hands.

He paused, regained his composure and said in slow, deliberate tones, "Cassie, I'll do it."

"Do what?"

"I'll take you out so Papa Charles can't."

"I don't understand, Holt."

"I'll take Charles Winters' action."

"Oh, I don't think you should."

"But it keeps your grandfather, your real grandfather, in the deal." She'd better not find out he'd told Porter Winfield he'd get control of the Charlemagne deal.

"Still—"

"Cassie, listen to me. Cassie, what did Mr. Winters offer for the land?" There was desperation in his voice.

"He asked me what I wanted, and I said sixty-five. Then he said, 'Since it's family, I insist you take seventy.' "

"Seventy?"

"Seventy million."

Holt flushed. He couldn't stop now. He was on a roll. "I'll give you seventy-five." He'd figure out how to sell it to Winfield.

"I don't think I can do that to my own grandfather," she said her eyes still lowered lest they betray her excitement.

This was his last chance to save himself and get in on the Charlemagne. He'd have to play her emotions once more. "Cassie, what do you owe Charles Winters? Hell, what has he ever done for you? He may even double-cross you, Cassie. He's famous for his tough deals. Kid, you've got to protect yourself. You've got to look out for yourself. You are number one. Don't let anybody step on you."

She lifted her head and smiled feebly. "Holt, thank-you for saying that. I really appreciate this support and advice. Do you think—do you really think—"

"Sell to me at seventy-five."

"It just doesn't seem right."

"All right. All right then." He had to take one more gamble. "Make it seventy-seven five." He stopped, then added quickly, ". . . but not a penny more."

She waited.

Minutes passed.

Finally she looked up at him, no emotion in her eyes even though she wanted to scream, shout, and jump for joy. Instead she said calmly, "Holt, I'll do it. I'll sell you the land for seventy-seven million five hundred thousand dollars if you'll sign now."

"What?" This child was mad.

"You'll have to draw the papers immediately and sign now. You see, I have Papa Charles's signed agreement to buy the land, and since I'm due in Porter Winfield's office at eight o'clock in the morning, I have to show a signed agreement to purchase the land. Then I'll be able to exercise my option. Now you know as well as I do that if the only paper I can produce has Papa Charles' name on it, I'll have to go ahead and sell to him."

He smiled. Wait until Winfield saw Holt's name on the agreement. And then wait until he found out where Holt's loan was going to come from. Holt gave her his hand and pulled her up from the sofa. She smiled. His palms were damp.

"Are we going to your office?"

He nodded.

He couldn't speak any more. In fact, Holt could scarcely breathe. It all rested on Cassie. What a double number she held. Two grandfathers fighting over her. She'd be like a grown-up Gloria Vanderbilt with two rich relatives vying to buy her love and loyalty. This was too hot to observe from the outside; you have to be a part of it, a big part of it. After all, he'd never said he hated marriage . . . he'd only said that for him at this time . . . but circumstances change . . .

At five A.M. Cassie went back to her apartment. She was too excited to sleep. She wanted to call . . . but was it too early? Who cared?

A bewildered Hilda answered the phone.

"Hilda, I did it," she crowed.

"Did? What? Who?"

"Saved the old plantation. Hilda, listen to me. Listen, I got us over seventy-seven million dollars so we can go ahead with the Charlemagne deal. Meet me in Porter Winfield's office at eight. Start renting office space at eight-oh-one. You're going to be the operator."

"Cassie, you're crazy. I don't know anything about operating."

"Then learn. We can learn anything, Hilda. You and I. We can do it all."

"Cassie, have you been drinking?"

"I don't think so. And if I'm asleep, I hope I never wake up."

"Is this the same Cassie I left a little while ago, the one who was broke and finished?"

"I left that Cassie out there someplace. Because since I last saw you, Hilda, something happened we never thought could happen. We've fooled them all, Hilda. All those smart men. And guess what? We're better than they are."

[291]

"We are?"

"Yes, and we're not only better at what we do, we're better at what they do."

"Are you sure?"

"Oh, yes. Hilda, I found out something very useful tonight. No man can lie, cheat, or steal better than a woman."

August 1977

Nothing is work unless you'd
rather be doing something else.
George Halas
Chicago Bears

XXXII

"DADDY. It's me. Cassie."

Bill Cassman looked at his watch. Noon. High noon. And Sunday. What did Cassie want on Sunday?

"Dad, are you there?" She sounded anxious.

"Sure, sure. How are you, Cassie?"

"Fine. I'm calling for a reason."

Of course she was calling for a reason. When you don't hear from your daughter for years unless you're both in the office, she must have a special reason for calling at home.

"Grandpa's going to be eighty in a couple of weeks—"

He was silent, not in the unspoken union of two people who need no words, but in the separateness of their feelings for that man.

"—so what I'm asking, Dad, is if you'll give the party at "21" with me."

He hadn't heard her words. He'd only listened to himself those minutes. "When? What? Tell me again, Cassie."

She repeated her plans: family and friends, no surprise, a week from Wednesday. She already had the Jack and the Remington Rooms. Would Bill be co-host?

He leaned back in his chair, put his feet up on the ottoman, reached for a cigar, and smiled contentedly. "No, Cassie dear, I won't give the party with you."

"Why, Daddy?"

"Oh," he said, the buttery tones oiling the next words, "I'm going to be in Europe that week. I've got a deal I'm working on with a group of Arabs—"

"Arabs?" she asked in a shocked voice.

"Well, one thing I learned from my dear father, Alexandra, is that you take the deals where you can make the deals."

"You won't even be here then?"

"No, I'm sorry, I won't."

"I can change the date."

"Don't do that. You see, Cassie, it's really too late for my father to change anything for me."

He put the receiver down, then picked it up a few minutes later. "Air France? This is William Cassman. Can you get me two tickets for Paris a week from Wednesday? Of course it's August, and everything's booked. But this is William Cassman . . . yes, Cassman Realty . . . and I need two tickets . . ."

The telephone awakened her.

"Get it, Stephanie," he growled in his best imitation of Sal Romano.

"Okay. Okay, Vince." She reached blindly. It was so dark. Vince liked the bedroom dark as night. The luminous clock dial said eleven o'clock. A.M. or P.M.? Must be A.M. She groped—r-ring, r-ring—knocked over a glass. Water spilled on the bed. No, not water. Ugh. The smell of old liquor.

R-ring.

"Hell, hello," she said in that little-girl voice that had taken her to places little girls weren't supposed to travel.

"Stephanie. It's me, Cassie."

"Oh hi."

"I'm not too early, am I? It's eleven o'clock out there. I called the shop, but they said you hadn't come in. Are you all right?"

"Sure, sure." All right? Who was all right, Cassie? Who besides you? Big-deal, hotshot New York woman. But I don't forget that you walked into it, Cassie. Everybody set it up for you. Neato, Cassie-o. Tra la.

"Things are all right at the shop, aren't they?" Cassie asked anxiously, a small knot forming in the pit of her stomach.

"Yes. Terrific." The shop. That was some laugh. They'd bought a needlepoint shop for her after the trial.

"Great. Great, Stephanie. I'm calling because it's Grandpa's eightieth birthday next week, and I'd like to have a birthday party for him at "21." Will you come home for it?"

"I don't know."

The knot in Cassie's stomach was throbbing. "What do you mean, you don't know? You can certainly leave the shop."

Oh, certainly. Even Cassie knew her shop was a no-income setup to let little sister masquerade as a businesswoman. A businesswoman just like her big sister. Oh well, Vince had put his daughter in there to run things. Who'd ever know the difference? Vince was still the contact between Las Vegas and the family in New York who paid her bills. And if Vince said Stephanie was in terrific shape, who would argue? Grandpa? Daddy? Who felt like coming out to Las Vegas to take another look at the kid? Nobody. That's who.

"Stephanie, did you hear me?"

"I heard you."

Cassie was desperate. Oh God, what was happening?

"Please come home, Stephanie. We'll be together. It'll be great. I want you here."

"Why, Cass? So the newspapers can report one big happy family?"

"Don't be like that."

"How should I be?"

"Is it the shop? You want to do something else?"

"Yes. There's something I really want to do. I want to stay home and give myself facials and take bubble baths and have a nice house."

"Isn't your house nice?" She didn't know what else to say.

"All right, then. I want to be a movie star."

Cassie's eyes filled. Stephanie was sick again. Really sick. Cassie recognized the sickness. It was the sickness she'd seen all her life. There was a whirl, a time machine gone awry. "Oh, Mother, don't talk like that," Cassie cried.

"This is Stephanie," her sister said coldly.

"Stephanie, what do you want? What should I do?" Cassie sobbed. Stephanie felt no emotion as she heard her sister. Instead she turned to look at Vince. His hairy body covered most of the double bed, although only his bald head was visible above the sheet. Thick, ugly features he had. Thick, ugly man he was. Not a romantic like Sal. Just another man who beat her up like Sal. She shivered in revulsion. He was snoring. "I'll come to New York," Stephanie said quietly. "When's the party?"

Cassie was both frightened and relieved. Whatever it was, at least the sisters could talk in New York. At least they'd see one another.

"It's next Wednesday. Why not fly out Sunday?" Cassie asked.

"Okay. See you then. Oh, where will I stay?"

Cassie paused. "With me. Of course with me."

Stephanie put the phone down.

"So you're goin' to New York," Vince said.

"I thought you were asleep."

"Vince Filippo never sleeps."

"Then how come Vince Filippo snores?"

"I liked it better when you were a dumb broad and didn't ask so many fuckin' questions." He shoved her toward the edge of the bed. "Where's my coffee?"

She slid her feet into satin mules, threw a robe around her nude body, and limped towards the kitchen. I'm the same kind of creep he is. That's why I'm with him, she told herself as she took out the mugs, measured the coffee. If it hadn't been for the accident—that's how she always thought about Sal's death, "the accident"—if it hadn't been for that, she'd probably have gone to Hollywood herself, made some films, some TV movies, had a fair career. Now it was all too late. She wasn't made for running a store and keeping books and carrying briefcases, and she wasn't into women's networking and all that stuff they talked about on the Phil Donahue show. She was Stephanie Cassman Romano, and she was washed up at twenty-eight.

Marcia couldn't believe her luck. If you took a close look at all she'd done, her story was even better than good old Cassie's. Of course, Cassie had a hell of a lot more press.

Marcia sprinkled herbs on the fish, adjusted the broiler, and wondered what to do next . . . next . . .

R-r-ring.

She caught the phone on the first ring.

"Marsh, it's me. Cass."

"You wouldn't believe it, but I was just thinking about you."

"Why?"

"Oh, wondering how you are." So, it was a little white lie.

"I'm good, Marsh. Really good."

"I haven't seen you for so long, Cassie. I called you then. You know, when that story was in the *Times*."

"I know you did, and I appreciated it, but after the big blowup in the papers, I had some work to do to pull things in shape. It all went well. Hilda was a godsend; she was really a true friend with it all—"

"And I suppose I didn't try?" Marcia interrupted.

"No, I don't mean that. I just mean that Hilda's in real estate, and you have your own career and everything—"

"I'm doing some super things, Cass. *Women's Wear Daily* called me the next Gerry Stutz."

"Terrific."

"I'll probably be one of the youngest department store presidents within five years—and a woman at that."

"Well, I guess being a woman works for us in that kind of position."

"But what about getting to that kind of position? I don't think you understand. After all, you're in a family business. What kind of jockeying did you have to do?"

"Sure. Right." Cassie wanted to punch her right in the mouth. Pow. Take that, dear old pal.

"But now that we're both doing so well, we ought to get together, Cass. After all, old friends and everything."

"Yes. Old friends. Well, I really called because I thought maybe you'd like to have dinner tonight."

"Sorry, Cass, but I've got this friend—"

"Oh?"

"He's coming for dinner."

"Well, maybe another time."

"Sure. I'll call you, Cassie."

Marcia put the phone back. Call you, Cassie? Never. You've screwed up my life enough already. Don't marry Steve Schwartz, you said. No, he's only an assistant buyer, and you'll look down on him six months after you marry him. Take your time. Have a ball. Don't rush into marriage. There's never been a better time for women. Terrific, Cassie. I took your advice. I said bye-bye to Steve, and he married some Park Avenue debutante. And where did I end up? In my kitchen, Cassie, cooking dinner for a work session with the sixty-two-year-old advertising director at the store.

Marcia's eyes filled. What was so terrible about marrying a man you cared for? Why did we all have to be such career kooks?

It would be the biggest gathering of the clan since Cassie's graduation. And they all knew it.

"This is some party," Grandpa said as he stood with Cassie just outside the elevator on the third floor of "21."

"It isn't a party yet, Grandpa. Nobody's here but us."

"They'll come. They always come. They're relatives."

"I thought you loved them."

"Cassie, even *I* can't love Aunt Sarah. Uncle Izzy, maybe. But Aunt Sarah? And those twins? Debbie and Doobie."

"Donnie and Donna, Grandpa."

"Donnie and Donna, Debbie and Doobie. So who cares? You know what happened to them?"

"I thought you didn't care."

"They're growing up to be geniuses."

"How wonderful."

"Wonderful? What's so wonderful? My brother Izzy deserves genius grandchildren? Why does he get the geniuses?"

"I'm doing okay, Grandpa."

"Smart, yes. But you weren't a genius, Cassie. I can't believe his grandchildren should be so smart. And that Izzy . . . first thing he always says to me is, 'So how's Stephanie?' Did he ever ask about Stephanie before the trouble? No, now that we have nothing but tragedy, my bighearted brother is worried about Stephanie."

"Grandpa, maybe we shouldn't have had—"

The elevator doors opened and Sam Cassman, his face wreathed in smiles, embraced his brother. "Izzy. Iz." He kissed him. "You came. I'm so happy to see you."

Uncle Izzy disengaged himself. "Listen, we're proud to be your family even if you've had a little trouble. So what's a family for if not to hang together? Right, Sarah?"

His wife nodded.

"Hello, Uncle Izzy," Cassie said. She kissed Aunt Sarah.

"Oh, the prize package. Cassie, your grandfather is so proud of you—" Aunt Sarah gushed.

"I know," Cassie interrupted. "And he's proud of Stephanie, too. She's right over there." Cassie's heart skipped a beat when she looked at Stephanie. "Stephanie," she called, "come join us; here's Uncle Izzy and Aunt Sarah."

"My brother never had a brain," Grandpa mumbled, "and now geniuses he's got. It's not fair."

Cassie laughed. "Grandpa, go in there with them and have a drink. Introduce Ruth—"

"Grandma Ruth, Cassie. She'd like it if you'd call her Grandma Ruth."

"Absolutely, Grandpa. Whatever you want." No doubt that was Grandpa's idea, not Ruth's.

One by one they arrived.

Uncle Dick and his children, Michael and Elizabeth.

Holt Hayward.

Jerry Farber, Cassie's first boss in the job that Grandpa had set up to keep her from going to Doubleday. What would've happened . . . what if?

Hilda Taylor, of course, and, "Papa Charles," Cassie said coolly as her other grandfather was wheeled from the elevator.

"Good evening, Alexandra," he said. There was no joy in his voice or his eyes.

It was the first meeting between grandfather and granddaughter since the winter night when she'd gone begging at his door, and he'd refused to help.

"Grandpa, Papa Charles is here," Cassie said loudly.

S.C. moved slowly. Let the man wait. He'd probably kept enough people waiting at Winters & Co. over the years. As he walked to greet Charles, Samuel Cassman was aware of the chill between his granddaughter and her other grandfather. He smiled. He really was richer than Charles Winters. He could afford to be magnanimous.

"Hello, Charles," S.C. said in his most expansive manner. "Sorry to keep you out here, but I don't move as fast as I used to."

"I don't move at all," Charles snapped from his wheelchair.

S.C. shrugged. What was there to say?

"Where's your son?" Papa Charles asked. "Where's Bill?"

Grandpa thought for a minute, then smiled benignly. "He's in Paris closing a big deal." Why should he let facts spoil his night?

Cassie's eyes widened. Bill hadn't been able to get tickets to Paris. She knew because Air France had called the office to say they were overbooked, oversold. Nothing was available. Still Bill wasn't around. Where had he gone instead? Maybe East Hampton. Maybe East Berlin. Who knew?

"If he closes this," Charles said, "it'll be the first time in his life he ever closed anything more than a window."

"He's doing very well these days," S.C. said. He looked at Charles. And since when was Charles's son Dick such a bargain? And what about Diane?

Charles turned the switch on the electric wheelchair. "I can manage," he said to Cassie as she moved to help. "I don't need anybody."

Stephanie, now standing in the doorway, said, "I wish I could say the same."

"Stephanie? That is you, isn't it, Stephanie?" Papa Charles asked.

"Yes, I'm still Stephanie."

"Well, it's nice you could make it. I wasn't sure myself I could be here. There was so much going on tonight. The people from the museum were at the house."

"Which museum?" Cassie asked.

"The Metropolitan, of course," Charles answered with some annoyance. "I'm going to set up the Winters Wing. It will be announced next month. We're waiting until we can get a big story, the right coverage. I want people to know the good my family can do instead of all these embarrassing stories."

Samuel Cassman disregarded the insult. "So what's going into your wing, under your wing?" he asked playfully.

"My collection," Papa Charles said with his customary hauteur. "The Winters family collection. With estate taxes the way they are now, there's no way my art can be left to anyone, so I'm making plans now, deciding where and how I want to leave my things."

[302]

Cassie looked carefully at Papa Charles. He was right. There was nothing for him to give her after his death because there was nothing he could give her during his lifetime.

By nine o'clock they sat down to dinner at six tables of six persons each in the Remington Room. The tables were covered in snowy white; bunches of snapdragons and zinnias in small baskets stood in the center of each table. Of the thirty-six people, only ten were family. The others were real estate agents, cronies, attorneys and hangers-on in the life of Samuel Cassman.

The guest list had been put together by Grandpa. "Do you want the mayor?" Cassie'd asked.

"If we weren't back in power, he wouldn't come," Grandpa said, "but now that we're on top, you can bet he'll show up."

Cassie looked around the room. As usual, Grandpa had been right. The mayor was entering now, to be seated at Cassie's left.

"What about Calvin Gardiner?" Hilda had wondered.

Cassie had thought for a moment and said no, "When I call him, it has to be because I'll take that room next to his grandmother."

And so the guest list had been screened and scrubbed.

Finally, together they'd come up with the idea of six tables and the hosts for each: herself, Uncle Dick Winters, Uncle Izzy, Cousin Herbert, Hilda Taylor, and Jerry Farber.

Cassie sat at the table in front of the fireplace with Grandpa on her right, Ruth, then Uncle Izzy, and the mayor.

As the evening wore on, Grandpa was in high spirits. Cassie didn't know whether it was wine or intoxication with the night. Eighty years old! How many men made it to eighty with all their faculties intact? He really was a remarkable man, not just because he was her grandfather. He was special.

Ruth was talking to Uncle Izzy. "Well, what can I say?" she shrugged. "Marriage isn't easy. No marriage is, but I come from a time when that's what a girl was raised to do. Get married. Frankly, I'm glad that's what it was like when I was young. I don't like all these decisions. There's a certain tranquillity—" Ruth laughed. "What am I talking about? Tranquillity? So far, Sam, you've been a barrel of excitement."

Sam Cassman threw his head back and boomed his laughter. "So!" he said to Stephanie, "How many eighty-year-old men live to hear their wives say such a nice thing?"

They all laughed, and then it was time.

Time to do what they'd come to do.

Time to toast Samuel Cassman and wonder at the power of it all.

Cassie rose, picked up a spoon and clinked her glass. The laughter and talk died down quickly. She began. "Mr. Mayor, Grandpa, Papa Charles." She paused. Where was her own father? "Thank you all for coming. I want to welcome each of you once again. This is a special night in the life of every person here. There isn't one of us who wasn't born—or hasn't lived the life we've lived—because this man preceded us. You haven't always been easy on us, Grandpa, and you certainly aren't an easy act to follow. But I wouldn't have it any other way. You are a wonderful man, Samuel Cassman. You're wonderful because you're eighty, and you haven't stopped growing. I don't suppose many people here know that your dream is to build the pyramids and that you love the Egyptian art in the Metropolitan. There are many different Samuel Cassmans. Unfortunately we've all had to deal with the Samuel Cassman of the media these last months."

She touched her grandfather's shoulder and looked down at him affectionately. "You didn't think I'd mention that tonight, did you, Grandpa? But I learned from you that you can't hide things, and you're in a stronger position if you don't wait for somebody to drop the shoe, but do it yourself. So let's talk about it, and then let's go on. It wasn't good, and it wasn't pleasant, but you didn't drown in those muddy waters, Grandpa. No, not you. Instead you came out shaking yourself off, and you actually said to me, 'This taught me a lesson. Don't think the world isn't looking and talking just because you don't want them to.' I learned your lesson, Grandpa, and I've learned a lot of other things, too, these last ten years. Some I learned from you, and some I learned from the people in my life.

"I've learned that we all work to create jewels of one kind or another. And the only way jewels are created is under intense heat and pressure. I've learned to understand that tension and to make it work to my advantage."

Holt shot her a dark look.

Now she looked directly at Holt. "I've learned that love is not all it's advertised to be. When it works, it's better than anything else in life, and when it doesn't it's a kind of death, a sentence. Not a prison sentence"—Stephanie winced—"but a sentence that begins, 'In twenty-four hours I can be away from him and this—'

"I have learned that families matter"—now her eyes shifted to Papa Charles—"families matter even when they're weak and stupid and an embarrassment. That's what makes them family.

"I know that nothing lasts, not the bad, not the good, and that the only important thing is to make the present a thing of beauty. You see, I believe in beauty. Our parents raised us in a beautiful house, and our mother taught Stephanie and me that it was possible to create some kind of beauty even if you had to deal with all kinds of ugliness in your own existence. Our mother had a sense of beauty and I never appreciated it until—until she wasn't around to hear me say it."

Cassie paused, eyes brimming, and saw her reflection in her sister's eyes.

"I've learned that people don't change; rotten is rotten. When Grandpa looks at a man and tells me he's no good, Grandpa knows something I don't. People don't really change at all; the boy who cheated on an arithmetic test in the fourth grade is the man who double-bills you later in life.

"Most of all, Grandpa, from you I've learned to dream. And from you I've learned that in all of life, dreams are the only reality. So I salute you on your eightieth birthday, Samuel Cassman. I am proud to be your granddaughter."

There was only one person in the whole room whose eyes were dry at the end of the speech, and he stood and patted his granddaughter on the head. "That's a nice speech, Cassie, but I think I knew most of those things when I was thirty, too, and I didn't have a grandfather like me. So listen, Cassie, don't give me too much credit. What happened to you would've happened with or without me. You'd be president of the company today anyway.

[305]

Maybe I made it happen a little differently. That's all. Just a little differently. Cassie, this is some crowd we have here tonight. A lot of heavyweights. Big stuff. The mayor. Top attorneys. Fancy people. Some of the smartest men in New York. Pardon me, Hilda, but to me you're a man. A pretty man, but still a man. At the age of eighty I don't need women's liberation telling me to call you persons. So listen, all you hotshots. Listen close. I'm going to tell you something you may not know. But I'll only tell you once."

Samuel Cassman stepped back, warmed his cigar, lit it and puffed twice while his audience sat in absolute silence waiting.

Satisfied and buoyed by their anticipation, Grandpa went on.

"Some night you—any one of you—will come home alone, pour yourself a drink, sit down in a nice big chair, and say to yourself, 'Good for me. I sold another building today.' And maybe you'll make the drink just a little bit stiffer to celebrate. But I ask you, is that what life is really about? Is it buying and selling? Nothing but buying and selling? And sitting in a chair smiling to yourself? Earlier this year I was drinking my drink, and I looked in the fireplace in my library. I saw ashes. I tell you, it made me shake a little. Ashes to ashes. All of a sudden I didn't want any more cold fireplaces. I didn't want to drink my drinks alone with nobody to talk to. I didn't want dinner with this lady one night, that lady another night. For the first time in a long time I was cold. I was cold like that when I married your grandma, Cassie, and God knows she kept me warm every day of her life. So if one woman could, maybe another could, too. I picked up the telephone and I called Ruth. Then and there, as God is my witness, I said, 'Marry me.' 'Sam, you're crazy,' she said. 'Probably I am,' I told her. 'But if you don't say yes now and make me marry you right away, I'll probably get cold feet. You don't need my money; I don't need your money. But I need somebody to sit by my fireplace with me and say, "So, Sam, how did it go today?" '"

He turned to his bride and kissed her gently. "Thank you, Ruth, for marrying me.

"Now let me talk about some other things. All week people have come up to me and asked, 'If you had to do it all over again, what would you do?' My answer, ladies and gentlemen, is this—if I had to do it all over again, I'd do it all, only bigger and better.

"The one thing people haven't asked me is the thing they're all afraid to ask. I'll ask it for you. There isn't a person in this room who doesn't want to come up to me and say, 'Sam, did you know the *Times* story was running that day? Is that why you left?' I want to tell you all, publicly, I didn't know. I had no idea—"

Cassie shook her head.

The old charmer.

Still a faker.

Who are you fooling this time, Grandpa?

I love you, but I'm not buying. But I'll do something you'll understand, Grandpa. You'll understand this because you'll call me tomorrow and laugh about it. And you'll know I've really grown up . . .

". . . and so," Sam Cassman said, "I do feel that I owe you all an apology because I made you go through such a hard time on my account, but I assure you I had no idea—"

It was then that Cassie stood and in full view of thirty-five astonished people walked away.

Samuel Cassman kept talking.

Cassie went to the telephone in the vestibule, picked up and dialed Calvin Gardiner's number. She heard his nice, comforting voice, and quietly she asked, "So, Cal, how did it go today?"

Then she threw her head back and laughed fully and deeply.

You could learn a lot from Samuel Cassman.